CONDEMNED
TO *Love*

USA TODAY BESTSELLING AUTHOR
SIOBHAN DAVIS

Printed by Amazon

Paperback edition © January 2021

ISBN-13: 9798595363969

Editor: Kelly Hartigan (XterraWeb) editing.xterraweb.com

Cover design by Robin Harper

Photographer: Sara Eirew

Cover Models: Quinn Biddle & Pamela Brisson

Formatting by CP Smith

Her teen crush is now a ruthless killer and powerful mafia heir.

Will one life-altering night unite or destroy them?

Bennett Mazzone grew up ignorant of the truth: he is the illegitimate son of the most powerful mafia boss in New York. Until it suited his father to drag him into a world where power, wealth, violence, and cruelty are the only currency.

Celebrating her twenty-first birthday in Sin City should be fun for Sierra Lawson, but events take a deadly turn when she ends up in a private club, surrounded by dangerous men who always get what they want.

And they want *her*.

Ben can't believe his ex's little sister is all grown up, stunningly beautiful, and close to being devoured by some of the most ruthless men he has ever known. The Vegas trip is about strengthening ties, but he won't allow his associates to ruin her perfection. Although it comes at a high price, saving Sierra is his only choice.

The memory of Ben's hands on her body is seared into Sierra's flesh for eternity. She doesn't regret that night. Not even when she discovers the guy she was crushing on as a teenager is a cold, calculating killer with dark impulses and lethal enemies who want him dead.

Understanding the risks, she walks away from the only man she will ever love, stowing her secrets securely in her heart. Until the truth becomes leverage and Sierra is drawn into a bloody war—a pawn in a vicious game she doesn't want to play.

As the web of deceit is finally revealed, Ben will stop at nothing to protect Sierra. Even if loving her makes him weak. In a world where women serve a sole purpose, and alliances mean the difference between life and death, can he fight for love and win?

Mafia Glossary

Bratva – The Russian mafia in the US.

Capo – Italian for captain. A member of a crime family who heads/leads a crew of soldiers.

Consigliere – Italian for adviser/counselor. A member of a crime family who advises the boss and mediates disputes.

Don/Boss – The head of a crime family.

La famiglia/famiglia – Italian for the family/family.

La Cosa Nostra – A criminal organization, operating within the US, comprising Italian American crime families.

Made Man – A member of the mafia who has been officially initiated/inducted into a crime family.

Mafioso/Mafiosi – An official member of the mafia.

Mob – The mafia/La Cosa Nostra/A crime family.

Omertá – The mafia code of silence. Breaking omertá usually means death.

RICO laws – The Racketeer-Influenced and Corrupt Organizations Act, a federal statute enacted in 1970. It allows prosecutors to seek tougher penalties if they can prove someone is a member of the mafia.

Soldati – Italian for soldiers.

Soldier – A low-ranking member of the mafia who reports to an assigned Capo.

The Commission – The governing/ruling body of La Cosa Nostra, which sits in New York, the organized crime capital of the US.

The Five Families – Five crime families who rule in New York, each headed by a boss.

The Outfit – The Chicago division of La Cosa Nostra.

Triad – Chinese Crime Syndicate.

Underboss – The second in command within a crime family, and an initiated mafia member who works closely with, and reports directly to, the boss.

Other references:

U of C – University of Chicago

Prologue

SIERRA

"**Y**OU COULD ALWAYS ask me to marry you," Saskia says, batting her eyelashes at Ben like she's sweet and innocent, and marriage-worthy, and not a cruel manipulative bitch who gets off on tormenting me any chance she gets. Her eyes dart over his shoulders, squinting in my direction, and I tuck my head back into the dark alcove, pressing my spine farther into the wall, praying she doesn't find me spying on her. There will be hell to pay if she knows I've been listening to her nauseating attempt to convince her boyfriend to put a ring on it.

"What?" he splutters, a choked laugh slipping from his mouth. "You can't be serious?"

The mounting panic sluicing through my veins slowly calms at the obvious disbelief in his voice. I rub a hand across my tight chest, wishing I could see his face, to know he's not entertaining her laughable suggestion for even a second. I've often wondered how Ben has put up with my sister for so long. I thought, for sure, he would have kicked her to the curb within those first few weeks of dating. But he has stuck it out for a year. If you ask me, he deserves a gold medal for putting up with my eldest sister for that long.

"Why the hell wouldn't I be?" Saskia snaps in a tone I'm more familiar with.

"Because you're twenty and I'm twenty-one, for starters," Ben replies in a more conciliatory tone.

"We're adults," Saskia huffs while I roll my eyes.

She loves to throw that one at me on the regular. *"I'm an adult, Sierra, and you're still a kid. You will do what I say, or I'll tell Daddy you're being a brat again."* I clench my fists at my sides, wishing there wasn't such an age gap between me and my sisters. Maybe, if we were closer in age, they wouldn't see me as their problematic little sister, and I wouldn't feel like such an outsider in my own family.

The only one who truly gets me is Mom.

To my sisters, I'm a nuisance.

To Father, I'm an unfortunate accident who continues to mess up his perfect life because I won't conform.

I might be only thirteen, and still discovering who I am, but I know enough about myself to want to forge my own path in life. Not to willingly follow the plan Father has mapped out for me—the same way he has done with my two sisters—just because we have to keep up appearances as the daughters of one of the wealthiest, most powerful, and most successful businessmen in the US.

Screw that.

I will make my own way in life, thank you very much.

And if he wants to cut me off, so be it. I would rather be broke and free to make my own decisions than miserable and rich.

"Old enough to vote, and have sex, and get married," Saskia adds, as I resume eavesdropping on their conversation.

Ben clears his throat. "Please tell me you're not suggesting we get married so we can have sex."

My cheeks warm at the turn in their conversation, and a foreign fluttery feeling swirls in my belly. It's the same sensation I get any time I daydream about Bennett Carver.

I'm sure there is some rule about not crushing on your sister's boyfriend, and maybe I'll be struck down for my naughty thoughts, but I can't help liking Ben because he is awesome. And freaking hot. I can't deny I have fantasized about running my fingers through his thick dark-brown hair like I've seen Saskia doing, or staring deep into his piercing blue eyes, or that I have imagined what it would feel like to touch him and kiss him. The warmth in my cheeks expands until it feels like they're on fire, and I press a clammy palm to my face, willing the flames to die down.

My sister is so lucky, because Ben is gorgeous. But it's not just that he's good-looking—he is sweet and kind and funny, and he treats me like I'm a person of worth, not like I'm something nasty clinging to the bottom of his shoe.

He *sees* me. Like Mom sees me. And I love him for that.

"I'm not suggesting it for that reason." Saskia's voice lowers, and the husky sound grates on my nerves. "In fact, I've decided I don't want to wait any longer. I want you."

To hell with the consequences. I need to see what's going on. Cautiously, I poke my head out of the alcove, smothering my pain as I watch my sister curl her arms around Ben's neck, rubbing the fine hairs on his nape, while she stares at his mouth like she wants to eat him alive.

"I thought you were waiting for your wedding night," Ben coolly replies, his tone giving nothing away.

"I've changed my mind," she purrs, pressing her body against his.

Ben's hands rest lightly on her hips, and I scowl, wanting to rush into the room and yank him away from her. "Why?"

"Why does it matter?" she says, an edge creeping into her voice. "I'll let you fuck me. Isn't that what you've wanted all along?"

Releasing her, Ben takes a step back, running a hand through his hair. "I've respected your wishes, Saskia, and I never put any pressure on you. Don't make out like I'm forcing you into doing something."

"Why does everything have to be such a big deal with you?" she hisses, folding her arms across her chest and glaring at him.

"What the fuck?" He cranks out a laugh. "You have the nerve to accuse me of that after you've just suggested marriage? Do you even hear how crazy you sound?"

"Don't make fun of my feelings." Her lip juts out in a pout, and I roll my eyes again. "I love you, and I know we belong together, so why wait?"

"Whoa." Ben takes another step back, dragging his hand through his hair again. "Enough with the heavy. I came to take you out to dinner, and it's feeling more and more like an ambush."

"Now *you're* being dramatic." Saskia pokes him in the chest with her finger, and I'm gonna give myself eyestrain if I roll my eyes any more.

"Maybe we should do this another night," Ben says, and Saskia's eyes widen briefly in alarm.

"Don't get your panties in a bunch." She closes the gap between them, placing her hands on his chest over his black button-up shirt. "We can't celebrate our one-year anniversary any night but tonight." She plants a faux sugary smile on her face that to me always makes her look like she's constipated. "Forget I said anything. We can talk about it later."

His sigh is loud in the silent room, but whatever he sees on her face seals the deal. "Okay. Let's just go out and have fun." He tucks a piece of her hair behind her ear, and I want to rip his fingers away from her. I hate that she gets to feel his hands on her. I wish I was older so I could fight her for him, because I would make a much better girlfriend.

"I need to finish getting ready," Saskia says, making a move toward the door.

I don't wait to hear the end of the conversation. I slip around the corner of the alcove and exit the room, racing in my bare feet toward my studio before she comes out and catches me.

Twenty minutes later, I have forgotten all about my sister and Ben as I paint swirls of vibrant color on the canvas in broad sweeping strokes.

Mom turned one of the extra reception rooms into an art studio for me a few years ago, and it's my safe haven in this monstrosity we call home. If I've had a bad day or something is bugging me, I lock myself away in here and vent my feelings through art. I don't discriminate and I don't restrict myself, experimenting with whatever appeals to my creative side. Mom indulges my whims, and I have taken classes in oil painting, watercolors, pottery, and jewelry making. Right now, I'm taking a photography class, and I'm enjoying getting a feel for the new Nikon camera Mom bought me for my birthday.

But today is a day for expressing myself through painting. The wide windows at the back of my studio face the rear gardens, and I love the view. I started out painting the beautiful manicured lawn and neat flower beds, but now it's evolved into a crazy burst of colors and strokes and dots on the canvas as I let my creative streak take control.

A firm rap on the door pulls me out of my head, and a massive

4

smile spreads over my mouth when the door opens and Ben sticks his head in. "Am I interrupting the genius at work?" he quips, flashing me a blinding smile that has my insides swooning.

"Yes, but I don't mind your interruptions," I say, setting my paintbrush down on the side of my easel. Grabbing a wet wipe from the pack, I clean paint off my fingers as I walk toward him.

Ben eases into the room, closing the door slightly but not fully shutting it. "Good, because I brought you something." His smile expands as he walks toward me, extending the small box.

A squeal escapes my lips, and I clap my hands. "They've reopened?" My favorite bakery had shut down without explanation a few weeks ago, and I'd given up hope of ever tasting their delicious cupcakes again.

He nods, handing me the box. "I noticed lights on in the bakery as I was driving here, and I had to pull over and grab a cupcake for my favorite firefly." He ruffles my hair, and warmth spreads over every inch of my body.

Opening the box, I let my long blonde hair hang around my face to disguise the blush staining my cheeks. "Red velvet. Yum." I swipe my index finger into the soft sweet frosting.

"It's your favorite, right?" He props his butt against the long table behind us.

"That and their…"

"Peanut butter truffle cupcakes," he finishes for me.

I beam at him as I suck icing off my finger. "You know me well."

"I think I do." He waggles his brows as his eyes scan the room. "Damn, Firefly, you've really taken to photography. Those pictures are amazing."

Every part of me melts at his compliment. I spin around, perusing the collection of photos stuck haphazardly to the far wall. "I'm still learning about technique, but it's fun. I'm enjoying it."

"You are so talented." He pushes off the table and walks toward the wall on the other side, his fingers brushing over the newest additions to my mural. I copied a scene from one of the Harry Potter movies, depicting the Hogwarts Castle elevated high above the ground with a lush green forest at the base. I've added to it over the months since I started it, as the mood took me.

"You added Harry," he says, looking over his shoulder at me.

"And Hermione and Ron." Walking to his side, I point at the small figures elevated in the sky upon broomsticks. "I had to add a quidditch game after we went on the ride at Universal Studios." My finger traces the circular edge of the golden snitch, and I smile as contentment sweeps through me.

Ben and painting make me happy, and I could burst with joy in this moment.

"You find inspiration everywhere, Sierra. I wouldn't mind seeing the world through your eyes."

"The world is one giant pool of inspiration. How could I not be inspired every second of every minute of every day?"

He leans down, bringing his gorgeous face close to mine, and I forget how to breathe. "I think you're the one who's inspirational, Firefly." Very carefully, he tucks some stray strands of my hair behind my ear, and my cheeks inflame. But I refuse to be embarrassed, holding his gaze as he smiles adoringly at me. "Never change."

"Uh, I won't," I croak, disappointed when he straightens up and steps back.

"I thought I might find you here," Saskia says, and I jump at the unexpected sound of her voice, emitting a high-pitched shriek.

"Oh my God. You frightened me."

She narrows her eyes. "It's not nice when people eavesdrop on private conversations, is it?" she asks, making it clear she knew I was spying on her earlier.

"Ben brought me a cupcake," I retort, waving the box at her.

"You'll get fat," she drawls, her gaze roaming me from head to toe. "And it's not like you can get away with packing on the pounds. You're already looking pudgy around the middle."

My face explodes, popping bright red with burning embarrassment. I fight tears, not wanting her to see how much she has upset me. How could she say that in front of Ben?

"Saskia. Don't be so cruel," Ben says, and I love how quickly he always comes to my defense. He's my hero, and I will always worship the ground he walks on. He turns to me, his features softening. "You're perfect just the way you are." He pats the top of my head, and my embarrassment puffs into thin air.

"I'm just trying to educate my little sister. The world is a cruel place," Saskia says, stalking across the room. She threads her fingers through Ben's, and I grind my teeth to the molars. "And only ugly old dudes want to fuck fat chicks." She pats me on the head, but her gesture is completely condescending. "So, eat your calorie-laden cupcake, *Firefly*, but don't blame me when you end up fat and alone."

Ben yanks his hand from Saskia's, but it only gives me a tiny bit of joy because her hurtful words and scathing look pierce the walls I hide behind, and her strike hits deep.

I know I have put on some weight lately, only because I haven't hit my growth spurt yet. I'm the smallest in my class with most of my friends towering over me. Mom said shouldn't worry about it since the weight will fall off when I grow taller. I usually pride myself on not being obsessed with my appearance, unlike Saskia and Serena who spend hours in front of the mirror, but I'm not strong enough to protect myself from such a horrid attack. I thought older sisters were supposed to protect their little sisters, not be mean and cruel for no reason.

"You are way out of line, Saskia," Ben says through gritted teeth. "Apologize to Sierra."

She huffs out a laugh. "You're my boyfriend, not my father, and I won't apologize for being honest. God knows Sierra doesn't stop to consider anyone else's feelings when she speaks her mind."

Ben opens his mouth, to defend me again, I assume, but I cut across him this time. "It's fine, Ben. I'm used to Saskia's personal brand of education. And I don't care what she says," I lie, stuffing the cupcake into my mouth while I spit fire at my sister through my eyes.

She pins me with a disgusted look, opening her mouth to insult me, I'm sure, but she stops, mouth open like a fish out of water, when Ben levels her with a dark look that is kinda scary.

"Can we be done with this?" she asks a few seconds later when she's composed herself.

Ben mutters under his breath, his chest heaving, before nodding.

Swallowing the delicious light spongy texture, I race to the table, snatch the painting I had set aside, and dash to the door before they leave. "Thank you for the cupcake," I tell him, thrusting the drawing at him. "I painted this for you."

He smiles as he takes the painting, his eyes carefully examining the picture I created especially for him. "A firefly, glowing with light and energy just like the little girl who drew it," he says.

I try not to feel disappointment at his "little girl" comment, but it's hard not to feel dejected. I know my feelings will never be returned, and comments like that shatter the illusion. Yet I'd rather dwell in blissful ignorance when it comes to Bennett Carver.

"Thank you, Sierra. I love it." He bends down, pressing a soft kiss to my cheek, and my legs almost go out from under me. Behind him, Saskia smirks, her haughty expression telling me she knows all about my crush on her boyfriend. "I will treasure it always."

Saskia rolls her eyes. "It's a stupid painting from an impressionable kid with a crush. Please don't pretend like it's some masterpiece."

"You're being a complete bitch, and my patience is in limited supply," Ben tells her, looking like he's two seconds away from snapping her neck.

I'm not sure I'd care if he did.

"Oh, relax." Saskia attempts to laugh it off. "You're so tense tonight." She grabs his shoulders, digging her hands in. "But I can help with that after dinner," she purrs, and my stomach lurches painfully.

"Would it kill you to be nice?" he asks, his eyes darting between Saskia and me.

"I *am* nice," she protests, and I barely resist another eyeroll. "And I really don't get why you bother. It's not like she's *your* little sister."

A muscle pops in his jaw, and I inwardly rejoice at the fact my sister appears to have foot-in-mouth disease tonight. Maybe Ben has finally wised up. Maybe he's planning to break up with her. God, I hope so, because he deserves so much better.

My joy is short-lived though as I contemplate what it would mean. I wouldn't see him anymore. He wouldn't bring me cupcakes from the Mountainview Bakery, and he wouldn't talk to me about my art or ask how school is, and I'd have one less person who seems to care about me in my life.

But I can sacrifice that if it means he is free of the witch and he finds someone nice who appreciates him.

"If I had a sibling," Ben says, "I would cherish him or her and do everything to build them up, not tear them down. You don't realize how lucky you are."

"And *you* don't realize how lucky you are being an only child," she retorts.

Ben shoves her hands off him, and I can tell he's working hard to control his temper. "Let's just get out of here before we miss our dinner reservation," he says after a few silent beats. He turns to me one final time, gracing me with a beautiful smile. "Good night, Firefly."

"Good night, Ben."

Maybe I had a sixth sense that night, but that was the last time I saw him. Less than a week later, Ben had mysteriously disappeared. Vanished without telling anyone, leaving his girlfriend behind without a word, fueling her anger and her heartbreak.

Over the years, I wondered what happened to him. Whether he was safe. Whether he was happy. Until he stopped occupying space in my head and I managed to forget him.

I never thought I'd ever see him again.

I never thought I'd need him to rescue me.

And I certainly never thought I'd grow to fear him.

PART I – EIGHT YEARS LATER

Chapter 1

SIERRA

"BOTTOMS UP, BABE!" Esme roars over the deafening noise of the club. "It's time to get officially drunk for the first time."

"It feels good to be legal now." No more fake ID's for me. Yay! Quickly licking the salt off my hand, I knock back the tequila shot, grimacing as it burns sliding down my throat.

"Now we're all twenty-one," Penelope confirms, shuddering as she drains her shot. "And the world is definitely our oyster."

I'm the last of my friends to celebrate this milestone, so we decided to celebrate in style. Hence why we are currently in one of the top nightclubs in Sin City, groomed to within an inch of our lives, and ready to party with a capital P.

"Says the girl who is already engaged," Esme replies, arching one elegant brow as she tosses her long wavy locks over one shoulder.

"What the hell has that got to do with it?" Penelope asks, narrowing her warm brown eyes at Esme.

"Nope." I shake my head, eyeballing them. "You two are not getting into it tonight. It's my birthday, and we're in Las Vegas, on a freebie, courtesy of my parents, and I'm deeming it an argument-free zone. No fighting on my birthday, capisce?" I wave my finger in their faces.

I love these girls to bits. They are more my sisters than Saskia and Serena, and they bicker as much as real sisters do. You couldn't find two more different women, but we've all been close since middle school, and I can't imagine my life without them in it. They have kept me from rocking in a corner when my family has driven me to the point of insanity.

"You just had to pull the birthday-girl card, huh?" Esme grins as she reaches over to grab the tray of cocktails from the waiter when he sets it down on our table. "Thanks," she mouths, pinning the hottie with one of her trademark flirtatious grins.

Esme is drop-dead gorgeous with thick dark-red hair and striking green eyes that are even brighter than my emerald peepers, but it's her winning personality that seduces every man who sets eyes on her. Esme is a woman who knows what she wants and goes for it. I like to think we share similar traits in that regard, but I'm less obvious when going after something I want.

"Fine. You win." Penelope readily concedes because she's not one to hold a grudge. With her big eyes, petite frame with voluptuous curves in all the right places, and her straight-talking attitude, Pen is no less of a catch than Esme. Leaning across the low black-and-red velvet couch, she kisses Esme on the cheek as she accepts a vodka cocktail from her. "Love you, babe."

"Right back at ya." Esme blows her a kiss before handing me a cosmopolitan. The other five girls in our party—a mix of friends from our hometown in Chicago and a couple of girls from college—snatch cocktails until the tray is empty.

We chat and laugh as we drain our drinks, and I'm nicely buzzed. Coming to Vegas was a genius idea, and I really owe Esme for organizing the entire trip. I know Pen helped out too, but she's in the thick of wedding planning, and Esme didn't want her stressing out so she did the bulk of the work. I would've helped, if I had been allowed, but the girls wanted the details kept a surprise until we arrived.

"Let's dance," Tammy says, tugging on my elbow as some of the girls stand, heading away from our table. We're in a reserved section of the lower level of the club, and Esme has paid for the table so it is ours for the night.

"Come on." I rise, lifting one shoulder, as I glance down at Pen and Esme. I'm not going dancing without my besties. The girls need little encouragement, polishing off their drinks before they follow us out of our section and into the main body of the large club.

The place is teeming with people. Although lighting is low, my eyes drink in the surroundings, admiring the attention to detail. I hope whoever designed this place got a nice fat bonus. They've gone with a fire theme, and the décor is a mix of different materials and colors, all in various shades of red, orange, black, and gold. Decadent crystal chandeliers hang over our heads, and it's obvious no expense has been spared. Multicolored strobe lights stretch across the room from the dance floor, providing bursts of illumination as we make our way through the main room.

We weave a path through the crowd and out onto the large dance floor. Pulsing beats reverberate off the walls from the large DJ booth at the top of the room. It's on an elevated platform, and a large screen projects illusory flames of fire across the dance floor at intermittent intervals. I grin as I stare up at the ceiling, joining my friends as we lift our arms, jumping in our heels as we try to touch the fiery projection.

We dance for a few songs, gathering some admirers, but there is no one who catches my eye enough to flirt with. I expand my search, scanning the other side of the dance floor for willing victims. "See anyone you like?" Esme inquires, noticing my perusal.

"Not so far, but the night is still young." I waggle my brows, and she grins, looping her arm through mine. "Let's go hunting. You definitely need to get laid. It's practically a rite of passage."

I roll my eyes, grabbing Pen's arm as Esme tows me off the dance floor.

"What are we doing?" Penelope asks when Esme stops beside the bar. Shoving her way through to the front, Esme grabs one of the bartenders, shouting an order at him, completely oblivious to the daggers embedding in her back from other thirsty patrons.

"Hunting for prey." I grin, scouting the guys hanging around the bar.

"I'll come with," Pen offers. "I know what you two are like if you are left to your own devices."

"You can help vet them," I agree because Pen has a great bullshit radar and she can sniff out an asshole from miles away.

"Don't you ever feel like you're missing out?" Esme rejoins us, handing out glasses filled with vodka cranberry.

"Esme." I caution her with a look. "You promised."

"I'm not stirring shit, I swear. I'm just curious."

"Is your issue with Eric or that I'm engaged at twenty-one?" Penelope asks, and I'm guessing they're having it out whether I lay down rules or not.

"It's not Eric. I like him, a lot. He's good to you," Esme says.

"Then why do you keep busting my balls?" Pen asks in between slurping her drink.

"I just think you're crazy getting tied down so young. I don't want to see you making a mistake."

I know this is coming from a good place, but I also know what's driving Esme's concern. "Pen isn't your sister, and Eric isn't that cheating asshole she married."

Pen's features soften. "I know you're only worried for me, and I love you for that, but I know what I'm doing. I love Eric. He's my soul mate, and I know there is no one else for me."

"Verity thought doucheface was her soul mate too, and look how that ended up. Now she's a struggling single mother with two small kids. He doesn't even see them anymore. He's too busy playing happy family with his new wife and baby son."

"That sucks for Verity," Pen says. "And that cockroach is the biggest slimeball to walk the planet, but just because that happened to her doesn't mean it will happen to me."

"I know I'm being irrational," Esme replies, chewing on the corner of her lip. "But I couldn't forgive myself if I kept my thoughts hidden and then something happened."

"Nothing will happen," I interject when I see the crestfallen look on Pen's face.

The last thing I want is Esme planting doubts in her mind. I get where Esme is coming from, and I know it's why she's insistent on playing the field and not getting attached to any guy, but she can't project her fears and insecurities onto others, because that's just not fair. "Saskia married Felix when she was twenty-one, and Serena was twenty-three on her wedding day," I remind her. "It's not unheard of to marry young."

"I'm not sure you should use either of your sisters as an example of matrimonial bliss," Esme replies, flashing a grin at someone over my shoulder.

"You're probably right." I doubt Saskia would be happy no matter who she married, and Serena shocked the hell out of me by marrying one of my father's oldest friends. She kept their relationship a secret from me, which still hurts, and we don't have much contact these days so I have no clue if she's happy in her marriage or not. All I know is she got knocked up pretty fast after the wedding and she dotes on my little niece Elisa.

"But neither of them were madly in love with their husbands," I add, wanting to reassure Pen. I rub her arm and smile. "It's clear you're head over heels in love, and Eric is a great guy. He adores you and treats you like a princess. You two are so good together, and if it feels right, that's all that matters. Do what your heart is telling you to do."

"Do you really believe that, or are you just saying it to keep the peace?" Esme asks, looking genuinely curious.

"I really believe that." I tuck a stray piece of my long blonde hair behind one ear before taking another mouthful of my drink.

"I wish I could." The smile slips off Esme's face, and a semi-tense silence descends.

"Hey, this is supposed to be a celebration, so no long faces." Pen nudges both of us in our sides. "You never know, both your soul mates could be in this very room. We should mingle."

Esme throws one arm around my shoulders and her other around Pen's. "I'm more in the market for a devil mate," she jokes. "But you can help." A mischievous grin appears on her face. "I'll just go after the ones you reject as unworthy."

"Lord help us." Pen shakes her head as I tap out a quick message to Tammy so the others know where we are. "One of these days, that attitude is going to get you in serious trouble."

"As long as we're there to bail Esme out, she's good," I say, slipping my cell into the small pocket of my black and gold dress.

We walk around with our drinks in our hands, scouting the talent, as we make a full circle of the room, checking out all the options. There is a mix of men here. Old. Young. Hot. Not so hot. A few groups of men whistle and holler as we stroll past, and we stop a couple times, indulging in mild flirtations before moving on. Maybe it's my mood, but none of the cute guys we meet are doing it for me.

"Oh my God." Esme slams to a halt, and I spill some of my fresh vodka cranberry on the hardwood floor. "Did you see him?"

"See who?" Pen and I ask in unison.

"Saverio Salerno." She licks her lips, and her eyes become alive. I can almost see the wheels churning in her head as she plots and plans.

"Should I know who that is?" I've never heard of the dude. I follow her line of sight to the back of a tall guy, heading toward the VIP door at the side of the room. He's wearing a black tailored suit that looks expensive, and his dark hair is cropped quite close to his head. His shoulders are broad, his arms straining the material of his suit jacket, so the guy is obviously ripped.

"He owns this place and a couple of casinos," she supplies, lowering her voice an octave. "It's rumored he's part of the mob."

Pen and I trade looks. Spotting the excitement on Esme's face, I already know we're screwed. "Please don't tell me you're interested in pursuing a man like that?"

"You know I love a bad boy and I thrive on a challenge."

"We also know you are reckless with little regard for your personal safety," Pen says, looking worried as she runs a hand through her quirky brown bob.

"You know I normally support your escapades," I say, "but if the rumors are true, he doesn't sound like the kind of man you should even look twice at, let alone sleep with."

I have a rebellious streak in me too—just ask my father. I'm sure he has a long list of bad behavior he could mention—but I know where to draw the line, and this is it. I wet my dry lips, tossing my soft blonde curls over my shoulder, as I contemplate how to divert this train wreck. "We should go to another club," I blurt. "Who knows when we might get to come to Vegas together again. We could go on a club crawl."

Esme winks. "Nice try, but I'm not leaving until I at least say hello to the man."

"This has bad idea written all over it," Pen mutters, eyeing the man's back with a wary expression. "I'd like to arrive home alive." She drills Esme with a loaded look. "As in, not wearing a body bag."

"My God, Pen. Chill out. You are totally overreacting."

I'm not sure she is, but what harm could it do to say hi to the guy? I know how stubborn Esme is, and if we keep resisting, it will only make her more determined.

"Let's say hi and then talk to the others and see if they want to stay or go?" I suggest.

"I can compromise with the best of them." Esme grins. Pen mumbles under her breath, but she gives up fighting too. Esme smooths a hand down the front of her short green dress. "How do I look?"

"Stunning, like always," I say.

"I'm not sure a man like that is after stunning," she muses, keeping her eyes locked on him as he stops to converse with a small group of men about ten feet from the enclosed VIP area.

"He's still a man, and they all think with their dicks." I tug the front of my strapless dress up, checking that I'm not showing more than a socially acceptable level of cleavage. I smother a snort of hilarity. If my father could hear my thoughts now, he'd be proud.

"This is a terrible idea," Pen mutters, looping her arm in mine as we follow Esme toward the man.

"We both know there's no talking Esme out of something once she has made up her mind. We can't let her approach him alone. If anything were to happen to her, we would never forgive ourselves."

"I know." Pen sighs. "I just worry about her. I'm all for sexual equality and exploring your options, but her penchant for fucking dangerous assholes could come back to bite her someday, and I don't want to see her hurt. Especially not on your birthday night. I want you to look back on this night with fond memories."

"And I will." I pat her arm in reassurance, hoping I'm right.

Spiking Tony's drink with sleeping pills might not have been the smartest play. If my father knew I was partying in Las Vegas without my bodyguard, he'd throw a hissy fit. He doesn't understand how restrictive it is. How it gets old having Tony trail me wherever I go. One would think I'd be used to it by now, because I've had a bodyguard for as long as I can remember, but I hate the intrusion and the attention it draws.

Being the daughter of the billionaire owner of Lawson Pharma comes with its fair share of perks *and* drawbacks. Lack of privacy being one. I wanted to come to Las Vegas and party with my friends without Tony breathing down my neck or having him relay every minute detail to my father.

Sometimes, I just want to be normal. A normal girl, out celebrating her birthday with friends, doing all the mad crazy shit normal twenty-one-year-old women do. Is that so bad to want? Honestly, if a genie appeared and granted me a wish to live a normal life in exchange for giving up the money and the trappings of wealth that come with our lifestyle, I would do it in a heartbeat. I wouldn't need to think about it. Not for a second.

I plan to get laid at some point during the trip, and Tony vetting any potential fuck buddies usually kills the mood and ends my fun.

Shove an NDA at a guy and see how fast he hightails it away.

It's the main reason I've only had one serious boyfriend and only had sex with two men.

Father is controlling as fuck. It's his form of OCD. One part of me understands it. His wealth and his notoriety draw all kinds of crazies, and he won't take any chances with his family. My sisters and my mother have designated bodyguards too, and Father travels with an entourage of two or three bodyguards. But sometimes, it seems like overkill, and I wonder how much of it has to do with my safety and how much with him knowing every aspect of my life and manipulating me so he's the one in control, not me.

He doesn't understand why I'm not obedient like my sisters. Why

I fight him on practically everything. He cannot grasp the concept I have my own plans, my own ambitions, and I want to forge my own path in life. I don't want to work for the family business like Saskia and Serena, and he went apeshit when I refused to enroll in the same business program my sisters attended at U of C. He threatened to disown me when I applied to study biomedical science with my sights set on alternative therapy as a chosen career, but Mom talked him into it.

"Earth to Sierra." Pen clicks her fingers in my face. "You spaced out, girlfriend."

"I did, but I'm back now." We almost slam into Esme's back as she stops unexpectedly. We are mere feet from the man, but he's engrossed in conversation with a bunch of dudes in suits, and I don't think barging our way in there will help Esme's cause.

"That conversation looks pretty heated," Esme says, keeping one eye on her target as she glances quickly at us.

"We should take that as our cue to leave." Pen makes one final effort.

"I'm not wasting this opportunity." A look of determination ghosts over Esme's face. It's a look I'm well-versed in. "I just have to time it carefully."

"Let's wait over there," I suggest, pointing at an empty high table just behind the men. "That way, he can't leave without us seeing."

"Good idea." She bobs her head vigorously, leading me around the men. Of course, she makes sure to stare at them as we pass, because subtlety and Esme do *not* go hand in hand. I look straight ahead, not wanting any of them to think I have any interest. From the brief glimpses I've seen, they are all way older, like my father's age, and the thought of any of them touching me makes my skin crawl. Esme has a thing for older guys, but they are not usually *that* old.

Esme slides onto one of the stools, strategically choosing the one which faces the men, while Pen and I claim the other two seats, happy to have our backs to them. We put our drinks down, talking in hushed tones for a few minutes, while Esme pointedly stares at the guy she has set her sights on.

"You're being obvious," Pen says.

"That's the point," I reply before Esme can.

"Exactly." Esme grins. "He's locked eyes with me a couple times, so it's working." She drinks noisily through her straw while maintaining eye contact over our shoulders. "And we're on," she adds, pulling her shoulders back, her grin expanding. "He's coming this way." She slants us a cautionary look. "Let me do the talking. 'Kay?"

"Trust me," I say, finishing my drink. "He's all yours."

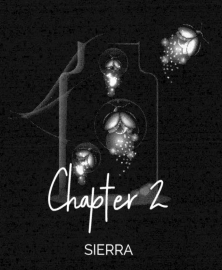

Chapter 2

SIERRA

"HELLO, LADIES." HIS deep, rich voice fills my ears while his breath fans the side of my face, and I automatically stiffen, straightening my spine as I stare straight ahead, refusing to look at him. Heat rolls off his body in noxious waves, and I jolt when his arm brushes against mine. Doesn't he understand the concept of personal space? And why is he standing so close to *me*? It's not like I'm the one eye-fucking him these past ten minutes.

"Hello to you too." Esme's broad smile drips confidence, and she doesn't shy away from holding his gaze.

"Are you enjoying my club?" he inquires, confirming he *is* the owner. I hope that's all Esme is right about though.

"Very much so," she replies. "This place is amazing."

"And your friends?" he inquires.

The air distorts as he repositions himself directly in front of me, forcing me to look up. Eyes as dark as night latch onto mine with immediate interest, and I smother my shocked gasp as he blatantly checks me out.

My assumptions were correct—he is definitely older. At least forty. It's hard to pin an age on him because his face is badly scarred and his skin is riddled with pockmarks. His Armani suit is tight-fitting, hiding little, and I can tell he is built but lean.

He lifts a brow, waiting for a reply. I'm not sure he's even noticed Pen, and considering she's mute and motionless beside me, it's up to me to answer him. "We are having a great night. Thank you," I say, hating how intensely he's scrutinizing my face.

"It's Sierra's twenty-first birthday," Esme supplies, and I shoot daggers at her. What the actual fuck? Why would she tell him that?

"Is that right?" he asks, maintaining eye contact with me. His eyes actually aren't black; they are a very deep shade of brown, but they are completely unnerving. The intensity of his probing gaze is like nothing I've encountered before, and I'm trembling inside. The man screams power and danger, and my internal alarm system is going crazy, urging me to run away. There is no disguising the hunger in his gaze as he drinks me in from head to toe, and it only adds to my anxiety.

I give him a curt nod, squirming in my seat, hugely uncomfortable with his singular attention. Didn't his mother ever tell him it's rude to stare?

Lifting his arm, he clicks his fingers, still staring at me like his eyes are glued to mine and he has no control over it. A waiter immediately approaches. "A bottle of our finest champagne for the beautiful birthday girl and her pretty friends," he demands.

"Coming right up, Mr. Salerno. Sir." The waiter scuttles off, looking petrified, and I know how he feels.

"That's very generous," I say. "But not necessary." I don't want to take anything from this man. He strikes me as the type who never gives anything away for free. There will be a price, and it won't be the usual currency.

"You can call me Saverio." He snatches my hand uninvited. "Miss?"

"Lawson," I croak, working hard to contain the shivers of disgust tiptoeing up my spine as he brings my hand to his mouth, kissing it. His eyes never leave mine as his lips linger on my skin. His gaze devours me, and he is unashamedly forward, shielding nothing. I can tell he's a man who is used to getting what he wants, and I'm fucking terrified at how much he seems to want me.

I am going to kill Esme for this.

"So, are you here on business or pleasure?" Esme asks, strategically propping her elbows up on the high table and leaning forward, granting him a clear view of her ample cleavage. She flashes him a seductive smile that normally has men falling at her feet.

He drags his gaze from mine, releasing my fingers, and I release the breath I was holding. The smile he gives Esme is downright scary. Pleasant at first glance. Until you see the irritation behind the tight pull of his mouth and the lethal glint in his eye. I don't think he's used to being interrupted, and he most certainly doesn't like it.

Esme's smile falters as she cowers under his intimidating gaze.

"Business," he says in a clipped tone. "Although meeting the beautiful birthday girl is definitely all pleasure," he adds, returning his focus to me.

Esme's shoulders droop for a split second before she shrugs, plastering a smile on her face again. It's not like her to give up so easy, but she's a pragmatist too. She knows a lost cause when she sees it. We also have a rule about never falling out over a guy. Although, I'm sure she can tell by my reaction that I have zero interest in this man.

I glance at her again, not surprised to discover she's now eye-fucking the man standing behind Scarface Salerno, oblivious to the mess she's caused. Saverio is ogling me with blatant desire, and I'm regretting my decision to drug Tony. For once, I actually wish my bodyguard was here. Underneath the table, Pen grabs hold of my other hand, squeezing it in support. I can't recall a time when Pen was ever this quiet, and it's telling.

"You are the most breathtaking creature, Ms. Lawson. Truly exquisite."

Creature. Really?

Panic returns when he raises his hand to my head, his thumb and forefinger rubbing a few strands of my hair like he has a God-given right to touch me without permission. If he was any other guy, I'd shove him away and tell him to take a hike, but this man is no ordinary guy—he's a predator of the worst kind—and only an idiot would risk his wrath, so I zip my lips and pray I can hide my fear.

"I have never seen blonde hair that's so golden, so pure, so mesmerizing."

"Thank you." I fake a smile. He continues rubbing my hair, and I bite down hard on the inside of my mouth, sitting on my hands to stop myself from slapping his hands away. A shudder works its way through me, and while I'm trying to keep my cool, it's hard to restrain the anxiety infiltrating my veins, creeping into every part of me the longer he continues staring at me.

He is freaking me the fuck out, and no one is calling him out on his batshit behavior either, so I'm guessing this is the norm. The more he ravishes me with his eyes, the more terrorized I become.

How the hell could Esme even consider hooking up with a man like this?

He is legit scary, and I find nothing attractive about him. Briefly, I wonder how he got those scars before pushing those thoughts aside because I'm freaked out enough as it is without adding my overactive imagination into the mix.

The guy is still staring at me, rubbing my hair, and salivating as his gaze rakes me from head to toe. Pen presses her body up against mine, offering silent support. Her body trembles, and I know she's scared too. I want to yell at him to stop undressing me with his eyes, but my vocal cords are paralyzed with fear, and I've resorted to praying for divine intervention.

Saverio looks like the kind of guy who would crush me with the slightest touch and the type of man who likes to rough it up in the bedroom. I know some women get off on being manhandled, but I'm not one of them.

"Boss." The man Esme has turned her attention to steps up close to Saverio's side, whispering something in his ear.

Saverio nods, dropping my hair and stepping aside as the waiter reappears with our champagne. "I must go. I have business to attend to."

Thank fuck. "It was nice meeting you," I lie, placing my hands on my lap. "And thank you for the champagne. It's very generous."

"The pleasure was all mine, Ms. Lawson." He clicks his fingers, and another man scurries over. His name tag says he's the manager in charge. "Mr. Landers. Please escort Ms. Lawson and her friends to the Givenchy booth, and get them whatever they want."

I open my mouth to protest when Esme kicks me under the table. She drills me with a look that begs me not to refuse. She clearly doesn't know me very well if she thinks I am accepting any more "freebies" from this man.

"Until we meet again." Saverio casts one last salacious glance my way before departing with his companions in tow.

I slump against the table, expelling my breath in spurts, relieved he's gone.

"If you would follow me," Mr. Landers says, sweeping his arm out wide and ushering me forward.

"We need to wait for the rest of our party," Esme replies, looking nonchalant as she swipes the bottle of expensive champagne from the ice bucket and proceeds to pour it into glasses. "They are on the way."

"Very well. I will return to escort you in a few minutes," he says before walking off.

Propping my elbows on the table, I lean over at Esme. "Text the others. Tell them we're leaving."

"Are you out of your mind?" She stares at me like my brain has just escaped my skull. "Do you know how many girls would kill to get into the VIP area? And he's reserving the Givenchy booth for us. The freaking *Givenchy* booth!" she squeals, clasping my hands. "It's usually reserved for celebrities. C'mon, Sierra. We can't pass up this chance."

"That man scares the shit out of me, and I want to put as much distance between me and him as I can," I tell her before sliding off the stool.

"I'm with Sierra," Pen says, climbing off her stool. "There are plenty of other clubs we can go to."

"He wasn't that scary," Esme protests.

"That's only because you were too busy eye-fucking that other guy to notice the vibes he was giving off." Pen grabs my arm. "The way he was looking at you creeped me out." She visibly shudders.

"Tell me about it." Planting my hands on my hips, I drill Esme with a deadly look. "It's my birthday and I'm pulling rank. I want to leave. Now, before he changes his mind and comes back for me."

"There you are!" Tammy shrieks, throwing her arms around me from behind. "We didn't know where you went," she adds, slurring her words as she steps around me, slinging her arm around Esme's shoulders.

"We might have run up the tab," Heather says, looking a little apologetic.

"Don't worry about it. My father's good for it."

Father put a ton of extra cash on my black card to cover the costs of this weekend, which is ridiculous and unnecessary as I already have enough in my account to feed a small nation. He forgets I'm not like my sisters. I don't waste thousands every month on designer clothes, bags, and shoes, and I'm not at the beauty salon or plastic surgeon every other day. Now they are married, at least Father is no longer footing astronomical bills.

If he took the time to talk to me, Father would know this about me. But he'd rather throw money my way than have to suffer my company. Both my sisters let him throw lavish parties for their twenty-firsts at The Drake Hotel. They were full of his old cronies, and I was so bored at Serena's party I fell asleep under the table. I didn't realize I was hidden by the tablecloth, and Father almost called the cops when they couldn't find me at the end of the night. He grounded me for two weeks after that. All because sixteen-year-old me had the audacity to fall asleep. So, when Mom offered me the same party option, I turned her down flat without having to think about it. I think she was relieved.

"Oh my, wow. That is freaking awesome! I've heard the VIP room here is sick." Tammy shrieks as I rejoin the conversation.

I groan. "Don't you start. You didn't meet the owner. He gives me the creeps."

"He wasn't that bad," Esme argues as she applies a fresh layer of gloss to her lips.

"He looks like the kind of man who devours puppies for breakfast," Pen says, looping her arm through mine.

"And pussies for lunch," Esme quips, throwing her head back and laughing. I pin her with a look. "What? She walked right into that one." She nudges me in the side. "You've got to admit it's funny."

"There is nothing funny about being trapped in that man's heated stare. Trust me. I feel ill just thinking about the way he looked at me."

"He's gone now, and you heard him, he has business, so you won't see him again."

"Nope. I want to leave." I'm not naïve enough to think he doesn't have plans to seek me out after his business has concluded.

A chorus of boos ring out, and I clutch Pen's arm as the other six girls beg me to stay. In the background, I see the irritated expression on the manager's face as he stands back while we debate it. "Come on, Sierra." Tammy puts her hands on my shoulders, fixing me with a pleading look. "Let loose! It's your birthday, and we're in Sin City, so *sin* a little; otherwise, why did we drug Tony?"

Valid point. But still. Maybe Scarface Salerno isn't in the mob. Maybe his looks earned him that reputation, but whether he is or isn't is beside the point now. I'm on his radar, and I'd prefer to disappear off it. Hanging around here won't do me any favors. "We can get into the VIP room elsewhere," I say, hoping my father's name is enough to swing it for me around here.

"Not at this late hour," Esme says. "You usually have to arrange it in advance unless you're a known celeb."

"We won't let that man anywhere near you," Heather says, and the others nod in agreement.

"There are seven of us, and we're not going to let him come within ten feet of you," Esme agrees.

"Don't treat me like I'm an idiot, Esme. That man always gets what he wants, and a bunch of girls won't stand in his way."

"Then how about this." Esme stuffs her lip gloss down the front of her dress and walks over to me. "Let's go for an hour, and then we'll leave. He has only just gone into a meeting, and I doubt it will be over before then. That way, we get to say we partied at the VIP room in Flame and you get to avoid he who shall not be named."

The others are looking at me with anticipation, excitement transparent on their faces, and I don't want to be a Debbie Downer. "Ugh." I shove my hands through my hair. My gut is telling me to run, but my heart wants to make my friends happy.

"Babe." Esme eyeballs me earnestly. "Do you honestly think me or Pen are going to let anything happen to you?" Excitement lights up her eyes. "Getting into the VIP room in a club like this is virtually impossible. I bet even your dad couldn't have organized it for you. You *can't* turn it down. Think of all the hot rich dudes and the free champagne. Your birthday weekend will live on in infamy. We'll still be talking about it when we're old and gray and have long given up our dancing shoes." She rests her hands on my shoulders. "It's just one hour. Please, Sierra. Please say yes."

I sigh, already knowing I'm going to agree. I glance at Pen, and I see the resignation on her face too. We are outvoted, and we both know it. "You're incorrigible. But you're going to be the best lawyer because it's impossible to say no to you."

"Whoop!" She yanks me into a hug, squealing with glee. The others pile around, and we engage in a group hug. "We're going to have so much fun," Tammy says. "You won't regret it!"

"I hope not," I murmur, nodding at the manager as I blatantly ignore the little voice in my ear screaming at me not to do it.

Chapter 3

BEN

I SIP MY bourbon slowly, wanting to keep my wits about me tonight. This is the first time my father is trusting me to represent him at an important meeting, and I can't fuck it up. It's taken long enough to get to this point, and I have no intention of regressing.

Salerno kept us waiting forty minutes, which pissed me off. Relations have been tentative between New York and Las Vegas for some time, but I intend to address that tonight. So, I force my aggravation aside, focusing on what I came here to do.

We are in the private basement in his club. It's an odd place for a business meeting, yet business and women seem to go hand in hand in Sin City. Leaning back against the plush velvet couch, I survey the room as Salerno and his men get comfortable.

A rotating mirrored bar is situated near the back wall on my left. On my right is a square dance floor, equipped with a small stage and a couple of poles. The rest of the space is made up of seated areas. Stylish low couches and comfortable high-backed armchairs surround small black glossy tables. The décor down here is similar to the main club upstairs—a mix of black, gold, red, and orange. Lighting is dim, and music is a steady hum in the background.

My eyes lift to the stairs on the far right of the bar, which lead to an upper level, housing a few bedrooms. Tales of Salerno's drug-fueled orgies are widespread. At least this time, I know what to expect, having attended one a few years ago when I was last here with my father.

"I'm surprised Angelo or the other New York bosses aren't here," Salerno says when he finally opens the conversation. He leans back in his chair as he stares at me. He likes to intimidate everyone he comes into contact with, and his dark glare is legendary. But it will take a lot more than that to put the fear of God in me.

He brought his underboss, Greg Gambini—a brute of a man with a reputation to match—his consigliere Fabrizio Russo, a few of his senior capos, and a handful of loyal *soldati*. There are eleven of them to our five, but I expected a show of strength on his home ground. With the exception of his soldiers, I've met the others before.

Salerno runs a small but tight ship in Vegas. He has his own set of rules, his own way of doing things, which is not always aligned to our thinking. On a personal level, I hate how they treat women, but in every other regard, they are moving forward with the times. Unlike a lot of the families in the US.

"They are attending similar meetings in Philly, Florida, L.A., and Boston," I confirm.

A muscle ticks in his jaw, and he straightens up in his chair. His men stiffen, their guarded expressions zeroing in on me. Behind me, I sense Leo reaching for the gun clipped to his hip.

"So, we're deemed not worthy enough of a meeting with one of the five?" Salerno says, his voice lethally calm, his face devoid of any emotion.

The atmosphere in the room takes a distinct nosedive.

"Bennett is the Mazzone heir and he will one day be the most powerful boss in New York," Leo coolly replies.

I'm glad he doesn't mention my plans to become the most powerful boss in all the US, because there's a fine line between confidence and arrogance. And a smart man never divulges his plan until the timing is opportune and the success inevitable.

"The fact Ben *chose* to come here should tell you all you need to know about your presumed value."

I hold up one hand, silencing my hotheaded underboss. Leo has many talents I'm grateful for. Diplomacy isn't normally one of them.

"I am here because we share a lot of the same values and ambitions for the future." I sip my drink as I cross my ankle over one knee, betraying no hint of emotion on my face.

"I thought you were here on Commission business," Russo says, eyeing me like I'm a bug he'd love to squash.

"I am, but the purposes align."

"I'm listening," Salerno says, his eyes drilling into my face.

"As you know, The Commission has been defunct for many years."

"Disbanded when Chicago broke away," Salerno supplies, as if I need a history lesson.

When I was dragged into this world, one of the first things I did was study the past, consuming everything I could about the families and our enemies.

"It's interesting you didn't mention them before," he adds.

"Relations between New York and Chicago are still fractured."

He barks out a laugh. "You speak like a politician, boy. The rumors I've heard are true."

Ignoring his outburst, I continue, swirling the bourbon in my glass as I eyeball the Vegas boss. "For now, Chicago is outside this process."

Salerno whistles under his breath. "You'd risk the wrath of The Outfit? You risk pissing off the Sicilians?"

"I said *for now*." I'm working hard to keep my temper in check. If the asshole would just let me speak without interruption, this might not take all night.

"Relax, boy." He waggles his brows, and I'm tempted to put a bullet in his skull. If he calls me boy one more fucking time, I just might do it. "I have my own beef with The Outfit."

That's news to me.

La Cosa Nostra originated in Sicily in the nineteenth century, but the organization in the US was only established during the prohibition era, and it operated completely independent of Sicily. Until Giuseppe DeLuca took power in Chicago almost thirty years ago and everything changed because the new leader of The Outfit refused to accept the ruling of The Commission, determined to do things his way.

The Commission was formed by Lucky Luciano in the nineteen thirties and served as a board of directors, so to speak, for the entire Italian American mafia organization. New York, as the only state with five families, had the controlling votes. Something The Outfit always resented. When DeLuca took control in Chicago, he did so from his permanent residence in Sicily, commanding his underboss, Gifoli, to run the show here in his stead. It was unheard of before, and The Commission wouldn't accept his authority when he refused to show his face.

A divide occurred, The Commission eventually broke up, and the families have operated independently since. To this day, DeLuca continues to rule through his underboss and none of the other bosses have ever met the man. It's perplexing, but everyone stopped trying to understand it years ago. Truth is, Chicago prospers, and it remains the second-largest organization behind New York.

After that, alliances grew between certain families, mostly to facilitate business. We have an arrangement with Salerno that enables the shipment of some of our drug supply into Las Vegas, and he organizes safe transport to New York. A lot of the families have similar arrangements, but this is the first time a more formal structure has been attempted. It's a bold move but one I feel we need to do. Finally, the five bosses agreed, and we are putting things in motion.

I arch a brow in silent question, wondering exactly what beef Salerno has with Chicago, but he dismisses my interest with a wave of his hand, further enraging me. Blood boils in my veins, but outwardly, I'm Switzerland. "The fact the Sicilians are outside of this plan only adds to the appeal."

He's already forgotten the "for now" part. If things with the Bratva escalate, as I suspect they will, we will need every family back in the fold. Including Chicago.

"New York wants to restart The Commission, initially through informal alliances that we will expand on in time."

"Why?" Saverio shrugs. "Things work so why try to fix something that isn't broken?"

"The Russians are an ever-increasing concern, and we need to unite all Italian American families if we are to contain the threat they pose." There are others to contend with too. The Irish, the Albanians, and the Triad could become a problem in New York. However, none of those factions warrant immediate action, because their numbers are small and their control is weak. But they are on my radar, and I'm keeping a close eye on things.

I take another sip of my drink, meeting Gambini's hard stare with cool indifference. He's got some Russian blood flowing through his veins. Distant, on his mother's side. His father comes from a distinguished Italian American family, but his Russian DNA leaves him open for target practice. He's eyeing me now, like he's just waiting for me to throw some slur his way so he has an excuse to stomp all over my existence.

The man is known for crushing opponents with his bare hands and his complete disdain for life. Sneeze on him and he's likely to kill you while barely breaking a sweat. What most don't know is he is sharp as a tack. A shrewd man like Saverio Salerno doesn't make a violent killer his underboss unless he has other considerable skills he's bringing to the table.

"The Russians are no threat," Salerno says, pouring more scotch into his glass.

Grabbing the twenty-thousand-dollar bottle of Old Rip Van Winkle, I top up my own drink before setting the bourbon back down on the table. "Their numbers match ours."

"They are unorganized, disloyal, and they aren't men of honor."

"That is all true, but for how long? I've received intel that concerns me. If the Russians mobilized, they could hurt us. We don't intend to give them the opportunity."

"I can defend my own territory. Why would I agree to resurrecting The Commission? To engaging in a bigger battle?" Salerno drains his drink, pouring another.

"You can defend your territory now, but for how long? This is going to happen, and those who choose to stay independent will be obvious targets. If the Russians unite and they attack you with the strength of their numbers, there is no way you won't fall. Strengthening ties makes sense."

"If the Russians land on my doorstep, I will kill every one of those motherfuckers myself," Salerno says, and I wonder if he really buys into that bullshit.

"And you'll either be dead or in a jail cell." I put my foot down on the ground and lean forward a little. "We can't continue to do things the traditional way, Saverio. Even with judges, lawyers, and law enforcement in our pockets, these RICO laws are restrictive. We can't go around killing anyone who breathes on us funny anymore." I side-eye Gambini, and the fucker growls. "La Cosa Nostra is no different from any other enterprise. We have to adapt, evolve, and grow, or we won't survive."

"I've heard about some of your endeavors," Salerno says, clicking his fingers at one of the men standing at the door. The man slips away by unspoken agreement. "I've heard what you're trying to do."

"Times are changing, gentlemen." I lock eyes with his capos, a curious Russo, and a reluctant Gambini. "It's adapt or die."

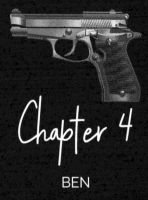

Chapter 4

BEN

"I AGREE, AND strengthening ties is smart." Salerno nods his agreement, and I want to smash my fist in his face.

The motherfucker was just testing me.

I clasp my glass tighter in my grip, talking myself off a ledge. For eight years, I've been on a prolonged test, and I'm sick of it. I thought as long as I paid my dues as a soldier, and worked my way up the ranks, I would earn my place at my father's side without question, without any further test, but it's obvious I am far from in the clear, and no one is finished testing me.

"Which leads me to our last piece of business before we move to the entertainment part of our night." He smirks, and I shift uneasily in my chair, knowing what's coming and wishing I could make my excuses and leave. To do so would dishonor our host, so I'm resigned to spending the night in the company of whores and sex slaves. Bile churns in my gut, and I gulp back a large dose of bourbon, welcoming the tart apple and caramel notes, and the comforting warm heat sliding down my throat. Getting drunk might be the only way I'll get through this night. "Does your father have a response to my proposal?"

Again, with this bullshit. I grind my teeth to the molars, counting to ten in my head before I reply. "I'm not marrying a child bride," I tell him bluntly. "And it's unnecessary. Forging stronger business alliances and uniting under the auspices of a new Commission is all that is needed to bind our families."

If I have my way, when I'm the boss, I will be petitioning to amend some of the old traditions, like the practice of arranged marriages. I'm not naïve. I know part of who we are is embedded in the old ways, and there are some things I won't get agreement to change, but the barbaric practices when it comes to women and their roles in our society is something I am passionate about.

I wasn't able to do anything for my mom, but maybe I can alleviate some guilt by ensuring other women are spared what she endured.

"I'm not sure I like your tone," Saverio says, a fresh layer of hostility filtering through the air.

"I mean you or Anais no disrespect, but I have already told my father I have no intention of getting married. I take my duties to *la famiglia* seriously and marrying *anyone* will weaken my position."

I'm expected to marry a beautiful well-behaved woman who will give me heirs to carry on the Mazzone legacy. Yet wives are little more than accessories. Caged birds who need to be kept in place, and I have zero desire to subject myself or any woman to that fate.

The reason why many men in our world agree to arranged marriages is so they can avoid caring too much. Lavishing affection on your wife is seen as a weakness, so our men rarely marry for love. And keeping a whore or two on the side ensures their wives are kept in check— should they harbor any romantic notions about their husbands.

Wives and children are obvious targets in our world, and I want no part of that. It's ironic our code of conduct supposedly reveres women, yet it's okay to disrespect them by kidnapping and killing them to make a point or to bed whores, as long as it's not flaunted openly.

Other families have even less regard for women, and Vegas is at the top of that list. Rumor has it, Salerno murdered his wife—eleven-year-old Anais's mother—because she objected when he moved three of his whores into their home. He's also amassed a large fortune from the sex trafficking trade, something we have stayed clear of in New York, out of principle and to avoid excessive heat. While I hate doing business with a man like him, we need his shipping and distribution routes, and he has other forward-thinking ideas I like.

"Be careful, boy. Change may be inevitable, but don't force change where it's not needed or wanted. I'm sure your father has told you to choose your battles wisely."

"Touché," I say, lifting my glass, returning his intense stare with one of my own.

His lips tug up at the corners, in the merest smile, as he raises his glass to me.

The sound of approaching footfalls in the corridor outside draws all our attention, and Salerno stands as the doors open and a group of scantily clad women are ushered into the room. Someone raises the volume on the music as the waiter deposits another bottle of scotch on the table alongside a bucket of beers.

"Relax, Messina." Salerno gestures at Leo. "Take a seat. Enjoy my hospitality."

Leo drops onto the couch alongside me, flashing me a grin. Unlike me, my best friend has no issue screwing whores. Removing my black suit jacket, I roll the sleeves of my white shirt to the elbows, forcing myself to relax on the couch.

Salerno greets the women as if they are long-lost friends, not prostitutes he's kidnapped and trained so he can pimp them out. He kisses and touches them while they pretend to enjoy his attention.

I don't care how rich and powerful he is; there is no way any woman can enjoy kissing that ugly motherfucker's face.

A couple of the women move over to the stage, gripping the poles as they start to shimmy up and down in time to the music. The rest descend on us like cocksucking vultures. Leo is the same age as me, and we are the youngest, and the hottest, by a mile, and it's almost comical how obviously the girls vie to reach us first.

I don't protest when a blonde with massive fake tits plops down on my lap, even though my instinct is to tell her to fuck off. Her arms snake around my shoulders as she purposely squirms on top of my cock. A thin brunette with boyish curves slinks onto Leo's lap, and his arms automatically encircle her waist. A slew of pouting girls drapes themselves over Gambini, Russo, and Salerno's capos, while the rest of our men, our *soldati*, stand around the room, keeping guard.

Leaning around the whore on my lap, I swipe two beers from the bucket on the table, silently handing one to her. I watch Salerno as the girl on my lap tries, and fails, to snag my attention. There is nothing stirring in my pants, but I'll make it happen when it gets to that point in the night. Salerno is staring at the door like he wants to riddle it with bullets. A dark look washes over his scarred face, and his eyes narrow at the single guard standing at the door. "Where is she?" he barks.

"On her way, boss. Renzo's gone to get her."

Salerno turns toward us as Leo helps himself to a beer. "I met the most stunning creature upstairs," he explains, pouring himself another scotch, before reclaiming his seat. He pulls a curvy redhead down on his lap, his hand diving underneath the band of her panties. She arches against him as he rips her panties off, the torn material falling to the floor while he openly finger fucks her. "She is all legs and golden-blonde hair with these big green eyes."

Gambini chuckles.

"Screams of innocence," Salerno adds, winking as he roughly thrusts three fingers inside the redhead. "She was fucking terrified, and I can't wait to smear her blood all over my cock."

"Virgin pussy." Gambini licks his lips as he fondles the naked brunette on her knees, between his legs, unzipping his pants. "Our favorite."

"I'm taking her first," Salerno says, continuing to finger the girl on his lap while his eyes remain glued to the door, waiting for his victim. "And Mazzone can take her next. Then she's yours to play with," he tells his number two.

I smirk as I lift the bottle to my mouth, draining half my beer. I have a role to play, whether I want to or not.

Commotion in the corridor pricks my ears as the blonde on my lap starts unbuttoning my shirt, pressing sloppy kisses against my neck. Beside me, Leo is slouched on the couch, with his thighs stretched open, a happy grin on his mouth as the brunette lowers her lips over his hard-on.

Crying reaches my eardrums as Salerno's soldier hauls two young women into the room. The small curvy woman with the short brown hair is openly sobbing while the taller, willowy blonde is wrestling against the man's hold, trying to pull herself free. "Let me go," she screams, and there's something familiar about her voice that has all the hairs on the back of my neck lifting. I try to get a good look at her, but it's hard from this angle, and masses of blonde hair shield her face from view.

The mousy brunette cries louder. Although she's pretty—if you're into that innocent girl-next-door look—it's obvious Salerno brought her along to ensure the blonde does his bidding because she couldn't be less his type. It's a classic carrot-and-stick approach.

Moving the whore to the side when she repositions herself on my lap—unhelpfully blocking my view—I watch as the willowy blonde pushes her hair out of her eyes. The man thrusts the girls forward into the room, and there's no hiding that face now. The vein in my neck throbs as blood rushes to my head. I stare at her, blinking a couple times to make sure I'm seeing what I'm seeing.

No. Fucking. Way.

"Ah, there you are, Ms. Lawson," Salerno says, pulling his fingers out of the redhead and dumping her on the floor. Stepping over her, he walks toward the trembling blonde.

A lump wedges in my throat as I drink her in. The minute I got a proper look at her face, I knew it was her. Salerno's words have just confirmed it. I bet it kills Saskia that her little sister grew up to be more beautiful than she is. Sierra bears a strong resemblance to her older sister. They both share their mother's blonde hair and green eyes, whereas Serena favors Joseph Lawson with her brown hair and hazel eyes.

Sierra might look a lot like my ex, but she is in a league of her own. Her features are more refined. Her hair is a dazzling shade of blonde, brighter than her sister's hair, and her figure is more alluring. Everything about her is authentic and natural in direct contrast to her sister.

Sierra is exquisite.

Like a goddess with her flowing blonde hair, her stunningly beautiful perfectly symmetrical face, legs that seem to go on for miles, and her slim body with curves in all the right places.

My little Firefly is all grown up, and it shows.

I never thought I would ever see her again.

Certainly not in a place like this.

Mr. Lawson was always extremely protective of his daughters, and I can't believe he has let his youngest wander freely around Las Vegas. I can only assume Salerno took care of her bodyguard. He's a man who lets nothing stand in the way of getting what he wants, and from the way he's devouring her on sight, I know he wants her badly.

Well, fuck him.

He can't have her.

My inner beast snarls as adrenaline surges through my veins.

I'm not sure how I can extract Sierra from the ruination Saverio has planned, but I won't stand by and watch him destroy her. I'm going to get her out of here, even if it's the last thing I do.

Chapter 5

SIERRA

FEAR HAS A vise grip on my heart, tightening and tightening until it feels like I can't breathe. Beside me, Pen is crying hysterically, and I have never seen her so scared. I focus on my friend, and the need to protect her, because it's the only way I won't fall apart. One of us needs to stay composed, or neither of us will survive this.

I knew I shouldn't have let the others talk me into going to the VIP room—I should have trusted my gut and ran. The second we reached the Givenchy booth, I knew we wouldn't be able to get them to leave.

Ironically, Pen and I only left the main room to go to the bathroom so we could discuss tactics for getting out of here. Scarface Salerno must've had men watching us, because his goon was waiting outside the bathroom when we emerged. I told him to get lost when he said he was there to escort us to Mr. Salerno's private club in the basement, but he wasn't shy about showing us his gun or threatening to hurt our other friends if we didn't go quietly with him.

I didn't feel like we had much choice.

"Let me go, you bastard," I hiss, as he drags me toward Saverio. The man's fingers are digging into my arm, and I know it will leave bruises. "You're hurting me."

A loud snort rips through the room. My eyes pop wide as a beast of a man turns his head, glancing over his shoulder at me, from the couch. Terror resurfaces when I spot the obvious lust on his face. "You'd better get used to the pain, *principessa*, because there's more of that coming your way." He undresses me with his eyes, licking his lips as his gaze fixes on my modest chest.

My eyes lower to the girl on her knees in front of him, sucking his dick, and my stomach lurches as nausea swirls in my gut. My gaze darts briefly around the room, and panic claws its way up my throat as I take in the scene.

There are several scary-looking older dudes in the room, all of them in various stages of intimacy with mostly naked women. The girls look much younger, but none of them look like they are being coerced. A couple of naked women gyrate against poles on a stage at the other end of the room while a group of ominous-looking guys stands off to the area at the back of the occupied couches. They are all dressed in black clothing and wearing gun belts.

What the hell is this place? And who are these people?

My heart thumps frantically against my rib cage as my panicked eyes scan the room for exit points, but the only way in and out of the place is through the main door behind us.

"Don't mind my friend," Saverio says, approaching us with the freakiest-looking smile.

There are some people whose smiles light up their entire faces. People whose smiles transform their features, elevating them from ordinary to extraordinary.

This man is the opposite.

His smile is like the murky depths of a cesspit, swarming with toxins that are hazardous to your health. I want to tell him he should never smile. That it does him no favors. But I expect a man like him would get off on that fact.

"We are all about pleasure here," he says, as low moans ring out from a man and woman at the end of the nearest couch. She is bouncing up and down on his cock while he tweaks her nipples in a way that looks more like pain than pleasure to me.

Saverio pulls me away from the asshole who has left indents on my skin, wrapping his arm around my waist and yanking me against him. Fear pummels my insides, and I can scarcely breathe over the tightness in my chest. Pen is hyperventilating as the asshole keeps a firm hold of her arm.

"You can't keep us here against our will," I protest, hating how my voice trembles.

A chorus of chuckles rings out around the room.

"Our friends will know something has happened when we don't return and call for help," I add.

Saverio's smile turns even more sinister, and I almost puke as his hand moves down around my hip, landing on my ass. I try to wrench away from him, but he shakes his head, tutting at me. "Do not offend me, beautiful." His voice drips with menace. "You really don't want to do that." He squeezes my ass, and tears prick the backs of my eyes. "Do not worry about your friends. My manager has given them a message." His hand moves lower again, slipping underneath the hem of my short dress.

Everything locks up inside me, and blood rushes to my head.

I can't believe I let this happen.

I can't believe I stupidly drugged Tony so I could get laid.

I can't believe I let the others talk me into staying in this club.

"They believe you have retreated to your hotel," he continues, his fingers creeping up the side of my thigh. "By the time they realize it's not true, they will be too high on the complimentary cocaine I've just delivered to their table or too smashed from all the free champagne to care."

His fingers brush the front of my lace panties, and a strangled sound leaves my lips. Movement on the opposite couch hits my peripheral vision, but I'm too panicked to make out the blurry shapes.

Pen's crying is louder, and I can tell from the irritated looks leveled our way from several of the men that they won't tolerate her much longer. Ignoring the callused fingers moving around to my butt, I focus on my best friend, pleading with my eyes for her to pull herself together before she ends up with a bullet in her brain.

A sort of resigned acceptance washes over me as Saverio's hands roam my body, and I prepare to retreat into my head, to block it all out. I've had years of practice tuning my father and Saskia's derision out, but this is on a whole other level. I can only guess what Saverio has in mind, but something tells me even my imagination couldn't conjure up the depths of the depravity he has planned for us.

I can't see any way out of this.

They have guns, and they could kill us.

I would rather agree and let them rape me in the hope I can get out with my life.

Pen screams as a naked man approaches her. His hideous old dick is erect, jutting toward her like a weapon. His skin tells a story—one I didn't want to be true. Scars litter his chest and his arms, and there's an obvious old bullet wound in his shoulder.

These guys *are* the mob, and we are so fucking fucked.

"I'll make you a deal," I blurt, as movement out of the corner of my eye momentarily distracts me.

Saverio chuckles as he slides his hand underneath my panties, palming my bare ass cheek. Nausea swims up my throat, and I'm a mess inside, but I try my best to hold it together. "I knew there was a reason I was drawn to you," he says before running his tongue up the side of my neck. A shudder works its way through me, and I'm not quick enough to hide it. He chuckles again, and I know my fear is only turning him on more.

Pen screams, and I watch in horror as the naked man wraps his hand around her throat, shoving her against the wall and holding her up a few feet off the ground.

"Let her go and you can do what you like to me!" I shriek, my chest heaving.

Pen's terrified eyes meet mine as her skin turns blue.

"You won't fight?" Saverio trails his finger along my chest, tracing the outline of my breasts with his rough skin.

"I won't fight." Because I can tell the bastard would get a kick out of that. "I'll cooperate. Just please. Please let her go. Let all my friends go and I'm yours." The words feel like poison on my tongue, but if it works, at least I will have saved Pen from this ordeal.

Saverio nods at the naked man, and he drops Pen unceremoniously. She slumps to the floor, gasping for air and clutching her throat.

"Renzo." Saverio calls over the man who abducted us outside the bathroom. "Escort the girl to her hotel and stay with her until I give you further notice."

"That wasn't part of the deal." I know it was the wrong thing to say the second the words leave my mouth.

"Quiet," Saverio snaps, wrapping his hands around my throat, forcing my head back. "If you want your friends to go unharmed, we do this my way. Your friends will be guarded until I'm satisfied they won't speak." Removing his fingers from my throat, he smirks. "After all, what happens in Vegas *always* stays in Vegas."

If he thinks I'm laughing at his effort of a joke, he has another think coming.

"Get her out of here," Saverio barks when Pen's sobs start in earnest again.

"Sierra!" she screams. "You can't do this!" Her sobs dry up as she levels Saverio with a frantic look. "Please just let us both go. We won't tell anyone. Just let us leave, and we promise not to say a word."

He dismisses her with a flippant wave of his hand.

"I love you," I mouth as she's lifted off the ground by the asshole.

"I'm sorry," she mouths back. Her cries and screams reverberate in my ears as she's carried out of the room.

"My ears thank you," the beast on the couch says, grunting as he fucks the woman sprawled across the table in front of him. "I think you're going soft, boss. I would've put a bullet in the bitch's mouth the second she entered the room."

"We've got a problem, Salerno," a deeply masculine voice says, rousing memories from the furthermost depths of my brain.

I spin my head in the direction of the voice, unable to believe my eyes.

Oh. My. God.

No way.

It can't be.

I examine every inch of his handsome face behind a layer of shock. He looks the same, yet different. Older and like he's properly grown into his skin. I crushed hard on Bennett Carver as a teen. I thought he was the hottest guy I'd ever seen, but either my memory hasn't done him justice, my thirteen-year-old eyes had blinders on, or he's just gotten even hotter.

Because this Ben?
He is sex on a stick.
So gorgeous it almost hurts.

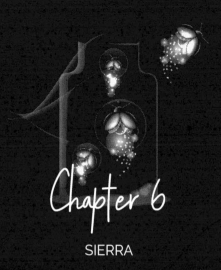

Chapter 6

SIERRA

IF I WASN'T on the verge of being violently assaulted, I'd swoon over Ben's piercing blue eyes, strong nose, that chiseled jawline coated in a sexy layer of scruff, and the thick glossy dark hair I used to fantasize about touching. He's bulked up too, looking broader in the shoulders with an impressive chest and defined biceps. His shirt is rolled to his elbows, highlighting his muscular arms with a dusting of dark hair I find so attractive in guys. The top few buttons of his shirt are undone, offering a glimpse of his toned chest with a smattering of dark chest hair.

"Ben?" I croak, finding my voice after the initial shock has worn off. "Is it really you?"

"Firefly." He smirks, arching a brow in a wholly arrogant way that is totally new. His eyes darken as he purposely drags his gaze over my body, inspecting me slowly from head to toe. "You're all grown up and so gorgeous."

Wait. What? I gape at him, and I'm sure my disbelief is written all over my face.

He moves right up in front of me, threading his fingers through my hair before twisting it around his fist, yanking my head back at an awkward angle.

My heart thumps erratically again, beating against my rib cage like it wants to escape. The Ben staring down at me—like he wants to devour me until he's sucked all the flesh from my bones—is not the Ben I remember. There's a cruel sheen to his gaze that wasn't there before. Or maybe it was, and I couldn't see it over the haze of infatuation.

Little sweat beads form on the nape of my neck, and my pulse throbs wildly as I try to work out whether Ben is an ally or a foe.

"You know the girl." Saverio isn't asking, and he looks irritated as fuck.

"Yes." Ben loosens his tight hold on my hair, and my neck welcomes the relief. Without subtlety, he pulls me away from the monster, tucking me in flush to his side. He stares at Saverio, no fear evident in his expression despite the naked aggression laid bare on Saverio's face. "And like I said, we have a problem. Two, really."

Another man approaches, clutching his unbuttoned pants to keep them up. He looks similar in age to Ben, if I had to hazard a guess. This guy is ripped with an impressive six-pack and a serious case of arm porn. His torso also bears the scars of a violent lifestyle, and I wonder if Ben looks like that when he's undressed. Which is kind of problematic when the man is holding me possessively like he can't decide if he wants to fuck me or kill me. I'd be totally down for the former—life-risking scenario aside.

"Who is she?" the stranger asks as he materializes beside Ben.

"Joseph Lawson's youngest daughter."

"Should I know who that is?" Saverio asks.

"He's Lawson Pharma," a man with salt-and-pepper hair and beady eyes says.

"He's well-connected and fiercely protective of his daughters," Ben explains. "If you hurt her, you'll pay a price. He's a billionaire with the resources to make your life hell."

Saverio shrugs. "I can handle a disgruntled businessman."

He clearly doesn't know my father.

"It's more than that though. She's my ex's little sister. I used to fantasize about doing her when she was older." My eyes pop wide, and Ben smirks again. "Don't pretend you weren't doing some fantasizing of your own, Firefly." He waggles his brows. "You drooled every time I came by the house, and I know you spied on Saskia and me."

Gripping my chin, he tilts my face up so I've no choice but to look at him. "Did you imagine it was you I was kissing? Did you lie in bed at night dreaming about me? Fingering your virgin pussy imagining it was my fingers inside you?"

A few chuckles ring out, and my cheeks inflame. I feel like I'm thirteen again, only this time it's Ben I want to murder.

A knowing laugh bursts from his mouth. "Grab my jacket," he tells his...friend? Colleague? Fellow deviant? I don't know who he is or how he knows Ben or even who Ben is anymore.

The man walks off, grinning as he grabs a tailored black suit jacket, returning with it in his hands.

"Open the inside pocket, retrieve my wallet, and remove the folded piece of paper," Ben instructs, and the man obliges. "Open it up."

A strangled sound leaves my mouth as the picture is revealed.

"You kept it," I whisper, fighting emotion. He kept the picture of the firefly I drew for him. It has my name and the date on the bottom right-hand corner.

"Aw, she must really love you," Ben's friend says, chuckling.

Saverio cracks his knuckles, looking ready to beat the crap out of both men.

"I know you had plans," Ben says, staring Saverio straight in the eye. "But she's not yours for the taking. I put dibs on her years ago, and I've waited for this night for a long time." He grabs my hip in a firm hold that hurts, fixing Saverio with a challenging look.

"You'd deny me?" Saverio drills a dark glare at Ben.

"You'd deny *me*?" Ben coolly retorts. "That wouldn't be a good start to our new working relationship."

The man beside Ben looks over his shoulder, and three of the men with guns move across the room, flanking our backs. Behind Saverio, a line of men forms, and the atmosphere shifts, tension palpable. Blood pounds in my head, alarm bells ring in my ears, and I'm afraid to even breathe.

"I don't take well to being insulted in my own domain," Saverio says, looking like he's ready to rip into Ben.

I want to say something, but I don't know what, and getting in between these two wouldn't be smart. I don't understand what's going on. I don't know who Ben is anymore. But I suspect he's trying to get me out of this, so I owe him my silence and my support. Very carefully, with no obvious visible movement, I place my hand on the small of his back. He stiffens, but it's subtle, and I doubt anyone noticed except for the guy with the muscles who is staring curiously at me.

Ben clears his throat. "I mean no disrespect, and perhaps we can come to an arrangement in relation to the girl."

"What arrangement?" Saverio grits out as I cast a quick glance at the seated area. The girls are all sitting dutifully on the couches, all still naked, looking bored as they stare anywhere but here. I wonder if they are drugged or just so immune to this world they don't pay attention anymore. At some point, someone lowered the music, and it's only soft background noise now.

"Let me have her, and I'll owe you a personal favor."

Ben's friend jerks his head up, looking alarmed for a split second, before schooling his features into a neutral line.

"It can be anything, and you can call it in at any time." Ben levels Saverio with a look I can't decipher.

Saverio stares at him for an indeterminable period of time before looking at the tall man with the salt-and-pepper hair. They share a silent exchange before Saverio swings his gaze back around to Ben. "Agreed."

I almost sag in relief, but I'm not out of the woods yet.

"But the girl stays and parties here with you." All the blood drains from my face when Saverio fixes me with a smug expression. "And you take responsibility for her and her friends. If any of this comes back at me, I will hold you personally responsible. There will be consequences to be paid."

"It won't come back at you. I give you my word. And I'll agree to your demands if you agree she's mine and mine alone." He levels a dark look at the beast. "No one else is allowed to touch her."

"Let me watch you fuck her and it's a deal."

What the what? Every cell in my body feels those words. A small squeak leaks from my mouth, and Ben pierces me with a ferocious look, warning me to keep quiet.

"Fine," Ben says, like he hasn't just agreed to fuck me with an audience.

In any other scenario, I'd be jumping for joy at this turn of events,

50

but there is no part of me that wants Ben to fuck me out of obligation, or protection, or guilt. And the thought of these disgusting old perverts seeing me naked and intimate with Ben makes me want to hurl. But it's better than being raped by the bastards. I have hope I can make it out of this night alive, which is more than could be said a few minutes ago.

"Hold on," Ben says, dragging me out of my head as he lifts me. My legs automatically wind around his trim waist, and my arms circle his shoulders as he walks us over to the couch. "Fuck off," he tells the naked blonde sitting on the end.

"Brandi!" Saverio hollers at her. "Get your whoring ass over here." Shooting daggers at me, she scampers over to Saverio as Ben sits down on the couch, keeping me on his lap.

Nerves blanket my skin and my heart is turning cartwheels as butterflies invade my chest.

Ben clasps my face in both of his large hands, taking his time drinking in my features. His thumb brushes across my lower lip. "So fucking beautiful." For a moment, a familiar adoring gaze sweeps over his face, but it's replaced by a look of cold fury so fast I'm not sure I didn't imagine it. "So fucking stupid." He shakes his head, glaring at me like he wants to throttle me. Clasping the back of my head, he holds it tight while he sits forward, moving his hot mouth to my ear. "Follow my lead," he whispers, "and don't say anything." He nuzzles his mouth into my neck, sending a wave of fiery shivers dancing over my skin.

I close my eyes, inhaling the spicy scent of his cologne when it swirls around me, drugging me, as his tongue darts out, tasting my flesh. A moan escapes my lips, and I writhe on top of him when I feel him hardening beneath me. His hands land on my hips, holding me steady, and I open my eyes, startled to find him staring at me with eyes as dark as the midnight sky. His nostrils flare, and his fingers dig into my hips as he stabs me with his smoldering blue eyes. When his gaze dips to my mouth, I forget how to breathe.

It's fucked up.

I know this.

I'm still in a precarious position, and Ben is clearly a dangerous man if this is the company he keeps. But I can't find it within myself to regret any of it, because the way he is looking at me now has obliterated all logic and sense of self-protection.

He's fighting an inner war, the conflict raging across his face, and I'm stuck between exhilaration and terror.

But the second his lips crash down on mine, there is no more thinking, just feeling, and I give in to it. Indulging my teen fantasy by opening myself up to Ben. Letting him do whatever he wants to me, even if I already know he's going to ruin me for every other man.

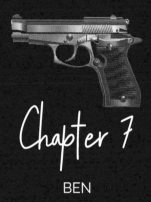

Chapter 7

BEN

IF I DIDN'T already know I was going straight to hell, this moment would confirm it. Sierra's soft lips glide willingly against mine, and the little sounds she's making are killing me. I'm only kissing her, and she's moaning and writhing on top of me like I'm fucking her. My cock is hard as steel, twitching with the need to bury itself balls deep inside her. She runs her fingers through my hair as we kiss, and her touch sets me on fire in a way I haven't felt in a long time.

I've worked hard to remain unattached. I have a short list of fuck buddies I call upon when I need pussy, and they all understand the score. I don't usually kiss women either. It helps keep things detached and purely about the physical act. With them, it's only sex.

But I can't do that to Sierra.

At least, that's the reason I'm telling myself why I'm currently kissing the shit out of her.

It would be easy to get lost in her, but I can't forget where we are. The danger hasn't passed. I feel Salerno's eyes burning a hole in the side of my skull while he pounds Brandi's ass over the arm of his chair. He has little interest in her. I've deprived him of the right to fuck Sierra—in his eyes—and he wants to live vicariously through me.

I've done a lot of bad things in my life, but deflowering the little girl I cared about, in front of a bunch of violent perverts, will not be one of them.

My plan is risky, and we could all end up killed if he realizes I have tricked him, but it's a risk I'm willing to take if it means keeping Sierra's virginity intact so she can give it to someone she loves. A guy who is deserving of her. No one in this room comes even close to measuring up.

"We back in kindergarten, boy?" Salerno grumbles in between pants.

Reluctantly, I drag my mouth from Sierra's, eyeballing the controlling asshole. "I'm warming *my* girl up," I coolly reply, emphasizing she's mine and he agreed no one else was having her. Sierra has gone still on my lap, and tension radiates from her body like it's a tangible substance. My eyes meet her gorgeous emerald gaze, shocked to see such naked desire in her expression. Her cheeks are flushed, her hair messed up, and her lips are swollen from my kisses, and damn, if that doesn't do something to me.

"Quit messing around," Salerno snarls. "Get her naked." His eyes drag the length of Sierra, and I want to gouge them from his eye sockets and stuff them down his throat.

Gripping her hips, I lift her onto the ground and stand, pulling her protectively into my side. "I fully intend to." I flash him a cocky grin as I lead her toward the stairs.

"Where the fuck are you going?" Salerno shouts, grunting loudly. I turn us around in time to watch him empty his load into Brandi's ass.

Sierra trembles, and I instinctively hold her closer. "Upstairs."

"Like fuck you are," Salerno hisses, yanking his dick out. Cum leaks from Brandi's ass, dripping down her thighs, and I know Sierra has seen it because she shivers violently against me. "The deal was you let me watch."

"And you still can. Unless you're saying the cameras have been removed from the bedrooms?" I quirk a brow, enjoying having the upper hand. One of the first things my father taught me was to always choose my words carefully, and it was good advice.

If Salerno had his gun close at hand, I'm pretty sure he'd shoot me. But we had a deal. We both gave our word, and he knows he can't do anything. He will still get to watch. Just not up close and personal like he assumed.

"I'd shoot you right now, boy, if it wouldn't start a war I couldn't win." A muscle clenches in his jaw as he swipes the bottle of scotch from the table, glaring at me. His gaze swings to Sierra, and she bravely holds his stare.

"Let's not overreact." I purposely reposition us so he's looking at her side profile. The last thing I need is him getting in her head before the plan has been fully executed. "You'll still get what you want. No blood needs to be spilled."

He says nothing else as we walk away, but his contempt stabs me in the back the entire way up the stairs. One of my soldiers silently follows, to stand guard, taking up position outside the middle bedroom I lead Sierra into.

Closing the door, I exhale heavily as I lean against it, praying I'm strong enough to do this. Sierra stands in the center of the room, looking uncertain but beautiful as fuck. Precum leaks from my cock as my erection strains painfully against my zipper, begging for release. It's been weeks since I fucked anyone, and I'm testing my self-control to the limits.

Sierra reaches around her back, and the sound of a zipper lowering is the only sound in the room.

"Not yet." I push off the door, stalking toward her, watching her eyes blaze with wanton desire and her lips part in expectation. "Keep the dress on for now," I instruct, brushing my fingers across her cheek as I drop down onto the bed. "Remove your shoes," I tell her, kicking off my own. Lying against the headrest, I pat my lap, gesturing her forward. She climbs slowly onto the bed, and I'm not sure if she's being deliberately seductive, but she is challenging my self-control with her sexy-ass moves as she crawls over my body, positioning herself in my lap again.

Yanking her head down, I lick a path up the column of her elegant neck, inhaling the gorgeous floral scent of her perfume. "Relax," I whisper into her ear. "I am going to take care of you."

"I trust you," she whispers back.

Still so stupid.

I reclaim her lips, and there's nothing gentle about this kiss. I brutalize her mouth, pushing my tongue past her lips and exploring. She tastes fruity, from whatever she was drinking, and it only adds to the appeal. Letting my hands wander her gorgeous body, I caress every curve and dip within reach. She moves on top of me again, thrusting her hips against mine, and more precum leaks from my cock. At this rate, I might even come in my boxers like I did as a horny teen.

Reaching between us, she unbuckles my belt and pulls my zipper down, sliding her hand into my boxers and palming my erection. I bite her lower lip, dragging it between my teeth as all the blood in my body rushes south. Her fingers curl around my shaft, and the urge to fuck her into next week is riding me hard.

"Remove your panties," I demand, leaning down to lick a line across the gentle swells of her tits. Scrambling off me, she lies back and shimmies black lace panties down her gorgeous long legs. She sits, but I push her back down, parting her legs and kneeling between her tempting thighs.

Fuck, I shouldn't be doing this, but I've got to make this look real. If it looks staged, Salerno will smell a rat, and the party will become a bloodbath.

Tracing my hands slowly and carefully up her legs, I keep my eyes fixed on her face, seeing nothing but trust and desire and need. I hover over her, pressing my lips to her mouth as my fingers sweep underneath her dress, trailing up her inner thigh. She shivers underneath me, and a light flush stains her cheeks. "So fucking beautiful," I repeat, kissing her again before I sit back on my heels.

Pushing her dress up to her waist, I immediately lower my head to her pussy so the asshole doesn't get much of a view. She's bare. All pink and glistening and mine for the taking. Parting her thighs wider, like a sacrificial lamb, she eagerly opens herself up, welcoming me.

I dive in, plunging my tongue into her pussy, while my hips grind involuntarily against the comforter. I forget where I am and who I'm with as I devour her, fucking her roughly with my fingers and my tongue. Her scent swirls around me, rousing my inner beast from slumber, and I lift her legs, draping them over my shoulders as her hips arch, granting me better access. I eat her out like a starving man at an all-you-can-eat buffet, vigorously rubbing her clit with two fingers while I fuck her cunt with my tongue.

The sounds coming from her mouth are insanely hot, and if she doesn't stop, I won't be able to resist fucking her. She explodes on my face, shoving her pussy into my mouth with no shame as she detonates, hips bucking and body spasming as her climax whips through her. I remove my pants and boxers as I watch her come down from her high. Without giving her time to recover, I spin us around until she's back on top of me. I'm careful to keep her dress on, positioning her pussy over my pubes with my dick nudging against her puckered hole. I groan at the feel of her crack against my hot dick, fighting the almost overwhelming urge to hammer her ass.

She tries to move down, and I subtly shake my head, digging my fingers into her hips to keep her in place. Confusion washes over her face, and I sit up, snaking my arms around her back to hold her body pressed against me. I fit my mouth to her ear. "This needs to look real," I whisper, placing a slew of kisses on her neck. "And you need to look scared."

Salerno would expect that of any virgin.

"I'm going to thrust my hips as if I'm inside you. Let me control the pace, but rock back and forth on top of me like we're fucking. You can whimper a little after a while."

"You're not going to fuck me?" she whispers. I detect something other than vulnerability in her tone. Tilting my head back, I look deep into her eyes. Sierra always wore her heart on her sleeve and the pain of my rejection is plain to see.

"I'm not going to take your virginity like this," I whisper over her mouth, as I thrust my hips up, not faking a groan when my dick pulses against her ass.

She pivots her hips against me, staring me directly in the eye as she whispers, "I'm not a virgin, and I think you should do this. I know you don't want to, and I'm sorry to force you into it, but if you don't, he will, and I can't bear the thought of that man coming anywhere near me."

I open my mouth to ask if she's crazy, but I stop myself from going there. Admitting I'm having a difficult time restraining myself and I wouldn't be forcing anything will only give her the wrong impression. She's a beautiful woman grinding on top of my dick, and I haven't had sex in weeks. Of course, I want to fuck her. And now I'm given the green light, I see no reason to hold back anymore.

Holding her face between my palms, I ask the question with

my eyes. Her answering expression is unrelenting and assuredly affirmative.

There's no going back now.

Salerno is expecting a show, and while I had initially planned to keep her dress on, to hide the fact we weren't really fucking, there is no need to take that risk now. She can be naked, and I can still shield her from his view so he's only catching fleeting glimpses.

Lowering the zipper on her dress, I help her out of it, tossing it aside, leaving her semi-naked. My eyes remain on Sierra's as I unclasp her strapless bra, letting it fall away. I peruse her body with a dry mouth and twitching hands.

She is utter perfection.

A work of beauty as if she was carved by the gods.

The craving to touch every inch of her is almost overwhelming. Her chest heaves as I drink my fill, and she drags her lower lip between her teeth in a nervous tell. Her tits are perfectly formed—not big but not too small either. Nice handfuls. Her nipples are neat rose-pink buds that demand to be sucked and plucked. My cock lies heavy between my thighs, precum lining the crown, and I can't hold back a second longer.

Shoving her flat on her back, I spread her legs and thrust inside her in one powerful move. She screams, and I lose whatever vestiges of civility I was clinging to. I fuck her, and fuck her, and fuck her. Pounding into her over and over, moaning and cursing as her tight walls grip my cock and I see stars behind my eyes.

Sweat adheres my shirt to my chest, and I rip it off, buttons flying everywhere. Flipping her over, onto all fours, I ram my cock back inside her, and she lets another scream loose. While one hand holds her steady at the hip to control my thrusts, I use my free hand to play with her tits. Alternating my attention, I flick her taut nipples, tugging and plucking as I plunge my erection inside her, slamming in and out, her body jolting with the movement.

Sweat glides down my spine as I fuck her harder, pushing her head down into the comforter and yanking her hips up more so I can thrust deeper. My fingers leave her tits, moving to her clit, and I rub her frantically as my balls tighten and lift and a familiar tingle whizzes up my spine. I roar as I spill inside her, driving in and out until my climax is exhausted and I've emptied my seed.

But I'm not sated. Not by a long shot. I need more.

"Fix yourself up," I bark. "We're leaving."

I hastily dress, leaving my ruined shirt on the floor, watching with hungry eyes as she gets dressed. Next time I fuck her, I want her heels on and her slim legs wrapped around my shoulders. I tap out a message to Leo as I slip my feet into my shoes. Then I swipe her stilettos, grab her hand, and pull her out of the room. My soldier follows us as we descend the stairs.

Leo and the rest of my men are waiting for us at the bottom of the stairs.

"Leaving so soon, Mazzone?" Salerno sneers from his position on the couch. The wide screen is lowered, the picture fixed on the bedroom we just vacated. The fucker let everyone watch. A few of the guys are fucking the whores while the rest are stroking their dicks, smirking at me to make their point known. I want to slice every one of their dicks off and shove them up their asses.

Pulling Sierra around so she's facing my front, I press her head to my chest, hoping she didn't spot the screen already. Rage pummels my insides, and it's not all directed at Salerno.

I lost control.

Enjoyed fucking her too much.

But there's no sense in beating myself up over it. What's done is done, and I can't rewind time or find it within myself to regret it because my dick is still straining against my zipper and screaming at me to bury myself in her wet warmth again. I just want to get her out of here now.

"You got what you wanted, and our business is concluded," I say, handing Sierra to Leo with a warning look. He nods, automatically understanding as he ushers her out into the corridor. One of my *soldati*, a smart guy who initiated a year ago, steps forward in his undershirt, holding his black button-up out to me. I slide my arms in the sleeves before walking to Salerno. I extend my hand. "I trust our personal deal is still intact and it remains between us." If my father discovers what I did, he will bust my balls, so I need to ensure this is contained.

"I'm a man of my word," Salerno says though it doesn't need to be spoken. We shake hands, and I nod. "It was a pleasure doing business with you," he adds, and I wish I could knock that smug grin off his face. He will most likely use the favor to force me into marrying his daughter, but he won't call it in for a while. A smart man would hold on to it for the right time. Anais is only eleven, and tradition rarely sees women married before eighteen, so I have a few years to come to terms with the consequences of saving Sierra.

"We'll be in touch." I offer a curt nod to Russo and Gambini before striding toward the exit, buttoning my shirt as I push through the doors into the corridor.

Leo is waiting with my men, his hand resting lightly on Sierra's shoulder. I scowl at him until he removes it with a grin. My hand wraps around hers, and I tug her forward. "Let's go." I need to put distance between me and that room before I change my mind and slaughter them all.

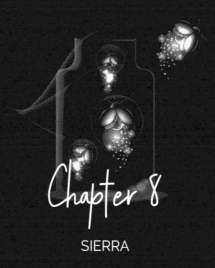

Chapter 8

SIERRA

I BLINK MY eyes open, wetting my dry lips as I take in my surroundings. This definitely isn't our suite at the Bellagio. I move in the bed, and my body aches deliciously, helping my memory to kick into gear. Turning around, I stretch my arm out, but the other side of the bed is stone cold. I sit up, clutching the black silk sheets to my naked chest, wondering where Ben is. Pushing the messy strands of my hair from my face, I scan the bedroom. Seeing it's empty, I climb out of the king-sized bed, my body protesting the motion.

I ache everywhere. There's a persistent throbbing between my legs, and my ass is a little sore. I yawn, knowing I haven't had much sleep, even if I have no idea what time it is. After entering the en suite bathroom, I pee before scrubbing my face clean of any lingering makeup and switching the shower on. Although I don't want to wash Ben's scent from my flesh, I'm sweaty and gross, and my skin feels icky.

My lips curl into a crazy smile as I stand under the hot water, tilting my chin up, letting water stream down my face. Memories of last night resurface in my mind as I shower. I should probably be focusing more on the predicament I found myself in—and offer thanks that I escaped unscathed—but all I can focus on is the mind-blowing sex Ben and I had repeatedly all night long.

It exceeded my wildest dreams and then some.

I presumed he was taking me to my hotel after we left Flame, but he took me to his hotel suite and ravished my body until we both collapsed from exhaustion. My nipples harden and my core pulses with renewed need as I recall the various ways he took me. His passion was a relentless train that sped along the tracks, going two hundred miles an hour, pulling me along for the ride.

There is no way you could call it making love.

He fucked me like we were wild animals with no boundaries. Like humans with the bare minimum of decency, and I freaking loved it. He pounded his cock into me with a savagery I never knew existed, and I became someone new, someone with no inhibitions and a rampant thirst for exploration.

I blush as I recall giving him my anal virginity, but I don't regret it.

I don't regret a single thing. How could I when he was the one guy I daydreamed about for years? My childish fantasies could never match the real deal. And my limited sexual experience couldn't prepare me for a man like Ben. Nothing could. I knew he would ruin me for all others, and I was right.

I can't imagine any man coming close to measuring up.

No night will ever be as magical as last night.

But I'm no longer some naïve thirteen-year-old, and Ben is no longer the same Ben I knew. We didn't talk last night—Ben's rough commands and his dirty talking don't count—and I have questions I need answers to. Like how he knows Saverio Salerno? Who are those men with him, and why does everyone call him Bennett Mazzone now? Where has he been all this time?

After my shower, I blow-dry my hair and get dressed in my clothes from last night before stepping out of the bedroom into the main body of the large suite with my high heels dangling from my fingers.

I spot Ben first, perched at the island unit in the kitchen. His face is buried in a laptop, and he's oblivious to my approach. He is wearing a white shirt and black pants, but his feet are bare. There is something so incredibly sexy about a man with no shoes or socks on that gets me horny like you wouldn't believe. My nostrils twitch as the scent of his spicy cologne slaps me in the face, and I can't contain my grin.

Coming up behind him, I wrap my arms around his torso, pressing the side of my face against his warm back. "Good morning." I place a kiss to the side of his neck, savoring the feel of his skin against my lips.

He visibly stiffens, lifting his head from his laptop but not turning around. "What do you think you're doing?" His voice is brusque and laced with an undercurrent I can't decipher.

I pull away, gulping over the sudden lump clogging my throat. Nerves fire at me from all angles as I move around the island unit so I'm facing him. "What do you mean?" My brows furrow in confusion.

His eyes narrow as he stares at me. One corner of his mouth tilts into a sneer. "Why are you still here? What makes you think you can talk to me? Touch me without invitation?" Hostility seeps from his pores like fog, and I take a step back as if that will protect me from the horrible vibes he's emitting.

My mouth opens and closes, but I can't form words.

"Cat got your tongue?" he taunts, and there is no warmth in his expression. No sign of the dark lust from last night evident in his cold ice-blue eyes.

"Why are you being like this?" I fold my arms protectively across my chest, feeling vulnerable.

"You told me you weren't a virgin, so I'm sure you're familiar with the concept of a one-night stand." His tone suggests he's already bored of this conversation, and he ignores me, lowering his gaze as he refocuses his attention on his laptop.

I bristle at his words and his clear dismissal of what we shared. Anger ignites a fuse inside me, and I glare at him, wishing he wasn't such a handsome fucker and my heart wasn't such a pitiful organ with minimal self-respect. "I know what a one-night-stand is, asshole. And last night wasn't one."

He lifts his head again, and the venomous look in his eyes forces me to take another few steps back out of sheer instinct.

Saverio is a man who prides himself on the monster within. A man who revels in displaying everything he is. As I look at Ben now, I see the same monster lurking behind his gorgeous exterior. I thought Saverio was the only man I needed to fear, but I see the error of my ways. Ben is everything Saverio is. He has just chosen to hide it. Most likely, it's on purpose—to lure unsuspecting victims in.

"You seem to be suffering from some delusions. Let me clear it up for you." Ben stands, and in my bare feet, he appears to tower over me like a dark shadow obscuring all the light.

Tension bleeds into the air as he steps toward me, and I take a step back.

"Ben." Someone calls his name, and my head whips sideways, only noticing the other four men now. His friend stands, walking toward us. He's the guy who escorted me out of the basement room last night. He didn't speak, regarding me with equal parts curiosity and wariness, but he didn't seem unkind. "I don't think—"

"If I want your advice, Leo, I'll ask for it," Ben says in a clipped tone. Leo stops walking, leaning against a pillar in the large open-plan room. "This is between *Firefly* and me."

He uses his pet name for me in a derisory manner, and it hurts. Ben has never spoken to me like this before, and I don't understand why he feels the need to be hurtful now. It was clearly just a one-time thing for him, and it's not like I had huge expectations. I live in Chicago and he lives…who the hell knows where. I wasn't anticipating walking hand in hand into the sunset, but I did expect respect and that we would at least part ways as friends.

This crap is bullshit, and he doesn't get to humiliate me.

Heat creeps up my chest and onto my neck, but I stop retreating, holding my chin up and fixing Ben with a deadly look of my own. Fuck him. He doesn't get to intimidate me. Not after everything we did last night. "Set me straight then," I hiss. "If you're such a big man."

An ugly sneer dances across his handsome face. "You're still just a little girl trying to fit into a world you don't belong in."

He knows how to hit hard, and those words penetrate deep, stabbing me clear through the heart. "You know nothing about me. About the person I am today."

He steps right up to me, drilling me with stony eyes, devoid of any human emotion. "I know you're a stupid little girl who found herself trapped in the lion's den. Tell me, what would you have done if I hadn't been there last night?"

I gulp, unable to answer, because the truth is, I was all out of options and we both know it. Some of my anger fades, remembering how he saved me. "Thank you for saving me," I say because I don't think I said thanks last night.

He scoffs. "You already thanked me."

I frown because I honestly don't recall saying those words.

The cruel sneer returns to his face. "You thanked me with your tight pussy and your virgin ass."

My cheeks inflame as anger returns tenfold. How fucking dare he say that to me, especially in front of his friends. "Fuck you, Ben."

"You already did, Firefly, and it wasn't all that memorable."

Tears prick my eyes, and my lower lip wobbles. Pain slices across my chest as his words cut deep.

"There she is," he says, gripping my chin tightly. "The vulnerable little girl who so desperately wants to be loved."

He is throwing acid all over my memories, and I will never forgive him for it. Never.

"You're not your sister," he adds, continuing to dig in the knife. "You will never be Saskia."

I've never wanted to be her, and he might think he's insulting me, but that's the greatest compliment he could ever pay me. I can't find it within me to be upset he favors her over me. Right now, I can't think of two people more deserving of one another. "Pity she's married now and you've missed your opportunity."

He barks out a laugh. "You think a little thing like a wedding band would stop me from taking what I want? I took you, didn't I? And it required no effort. It's probably why it wasn't enjoyable. Saskia always presented a challenge."

I slap him across the face, and the three men on the couch hop up, hands automatically going to the guns strapped at their hips. Leo shakes his head, and they hold their ground, not sitting back down but not coming over here either.

"I'll give her your regards," I say, spinning on my bare feet, ready to get the hell out of here when he yanks me back. He pulls me flush against his body, and his arm wraps around my neck, locking tight under my chin, restricting my airflow and holding me in place. Panic jumps up and bites me, and I work hard to control my breathing, stowing whatever oxygen I have left in my lungs.

"Listen carefully, Firefly. You will not breathe a word of last night to anyone. No part of what happened will leave your lips. As far as anyone is concerned, last night was a figment of your imagination. You might think I'm an asshole, but Saverio Salerno is a different kind of asshole. One you don't want to unleash. Don't make me hunt you down." He shoves me away, and I gasp, clutching the side of the island unit to stop myself from falling as I suck in air. "Now get out and don't come back."

I don't need to be told twice, rushing out of his suite, swiping at the slew of hot angry tears as they course down my cheeks.

Chapter 9

SIERRA

I STOMP THROUGH the lobby of the prestigious Venetian hotel, uncaring that I'm doing the walk of shame because fuck those gawking bystanders. I don't know who they are, and I won't see them again. I flip my middle finger up at an older couple who are shaking their heads and looking at me with disgust as I pass by. Father would be furious if he saw me now, but I'm too freaking mad and upset to care about anything except getting the hell out of here.

When I step onto the sidewalk, I realize I have no purse, no cell, and no money. I can still get a cab and make the driver come up to our suite so I can pay him. I'm walking toward an empty cab when a man wearing a smart black suit steps in front of me. "Miss Lawson?" he inquires, and I peer at him, narrowing my eyes suspiciously.

"Who wants to know?"

"Mr. Mazzone asked me to drive you to the Bellagio." He opens the door to a black Mercedes with fully tinted windows, lifting a brow when I don't move a muscle. I'm tempted to tell him where he can stick his ride, but there's no point being stupid about it, so I climb into the back seat and let him drop me at my hotel, fuming the entire journey.

"Thank God!" Pen screeches, rushing me the instant I step foot in our suite. "I've been going out of my mind with worry." Flinging her arms around me, she hugs me tight. I cling to her, needing a friendly hug so badly. She eases back, examining me from head to toe. "Are you okay? Did they hurt you?"

"I'm fine. I'm not hurt." Much. I glance around the empty suite, frowning. "Where is everyone?"

"Esme is showering, Tony is freaking out someplace, and the rest of the girls are in the casino."

Shit. I scrub my hands down my face. I'd forgotten about my bodyguard. It's no wonder Tony is going crazy. I need to find him before he calls my father. I'm hoping the fact I was MIA means he hasn't called him yet—Father would blow a gasket if he knew I was lost in Vegas without protection, and Tony would be out of a job. I'm hoping his sense of self-preservation is strong enough to have held off making that call.

Pen touches my arm, and worry lines furrow her brow. "Are you sure you're okay?"

"I am. I promise." I notice the bruising shadows under her eyes, and I can tell she's had a sleepless night. "Are *you* okay? And what happened after you left?" I remember how terrified she was last night.

"I'm fine. Look, why don't you get changed, I'll order us some room service, and then the three of us can talk."

I nod. "Sounds like a plan."

I conduct a quick search for Tony, but he's not in the suite. Going into my room, I change into yoga pants and a slouchy shirt that rests just below my ass. I tease my hair into a messy topknot before slipping my feet into fluffy slippers. I find my purse on the bedside table, and I'm grateful one of my friends made sure to bring it home. I check the contents, and it's all there. My cell is dead, so I plug it in to charge as someone raps on my door. I open it, revealing a furious Tony. I sigh, not in the mood for a lecture, but there's no point in delaying the inevitable. And it's not like I don't deserve it. "Come in."

He storms into the room, brushing past me with his nostrils flaring. He is red in the face like he ran up all thirty-six floors. "Jesus fucking Christ. You are going to be the death of me." He sighs heavily while examining me from head to toe. Satisfied I'm in one piece, he grips my shoulders. "Where the fuck were you?" he barks.

"Out partying?" I shrug, smiling sheepishly, because I'm not sure how to handle Tony when he's like this.

"Don't act cute." He lowers his hands from my shoulders, dragging his fingers through his short hair. "Don't you know how worried I was? I've been frantic, searching everywhere for you." He glares at me, and I can tell he'd love to throttle me right now. "You have a lot of explaining to do, Sierra. Your father will not be pleased."

I almost choke on my tongue. "Please tell me you haven't spoken to my father," I splutter, flopping onto the edge of my bed.

He rubs the bridge of his nose. "Not yet, but he's been blowing up my phone, and I need to return his call."

I sit up straighter. "You can't tell him. He'll just ground me for eternity, and you'll get fired." I might be twenty-one, but I'm still living at home, and my father has numerous ways to make me suffer.

"Do you think your father pays me to protect you as some kind of joke?" he shouts.

"No. Of course not."

"Do you have any idea how much danger you were in last night?" He shakes his head, staring at me with a mix of anger and concern.

Eh, yeah, buddy. I was aware of how close I came to being raped and murdered. I can't say that though, so I press my lips together, happy to let him vent and hopefully get it all off his chest.

"Do you hate me then?" His brows climb to his hairline. "Is that it? You want to get me fired, or you were hoping to kill me?"

"Don't be ridiculous." It's not like Tony to be dramatic. "I might hate what you represent, but I don't hate you personally. Giving you a few sleeping pills is not the same as poisoning you, which is what I'd do if I wanted to kill you."

"Don't you dare make light of this. This is no laughing matter," he snaps, and it's uncharacteristic because Tony is always calm and he's always been nice to me. "I didn't wake until six a.m., Sierra. I was knocked out cold for twelve hours. Anything could have happened to you in that time. I had no choice but to take Pen's word that you were safe. Knowing you were out there with some guy I hadn't vetted, without your purse or your cell—" Scrubbing a hand across his stubbly chin, he shakes his head, pinning me with pained eyes as he sighs. "I've been worried sick."

I'm instantly chastised because I see the truth written all over his face. I lean forward on my elbows, looking him straight in the eye. "I'm really sorry, Tony. It was a totally shitty thing to do. This wasn't anything personal. I swear. I just wanted to let loose and have fun without you watching my every move and reporting it to my father."

"And did you?" he asks.

I frown. "Did I what?"

"Have fun?" His features soften a little as he looks at me expectantly. Reading between the lines, I can tell he understands why I did what I did, maybe even approves on a subconscious level. Warmth spreads across my chest. I'm glad Tony is my bodyguard. Because he knows me, understands me, and while he still wants to throttle me for putting myself at risk, he gets it.

I smile, nodding. "I did." Mostly.

He crouches over me, and his brow puckers as he gently brushes his fingers against my neck. His eyes narrow as he zones in on the slight finger-sized bruising around my throat. "Did someone hurt you?" Anger and fear replace the previous emotion in his eyes, and he looks ready to flatten someone.

"No. It's not what it looks like." I inwardly cringe. "It was consensual."

"You're sure I don't need to beat someone's ass?"

I cough out a laugh at the very idea of Tony trying to take on Ben and his gun-toting friends. "I'm sure."

He stands. "This can't happen again, Sierra. I'm charged with protecting you for a reason. There are plenty of crazies out there who would love to get at your father through you. If anything had happened to you last night, I would never have been able to live with it. Your safety is more than just a job to me."

Without hesitation, I jump up, flinging my arms around him. He doesn't hesitate to return my hug, and we enjoy a rare, brief embrace. "I care about you too. And I am really, genuinely, honestly sorry. I promise I will never do that again."

"Okay." Air whooshes out of his mouth, and the last vestiges of his anger disappear.

"So, we're gonna keep this between us. Yeah?" I offer him my best puppy-dog eyes.

"Yeah." He sighs, running a hand across the back of his neck. "But don't make me regret it. If your father finds out what happened, and that I hid it from him, he won't just can my ass."

"He won't find out. I promise." I know Pen and Esme will carry the secret to their graves. The other girls are never at my house, and Father doesn't even know their names, so we're good. I breathe a sigh of relief. At least that's one problem diverted.

I follow Tony out, joining my two best friends in the living room, watching as he exits the suite to stand guard in the corridor.

"I didn't know what you wanted, so I ordered a bunch of things," Pen says, waving at the array of cold and hot foods on the long coffee table.

My stomach rumbles appreciatively, reminding me I haven't eaten since dinner last night. "What time is it anyway?"

"It's just after two," Esme says, pulling me into a hug. Holy shit. I guess I got more sleep than I thought. "Pen woke me at eight to tell me what happened." She holds me at arm's length, staring at me with tears in her eyes. "Are you okay?"

"I'm fine," I assure her.

"This is all my fault. I'm so, so sorry. I should never have gone after that man."

"You shouldn't have," I agree, stacking a mountain of fries and a chicken burger on my plate. I add some salad to offset the coronary-inducing feast.

If I wasn't so pissed at Ben, I would be angry at my friend now. Truth is, Esme's recklessness almost cost me and Pen our lives. If Ben hadn't been there, who knows if either of us would be standing here right now.

"Are you sure you aren't hurt?" she asks, biting down on her lower lip.

"I'm not. At least not physically." I proceed to fill them in on everything as we eat, and they listen attentively. Esme interrupts, cursing like a sailor when I get to the part where Ben insulted me and then basically kicked me out of his place.

"That fucking bastard," Esme seethes. "I've a good mind to head over to the Venetian and give him a piece of my mind." And there's that reckless streak again.

"It's not worth it, and it's far too dangerous." I doubt Ben and his friends carry guns as accessories. "Besides, I never want to lay eyes on him again."

"That sucks, babe." Pen pins me with a sympathetic look. "I remember how badly you were crushing on him."

"He wasn't worthy of your devotion," Esme says. "But it's weird he keeps your picture in his pocket."

"Do you think he knew we would be there?" Pen asks, looking newly concerned.

"I don't see how." I stuff the last couple fries in my mouth. "Esme made the booking in her name, and we only stumbled across Scarface Salerno by accident."

"Then, shocker, I agree with Esme. It's weird he'd be so cruel when you clearly meant something to him. He wouldn't have kept the picture otherwise."

"And it's not like you were a shit lay," Esme supplies, and my mind instantly recoils in horror. "Babe. Stop freaking out." She squeezes my hand. "No guy fucks a girl all night long unless he's really into the sex. He came, right?"

I nod. "Multiple times. On me and in me."

"So, it's not that." Esme taps a finger on her chin.

"It doesn't matter anyway." I set my empty plate down on the table. "I don't want to think about Ben anymore. As far as I'm concerned, he's dead to me now." I uncap a bottle of water, glugging a few mouthfuls. "He wants me to forget last night ever happened, and I'm A-okay with that."

"That guy he sent here said the same thing," Pen says, and I almost spit my water all over the floor.

"What guy?"

Pen glances over her shoulder to ensure no one is listening. She lowers her voice. "That dickhead Renzo brought me back here, and he insisted on taking my cell and disconnecting the phone in the suite so I couldn't call anyone. I was losing it, close to breaking point, when Ben's friend Leo showed up." Her cheeks flush, and I arch a brow.

"You didn't give me any of these deets earlier," Esme says, wearing a curious expression. "Spill."

Pen purses her lips, but she can't contain her grin. "He was hot and ripped and a bit scary but super sexy."

"Poor Eric." Esme licks yogurt off the back of her spoon.

Pen elbows her in the ribs. "Poor Eric nothing. I still love my fiancé, but I can acknowledge a hot guy when I see one."

"What did he want?" I ask, keen to get to the meat of the story.

"He got rid of Renzo. Told me not to worry, that you were safe, with Ben, and he would take care of you. He stayed with me, disappearing for a few minutes when the others arrived back totally smashed."

"I have the headache to prove it," Esme says, dumping her empty yogurt carton in the trash.

"I got everyone to bed," Pen continues, ignoring Esme, "and when I came back out, Leo had made coffee."

"How cozy." Esme waggles her brows, and Pen flips her the bird.

"He was pretty vague, yet he still managed to drive his point home. Basically, he said what Ben said but in a nicer way—those men from the basement are dangerous, and we need to keep quiet about last night. It's why I only told Esme the truth. All the others know is you met a random guy and went back to his hotel."

"Thanks, Pen. I think we're all agreed we need to keep it a secret."

"You're preaching to the choir," she says, her face turning pale.

I take her hands in mine. "I know you were petrified last night. Are you sure you're okay?"

Tears pool in her eyes. "I have never been so scared. I was sure they were going to rape both of us and then slit our throats when they were done." She looks away as a single tear rolls down her face. "I'm so sorry I left you there, Sierra. I'm a shitty friend."

"Stop that." I tip her chin up with one finger. "You're not and it wasn't your fault. I made the decision, and you shouldn't feel guilty about that. If you had fought, they might have shot you."

"That's what Leo said," she whispers. "He said I was bait. That it's Scarface's MO. He was always going to use me to force you into staying."

I hadn't considered that last night. I was too panicked. But it makes sense. He readily agreed to my plan and let Pen go without argument.

"The most important thing is we are all safe and no one got hurt," Esme says.

"Except for my bruised pride." I shrug, trying not to feel dejected.

"Look at it this way," Esme adds, pulling her knees into her chest on the couch. "You got to screw your crush and he was a fucking beast in bed. He gave you multiple O's, popped your anal cherry, and you won't forget your twenty-first birthday in a hurry."

"For fuck's sake, Esme. Are you stupid?" Pen snaps, glaring at our bestie. "You need to wake the fuck up and stop talking crap. Stop acting without thinking. This is no joking matter. You weren't in that basement. Sierra is lucky Ben was there. I shudder to think what state she would be in now if he hadn't been able to stop it."

Esme looks instantly chastised, and her voice is quiet when she speaks. "You think I don't know that, Pen?" Tears swim in her eyes. "If you think I'm not torn up over this, you're mistaken."

"It's okay," I say, reaching out to both my friends, taking their hands. I know Esme isn't as carefree and unthinking as she'd have us believe. She struggles to process things, and she uses humor and detachment to avoid facing hard facts. I know she's remorseful, in her own way, and she'll try to make it up to me. "We're not playing the blame game. Yes, there are lessons to be learned from last night, but I'm choosing to focus on the positives and not dwell on the what-ifs. All I ask is you both try to do the same."

They nod, and I slump against the couch. "One thing's for sure," I say, in parting, a wry grin spreading across my mouth. "This is definitely one weekend I'll never forget."

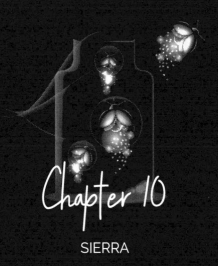

Chapter 10

SIERRA

Life returns to normal in the weeks that follow the Vegas trip, but the events of my birthday weekend are never far from my mind. I'd be lying if I said I didn't think about Ben. The first couple of weeks were a bit of a haze, as the full extent of the danger I was in finally registered, and I existed in a state of delayed terror. I vented my emotions in my studio every night, painting until my soul was cleansed and I found my inner Zen again. After I moved past that, my thoughts became preoccupied with Ben.

His cruel dismissal still hurts, but most of my anger has faded. I had a near escape, and he saved me from a fate that would have either killed me or traumatized me for the rest of my life. Relief and gratitude are my overriding emotions now, and I can't find it in my heart to hate him. Maybe I'm naïve, but I want to remember the good in him, and he showed me that weekend he still has plenty of that.

Christmas is the same old parade of stuffy parties and events with my family, and the strain of keeping up appearances, making small talk with lecherous bores and their Stepford wives, almost kills me. It's only the few college parties I manage to sneakily attend that keep me sane over the festive period. Pen and Esme notice I'm distracted, but I deflect their concerns, blaming my odd mood on the stress of having to play the role of dutiful, meek Lawson daughter.

Spring semester starts, and I attend classes, throwing myself into my studies while I continue to deny the truth. Until I can't deny it any longer, and I pull on my big girl panties and buy a pregnancy test.

I slump to the ground on the tiled floor of my personal bathroom, staring in resigned acceptance at the word on the digital stick.

PREGNANT

I've been expecting this result, but I'm still floored. *Literally.* My periods are always erratic, so when I missed one in November, I didn't dwell on it. However, when my period failed to arrive again in December, I knew. Deep down, I knew. But I couldn't face it, so I wallowed in la-la land for another month until I woke this morning with sore breasts that are definitely bigger. It is the slap in the face I need to stop burying my head in the sand.

A few silent tears roll down my face, but they're not unhappy ones. Sliding my hand to my stomach, I rest my palm there, smiling as I think of the little life growing inside me.

I'm scared shitless.

Terrified to the point of puking, but that could be pregnancy hormones.

Yet, I'm not displeased. Unhappiness has not been the emotion driving my refusal to accept reality—that was all fear.

Fear of telling Ben.

Of facing my family's furious reaction, because this news will not be well-received.

Fear of the unknown—I haven't a clue how to take care of a baby, and I'm scared I won't be good enough, especially if I end up doing this alone.

But I'll learn.

And I'm luckier than most women who find themselves in this position. So, it's time to wake up and own my situation.

I *can* do this.

I know I can.

I refuse to cower from the truth anymore. There is a new life counting on me, and I won't let him or her down. Swiping my tears with the back of my sleeve, I stand tall, radiating determination as I stare at my reflection in the mirror. My cheeks are flushed, my eyes wide and bright, and I look different yet the same. It's hard to articulate it. Apart from missed periods and feeling more tired than usual, I haven't suffered any ill effects of being pregnant. Mostly, I feel great. I'm not surprised it agrees with me because I've always wanted to be a mother. That has always been a part of my life dream.

Did I plan to be a young single mother? No. And even though I'm scared of what the future might hold, I'm excited too. I don't know why I denied the truth for so long when a certain sense of contentment has lodged deep in my bones now I have faced up to my new reality.

It was selfish not to have done a test a few weeks ago when I first suspected. There isn't just me to consider now. I'm nurturing this little life, and I need to take care of him or her. I vow to make a doctor's appointment ASAP, and I make a mental note to download a couple of pregnancy books on my e-reader. "It's you and me, kiddo," I whisper, running a hand across my stomach. "I might not know the first thing about being a mom, but I promise I will learn and I will try."

Wiping all trace of tears from my face, I swipe my purse, jacket, and car keys, stopping by the sunroom where Mom is reading to let her know I'm heading out. Tony trails me out the front door, and I hand him the keys to my black Lexus SUV, happy to let him drive for a change. He stares at me like I've grown an extra head, and I laugh. I get it. I hate having anyone do anything for me, and I usually insist on driving myself everywhere. But I'm still a little dazed, and I need time to try to make sense of my muddled thoughts.

I message Pen from the car, praying she's at home and that Esme is with Mikel, her latest fuck buddy. I don't plan on keeping it a secret from her. I just need advice from my straight-shooting levelheaded best friend right now.

Esme will freak out when she discovers I'm pregnant. She sees how hard her sister struggles as a single mother, and she won't be calm or reticent about vocalizing her opinion. I can't handle that yet.

Pen's immediate reply states she is home alone, and I settle back in the seat, thinking over my options as we drive toward the city.

"Hey, you." Pen greets me at the door with a hug, which I readily fall into. "Come in." She steps aside to let me enter the three-bedroom condo she shares with Esme and another friend from U of C while Tony takes up guard in the corridor. Pen drags a chair out for him to sit on, handing him a bottle of water. He nods his appreciation before sitting.

Pen closes the door behind us, and I pull off my jacket, dropping it on the arm of the couch. I survey the homey open-plan living area with a pang of envy. I wanted to room with my besties, but Father put his foot down, and Mom sided with him. She fought tooth and nail to get him to agree to let me attend Loyola, and she educated me in the fine art of compromise. So, I had to sacrifice living an independent college life in pursuit of my career of choice. After this semester, I have one more year before I'll graduate with my biomedical science degree, and then I have another two years to specialize in acupuncture and homeopathy.

"You look gorgeous," Pen says, cocking her head to the side as she examines me. "Did you do something different with your hair or have you found some new miracle skincare products because, girl, you're glowing."

"That would be the pregnancy hormones," I deadpan, flopping down on the couch.

Pen stumbles back, clutching the sideboard to steady herself. Her eyes are almost bugging out of her head, and her mouth is gaping open.

"I probably shouldn't have blurted it out like that," I admit, shrugging. "But there's no easy way to say I'm knocked up."

"Oh. My. God." Composing herself, she rushes to my side. "Stupid question, but are you sure?"

"Yeah. I took a test, but I've known for a few weeks. I was just too chicken to confirm it until now."

"Wow." She sinks into the soft couch beside me. "What are you going to do?"

"I'm not sure—except I'm keeping it." An involuntary smile ghosts over my lips as my hands automatically move to my stomach.

"I already knew that part." She twists around so she's facing me. "You were born to be a mother, Sierra. You're strong and patient, and you have that legendary Zen energy working in your favor."

"I'm scared," I admit. "When I imagined myself as a mom, there was always a dad, a husband, in that picture, and I was older."

"Age doesn't make a mother, and who says there won't be a dad? A husband?" She twiddles the small engagement ring on her finger as she arches a brow.

Pen knows who the father is because I haven't as much as kissed any other guy since Vegas. It's not for lack of attention. There were a couple of guys I met over the Christmas break, at college parties, who would've happily taken me to their beds, but I already suspected I was pregnant, and I had zero interest in further complicating the situation.

"I'm not a little kid with a crush anymore, and I won't entertain delusions. Ben might be willing to sign up for parental duties, but there's no way he's interested in being my husband."

"You won't know until you talk to him." She purses her lips for a moment. "You are planning on telling him, right?"

I nod. "He has a right to know, and I owe it to my child to tell him. How he reacts and deals with it is on him then." Kicking off my shoes, I rest my back against the arm of the couch, tucking my knees into my chest. "But I am scared that involving him could mean I'm opening me and my child to a world I know nothing about. You saw those men he was with."

"I know, and you're right to be concerned."

Silence engulfs the room for a few minutes. "Do you think I should leave it alone then? Just do this myself?"

She drags her lower lip between her teeth. "I don't envy your position, Sierra, but I can't tell you what to do. It's got to be your decision." Reaching out, she clasps my clammy hands in her warm ones. "Just know that whatever you decide, you have my support, and I will help you as much as I can."

Tears prick my eyes. "Thank you, Pen. I really needed to hear that." I sniff, wiping a couple of errant tears from my cheeks. Pregnancy hormones are no joke. It's like they are directly connected to my tear ducts. "I was thinking about this on the way over. I feel like I must tell him. At some point, my child will ask who their daddy is. How could I live with myself if I kept him or her away from Ben because of my suspicions? I could be wrong. Just because Scarface Salerno is clearly part of the mob doesn't necessarily mean Ben is too." I know I'm likely grasping at straws, but I'm trying to justify it so I do the right thing.

"Do you know how to reach him?"

I shake my head.

"We can Google him." She grabs her iPad from the side table. "If he's got connections to the mob, there's bound to be something online about him."

"I've been tempted to Google him plenty of times," I admit. "But I've held back because he told me to forget about him, and I worried I might find something I didn't like."

Whether he is in the mafia or just has mafia connections, Ben *is* a dangerous man. I saw enough to know it, and I hope I'm doing the right thing here. Because protecting my baby is my only priority, and if that means I end up having to keep this a secret from my baby daddy, then I won't hesitate to do it.

Chapter 11

SIERRA

I MOVE IN closer to Pen on the couch as she Googles his name, watching pages upon pages uploading.

"He sure gets around," Pen mutters. There's an edge to her tone and a look of disgust on her face as she scrolls through images of him with various women. The photos are taken at prestigious events or glitzy balls, and the women are all stunning. It's no wonder he dismissed me so readily if these are the type of women he usually dates. Models, politician's daughters, socialites, and successful businesswomen. Blondes, brunettes, redheads. He doesn't appear to discriminate, as long as they are beautiful.

Ignoring the sinking feeling in my gut, I urge Pen to move forward, pointing at an article in a leading business magazine about Caltimore Holdings. I read it aloud.

"Bennett Mazzone, son of Angelo Mazzone and the late Jillian Carver, has been making waves in New York as the newly-appointed CEO of Caltimore Holdings. Caltimore Holdings is the business empire founded by his great-grandfather in the nineteen twenties. Initially focused on construction, shipping, and transportation, under Angelo Mazzone's stewardship, the company also ventured into the retail and service industry, being full or part owner in a host of different restaurants, clubs, and casinos. In a surprising yet bold move,

Bennett Mazzone's first maneuver as CEO was a hostile takeover of IT company FistMine. Does this signal plans to move Caltimore away from its traditional core businesses or is Mazzone supplementing their existing billion-dollar empire with smart investments in tech-savvy industries with huge growth potential? Only time will tell. Key Caltimore employees we spoke to said Mazzone has ambitious plans for overhauling every aspect of the company and strong ideas about modernizing the brand. Feared as much as he is admired, it's clear Bennett Mazzone is a force to be reckoned with and a man to be watched."

"Huh." Pen rubs a spot between her brows. "It seems like he's a legit businessman."

"And a CEO at twenty-nine." I can't help but be impressed. "Still, you can't believe everything you read on the internet."

We spend another half hour trawling through the web, but we don't find anything linking Ben to the mafia. There is also no mention of how he came to find his father or why he just disappeared from Illinois eight years ago. The Caltimore Holdings website has a run-of-the-mill bio that says plenty but tells you nothing.

Pen prints off the address to the main Caltimore Holdings offices in Midtown Manhattan. "Considering we can't find any personal address for him, you'll have to go to his place of work and hope you can get a meeting with him."

"I'll hang around outside until he makes an appearance if it comes down to it."

"I bet someone in the IT department of Lawson Pharma has skills you could use," she suggests.

I bark out a laugh. "You're not seriously suggesting I tell my father before I tell Ben?"

"I was more thinking out loud," Pen says, pulling her legs up onto the couch. "When are you planning on telling your family?"

"Never?" I joke. "If I thought I could get away with it, I'd abscond overseas. Get a fake ID and hide."

She shoots me a sympathetic look. "They'll come around."

"Have you met my father?" My voice betrays my disbelief. "There is no part of him that will ever be okay with any part of this. Ever." I might not know how Ben will react to the news, but I know with certainty that my father will hate this. "I'm the mistake they were never meant to have. In his eyes, his mistake will just be giving birth to another mistake. You know how anal he is. Having a child out of wedlock is committing a mortal sin to him. It's just another way I'm making him look bad in front of the world."

"Your father is an ass."

"Yup. And he'll never change. He'll probably disown me. God knows, he threatens to kick me out at least once a month."

"Oh my God." Pen sits up straighter, her eyes popping wide. A wicked grin slips over her mouth. "Saskia is going to throw an epic hissy fit when she discovers you slept with Ben and now you're having his baby."

I sigh. "I know. It will be a real sore point because she hasn't had a baby yet." As much as I dislike my sister, and we aren't close in any way, I never want to deliberately hurt her. And this *will* hurt her. She's been married to Felix for over seven years, and according to Mom, they've been trying to have kids for the past four years with no success. "Knowing Saskia, she will accuse me of doing this on purpose just to piss her off."

"Damn straight. She has always been competitive with you. I think it's jealousy."

I crank out a laugh. "Are you kidding? Why on earth would she be jealous of me? She's the one with the business degree from U of C, a rich, handsome husband, gorgeous house, and a promising career at Lawson Pharma. She is also the apple of our father's eye. As far as he is concerned, she can do no wrong."

"She's a fucking bitch," Pen seethes.

"Of the highest order," I agree. "Dishonesty and sucking ass are traits my father seems to covet over truth and authenticity." I check the time on my watch, and it's getting late. I swing my legs around. "Saskia is the least of my worries now." I'll deal with my problems, one at a time. "I need to book a flight to New York and prepare to tell my teen crush he put a bun in my oven."

"You're what?" Tony stares at me like I'm pooping rainbows from my ass.

"Pregnant. I'm having a baby."

He blinks profusely as horror washes over his face. I know he's wondering why I'm telling him this. "The guy in Vegas?" he surmises.

I nod. "I'm sorry, Tony." We both know what this means for his job.

"Don't apologize." He drags his hands through his hair. "Shit." His Adam's apple bobs in his throat as he leans his elbows on the Formica tabletop.

"Hot tea and a cappuccino," the waitress says, setting our drinks on the table.

"Thanks." I offer her a terse smile.

"Lemme know if you need anything else." She saunters off, swaying her hips.

We're tucked into the back booth of my favorite little coffee place, a few blocks from Loyola. It's quiet at this time of night, like I knew it would be.

"How long have you known?" he asks as I slide his coffee to him.

"I've suspected for a few weeks, but I only took a test earlier today." I blow across the top of my mug.

"Will he stand by you?" he asks before taking a mouthful of his drink.

"I don't know. I need to go to New York to tell him." I wrap my hands around my mug, letting the warmth sink into my skin. "Which is where you come in. I was hoping you'd come with me and that we can keep it from my father." He opens his mouth to speak, and I raise one hand. "Just hear me out, please."

He clamps his lips shut, nodding.

"You know as soon as my father hears I got knocked up, he is quite likely to murder both of us. So, I have a plan." I take a sip of my tea, watching the wariness creeping into Tony's eyes. "Hey, give me some credit here. I could've escaped and traveled to the Big Apple alone, but I promised you I wouldn't sneak off again, and I keep my promises." I lean across the table, glancing around the room, ensuring no one is paying us any attention. "Here's what I'm proposing."

I lower my voice. "You will help me plan this trip without anyone knowing. You'll come with me and cover our tracks. After, I'll return to Illinois alone. You should stay in New York and keep far away from Chicago. I'll give you cash to keep you on your feet until you find a new position."

He stares at me in shock for a minute. "Why would you do that for me?"

"Because you've been good to me and you don't deserve to suffer the consequences of my poor decision-making. Father won't just fire you. He'll ensure your name is blacklisted so you can't find work in Chicago. There is no point returning to face that. Let me help you. I have more than enough money to make sure you're comfortable."

Mom's parents were billionaires. Lawson Pharma was their company until they died in a car accident a couple of years after Mom married Dad, and then Father took over as CEO. My sisters and I were left a substantial inheritance, because Mom was an only child and there was no one else for my grandparents to leave their wealth to. They set up a group trust fund, leaving instructions to divide it equally among their grandchildren. I only found out about it when I was sixteen, and when I turned twenty-one, I got access to the money. Between that and the allowance my parents have been paying me every month, I have more than I know what to do with.

I know I'm fortunate. If I'm on my own with this baby, at least I won't have any financial worries.

"Sweetheart." He pats my hand over the table. "I'm touched you would be willing to do that for me. But I won't run from my responsibilities. I will face your father like a man and accept the consequences of my actions."

I open my mouth to argue, but he shakes his head.

"You won't dissuade me, Sierra. But I *will* help you. I have nothing left to lose. My allegiance is to *you*. I will make the necessary arrangements and escort you to and from New York. Keeping you safe will remain my priority until your father strips me of my duty."

"Thank you." I squeeze his hand. I will miss Tony. "I would like to leave on Friday morning and return Saturday afternoon." I will tell my mother I'm going out with Esme and Pen after school and staying the night at their place. She won't question me as it's a normal occurrence.

"As you wish." Tony nods.

There's no going back now. I have no clue how the conversation with Ben will go down. All I know is my life is going to change either way.

Chapter 12

SIERRA

"IT'S RIGHT THERE," I tell Tony, pointing at the impressive glass high-rise on the corner of 57th Street between Fifth and Sixth Avenue.

"Trust you to get knocked up by a Caltimore Holdings employee," he mumbles under his breath. He had a funny look on his face earlier when I gave him the address to input into the GPS.

"Why? What do you know about this company?" I don't bother correcting his error. He'll find out it's the CEO, and not an employee, in due course.

"They are shady as fuck," he cryptically replies. Tony clearly knows something, but I don't have time to drill him for intel now.

"I'll see if I can make an appointment while you park," I say, opening the car door before he can object and stepping out onto the sidewalk.

"Don't move from here." He jabs his finger in my direction. "Stay put until I return."

"I'll wait in the reception area while you park the rental. I promise." I doubt I'll be in any danger in such a public place. I close the door, and he glides out into the traffic.

The building must have been renovated in more recent years, I think, as I stride in the direction of the swinging entrance doors. It's very modern looking with full floor-to-ceiling windows, and it extends high into the sky, beyond my eyesight. I'm betting there is an exquisite view over the city and Central Park from the top floor. I'm also betting that's where Ben's office is located.

I'm a few feet from the door when a group of three men and one woman emerges from the building through a side door. I instantly spot Ben, with his cell to his ear, walking in between two bulky dudes. All three men are wearing black suits and dark expressions. The woman is talking animatedly to Ben, looking harried as she points at papers in her hands while struggling to keep up with the men's long-legged pace in her tight skirt and high heels.

Shit. I'm too far away for him to notice me, and I don't want to call out to him and cause a scene. I was hoping for a private meeting where I could tell him the news with just us in the room.

I'm undecided on what to do when I see a large black SUV pull up to the curb. My legs act of their own accord as I turn around, walking briskly toward the line of taxis idling by the curb at the side street. I can't let Ben leave without following him. It's after two on a Friday. He might not return to the office, and I don't know if he works weekends. This could be my only chance to talk to him.

I call Tony on my cell as I watch Ben get into the blacked-out SUV. Tony answers just as I reach the first taxi. "Wait a sec," I bark into the phone, holding it to my chest as I hop into the back seat, instructing the driver to follow the SUV. "Sorry. Change of plans," I tell Tony, holding the phone out from my ear as he lets loose a string of expletives. "He's on the move, and I have to follow him. Use my cell to track my location. I'll wait for you when we reach our destination."

I hang up before he can berate me for my reckless reaction. I had to make a split-second decision, and I'm not sorry I made this call. If I had waited for Tony to come back, we would have lost Ben. I don't want to have to return to New York. It's taken a lot this week to psych myself up for this meeting, and I just want to get it over and done with now.

If the driver thinks it's weird I asked him to follow another car, he keeps those thoughts to himself.

Traffic is shit, and it takes forty minutes to drive less than thirteen miles. Eventually, Ben's car turns off the busy roads, driving up and down successive side streets before pulling into the parking lot of a two-story building in Queens.

The property is on its own contained lot, distancing it from other bars, clubs, and stores in the area. There is an overgrown park on one side, and the Hudson River is only a couple of streets away according to Google Maps. Requesting the taxi driver to pull over to the curb at the corner, I watch Ben's SUV as it parks right in front of the building while I phone Tony. "Where are you?"

"I'm about ten minutes behind you."

"Okay. Hurry." I hang up, chewing on the inside of my mouth as Ben's driver opens his door and he gets out. He has left his coat and suit jacket inside the car, emerging in a crisp white button-down shirt, expensive black pants, and matching dress shoes. I can only see him from behind, but his form is every bit as impressive as I remember it.

Images flash vividly in my mind.

I see his large warm hands grazing the length and breadth of my body. I feel his skillful fingers and tongue sending me into a frenzy of unleashed desire. I shudder at the remembrance of his monster cock pounding inside me as we created a new life. Heat creeps up my chest and onto my neck, and I shake myself free of all nostalgic thoughts. This isn't the time or place.

The two men in suits, still wearing ferocious expressions, accompany Ben into the building while I contemplate my options. I know I should wait for Tony. He's only ten minutes away, but my gut is telling me to go in there after Ben now.

"Please wait here," I tell the driver, handing him a fifty. "I will give you another one of those and a generous tip when I return." I don't want to go into that building without a way of getting out of here, just in case Tony is delayed or I need to make a rapid exit.

"Lady, you sure you want to go in there?" He glances over his shoulder at me.

"My friend is on his way. He'll be right behind me."

I climb out of the back seat before I can second-guess myself, tying the belt of my three-quarter-length pink woolen coat firmly around my waist. I'm glad I dressed warmly because it's freezing in New York today. At least there is no rain or snow, so I'm grateful for small mercies. Holding the strap of my Michael Kors purse, I walk quickly across the road in my black pantyhose and stilettos, heading toward the building Ben went into.

The building is in need of TLC, a lot like the area. Gray shutters are pulled down against the windows, and paint peels off the overhead sign. Weeds poke up between the asphalt as I stride across the parking lot. Besides Ben's SUV, there are four other vehicles here, but the place appears virtually deserted.

Nerves prick at my skin as I approach the grimy front door. What the hell is this place, and what is Ben doing here? Wetting my dry lips and tucking my long blonde hair behind my ears, I draw a brave breath and open the door.

Music greets me as I step inside, but it's low, just background noise in the dingy, dimly lit room. It's a bar or club of some sort with a mix of booths and open seating areas surrounding an elevated section in the center of the room, resembling a runway with the addition of stripper poles.

Classy. Not.

It's like the eighties threw up in here with its brick walls, tired décor, and dark wood furniture that looks like a throwback to *Cheers*. I scan the space, spotting the back of Ben's head as he enters a rear door at the far side of the room. A burly guy with a shaved head and a scowl on his face stands guard in front of it, so I wander to the bar and pull up a stool to wait for Tony.

A lone bartender is working behind the bar, and he looks up when I sit down, gawking at me for a few seconds. I know I look out of place in a joint like this. I thought I was meeting Ben in a plush office in the middle of the Central Business District, and I dressed accordingly in my fitted long-sleeved black knee-length dress, black pantyhose, and skyscraper black Louboutins. Add the expensive pink coat and patterned silk scarf, and I stick out like a sore thumb in here.

"What can I get you, Miss?" he asks, masking his surprise.

"I'll take two sparkling waters. Pellegrino if you have them." He stares at me like I have spoken a foreign language. "Two bottles of water. Any will do," I rephrase. "My colleague will be joining me shortly."

Without saying a word, he retrieves two bottles from the fridge, placing them in front of me. I slap a twenty down on the counter. "Keep the change." He tips his head and swipes the cash but otherwise ignores me.

Feeling eyes on me, I look right, noticing the two old perverts seated at the bar watching me with blatant curiosity. Apart from them and the two staff members, there is no one else around. I glance at my watch, willing Tony to hurry the fuck up, when the rear door opens and one of the guys who came in with Ben pops his head out, speaking to the man standing guard. The bodyguard nods and walks off across the room, exiting through a different door, while the other guy disappears back to where he came from.

The bartender is crouched down behind the bar, stacking drinks on shelves, so the only witnesses are the two perverts at the end of the bar. Sliding carefully off the stool, I walk on the dirty threadbare carpet in their direction. Handing each of them a hundred-dollar bill, I tap the side of my nose. "You didn't see anything," I tell them in a low voice, ignoring the fluttery feeling bouncing around my chest cavity and how all the tiny hairs on the back of my neck are standing at attention. I'm definitely channeling Esme right now, and Tony is going to string me up, but I'm not wasting the opportunity.

Keeping one eye on the bar, I walk quickly toward the rear door and slip inside, surprised to find stairs leading to a lower level. Blood rushes to my head, making me dizzy, and I clutch the wall until it passes. My heart is thumping wildly against my rib cage as I remove my shoes. Holding them in one hand, I slowly descend the stairs. My legs feel like they might go out from under me, and when a guttural scream rings out, I stall midway down the stairs, blood pounding in my skull as bile travels up my throat.

My cell rings in my pocket, and I about die, scrambling to mute the sound before someone hears. But I doubt anyone could hear over the incessant roars emerging from downstairs.

I'm frozen.

Rooted to the spot.

One-half of me is screaming to get the fuck out of here before I become that stupid person in every horror movie. You know, the one who just has to investigate and usually ends up paying for their curiosity with their life?

The other part of me needs to know what's going on, and that part is overriding all sense of logic and self-preservation. My gut tells me to press on. That it will be okay.

Unless there's another exit point in the basement level, Ben is down here. He won't let anything happen to me. No matter how dangerous he is, he has protected me before, and I know he will keep me safe again.

Chapter 13

SIERRA

PUSHING THROUGH MY fear, I force my limbs to move and continue forward. When my foot hits the floor, I have no choice but to turn left because it's the only option. Keeping my bag clasped tightly to my chest and my shoes secured in my free hand, I flatten my body against the closest wall and move stealthily down the long corridor. Successive doors are on the left, all closed except for two in the middle that are slightly ajar.

Lighting is scant, and the only illumination comes from a flickering light bulb dangling from the cracked ceiling. Cobwebs cling to the corners of the walls, and I shudder as a blast of cold air swirls around me. The concrete floor is like ice under my shoeless feet, my pantyhose offering little protection.

My nostrils twitch as a godawful smell slaps me in the face. It reeks of sweat, stale piss, vomit, and other indistinguishable smells. I press my lips together and scrunch my nose, and it marginally helps to keep the grossness at bay. My stomach lurches, and I pray this isn't the moment my pregnancy nausea kicks in.

Soldiering on, I take slow careful steps forward. I startle, as more roaring and screaming echoes through the basement, slapping a hand over my mouth to stop myself from reacting and giving myself away.

This is a bad idea.

But something is still prompting me to keep going, not to turn around, so I persevere, ignoring the vicious trembling in my body and the rapid beating of my heart.

As I approach the first open door, I press my spine flat to the wall, pricking my ears to determine if I hear movement in the space. I hear voices, jumping when another shout rings out, but it doesn't sound like it's coming from the room right beside me. The shouting is muffled, not piercing like it was when I first heard it on the stairs. Wherever it's coming from, I don't think it's this room.

Making the sign of the cross, I risk a peek, relieved when I discover the empty room. I sneak inside, softly closing the door but not all the way. I stuff my hand in my mouth, blocking the scream ready to let rip when I lift my head, staring at the glass window in front of me. It looks right into the much larger room inside, and I'm waiting for one of the five men in that room to notice me, sure it's about to happen when Ben's friend, Leo, stares right at the window, straight at me. I stop breathing as I wait for him to call me out, but he turns back around, expression unchanged, as if he hasn't seen me.

This must be an observation window, like they have in police stations. I release a shuddering breath, relieved they can't see me and they don't know I'm here.

"I can do this all day, Sergei. And we know enough to determine the Irish are meeting your Bratva bosses," Ben says, rolling his sleeves to his elbows as he stares at the man strapped to a chair in the middle of the room.

Although calling it a room is a bit of a misnomer. It looks more like a dungeon or a torture chamber. The bare brick walls and concrete floor are spattered with dark stains, and various hooks and chains dangle from some steel contraption secured to the ceiling. A trickle of urine leads from the man in the chair to a large vent in the floor. That explains part of the woeful smell. The man is naked, bound at the ankles and wrists to the chair with silver cable ties. He has several lacerations across his arms and his chest and a deeper gash in his thigh. Blood drips onto the floor from his shredded skin, yet he spits at Ben in defiance, spouting something in a foreign language. Given his name and Ben's mention of Bratva, I'm guessing it's Russian.

Bright strip lighting grants me a prime view of the proceedings, and I watch the scene unfold in a state of dazed numbness. It's almost like it's not real. Like I'm watching a movie or show and these are just actors playing a part. That's not real blood. And it's not my baby daddy getting ready to beat a man bloody.

My heart is lodged in my throat as I watch it go down.

Ben coolly removes a set of pliers from a steel unit wedged against the wall. Both shelves are full of weapons and instruments of torture, all clean as if lovingly cared for. The pulse in my neck throbs when Ben turns around and I see the front of his shirt for the first time. His pristine white shirt is now smeared with blood, and it turns my stomach. "I won't ask you again. This is your last chance, Sergei. Why were you meeting McDermott? What business do the Russians have with the Irish?"

"Fuck you, Mazzone, and your dead whore mother."

Ben's sinister smile sends chills creeping up my spine. I expect him to lash out at the man for the comment about his mother because I know a little of the history there. But he is the epitome of cool, calm, and collected as he applies the pliers to the man's hand, breaking his fingers, one at a time.

Panic is racing around my chest as I watch the man I crushed on as a kid slowly and methodically remove each one of Sergei's fingers. Gargled sounds escape the man's mouth as he grinds his teeth together. Blood spurts from his stubby hands, and I'm rooted to the spot again, staring in horror as Ben sets the pliers down on the table, picking up a bloody knife this time.

"You know, I'm building a new organization. Changing the playbook," Ben says. "It's not too late to change allegiance. We could use another couple of spies within the Bratva."

"Fuck you, Italian scum bastard."

Ben shrugs before gesturing to Leo. Leo grabs the man's head, forcing his mouth open. Sergei thrashes on the chair, refusing to do this quietly, until one of the other men presses down on the oozing wound in his thigh, stalling his movements. Piss leaks from Sergei's flaccid cock, soaking the front of Ben's pants.

Ben looks down in clear annoyance. "You will pay for that." His voice is monotone, devoid of any emotion, and he barely looks human with the dark glint of mad rage glittering in his eyes and the complete lack of decency.

It's clear Sergei is not getting out of here alive. He could shoot him. There are several guns on the table, but Ben is *choosing* to torture him.

I don't understand why I'm still here. I've seen enough to know I'm not letting this man anywhere near my baby. But I can't make myself move. Stunned into watching this play out by some morbid fascination.

Ben slices Sergei's tongue off in one fast motion, flinging it across the room. Nausea swims up my throat, and I clamp a hand over my mouth to stop myself from puking. Ben looks every bit the monster as he lays into the man. He slices Sergei's skin with the knife, over and over, until his chest is a bloody mess, his internal organs hanging out. I gag as I struggle to hold on to the contents of my stomach.

The man yells in agony when Ben slices his dick off, and the moment he shoves it in Sergei's mouth, I wake the fuck up. I can't witness any more of this brutality, and I need to get out of here before I'm the next person strapped to that chair.

I no longer trust Ben to keep me safe.

I'm in a shocked, terrified daze as I get out of there, but I haven't lost all sense of reality, carefully edging out of the room and tiptoeing up the stairs so I'm not heard. I concentrate on the rapid thumping of my heart to keep myself grounded, barely hearing the gunshot as I ascend the stairs and open the door to the main room.

Which is now strangely empty.

Fueled by a fresh injection of anxiety, I race across the main room, desperate to see the back of this place. I burst through the front door hyperventilating as I stagger to the corner of the building and puke my guts up.

A hand covers my mouth from behind, as I straighten up, and I swing my arm around, lashing out with my stilettos, ready to inflict damage, when a familiar voice says, "Don't scream. It's me."

I slump against Tony, and the dam breaks. Strangled sobs leak from my mouth as I turn around, flinging my arms around him, so grateful he's here.

"Are you hurt?" He holds my face firmly in his cold palms, jerking my head up.

"No," I pant over a sob.

"We need to get out of here." He grabs my hand. "You didn't leave anything inside, did you?"

I shake my head. I'm still clutching my purse and my shoes for dear life.

He tugs me around the corner of the building, clamping his hand over my mouth again when I move to scream at the sight of the five bodies piled on top of one another at the back of the yellow taxi.

"Don't make a sound, Sierra," Tony warns. "Not if you want to live."

I stare at him in shock, and he lifts me over one shoulder, racing through brush at the back of the building toward the rental, which is parked at the corner of a back alley.

He places me in the passenger seat before getting behind the wheel and flooring it out of there.

We don't speak for ages.

I'm not sure I have the ability to form a coherent sentence or a coherent thought. Tony is tense, glancing in his mirrors constantly, checking to see if we're being followed. Every so often, he casts a fleeting look in my direction, his expression troubled. He doesn't stop his incessant monitoring until we are out on the highway, heading toward JFK.

Pulling my knees to my chest, I look sideways at him, wondering if I know who this man is at all. "You killed them," I whisper. "Why?"

"I couldn't leave any witnesses. No one could know you were there."

I stare at him numbly before mumbling, "I don't understand."

Traffic slows down until it comes to a standstill. Tony turns to me, keeping one hand on the wheel. "What did you see in that building?"

"Monsters." I look him dead in the eye. "I saw monsters." Ben might have been the one doing the torture, but it was clear from the state of Sergei's body and the smells clinging to the walls that he had been there for some time. Ben just finished what the others started.

"You should've told me the man you were with in Vegas was Bennett Mazzone."

"How did you know it was him?"

"I didn't until I got here and I couldn't find you. I forced one of his goons to talk. He told me Mazzone had just arrived, and I connected the dots."

"You know who he is."

He nods, easing the car forward when the traffic starts moving again.

"He's part of the mafia, isn't he? That legit businessman image he projects is just a front."

"He is mafia royalty, Sierra."

"How do you know that? There is nothing online that even hints at him being mafia."

"I'm from New York originally, and there are very few people in this city who don't know the Mazzone family is the most powerful mafia family in the US."

"Why didn't I find anything online?"

"Ben is smart. He has skilled IT resources in his pocket, and these people know how to control what information is put out there about him. Caltimore's takeover of FistMine is the first of many, I predict. Ben is changing the way things are done."

"I just watched him torture someone. So, I wouldn't say he's changing everything up," I say, and it's as if someone else is speaking the words. I gulp over the messy ball of emotion in my throat. "He was so cold, and from the expert way he inflicted pain, I know this wasn't his first time."

Tony pins me with a sympathetic look that makes me feel like a stupid, naïve thirteen-year-old again.

"He's a killer. My baby's daddy is a ruthless killer." I place my palm on my stomach, fighting tears again.

"I can't believe the man you slept with in Vegas is Ben." He signals to take the next exit off the highway, toward the airport. "I knew you had a big crush on him when Saskia was dating him, but I had no idea you were still in contact with him."

God. I never realized I was so obvious. Does everyone know I had the hots for him?

"I wasn't." I proceed to tell Tony everything that went down in Vegas, holding nothing back.

By the time we pull into the parking lot at JFK, he is as white as a ghost. "Sierra." He grips my shoulders almost painfully. "Tell no one who the father is. *No. One.* Not Ben. Not your father or anyone in your family. Warn Esme and Pen to keep their mouths shut too."

"Trust me, you don't have to convince me after what I saw today."

"Sierra." His voice elevates a few notches, and he looks seriously rattled. "I mean it. This can't ever come out. To do so would place you and your child in untold danger."

"You're scaring me."

"You should be scared. Those men are dangerous men existing in a dark world with few rules they abide by except loyalty and honor to *la famiglia*. Dangerous men always have dangerous enemies. If anyone found out, they could use you against him."

"No one will find out. I'll carry the secret to my grave."

"Promise me you won't take risks." He drills me with a look.

"I won't. It's not just me anymore," I add, rubbing my tummy. "I won't place my child in harm's way. I will do everything in my power to keep him or her safe."

"You know, if I had ever married, I would have wished for a daughter like you," he says, leaning in to kiss my cheek. "Your father is a bastard for the way he's treated you. He appreciates all the wrong things. Whatever happens, don't ever lose sight of the person you are."

"This sounds very much like goodbye," I say, eyeing him warily.

"I've never broken my word to you, Sierra, and I don't want to break it to you now, but I know too much. Returning with you is too dangerous. This is where we will part ways."

"What do you mean? Why do I get a sense there is a lot I don't know?"

"There is so much you don't know. Things I wish I could tell you, but it's not safe. Trust me when I say you are better off not knowing."

"Ignorance is debilitating if it means I can't protect myself. Knowledge is power, Tony, and if it's something I need to know, then tell me," I plead.

"The only truth you need is Bennett Mazzone is bad news. He's no good for you, and you need to steer clear of him." Planes fly overhead, reminding me I have a flight to catch. "You should go. You can't miss your flight."

"You're really not going to tell me?"

He shakes his head. "It's better this way."

I recognize defeat when I see it, and I trust Tony. I know he has my best interests at heart. Sucks to be excluded from the truth, but I have no choice. "I don't like being kept in the dark, but I'll drop it." Reaching into my purse, I withdraw the bulky brown padded envelope. "This is for you." I offer it to him. "Fifty K is all I could get at short notice, but it should keep you afloat for a while."

"I don't want your money." He pushes my hand away.

I shove the envelope at his chest. "Take it, Tony. I know you'll need it." There is no way he can stay in New York now. It's too risky after he just took out five men. I still can't believe it. I've never seen Tony harm a fly, and he took out five men like he was a hardened killer.

Is everyone?

"I never really knew Ben, and I'm guessing I never really knew you either," I say, memorizing his face because I'm pretty sure we'll never see one another again. "Irrespective of who you are or aren't, I know everything you have done has been done to protect me, so thank you. Thank you for keeping me and my unborn child safe."

"I hope you know it's been an honor protecting you. An honor to watch you grow up. I wish we didn't have to part ways like this."

"Me too," I whisper, fighting to keep the tenuous hold on my emotions. Pregnancy hormones are riding me like a bitch, and I wonder if this is what the next few months have in store for me.

"Stay strong, Sierra." Tony pulls me into a hug. "And stay safe."

Chapter 14

SIERRA

AFTER ROLLING MY yoga mat and putting it away, I wipe the light sheen of sweat from my brow as I stare out the window of my bedroom at the rear garden of our house. Rain drops from the sky in painful sheets, pummeling the ground below, coating the shrubs, flowers, and plants in a heavy layer of water. It's beautiful. Like Chicago is taking a giant communal shower. If I didn't have to get ready for our usual Sunday family dinner charade, I would paint this view. I might be weird, but I love the rain and snow, and I would happily vacation in a colder climate over a hot one.

I pop my vitamins before stripping out of my workout clothes and stepping into the shower. I'm calm as I go over everything in my mind while I soap my body and wash my hair.

It's been one week since I returned from New York, and I've been busy putting my plans in motion. My cases are already packed and loaded in the back of my SUV. I only took the essentials from my wardrobe and my studio. I can buy anything else I need. I've rented a small apartment in the city, close to Loyola, that I will use in the short-term.

After I'm dry and my hair is blow-dried straight, I pour myself into a red bodycon dress and slip my feet into my black Louboutins. I was tempted to paint a big scarlet A and stick it to my chest, but I don't think anyone would appreciate the humor.

Stepping into the formal living room, I see my sisters are already here with their husbands. Elisa's cute dark head is bent over her doll as she sits on the carpet, playing, in front of Serena's feet. I wish I had spent more time with my niece when she was a baby. That I had put aside my differences with Serena and offered to help. While my relationship with Saskia has always been fractured, there was no contention or falling out with Serena—we're just not close.

Serena tended to do stuff with Saskia because they were the closest in age. There are eight years between me and Saskia and five years between me and Serena, and I was a little kid when they were teenagers, so I was naturally left out. However, Serena has never been cruel in the way Saskia is cruel. It's more that I felt invisible around her growing up, and I didn't bother trying to get close to her when I became an adult. Relationships are two-way streets though, and in this moment, I realize I have made no effort with my sister. Something I hope to rectify someday.

"Why are you always the last to arrive? Every Sunday is the same," Saskia says, pinning her cutting green eyes on me. I hate the whiny parental tone she has always used around me. "You live here, and you have no one to attend to but yourself, so there's really no excuse."

"Maybe I do it to piss you off," I quip, shaking my head when Maria—one of the many maids Mom employs to run the household—attempts to hand me a glass of wine. "I'll have a water, please."

"Do you hear this?" Saskia eyeballs my father. He's seated in one of the high-backed leather armchairs in front of a roaring fire, discreetly talking to Alfred and Felix.

"Don't interrupt, darling," Felix says, sending his wife a pointed "shut the fuck up" look I already know she'll ignore.

"Daddy." Saskia pouts. "Are you going to let Sierra speak to me like that?"

"Are we really doing this again?" I sigh. It's the same old tired crap every week.

"Stop winding your sister up," Father says, not even looking in our direction as he continues his conversation with the men.

Saskia's mouth pulls tight. She hates when she can't claim his attention, but she would never call him out on it. She knows how to pull his strings, and she pulls them with practiced ease.

I smile at Maria when she hands me a tall glass of sparkling Pellegrino with lemon, lime, and crushed ice, bracing myself for Saskia's next assault because I know it's coming.

"This is what happens when you let your children run wild. Take note, Serena. Don't make the same mistakes Mom made with Sierra."

"Watch your tone, Saskia. I don't care much for it," Mom says, brushing a stray blonde hair back into her chignon. She is perched on the end of the couch beside Serena, gazing adoringly at her only grandchild.

Elisa holds a doll in each hand, and she's babbling away, moving them as if they are talking to one another. It's cute, and I remember doing something similar. Though I was mostly into Barbie dolls. I loved experimenting with their looks, and I can still remember Saskia's horrified expression the day I decided to give all my Barbies a makeover, hacking off and coloring their hair different colors. Fun times.

I wonder if I came out of the womb predetermined to disappoint and annoy my oldest sister.

"The truth hurts, Georgia." Saskia smiles sweetly at Mom as she sips her glass of Sancerre, using her given name on purpose to be spiteful.

"Respect your mother," Felix admonishes when it's obvious my father won't.

I can't figure my parents' relationship out at all. There are times Father lavishes attention on Mom and worships the ground she walks on. And there are times when she's as invisible as me. Championing my causes over the years hasn't done her any favors, but she was my only support in this house growing up, and I love the sacrifices she made for me.

My heart swells with love for my mother. She's not perfect. She's made mistakes, and she didn't always stand up to Father or do the right thing, but her intentions were honorable, and she selflessly put us first all the time. If I can be half the mother my mom is, I will be okay.

"Do not tell me what to do in front of my family," Saskia snaps at her husband.

"Saskia." Father's stern voice rings out around the room. "That's enough." Oh, the irony. He doesn't give a rat's ass if Saskia disrespects me or Mom, but the second she disrespects her husband, he has a problem with it.

It's priceless. Honestly, it has to be seen to be believed.

The bell sounds for dinner, and we make our way into the dining room. My heart is slamming against my rib cage, and nervous adrenaline flows through my veins, but I'm ready to do this.

At least today's Sunday dinner will be entertaining for a change. I doubt there will be anything usual or boring about it once I drop the mother of all bombs—pun intended.

The sumptuous dinner tastes like sandpaper in my mouth, and it's a miracle I can force any food into my stomach. I'm quiet, contributing little to the discussion, biding my time before it's my moment in the spotlight.

Saskia's grating voice gets on my nerves as she monopolizes the conversation, like always. She spouts off about her accounting position at Lawson Pharma, suggests Serena should start Botox to eliminate imaginary lines on her face, and spreads salacious gossip she picked up from her bitchy friends.

I tune her out, visualizing the homey bungalow on Elm Street I just made an offer on, while I steady my nerves. I'm waiting to time this to perfection so I deliver my news with maximum effect. I know it won't be well-received, so I might as well do this the way I want to do it—with zero fucks given.

Elisa's nanny removes her from the table after she's finished eating, taking her away for her nap. Judging by the mess on her highchair and the floor, I'm figuring most of her dinner bypassed her mouth. I enjoyed watching her eat, having a newfound appreciation for my niece. If Serena is still talking to me after today, I'm going to offer my babysitting services. I'm embarrassed I haven't taken more interest in Elisa, and I want that to change.

I clear my throat, wanting to say my piece before dessert is wheeled out. "I have some news," I say in a loud voice, projecting around the table so I capture everyone's attention.

"This should be good." Saskia rolls her eyes, sitting back in her seat with a smirk.

I don't even care that I'll wipe it off in a second, replacing it with one of pain.

Folding my hands in my lap, I tilt my chin up, eyeballing my father as I say, "I'm pregnant, and I'm keeping my baby."

Initial shocked silence greets my announcement, and then chaos rains. Predictably, my father is the first to have a go at me. "I must have a problem with my hearing," he says, drilling me with a pointed look. "Because I couldn't have just heard my youngest daughter telling me she's pregnant with a child out of wedlock."

I grin. "Nope, there's nothing wrong with your hearing. I'm knocked up. And I don't even have a boyfriend. But guess what, *Daddy*?" I lean into the table, my eyes blazing with moral righteousness. "It's not the Dark Ages. Single women have babies all the time. Some even *choose* to raise a family that way."

He thumps his clenched fist on the table. Glasses and silverware rattle. "Not in this house!" he roars. "Over my dead body will you embarrass our family like this."

That could always be arranged.

"It's not up to you," I coolly reply, taking a sip of my water. Out of the corner of my eye, I spy Mom jumping up, stopping the maids from delivering dessert.

"How far along are you?" Serena asks, smiling softly at me. Apart from Mom, she's the only one not looking at me like she wants to stab a fork in my uterus.

"Thirteen weeks." I visited my ob-gyn yesterday and she explained how they count the forty-week gestation from the date of my last period.

"There is still time to get an abortion," Father barks, and I see red.

Esme uttered those exact same words to me, and we had an almighty argument. I know she believes she's helping by bringing up all my options, but she can't project her opinions on me because of what happened to her sister. She knows me well enough to know I would never do that, so she should have kept her mouth shut. She didn't appreciate me telling her that, and the conversation rapidly deteriorated. I ended up stomping off, and I'm still not speaking to her.

"Maybe you *are* hard of hearing," I say in a clipped tone. "Because I clearly told you I'm keeping my baby." I place my hands protectively on my stomach, grateful the baby isn't privy to this conversation.

"That's nonnegotiable." Everything is. Which he will learn in due course.

Father's nostrils flare, and his fists are clenched on top of the table. I've seen him mad plenty of times before, but I've never seen him look at me like he wants to murder me.

Unease trickles up my spine, but I hold my ground, keeping my chin raised defiantly.

A muscle pops in his jaw as he addresses me again. "If you insist on this madness, then I insist the father marries you."

Yeah. I figured that one was coming. Even if I didn't need to keep Ben's name a secret, I would be doing it for this very reason. "I don't know who he is," I lie, shrugging because I know how much this is going to enrage him. "He was just some random hookup my birthday weekend in Vegas." I wet my lips, praying I won't go to hell for this. "I didn't even get his name. I was too busy fucking his monster cock to form a coherent sentence."

Mom rips me from my chair, dragging me back to safety as my father roars, jumping up and shoving the table over. It crashes to the ground with a large thud. Glass shatters, and water seeps onto the floor from the broken vase, flowers flying across the room along with silverware.

"Are you happy now, you little slut?" Saskia's hateful face materializes in front of me, and it's all I see before I feel the stinging pain lance across my cheek.

"Saskia!" Mom hollers, pulling me away from my sister. "Don't you dare hit your pregnant sister!"

I rub my sore cheek in a daze, too startled at the sight of Alfred and Felix frantically whispering in my father's ear, their words seemingly the only thing holding him back. He's ready to throttle me, and the only thing stopping him are my two brothers-in-law.

"How could you be so reckless, you fool!" Saskia yells, invading my personal space again. "If you insist on acting like a common whore, you could at least make them wear condoms. Have you no self-respect at all?"

"I was on the pill!" I retaliate.

"No single method of contraception is one hundred percent reliable, and what about STDs?" She rakes her gaze up and down my body with derision. "You're probably riddled." She glances over her shoulder at our father. "If you thought finding a man to take her off your hands was a problem before, you can forget about it now. No decent man wants used goods. You should cut her loose. She doesn't deserve to bear the Lawson name."

I see the renewed flint in her eyes when she refocuses on me. "How many guys have you let into your saggy cunt?" She prods my chest with one bony finger. "How many degenerates did you let fuck you in Vegas?"

"Hundreds," I hiss, just to piss her off. "I spent the entire weekend flat on my back." I return her derogatory glare with one of my own. "Jealous you're tied to one dick for life?" While I don't think Saskia's marriage is a happy one, she is stuck with Felix because it's clear Father would never tolerate a divorce. Appearances mean everything to him, and having a divorcée for a daughter is almost as bad as my single mother status.

Saskia moves to slap me again, and I grab her wrist, ready to inflict pain if she dares lift a finger to me. "I'm not some little kid you can bully anymore. I put up with enough of your shit growing up, and you don't get to take your anger out on me. You made your own life choices. Deal with it." Her entire body vibrates with barely concealed rage as I release my hold on her, pinning her with a challenging look. "Hit me and I'll hit you back ten times harder."

"That's enough." Father's rageful boom carries across the room. Jabbing his finger in the air, he glares at me. "Is this connected to Tony's disappearance?"

He grilled me last weekend when Tony's MIA status became obvious. I smirk. "Supposedly, you're a smart man. You figure it out." My spine stiffens, and my jaw tenses as he stalks toward me.

"You need to get out of here," Mom whispers in my ear, and I feel her trembling against me.

He grips my chin, digging his nails into my skin, but I refuse to show any emotion. "Where is Tony?" he hisses, spittle flying from his lips, hitting me in the face.

"I don't know," I truthfully reply. He's long gone from New York by now, I'm sure.

He slaps me, and the sting of his hand on my cheek is far harsher than my sister's efforts. "Don't you lie to me." He raises his hand again, but Mom intervenes, yanking me behind her. Father's nails draw blood on my chin as I'm dragged away from him.

"I know you're angry, Joseph, but you can't hit her. I won't allow it."

"Saskia is right," he fumes. "This is all your fault, Georgia. You were always too lenient on her. I let you pander to her whims to keep the peace, but it was a mistake."

"It isn't fair!" Saskia cries, and I drag my gaze from my father, almost keeling over at the sight of my sister with tears streaming down her face. I have never seen Saskia cry. Never.

"Darling." Felix comes up behind his wife, wrapping his arms around her. I expect Saskia to push him away, like she does the rare times he indulges in PDAs, but she turns in his arms, sobbing into his chest.

"How is it my slut of a sister can get pregnant without even trying and I can't?"

Her words are muffled against his chest but clear enough to be heard. I'm guessing that was the intent. I am done with her calling me a slut. At twenty-one, I have had sex with three men. That's hardly whore-worthy.

I'm so mad at her I'm tempted to tell her it's Ben, just to see the look on her face. But this isn't about me anymore, and I have a child to protect. The thought is sobering.

I'm not religious, despite being raised in a Catholic household and forced to attend church every Sunday until I turned eighteen and put my foot down. But I have wondered if Saskia has ever considered why God isn't blessing her with a baby. My guess is he doesn't want to inflict that kind of suffering on any innocent child. I don't even know why Saskia wants to be a mom so badly. She's self-centered and absorbed in her career and her busy life, and I can't see her sacrificing her lifestyle for a child. My sister is the type to give birth and immediately pass the child to a nanny to raise.

"I am not a slut," I say, disengaging from Mom's protective stance. I'm glad my voice is level and my resolve is intact. "And I'm done with being judged unfairly by this family." I face my father. "You've never wanted me, and I know you hate me. That I've been a constant disappointment. See this as the perfect opportunity to disown me. None of your cronies will disagree now I have shamed you."

"I couldn't have put it more perfectly," he agrees, pinning me with a hateful expression. "You are no longer a daughter of mine and no longer welcome in this house."

"Joseph. No." Mom's voice cracks, and I know this has the power to hurt her the most.

I turn to her, ignoring my father and my older sister, saying all I need to say. "It's okay, Mom. It's for the best, and I expected this. I have a place, and I have my things in the car. I will call you." I disposed of the cell my father gave me. I'm not naïve; I know it wouldn't take much for him to get my new number or to discover my new apartment or the address to the new home I'm in the process of buying for me and my child, but I'm banking on the fact he just doesn't care anymore.

For the first time in my life, I will be completely free of the ties that bind me to my family, to the Lawson name, and it feels invigorating.

As I walk out of my family home for the last time, I can't help thinking this is meant to be. That I am exactly where I should be, and despite the lingering fears bubbling in my chest, I am excited for what the future will bring.

PART II – SIX YEARS LATER

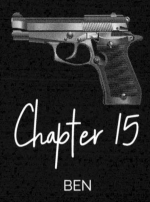

Chapter 15

BEN

"ETA IN FIVE minutes, boss," Alessandro says from the driver's seat of my armored SUV.

I acknowledge him through the mirror before I resume staring out the window. Fourteen years. That's how long it's been since I was last in Illinois. I left less than a week after my disastrous anniversary dinner with Saskia. Not by choice. But I refuse to live a life of regrets. I might have detested Angelo Mazzone when he first dragged me, kicking and screaming, from Chicago, but he did me a favor. My relationship with my old man is complicated and underscored with deep-seated resentment and hostility, but I don't regret he plucked me from a dead-end life to the one I live now.

The man whose funeral I'm here to attend is the last remaining tie I had to my old hometown. Terry Scott was the only decent man my mother ever hooked up with. If she hadn't been so wasted on booze and drugs, she might have realized it and tried harder to make things work with him.

Addiction is a terrible disease. I watched it devour my mother from the inside until it consumed her life. She OD'd when I was twenty. That I couldn't save her is one of only two regrets in my life.

Jillian Carver's demise is the main reason I control my liquor consumption carefully and I never take narcotics. I drill it into my men and our staff not to touch the drugs we supply to a wide network of VIP clientele. Addiction is a one-way road to hell, and I won't tolerate any mishaps in my organization. You use? You're out. It's as simple as that.

When we pass the sign for Sierra's hometown, I ponder my only other regret. I wish I'd never fucked my ex's little sister because I can't erase the memory of that night from my brain no matter how many years have passed or how many women I screw. It's as if she imprinted herself on a part of my soul, and I can't get her out. I've been tempted to look her up, during certain weak moments, but I have always resisted.

Radiant goddesses like Sierra Lawson have no place in my world. Even more so now. Angelo's condition is worsening by the day, and it won't be long until the entire empire is officially mine. At thirty-five, I will be the richest, most powerful boss in the US and one of the most successful businessmen to boot. I'm proud of my achievements, but it has come at a high price.

"Have you reconsidered contacting Gifoli while we're in town?" Leo asks, from his seat beside me.

I shake my head. "The timing isn't right." I eye the two *soldati* in the front seats so Leo doesn't say too much.

Alessandro is my most promising soldier and a man I trust with my life. He's only twenty-six but smarter and more observant than men who have been killing for longer than he's been born. It's why I elevated him to my personal bodyguard a year ago. The other man in the car is Frank, Leo's younger brother. Another soldier with strong potential. I trust them, but there are plenty of things that can't be discussed in front of them.

They are aware my father is very ill, and they know to carry the secret. Keeping Angelo's stage-four-cancer prognosis from becoming public knowledge is critical. We are at a pivotal juncture within the organization, having united most of the *famiglia* across the US under

The Commission's governance, and we have consolidated forces to help in the upcoming war with the Russians. Chicago and Florida are the only two *famiglia* on the outside, but we are hoping to bring them into the fold in due course. The Russians are mobilizing, restructuring, and getting organized. It's only a matter of time before they make a move.

If the Bratva or any of our other enemies discover my father is dying, it leaves us exposed. With the right persuasion, it could weaken The Commission at a time when we are not fully united. And if The Outfit discovers the truth, it could tempt them to push for ultimate control. Right now, I'm acknowledged as the Mazzone heir apparent and acting boss, but they assume Angelo is still calling the shots.

He's not. I'm in charge in everything but name.

"We're here, boss," Alessandro says, swinging the blacked-out SUV into the church parking lot.

"Damn. This takes me back." I peer out the window at the familiar gray brick church.

"You went to church?" Leo asks, disbelief evident in his tone.

"Angelo ensured I was baptized before he abandoned my mom," I admit. "I don't know if she felt some sense of obligation, but she frog-marched me in that door every Sunday. Half the time she was too high to even realize what she was doing. I often wondered if she felt it might absolve her of her sins."

I don't talk about my mother much. Leo knows the full story. Frank has heard bits from the Messina family over the years, no doubt. And Alessandro can be trusted to keep his mouth shut.

It's no secret I'm Angelo's bastard son. Everyone knows he only looked me up when Mateo—the half-brother I never met—was gunned down in cold blood in the streets of Manhattan. To this day, no one has been charged with his murder. My father suspects the Russians or the Irish were behind it. Without proof, he couldn't go after them. Not without inciting a full-blown war. I'm sure that sticks in his gut, but he never mentions it to me. He never talks about his firstborn son. Not even with my sister Natalia.

"You want us to come in, boss?" Alessandro asks, glancing over his shoulder at me.

I shake my head as I slip on my suit jacket. Early September is still warm enough in Chicago not to need a coat. "That won't be necessary. Leo and I have this."

It's not like I'm expecting a shoot-out in church. New York might have beef with The Outfit, but it has never turned violent. We find other ways of taking potshots at one another.

We pay our respects and attend the burial, and a couple hours later, we head back to the car. Frank is outside by the hood, smoking a cigarette as he scans the dispersing crowd.

"Any issues?" I inquire as we come up to him.

"It's all quiet on the home front, boss."

We climb into the car, and I'm ready to split for the private airfield, but we're hungry, so I direct Alessandro to Glencoe. It's the most affluent city in Chicago and prime real estate, bordering Lake Michigan. The historical village has an abundance of top-class restaurants, which better serve our needs.

The fact it's Sierra's hometown doesn't factor into my planning.

Alessandro whistles as we drive through central downtown. "Wow, this place is nice."

"Glencoe is the eighth richest town in the US," I explain as I stare out my window, watching people going about their daily business. "It was developed as a planned community back in eighteen sixty-nine, and nowadays, it has one of the most attractive business districts along the North Shore."

"You sound like a talking encyclopedia," Leo says, smirking.

"I dated a girl from here. Spent a lot of time socializing in the village."

"You sound nostalgic," Frank says.

"Not in the least." I grit my teeth. "Most of my memories are not pleasant." As we round the bend, I spot a familiar blonde head outside the private kindergarten.

Speak of the devil.

"Stop the car." I'm not sure why I do it, but Alessandro pulls up alongside the curb before I can change my mind. Leo frowns, but he gets out of the car alongside me without asking questions.

"Rowan! Hold my hand," Saskia says to a little dark-haired boy at her side. He is wearing a school uniform and a sulky grin.

"I want Auntie Serena," the boy replies, stubbornly folding his arms across his chest. "She always gets me candy on Fridays," he pouts.

Saskia grabs his hand. "Candy will rot your teeth, and Auntie Serena should know better."

"Still laying down the law, I see," I say as we approach my ex and her son.

Saskia stares at me in confusion for a few seconds before her eyes pop wide. "Ben?" Disbelief drips from her tone. "Bennett Carver? Is it really you?" Her appreciative gaze rakes me up and down, and she angles one hip, thrusting her chest forward. Saskia had big tits when I knew her, but it's like two melons are propped on her chest now. Enhanced lips and a suspiciously smooth brow confirm her tits aren't the only cosmetic surgery she has indulged in.

It's fitting that the fake exterior matches her fake personality now. Saskia was always beautiful on the outside—it's what initially drew me to her—but completely ugly on the inside. By the end of our relationship, I could barely tolerate being in the same room as her.

"It's me," I say, glancing at the little boy. His head is tilted to the side, and he's staring intently at me, studying me with these wide big blue eyes, like I'm a puzzle he wants to figure out.

"I have a bone to pick with you," she says, licking her lips and batting her eyelashes. Her gaze veers to Leo, and her grin expands as she gives him a brief eye-fuck. Man, is she still using those tired moves? The flashy rock on her ring finger is clearly no deterrent. "You just upped and left, Ben," she adds, refocusing on me. "Vanished off the face of the Earth. I was so worried."

Yeah, I'm sure she was. Worried about how it made her look. "We broke up, and I left town. I thought it would've been apparent."

Her lips purse, and a flash of anger glints in her eyes before she disguises it. "It's water under the bridge now anyway." She forces a sweet smile on her face. "Life has clearly been good to you. You look great." Her eyes drift up and down my body again. Her blatant undressing feels like a violation, and I barely contain a shudder. Her little boy tugs on her hand, getting bored, but she ignores him.

I shoot him a pitiful smile. Poor kid. I know what it's like to be saddled with a shitty mother.

"We should meet for coffee. Catch up." She reaches out, touching my arm uninvited.

I purposely stare at her hand on my jacket until she removes it. "I'm only passing through town."

"Auntie Saskia," the little boy says, peering up at her with pleading eyes. "Can we go for candy now? Puh-leeeze."

All the hairs on the back of my neck lift at his words. Schooling my features into a neutral line, I examine the child more closely.

"Not now, Rowan," she hisses, working hard to shield her impatience from Leo and me. "Be quiet. The adults are talking."

She dismisses him like he's a nuisance, rolling her eyes as she gives me her undivided attention. "Sorry about that. His manners leave a lot to be desired."

"He's not your son?" I ask, doing some math in my head.

A fleeting glimmer of pain races across her face. "Oh my God. No." She slaps a hand across her chest. "No child of mine would ever be so unruly." Rowan scowls, and I don't blame him. Saskia is as brash and rude as she has always been. "He's Sierra's bastard," she volunteers without me having to ask.

While she may not be aware I'm the bastard son of the notorious Angelo Mazzone, she knows I grew up in a single-parent household, with a junkie mom, knowing nothing about my father, so I take huge offense to her words. Pinning her with a lethal look—one I normally reserve for men I'm about to interrogate or murder with my bare hands—I keep my tone deliberately low so the child doesn't overhear. "Tread carefully, Saskia, before you insult *this* bastard son."

She gulps audibly, her eyes popping wide with a combination of fear and panic. "My comment was in no way directed at you." Rage filters through my veins, but she blathers on, oblivious. "And look how well you have done for yourself. You should be so proud of how far you have come."

I shove my hands in my pants pockets before I'm tempted to hit a woman for the first time. "Who is his father?" I ask, ignoring her condescending remarks because I'm fast running out of patience. I want to get the pertinent facts and get the hell away from her.

"No one knows. Not even Sierra." She makes no attempt to lower her tone, and my jaw pulls taut with the strain involved in holding my tongue. If things are as I'm beginning to suspect, then maintaining a blank face in front of my ex is essential. I won't give her any reason to start connecting the dots. "The slut came back from Vegas knocked up at twenty-one," she continues, confirming my suspicions. "Not that I was surprised—"

I tune her poisonous tirade out, focusing on the little boy instead as my mind grapples to process this bombshell. Crouching down, I stare at him up close, and the resemblance almost knocks me flat on my ass. My heart is pounding behind my rib cage. Blood thrums in my ears. "Hey, Rowan. I'm Ben." My hand is shaking as I offer it to him, and I hope Saskia doesn't notice. "How old are you?"

Rowan eyes my hand like it's infected. Wrenching his hand from Saskia's, he folds his arms again, regarding me warily. "Mommy says I'm not to talk to strangers." His confident little voice tugs at my heartstrings.

Clearing my throat, I hope my smile looks genuine and that it masks my growing shock. I let my arm drop. "Your mommy is smart. I used to know her when she was a little girl."

Rowan looks up at his aunt for confirmation. Smart kid. I feel the burn from Saskia's heated stare, but I refuse to look at her.

"My mommy is smart and beautiful and the bestest mommy in the whole entire universe." He flashes me a toothy grin.

"The entire universe, huh?" I chuckle, not doubting his statement for a second.

He vigorously bobs his head, and I can hardly speak over the messy ball of emotion clogging the back of my throat. "She sounds amazing."

"She is. I love her this much." He extends his arms wide, hitting Saskia's hip in the process.

"For God's sake, Rowan. Stop hitting," she snaps, and I watch the exuberant smile slip from his face. I want to lash out at her. Wrap my hands around her throat and squeeze until she turns blue, but I grind my teeth to the molars, caging my rage. For now.

"I didn't mean it," Rowan says, his lower lip jutting out.

"Auntie Saskia knows it was an accident," I say through gritted teeth. If she makes one more snide remark, all bets are off. I will squeeze the life from her pathetic body in broad daylight with zero fucks given.

"We need to go," she says, her tone clipped as she snatches Rowan's hand again. Perhaps she has some self-preservation skills after all.

"It was nice meeting you, buddy," I say, lifting my clenched fist for a knuckle touch.

His skin is soft and warm when his small knuckles brush against mine. "You too, buddy."

"It was great seeing you again," Saskia says, as I straighten up, all anger replaced with sultry enthusiasm. "Look me up when you're next in town." She slips a business card in the pocket of my suit jacket. Leaning in, she presses her mouth to my ear. "Or call me and we can arrange to meet someplace central for both of us."

Ignoring her, I grab a twenty from my wallet and hand it to Ben. "Maybe your auntie will let you get candy now."

His eyes dance with excitement, and he jumps around. "Yay. Thank you!"

Saskia sways a little on her heels, not disguising her frustration, but I couldn't give two shits about her. "Goodbye, Bennett." She gives me one last lingering glance before dragging Rowan away.

"Bye, Ben," he calls out, waggling his fingers at me.

I return his wave as the storm grows to epic proportions inside me. Crumpling the card in my pocket, I remove it and toss it in the nearest trash can. I stare after them, watching Saskia scold Rowan again, and I'm two seconds away from going after her when Leo steps in front of me. "Did that just happen?" His brows climb to his hairline in disbelief.

"You know?"

He nods, still looking shell-shocked, and I can relate. The news hasn't sunk in yet. "Despite the shit she's injected in her face, it's obvious Saskia is Sierra's sister and then she mentioned Vegas." Leo drags a hand through his hair, glancing over his shoulder as Saskia and Rowan cross the street. "You don't need a DNA test to confirm it. Rowan is the fucking image of you. He's got your dark hair and your eyes. I see little of his mom in him."

I scrub my hands down my face, blindsided in a way I rarely am.

I have a son.

I'm a father.

And my little Firefly never told me.

Joy, confusion, regret, fear, and anger are a heady mix swirling inside me.

"What are you going to do?" Leo asks.

I exhale heavily. That's the million-dollar question. And I don't have the answer yet, except for one overriding conviction. "Protect them." Shaking the fog from my brain, I stride toward the car, jumping in the back seat. Leo slides in beside me.

"Change of plans," I supply, looking at Alessandro through the mirror. I point across the street at the sleek silver Mercedes Saskia and Rowan are getting into it. "Follow that car."

Chapter 16

SIERRA

I AM GOING to murder Serena with my bare hands for this, I think as I drive up the driveway of Saskia and Felix's plush home. What the hell was she thinking asking Saskia to pick Rowan up? If there was an emergency and she couldn't pick up my son, she should've called me, and I would have asked Pen or Esme to drop by the school. Ordinarily, Dion could have kept him until I arrived, but he's finishing work early today because he's flying to New York with some of his buddies for their friend Abe's bachelor party.

Rowan doesn't like Saskia, and it's not because of anything I have said. I would never do that. No, my son is astute, and he has picked up on the vibes she emits. Or maybe it's the short, impatient way she speaks to him during the rare occasions we attend Sunday dinner at my parents' house that has rubbed him the wrong way.

Father ignored me the entire way through my pregnancy—it was bliss—but as soon as I gave birth, his tune changed. I still don't know why. It's not like he pays Rowan much attention, and for the most part, when I visit, he ignores me, which suits me fine.

I only make the effort for Mom's sake and for my son.

My family is the only family Rowan is likely to know, and I won't deprive him of a loving Grandma, or his cousins. So, I suffer my father and Saskia in small doses to ensure my son doesn't miss out. It's a small price to pay, I remind myself as I park and stomp up the steps to Saskia's front door. I ring the bell, chewing on the inside of my mouth as I wait for the door to open.

"Mommy!" Rowan rushes me the second I step foot in the kitchen, clinging to my legs.

Mrs. Smith, the housekeeper, smiles warmly at him as she packs up his pencil case, stowing it and his books in his backpack.

"Hey, Firecracker." I kneel, pulling him into a hug. The instant his small arms wrap around me, a deep sense of contentment washes over me. I was excited to be a mom, but I couldn't have predicted how much I would adore it.

Or maybe it's all down to Rowan.

Because he is the most amazing child and he has brightened my world in ways I could never have imagined. From the second he was born, I was high on the most intense love drug. My heart swelled to bursting point the first time I looked at him, and it hasn't deflated any time since.

Rowan is my greatest achievement. The most precious person in my life. The main reason I wake up happy each day. I would go to the ends of the Earth and back to ensure he is safe, happy, and healthy. I truly adore being his mother, and I'm so blessed I get to share my life with him in it. He is my pride and joy. My happy place. My everything.

I dot kisses all over his cute face until the strain eases from his gaze. "Ready to go home?"

He bobs his head. "Can you carry me?" he asks, and my heart aches. Rowan is fiercely independent, and while he is also hugely affectionate, it's not like him to want to be carried in the middle of the day. That's how I know he was feeling vulnerable here. I don't blame him. This house may have been highlighted in celebrity magazines, but it's a show home. There is nothing warm or inviting about it.

I can't even get mad at my sister for dumping my son in the kitchen with her staff because at least Mrs. Smith is kind, and she looks like she enjoyed his company.

Saskia and Felix never had kids, and they have given up trying.

The world is a better place for it, if you ask me.

Rowan wraps his legs around my waist, and I hold him close as I stand. Mrs. Smith walks with us to the car, carrying his backpack. Saskia is nowhere to be seen, and I'm glad because I'm not sure I could restrain myself, and I hate losing my temper in front of my son.

"What do you say to Mrs. Smith?" I ask Rowan as I strap him into his car seat.

"Thank you for looking after me," he sings, giving her a big goofy smile.

"You're very welcome." She sets his backpack down on the floor of the back seat. "You take care, Master Rowan."

He giggles, and I mess up his hair. "Love you, Firecracker," I say, kissing his brow.

"Love you too, Mommy."

Offering endearments wasn't something that happened often in my house growing up as my father frowned upon my mother when she showered us with affection. He believes love makes you weak, and loving words and displays were pretty much banned in the Lawson household. Mom still told me she loved me when we were alone, but it always felt off. Like it was wrong. I know better now, and I'm determined my son will always know how much he is loved and cherished, so I make a point of telling him at least once a day that I love him.

We wave to Mrs. Smith, and I power up the engine, keen to get the hell out of here.

"Mommy?" he asks when we are halfway down the road.

Out of the corner of my eye, I spot a blacked-out SUV pulling out onto the road a little farther back. "Yes, Rowan."

"Auntie Saskia wouldn't let me get candy."

Of course, she wouldn't. I'm strict with sugary treats, but Serena knows Rowan is allowed a visit to the candy store on Fridays after school. I'm much closer to my middle sister now, and I'm positive she would've told Saskia this.

"I'll drop by the store on our way home," I assure him, eyeing him through the mirror.

"She wouldn't let me keep the money her friend gave me either."

Oh my God. If Saskia had one of her airhead bitchy friends near my son, I will string her up. And what kind of heartless monster takes money from a child? Just when I think Saskia really couldn't sink any lower, she finds new ways to surprise me.

"It's okay. I will talk to Auntie Saskia and get it back for you. For now, I'm good for it." I waggle my brows, and he sits back, looking happy and content. I hook my cell up to the sound system in the car, and we sing along to some kids' songs I keep on my playlist while we drive.

After a detour at the candy store, we head home to our bungalow. I pull into our small driveway and kill the engine, noticing a large black SUV park at the curb a few doors down. I could swear it's the same one I saw earlier. Apprehension trickles up my spine, and I rub a hand across my chest, hoping to ease the sudden anxious fluttery feeling.

"Mommy." Rowan thrusts a sugary hand out. "Want some?"

I pop a couple Sour Patch Kids in my mouth, my cheeks puckering automatically as the sour, tangy, fruity candy bursts in my mouth. I don't know how he can stomach those things.

"Want to bike to the park to look for bugs?" I ask as I unbuckle him from his car seat.

"Yes, yes, yes." He jumps out, flinging himself on me, and I almost take a tumble.

I laugh, nuzzling my nose into his hair, inhaling the strawberry smell from his shampoo. I look down the road, but I don't see the black SUV anymore. Air whooshes out of my mouth in grateful relief. I was obviously imagining things. "Let's get changed out of our uniforms, grab some water, and then we'll hit the road." I snatch his backpack and my purse, slinging them over one shoulder as I lock the car with the key fob while Rowan slides his sticky hand into mine.

"How was school?" I inquire as we walk across the gravel toward the front door.

"Great." He beams up at me. "Mr. Stewart let us paint, and then we watched *Dr. Doolittle*."

"That sounds fun."

"It was," he agrees, racing into the house while I turn off the alarm.

"Be careful," I shout after him because he's a little accident prone at times, especially when he's running around the place at full speed. Rowan is full of boundless energy, which I never want to tame, but I need to strike a balance to ensure his safety.

Depositing his backpack on the floor, I dump my keys and my purse on the hall table, stifling a yawn as I pad through our combination kitchen and dining room and out into the corridor at the back that leads to the three bedrooms. Over on the other side of the house is a large living room, a small sunroom, and an art studio, but my favorite part of the property is the large garden at the rear. I added some swings, a slide, and a climbing frame for Rowan, plus we have a vegetable and flower garden, a sand pit, and a small, covered pond with some colorful fish.

Walking into Rowan's room, I chuckle as I watch my rambunctious son wrestle with his school shirt. "Here, let me help." I kneel on the carpet, pulling the tangled shirt back down over his torso. "It's quicker to unbutton it, Firecracker." I tweak his nose, smiling, as I quickly flip the buttons. I leave him to strip out of his pants while I remove sweatpants, a T-shirt, and a hoodie from his closet. It's still relatively warm out, but it can get distinctly chilly in the evenings.

I leave my son to get dressed while I strip out of my black work top and pants.

I managed to graduate from Loyola two years after I had Rowan, and then I took the acupuncture program part-time at night and online. I don't want to miss a minute with Rowan, so studying when he's in bed is my only option. I'm working part-time at a local practice in the village, and I've put my studies on hold for now. When Rowan starts elementary school next year, I'll probably sign up for the homeopathy program.

"Ready!" Rowan vaults into my room, announcing himself loudly.

"Well, I'm not," I say, standing in my underwear. "Why don't you fill two water bottles while I get dressed." I hurriedly pull on a pair of yoga pants and a long-sleeved T-shirt of Dion's before lacing my sneakers tight.

Ten minutes later, we are on our way. This neighborhood is quiet and peaceful, and there isn't much traffic on this side of town, but I still ensure we stick to the footpaths and the bike lanes until we arrive at the park.

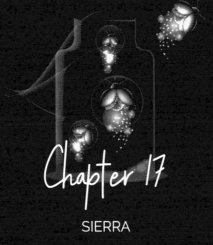

Chapter 17

SIERRA

WE SPEND AN hour at the playground before exploring the small woods where Rowan finds another worm, beetle, and butterfly to add to his ever-growing insect collection. He wants to delve deeper into the woods, but I'm on edge for some reason. I can't put my finger on it, but all the tiny hairs keep lifting on the nape of my neck when we are alone in the forest, and I can't shake the feeling of eyes on my back.

I don't know what's gotten into me today, but I'm spooked in a way I'm rarely spooked anymore. I haven't had a bodyguard in years, and I have almost forgotten what it was like when I had Tony trailing me everywhere. My mind wanders to my former bodyguard, as it does from time to time, and I wonder where he is. I never heard from him again, and I hope he's happy, wherever he is and whatever he's doing.

When I first brought Rowan home, Father foisted another bodyguard on me, claiming it wasn't safe for either of us without one. I didn't fight him on it because I was too preoccupied with my son. After a year, he removed the man out of the blue, stating we didn't need protection anymore. Honestly, half the time, I wonder if Joseph Lawson is getting early-onset dementia or his OCD is just that whacked. Anyway, I can't say I've missed having a bodyguard until small moments like this, when I wouldn't mind having someone around for my peace of mind.

I coax Rowan out of the woods, only relaxing when we are back on our bikes and heading home. We stop at the small neighborhood bakery on the way, and I buy a fresh loaf of crusty bread to go with the pasta I am making for dinner.

After my little Firecracker has consumed his body weight in pasta, I bathe him and dress him in clean pajamas. Then I snuggle into bed with him, reading another few pages of *James and the Giant Peach*. When his eyelids grow heavy and he is struggling to keep his eyes open, I set the book down and press a kiss to his brow. "Good night, sweetheart. I love you. Sleep tight."

"Night, Mommy," he whispers in a sleepy tone. "Love you, too."

I finish cleaning the kitchen, and then I take a nice long hot shower. Emerging from the bathroom, I notice I missed a call from my boyfriend, so I call him back while I pull on sleep shorts and a tank. Nightfall has descended, and I pop my cell on speaker while I walk around the house, pulling down the blinds. Dion answers just as I'm about to hang up. "Give me a sec," he shouts, loud music blaring in the background.

Wandering into the kitchen, I flick the overhead light on as I pad to the refrigerator, removing a chilled bottle of wine. I set my cell down on the marble countertop while I pour myself a much-needed drink. Noise mutes on the phone, and my ears give a silent thumbs-up.

"Hey, babe," Dion says. "Sorry about that. We're at this sports bar a block from our hotel and it's freaking crazy. The Yankees are trouncing the Cubs and the whole place is going nuts."

"It's cool." I secure the cap on the wine bottle, popping it back in the refrigerator. "I wouldn't have disturbed you except I saw your missed call."

"I called to let you know I landed safely in New York and that I miss you already."

I laugh softly. "You only saw me last night."

"And your point is?"

"It's too soon to miss me."

"I miss you the second I drop you home after our dates."

I smile into the empty room. This man is so unbelievably sweet. "You're crazy."

"Crazy about you."

"You're such a charmer. I have no idea how you reached thirty without some woman tying you down." The words are out of my mouth before I can reclaim them.

"I just hadn't met the right woman," he replies, and my smile fades. I like Dion.

A lot.

He's a gentleman, and he treats me with respect. He's hot, and funny, and smart, and Rowan already worships the ground he walks on. Although, my son isn't aware that I'm dating his teacher because I won't introduce any man to him until I know it's serious.

I made a mistake when Rowan was three and introduced him to the guy I was dating then. When things ended, Rowan was devastated because he had grown close to Julian.

So now, I have strict self-imposed rules.

Rules Dion knows about and has always supported, but lately, he's asking me when we can make it official with my son, forcing me to confront the reality of our relationship. I tried arguing it's risky to let Rowan know about us, as Dion could get in trouble with the school for dating a parent, but he said it's a risk he's willing to take.

Truth is, Dion is perfect on paper, and I'm enjoying spending time with him, but he doesn't set my heart racing or ignite a flame with his touch. Not like...

"Sierra. Are you still there?"

Dion pulls me out of my head. "I'm here. I should let you get back to the guys."

"I freaked you out again, huh?"

"No, it's just—"

"It's okay, babe. You don't need to explain, and I'm sorry if I'm rushing you. I don't mean to."

"I know you don't, and let's not stress about it. We can talk when you're back."

"Our flight gets in late Sunday, but I could drop by Monday night after Rowan is asleep?"

"I'll cook a late dinner."

"You don't have to do that."

"You know I enjoy cooking. It relaxes me, and I want to cook for you."

A door bangs in the background, and a hushed conversation ensues. I sip my glass of wine while I wait for Dion to speak. "Sorry, babe. We're heading to another bar. I gotta go."

"Have fun. I'll see you Monday."

Like the coward I am, I hang up before he can tell me he loves me. I wonder if there is something wrong with me. Some vital missing piece that has screwed up my internal wiring.

Dion is perfectly sweet and romantic, and the sex is good. He loves me, and he loves Rowan, and I know if I made more of a commitment that a proposal would be forthcoming, yet the very thought makes me break out in hives.

I haven't told Dion I love him because I don't have those feelings for him. I don't know if I ever will. I like his company, and we have fun. Our relationship is nice. Easy-breezy. Comfortable. Borderline boring. But there is a certain predictability with boring that is reassuring.

Yet is that enough reason to continue dating him? Am I settling? Or will every guy I meet always fall short compared to Ben. And how ridiculous is it to still fixate on a man who tossed me so easily to the curb?

Ugh. I take a big slurp of my wine, wishing Dion was enough. I feel like I'm shortchanging him and cheating myself. Now that he is pushing to take things to the next level, I'm feeling like I should probably break things off before they get messy. The last thing I need is things getting complicated with Rowan's teacher.

Sighing, I pad into the dark living room with my wine in one hand and my cell in the other, planning a night with some *Friends* reruns. I'm in desperate need of a little light relief and Joey, Chandler, and crew are the perfect remedy.

I'm moving toward the couch, in the direction of the large freestanding lamp, when a subtle motion in the corner of the room sends my blood pressure skyrocketing. Out of the corner of my eye, I detect a shape hiding in the shadows beside the fireplace.

Holy fuck! Someone is in the house!

Panic powers through my veins, and my heart jumps, pumping frenetically, to the point I fear I'll have a heart attack if I can't slow it down. Rooted to the spot, I silently talk myself off the ledge. If someone *was* in here, they would have made themselves known by now, and the alarm would have sounded. I'm probably just freaking myself out for no reason. Like in the woods earlier.

With my heart jackhammering against my rib cage, I slowly turn around, ready to confront my torrid imagination, because I have convinced myself I'm just imagining things again.

A blur rushes past me, and I open my mouth to scream when a hand clamps down hard over my lips. My cell phone and my wine slip through my fingers, crashing to the ground. Glass smashes on the hardwood floor, and liquid splashes my bare legs. Blood rushes to my head as my heart tries to beat a path out of my chest. Warm breath fans across my cheek as I'm hauled against a solid body. I can scarcely think over the screaming in my head and the frantic pounding in my chest.

Rowan!

That's the first thought skating through my mind as the intruder wraps his muscular arm around my waist, lifting my legs and pulling me back from the broken glass and spilled wine on the floor. I don't fight, even though my instinct is to buck and writhe in his arms, to bury my teeth in his arm until he releases me. But I can't do it. I won't struggle because I don't want to risk Rowan waking and barreling into the middle of this.

I will give this man whatever he wants—my car, money, *me*—as long as he leaves my son alone.

The man's lips brush against my earlobe, and every bone in my body locks up tight. "Hello, Firefly," he says in a sexy voice that continuously torments my dreams.

No freaking way! It's Ben!

I almost collapse in relief against him until I recall the last time I saw Bennett Mazzone and I remember the truth I have denied him. Ben's flesh and blood is asleep only a few feet away, and if he's here now, it means *he knows.*

Somehow, Ben found out I gave birth to his son, and from the way his body radiates angry waves of aggression, I know I'm about to suffer the consequences of my silence.

"You and I need to talk," he says, his voice dripping with barely controlled rage. It's more of a threat than a request, and an icy chill slithers up my spine.

Oh fuck. I am royally screwed.

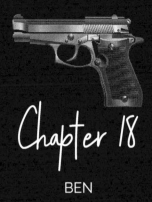

Chapter 18

BEN

KEEPING A FIRM hold on Sierra's slim waist, I lift her away from the broken glass on the floor, over to the other side of the living room. I'm working hard to control my temper so I don't accidentally kill my little Firefly. It's not easy though. I think I've gone through a whole gamut of conflicting emotions in the past few hours. Shock. Grief. Pride. Happiness. Relief. Remorse. Fear. Anger. With the latter being the overriding emotion this past hour as I've hidden inside her house—my son's home—listening to everything.

"Start talking," I growl, invoking huge self-control as I gently place her feet down on the ground. Walking to the lamp, I turn it on, casting a faint light over the proceedings. Then I back her up against the wall, clenching and unclenching my hands as I glare at the woman who hid my child from me for over five years.

The first thing I did while Alessandro tailed Saskia from the village was to call one of my tech guys and request a full background check on Rowan and Sierra. Within an hour, I had everything I needed to know, which only added to my rage. It was too easy to find them, and it's a fucking miracle no one has discovered them or made the connection to me before now. If Saskia wasn't so stuck up her own ass, she would have connected the dots today. Thank fuck, she was too busy ogling me to notice.

Looking at the photos of my son in the electronic file Phillip sent me is like looking at a photo album of myself as a kid. The resemblance is that strong. Not that there are many photos of me as a kid. There actually weren't that many of Rowan online either. I'm assuming that's because Sierra didn't want me stumbling across an image of him. But it doesn't matter. All it takes is one photo.

"Cat got your tongue again, Firefly?" I hiss, rotating my neck from side to side to loosen the tension sitting there.

"How did you find out?" she asks, her tone betraying no trace of the fear plainly etched upon her face.

"That doesn't fucking matter," I say, through gritted teeth. "What matters is you kept my son's existence from me. That I missed his birth. Missed the first five years of his life," I snap, losing the tenuous control on my emotions, which is most unlike me.

I am *always* in control.

It's how I have run my life for the past fourteen years since my father upended it so completely. I have learned to shut my emotions off. To not care. And today is testing my whole belief system and challenging my entire way of living.

"You left me no choice," she says, and I see red.

Advancing on her, I wrap my hands around her throat and squeeze. My nostrils flare, and fire charges through my veins, infusing my anger with self-righteous indignation. "There are always choices, and you made the wrong one."

Terror dances across her green eyes as she claws at my hand.

"How fucking dare you deny me the opportunity to know my son. How dare you let your stupid fucking pride get in the way of what is right for an innocent child." I know I was cold and cruel to her the morning after the night we spent together in Vegas, but that was necessary to ensure she walked away for good. If I had known it would stop her from telling me she was pregnant, I might have handled the situation differently.

She raises her leg, to knee me in the balls I'm guessing, but I won't give her the opportunity or the satisfaction. I lift her up by the neck, her legs thrashing against the wall as her skin turns a pale shade of gray. "You know I grew up without a dad." Mom had only died a few months before I met Saskia, and I remember a painful conversation over dinner one time where Joseph Lawson grilled me clinically over her death and the absence of my father. Sierra was there, lapping up every word. "Did you ever stop to think this is the very last thing I would want for my son?"

Pain slices across my chest as I consider my child lying in bed at night wondering why his father doesn't care enough to know him. My fingers tighten around her neck, but then I let her go before I kill her in a blind rage.

She slumps to the ground, sucking greedy mouthfuls of air into her lungs, working hard to quiet the strangled sounds coming from her throat, as silent tears spill down her cheeks.

I crouch over her. "I could fucking kill you right now, Sierra, for depriving me of my rights. I have already missed out on so much of his life." I sit back on my butt, crossing my legs in front of me as I hang my head, willing my errant breathing to steady.

I hate feeling out of control.

It's unsettling.

Her quiet sobs are the only sound in the room for a couple of minutes while I grapple with my anger. I didn't come here to kill her. From watching her with my son today, it's clear Rowan loves and adores Sierra.

To hurt her is to hurt him.

That's not part of my agenda, and I need to remember that.

I came for answers, and to start making things right.

When I feel calmer, I lift my head, not shocked to find her bloodshot eyes shooting daggers at me. "Who the fuck do you think you are to break into my home and threaten me?" she says, her chest heaving. Her voice is hoarse and borderline hysterical. "I was right to keep him from you. You're a fucking monster."

My lips pull into a snarl, and I invoke every ounce of self-control to avoid lunging at her again. "Choose your words carefully, Firefly. You have no idea who you are dealing with. I will not be spoken to like that."

"And I will not be abused in my own home!" she shrieks, quickly clamping a hand over her mouth, her eyes darting to the door.

She is trying to stay quiet so she doesn't wake Rowan. That helps to tamp down my anger a little. Listening to her with him earlier helped too. She's such a good mother. Kind, fun, and loving. The exact opposite of the way Saskia was with Rowan earlier. She reminded me of how my mom was at one time before she fell prey to her addictions.

However, any goodwill she engendered disappeared the instant I overheard her talking to that asshole boyfriend. Fuck buddy. Whoever he is to her. Anger returns and I pin her with a dark glare that has caused grown men to piss their pants.

It doesn't have the desired effect though. It only seems to enrage her further. If looks could kill, Sierra would have just buried me ten feet under with the force of her resentful glare. She tucks her legs into her chest, glowering at me like she wishes she could riddle my body with bullets.

Where the hell does she get off being furious with me? I'm the one who has been wronged here. If I haven't made that point clear enough, I'm about to. "You better not have had any other man around my son. I will fucking murder any asshole who thinks he's taking my place."

Her face turns as white as a ghost, and she's not looking so self-righteous now. Her eyes pop wide with renewed terror. "No one has taken your place," she croaks. "I'm strict about keeping the men I'm dating away from Rowan."

A growl rumbles from my chest, and an unwelcome surge of jealousy floods my system as I think of her with anyone else besides me. It's irrational, and it's not like I haven't considered this in the years since Vegas. Sierra is stunning and free-spirited, and she can't help but draw people to her. I knew she must be dating. When I really wanted to torture myself, I imagined she was married. So, this isn't news. But it's completely different now I know she has had my son this entire time. A fresh layer of murderous rage sweeps through me at the thought of any man even coming into proximity with my flesh and blood.

"What about the asshole on the phone?" I bark.

Her eyes narrow as anger, once again, replaces fear. "Rowan doesn't know I'm dating Dion."

Dion. An asshole's name if I ever heard one. "But Mr. Stewart knows Rowan. From what I hear, he's his favorite pupil. I wonder why that is." It's ironic the douche is in New York this weekend while I am here. I could send one of my men to relay a message, but I'd much rather deliver it in person. I think I'll organize a nice little welcoming party for Mr. Stewart on Sunday night at the airport.

Her face pales again. "How do you know that?"

"It's my job to know everything, and it didn't take long to dissect every aspect of your lives here."

She shivers, and her lower lip wobbles. "Rowan loves his teacher, and Dion is a great guy," she whispers. "Don't do anything to hurt him."

I'm surprised she has gone straight there. Then again, she was around Salerno and his men in Vegas, and she would have noticed my *soldati* carrying weapons. It wouldn't take much for her to piece things together. I doubt she knows exactly who we are, but she knows enough to understand we are dangerous. That *I'm* dangerous.

Good. That should make this easier.

"That all depends on you." I expect her to ask how, but she surprises me again.

She clears her raspy throat. "I never planned to keep my pregnancy a secret. I wanted to tell you. I even flew to New York to see you in person."

If I wasn't already sitting down, that statement would've flattened me on my ass. I examine her face for lies, but she is telling the truth. "When?" I grit out.

Her tongue darts out, wetting her dry lips, and I try not to think about how good it felt to have her tongue slide up and down my cock. My dick swells behind my zipper, but I ignore it. While angry fucking her has a certain appeal, I never force myself on women, and there is no way Sierra will let me touch her after I broke into her house, scared the shit out of her, and almost choked the life from her body.

"It was the January after Vegas, the first week of spring semester," she explains, coughing a little. She lifts a hand to massage her throat, and a small pang of guilt accosts me.

Wordlessly, I get up and walk to the kitchen, grabbing a couple waters from the refrigerator. She hasn't moved when I return. She's just sitting, staring off into space, lost in thought.

I sit down on the floor in front of her again, handing her a bottle. Sitting cross-legged, she stretches her arm toward me. Her fingers brush against mine as she takes the bottle from me, and a jolt of electricity shoots up my arm. She jerks her arm away, her expression a mix of lust and hate—a lethal combination that only swells my cock to the point of pain. I blatantly rake my gaze over her sexy body as she drinks, noticing she has filled out more.

Her thin pajamas conceal little, and she may as well be naked. She's not as slender as she was when I saw her in Vegas, but she is still slim with curves in all the right places. Her legs look endlessly long and smooth, and my fingers twitch with a craving to explore every inch of her silky skin. I lift my eyes, spotting her nipples poking through the flimsy material of her tank. Her tits are definitely bigger, but unlike her sister's, they are clearly not fake. I imagine tearing her top from her body and sucking her neat rosy nipples into my warm mouth while she strokes my cock.

"Do you mind?" she hisses, pinning me with a hateful look as I'm dragged from the pleasant visual in my head.

I smirk as I uncap the lid from my bottle. "I don't mind at all." On purpose, I let my eyes linger on her chest and adjust myself in my pants, making sure she sees.

Her eyes lower to my crotch for a couple of seconds before she collects herself. Scowling, she rubs a spot between her brows. "Do you want me to explain or not?" she snaps, eyeballing me.

I wave my hand dismissively in the air, knowing it will infuriate her. "Continue."

Her nostrils flare, and her eyes scrunch up, and I'd love to kiss that defiance off her beautiful face. But we are a long way from that point. I'm still mad at her, and she's spitting blood.

"I went to the Caltimore Holdings office, but you were leaving as I got there, so I hopped in a taxi and followed you to some seedy club in Queens, a couple blocks from the Hudson."

I know the place she's talking about. I sold it and the rest of the old strip joints four years ago because they didn't fit into my new business model. Now, I own a string of high-end casinos and clubs—some regular clubs, some sex clubs—catering to an exclusive VIP clientele who have big pockets, big desires, and an even bigger need to keep their activities on the down low. But that is only one small part of my business empire. An empire that has doubled in value in the past six years, largely due to my ambition and my meticulous execution. I run a very tight ship, and I have considered every possible angle.

Except for a child.

"And?" I arch a brow, urging her to continue while I drain my water in a few mouthfuls.

She rubs a hand across her chest as potent fear returns to haunt her troubled eyes.

I tilt my head to the side, curious now.

She stares at me. "I saw you torture a man," she blurts, and all the blood drains from my face. I nod for her to continue. "It was in the basement. He was Russian. Sergei. You ripped his fingers off one at a time, and then you slashed him with a knife." Her voice lowers to a shaky whisper. "His insides were hanging out." She gulps, pausing for a second as if she might puke. "It was the most shocking thing I have ever seen." When she raises her eyes, they radiate with sheer terror. "I barely remember getting out of there. I was that scared."

"You brought your bodyguard with you," I surmise, remembering the mess he left for me to clean up.

Death doesn't scare me, and my hands have plenty of blood on them. I don't remember all the dead bodies I am responsible for, either by my own hands or by another's hands, but I remember every innocent life that has been needlessly lost. I didn't kill those two old men drinking at the bar, my bartender, one of my soldiers, or the taxi driver, but I have carried the weight of responsibility with me since that day. I never understood why. We didn't keep cameras in the strip clubs, for obvious reasons, and whoever killed them left no trace. I knew it was a professional hit. But I never knew why or could find out who did it. At least that mystery is solved.

She nods, dragging her lower lip between her teeth for a second. "Did you…did you hurt him?"

I shake my head. "I never knew who did it or why."

Her shoulders relax a little.

"You still should've told me. You had no right to keep it from me."

Fire blazes in her eyes. "Are you for real?" she shouts before cussing and clamping a hand over her mouth. I glance over my shoulder, but there isn't a peep from the other side of the bungalow. "Why the fuck would I tell you after that?" she continues. "I put aside your cruel treatment of me in Vegas to do the right thing for my unborn child, but after witnessing you torture and kill a man, I wanted to run as far away from you as I could. There was no way in hell I wanted you anywhere near my son, and that hasn't changed." She tips her chin up defiantly, and I grace her with a wry smile as I climb to my feet.

I loom over her as I lay down the new law. "I don't give a fuck what you want. He's *my son,* and I have a lot of missed time to make up for."

She scrambles to her feet, inching away from me.

I flash her a deadly smile.

"You're dangerous, and I want you nowhere near him."

"I am, but there is nothing you can do to stop me. I will drag you through the courts if I have to." Hell will freeze over before I'd publicize her and my son in such a blatant way, but she doesn't need to know that.

"You can't do that!" she cries.

"You can't keep me from my son. I won't hurt him," I add, seeing the abject fear reappearing on her face. "I will protect you both, but I can't do that from New York."

Her brows pucker as suspicion creeps into her tone. "What exactly are you saying?"

"You have this weekend to pack up your shit. Rowan and you are moving to New York with me."

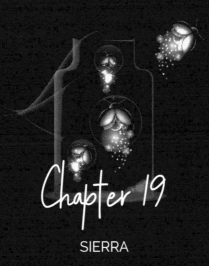

Chapter 19

SIERRA

"THE HELL WE are," I tell him. Has he lost his ever-loving mind? "You don't get to show up here and start dictating things to me."

"You better start listening carefully, Sierra, because I am not in the habit of repeating myself." I'm not sure if his cold tone and emotionless expression is better or worse than the naked rage which contorted his face when he first showed himself. "You will not keep me from my son, and you are in no position to argue with me. You lost that right the day you fled New York without telling me the truth."

"I'll go to the cops," I blurt. "I'll tell them what I saw."

He barks out a soft laugh, and I'm grateful he's careful not to wake Rowan. Not that I'm telling him that. "The cops won't touch me. There is no evidence."

"I'll tell them what kind of man you really are." It's a weak argument, and we both know it.

"What kind of man is that?" he teases, fighting a smile, and I want to ram my fist in his smarmy face.

"The kind who hides his criminal activities behind legitimate businesses. I'll tell them how you have strategically targeted up-and-coming tech companies to foster your agenda, like using your staff to invade people's privacy," I snap, hating that I have just let him know I have kept tabs on him over the years. He also knows my statement is conjecture because there is still nothing shady reported online. I'm grasping at straws, and I bet he can tell.

Frustrated, I cross my arms, wishing again that I wasn't wearing such flimsy pajamas. He enjoyed drinking his fill earlier, and I'm embarrassed to admit how much his intense, heated stare turned me on.

I hate him.

He's a predator of the worst kind.

Hiding in my house. Eavesdropping on my conversation with Dion. Spying on Rowan and me as we went about our normal nightly routine completely unaware of the monster lurking in the shadows.

He's a cold-blooded killer and a man who can't be trusted. He almost choked me to death earlier. My throat throbs, as if on cue, helping to remind me. I might feel guilty because I have denied him his son and I have denied Rowan his father, but I did what I believe was in the best interests of my child. Rowan is the priority, and he always will be. Keeping him away from Ben is still the right thing to do.

He's staring at me with that cold, harsh gaze, awaiting my response, so I tell it as I see it. "The kind who maims and kills and doesn't lose a wink of sleep over it."

"I am all that and more," he agrees, stalking toward me, eating up the small gap between us. I retreat until I hit the end of the wall and I can't retreat any more. "And you would do well to remember it." The tips of his fingers brush against my sore throat, and I detest the flurry of fiery tingles his touch invokes against my sensitive flesh.

Why can't I feel this when Dion touches me? Why do I have to crave the man who would sooner crush me than treat me with any kindness? I am under no illusion here. Ben wants Rowan, and I'm only part of the package because he knows he needs me to take care of his son while he's off building his crooked business empire.

"I'm not scared of you," I lie. He chuckles, and I'm back to wanting to punch him again. "And I won't apologize for doing what I did to protect my son."

All humor fades from his face as a familiar thunderous darkness washes over his features. His piercing blue eyes—the same ones his son shares—penetrate my skull as if his gaze is a knife slicing through skin and bone. He presses his body flush against mine, forcing my chin upright. "My son does *not* need protection from me." A muscle pops in his jaw. "But he does need protection from my enemies. You both do. If word got out, they would come for you and Rowan. You are both targets now."

Fear whittles through me, but I compartmentalize, focusing on damage control. I won't agree to this, but I'm not stupid either. Ben is a powerful, dangerous man with considerable resources at his disposal. If I refuse, he will just take Rowan anyway, and I cannot bear the thought of him being separated from me. My only option is to appeal to whatever sliver of humanity still lingers in his bones.

"No one knows, Ben. Your name isn't on his birth certificate, and only two of my friends know the truth, and they will take the secret to their graves. You can leave and no one will be the wiser." He opens his mouth, to spit more hatred at me, I'm sure, but I talk over him. "Rowan is happy here. He loves school, and he loves this house, and he is best friends with his cousin Romeo. Pulling him away from everything he has ever known will unsettle him." I peer deep into his eyes, pleading with everything I've got. "Please don't force me to do this. I'm begging you."

"You should never beg, Sierra," he says, but the hard edge to his tone is missing.

A little surge of hope springs to life inside me.

Releasing my chin, he steps back, rubbing his hands down his cheeks. "I don't want to upset him or unsettle him, but you can't ask me to turn my back on him. I cannot do that, Sierra. I know what it's like to grow up without a father, and I'm not inflicting that suffering and guilt and self-doubt on my child." Pain flares briefly in his eyes. "You said no one knows, but two people do."

"My friends would never tell."

"Our enemies have ways of torturing the truth from hardened men who have been trained to keep secrets. If they get their hands on Esme or Penelope, they will sing like a canary."

He references my besties with the confidence of someone used to extracting truths. If he can make the connection that easily, it doesn't bode well for others who might come looking. "How would anyone even know to come here? Know anything about me?"

"Have you forgotten the men in that basement in Vegas?" he asks. A shudder works its way through me. "I haven't forgotten a single thing about that night," I say, scowling when his lips curve into a salacious grin. "Are you saying Scarface Salerno is your enemy now?"

He shakes his head, propping his butt against the arm of my couch. "Vegas is an ally, but situations can change overnight. He knows who you are. No doubt he still has the recording from the bedroom." Ben smirks. "He probably jacks off to it nightly."

My face pulls into a grimace. "Not helpful, and can we stay focused."

I'm getting hot thinking about the more pleasant aspects of that night, and I won't let him distract me.

"The point is, your friends knowing is a risk. If you stay here, you put them at risk as well as yourself and Rowan."

"We have lived here for five years, and nothing has happened," I protest.

"That doesn't mean it will last forever." Exhaling heavily, he stands. "Look, it's late. Let's sleep on it and talk again tomorrow."

I know he has no intention of letting it go. I see the determination glinting in his eyes. Yet, buying some time to think of options is better than the alternative right now. "Okay." Briefly, I consider packing Rowan up and fleeing in the night, but I doubt I could find any place on the planet to hide where Ben wouldn't find us. A life on the run, constantly looking over our shoulders, is not the kind of life I have in mind for my son.

He taps out a message on his cell phone. "Walk me to the door," he demands, and I barely resist the urge to flip him off. He's so damn bossy.

I startle when I open the front door, finding a tall guy about my age standing right there. "Fuck." I slam a hand over my chest, sure my heart is going to short-circuit this time. There are only so many frights it can handle in one night.

The guy looks me up and down.

"Eyes on my face," Ben snaps, and I jerk my head up.

"Sorry, boss." The man sounds contrite, but you can't tell from his face which is a master class in nothing. He obviously attended the same school as Ben—both have the art of emotionless expressions down pat.

"This is Alessandro," Ben explains.

"Hi. I'm Sierra." I don't smile, but my tone is pleasant.

"It's nice to meet you," he says, offering me a slight smile. He's good-looking with dark hair and warm brown eyes, and I'm betting he does well with the ladies. He has that whole moody, broody vibe working for him.

"Alessandro will guard you overnight," Ben says. I open my mouth to protest, but he places his fingers to my lips, silencing me. "It's not just that I don't trust you to not make a run for it," he says, and my cheeks flare up as I remember my thoughts from a couple of minutes ago. "It's for protection."

"It's past midnight." I poke my head out, looking left and right. "The neighborhood is dead. Everyone is asleep."

"Arguing is pointless," Ben says, stepping out of the house. He stands beside Alessandro. "Either Alessandro keeps watch out in his car or I guard you from inside. Your choice."

"That won't be necessary." There is no way I want to explain his presence to Rowan. I face Alessandro. "Do you need to use the bathroom, or can I get you anything to eat or drink?"

"I'm fine, but thanks." With another small smile, he returns to the black SUV now parked directly outside my house.

"Don't make plans for tomorrow," Ben says as a sleek black Mercedes pulls up to the curb. "We have lots to discuss."

"I don't want you to meet him yet," I say, steeling myself for another argument. "I will drop Rowan off at Serena's in the morning, and he can play with Romeo until we are done."

"You can't keep him from me forever, Sierra. I have a right to know my own child, and he has a right to know I'm his father."

"I'm not saying that."

"Aren't you?"

"We can't just spring this on him is all I'm saying."

His shoulders stiffen. "We will talk more tomorrow." He walks away but stops, turning back around. "He's a great kid, Sierra. You've done a wonderful job with him."

"It's not me," I rasp, barely able to talk over the lump clogging my sore throat. "It's all Rowan. He makes it so easy to love him."

"I wish I knew that firsthand," he says as a new wave of anger skates over his face. "Good night," he clips out, his jaw tensing as he walks off.

Leo gets out of the car, holding the door for Ben. His eyes are hostile as he stares at me while Ben climbs into the back. Having withstood enough hostility tonight, I slam the door shut and walk into the kitchen, grabbing a broom and dustpan. I walk on autopilot into the living room, cleaning up the mess and washing the wooden floor, only heading to bed when I'm sure every speck of glass is gone.

Sunlight is creeping through the blinds in my bedroom when I finally fall asleep hours later. But my dreams are troubled, and I toss and turn fitfully, hating that everything is about to change yet understanding I am powerless to stop it from happening.

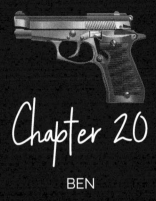

Chapter 20

BEN

At least hanging around Chicago for the weekend gives me the opportunity to meet with Gifoli to open proceedings. The news this morning from my father's medical team isn't good. He only has six months, max, left to live, and there is still much to do. We need to secure Florida's and Chicago's commitment to The Commission before Angelo Mazzone dies. It's the only way to ensure we survive should the Russians use my father's death as the catalyst to make their move. I'm hearing all kinds of rumors of planned attacks and attempts to forge alliances with other criminal entities, and they aren't mobilizing without a goal in mind. While they don't know about his condition, I am sure they are watching and waiting for the perfect moment to present itself for them to strike. It's what I would do in their shoes.

Hence why I reached out to Alfredo Gifoli—the underboss in charge of The Outfit in Chicago—a couple of hours ago. One of the other New York bosses—Gino Accardi, my brother-in-law—is dealing with the stubborn don in charge of Florida.

I had Phillip send me a file on Gifoli this morning, and I was shocked and more than a little concerned to discover Serena Lawson is now Serena Gifoli. I dug a little deeper, discovering Saskia is married to Felix Barretta. Felix's father Thomas is the consigliere to

Giuseppe DeLuca, but as DeLuca rules his domain from his residence in Sicily, Barretta effectively reports to Gifoli. Felix stands to become consigliere when his father retires, as is tradition.

"It's no accident Joseph Lawson married two of his daughters to men of power within the mafioso," Leo deduces as he drives me from our hotel to Sierra's house.

One of my soldiers is normally on driver duty, and it's not often a task asked of my underboss, but circumstances necessitated it today. I would have driven myself except Leo refused to let me go anywhere without him now that I have assigned Alessandro as Sierra's bodyguard.

I nod. "It's widely known Lawson Pharma has been laundering money for The Outfit for years. Lawson has hundreds of reps on the road dealing directly with doctors and small-town pharmacies, and they favor cash payments purely so they can wash money for DeLuca's organization. In return, The Outfit uses their contacts and influence inside the government to ensure significant R&D funding goes to Lawson Pharma and that key legislation is passed to enable them to rush trials through as quickly as possible."

It's genius, really. No one would suspect a pharmaceutical giant of money laundering. The mob usually uses clubs, bars, hotels, and casinos to wash their cash, and that's what the authorities focus on when they are trying to find something to charge us with. One of the reasons I'm putting a lot of my energy into the construction division of our business is so we can wash cash. Focusing on high-end multimillion-dollar projects in prime locations is strengthening our redeveloped brand and enhancing our reputation within legitimate business circles as well. We still clean some money through the casinos, but it's carefully laundered in a way that can't be traced.

"I see the attraction for Lawson," Leo adds, taking the next exit for Glencoe. "What I don't understand is why powerful men like Gifoli and Barretta would agree to it."

Arranged marriages are fairly common within *la famiglia*, most usually at the higher levels, as a way to forge bonds, foster loyalty, and to ensure the bloodline continues. It is rare for Italian men to marry non-Italian women. "Both enterprises have grown wealthier over the years, thanks to the alliance. Money is a powerful motivator, and it's the only leverage Lawson has." I flick a piece of lint off my pants. "Gifoli must need him badly enough, or perhaps I'm not the only one challenging traditions."

It might come across like I'm making light of it, but I'm not. It *has* raised some suspicions in my mind.

Leo eyes me through the mirror as he drives through downtown Glencoe. "Sierra getting pregnant must have saved her from a similar fate."

"I have no doubt that's true."

"When Lawson discovers the truth, he will use that to his advantage," Leo warns.

"Only if we make peace with The Outfit. He wouldn't dare risk their wrath by insisting I marry Sierra if The Outfit remains outside of The Commission's control." He pulls onto Elm Street, and I smooth a hand over my hair.

"They are in even greater danger." Leo acknowledges what I already know as he guides the car to a halt outside the small bungalow my son calls home.

"Lawson can't know yet," I supply. It has thrown my plans into disarray. I can't whisk my family away now. Not without tipping Lawson off. If he finds out before things are agreed with The Outfit, he might do something to hurt Rowan or Sierra. I remember how little regard the man had for his youngest daughter, and I can't believe her status as a single mother has elevated her higher in his esteem. Joseph Lawson has always been a heartless cruel bastard. If he believes Sierra's connection to me might damage his business arrangement with The Outfit, he will take steps to eliminate the problem.

Leo kills the engine and turns around to face me. "Either way, this only means one outcome."

I pin him with a pointed stare. "I'm well aware of what it entails."

A smirk creeps over his mouth. "How the hell do you plan to marry two women?"

"I'll become a Muslim and move to Africa," I dryly state.

He loses the smirk, addressing me with a serious tone. "Salerno will never accept it if you marry Sierra."

"Saverio hasn't called in his favor yet," I remind him, staring out the window at the bungalow. My son's bike is propped against the side wall, and a messy ball of emotion catches in my throat.

"It's only a matter of time. The girl will be of age next year."

Tearing my gaze from the blue and yellow bicycle, I eyeball my friend. "Maybe this was the solution all along." Saverio might lose his shit if I marry Sierra before he can ask me to marry his daughter, Anais, but it's not my fault he delayed calling in his favor, and we never discussed the specifics. I have made no commitment to marry Anais, so he can't hold it against me, even if he is pissed. I'll be thirty-six next year, and I have zero desire to marry a bride half my age.

"You have always been adamant about not getting married," Leo adds.

"As have you."

He stares wistfully into space. "For different reasons," he mumbles, and I nod.

I know why I have never considered it—loving a woman will weaken me in the eyes of my enemy and any wife I take will be an obvious target. I have never wanted the distraction or wanted to put any woman in that position. Everything has changed now. As the mother of my child, Sierra is an automatic target whether I marry her or not. At least as my wife, I can offer her some additional protection, while ensuring my son is well-guarded and a permanent fixture in my life.

I want to get to know him, and that means Sierra is a natural part of the deal. I'm still mad at her, but I would never take her away from her son. I want Rowan to grow up with both parents in his life, enjoying a stable, secure family home where he will be loved, supported, and nurtured. I want him to have all the things that were lacking in my life when I was his age.

When I talk to Sierra about this, I will make it clear my decision is a way of keeping her safe and nothing more. I have no time for love, and she needs to understand that at the outset. I won't cheat or take a mistress as long as she agrees to sex. She's adventurous and responsive in bed, and I will enjoy fucking her. I will ensure she is satisfied, cared for, and not wanting for anything, but love is off the table. I don't have time for it, and I can't afford the distraction.

Leo is still pensive, staring at nothing. I know why he no longer considers marriage an option—because he lost the only woman he would ever consider marrying to another. Not that he will ever admit it, but I know. I have always noticed the way he looks at Natalia. "It's a moot point right now," I say, and his gaze snaps to mine. "If I told Sierra my intention is to marry her, she would go for my jugular."

Leo chuckles. "Something tells me you will have your hands full with that one."

"Don't I know it." Sierra is not going to make any of this easy for me. Her reaction last night made that very clear. Losing my temper and almost choking her to death didn't help either. I sigh, curling my hand around the door handle as my cell pings. Extracting my phone from the inside pocket of my suit jacket, I read my new text. "Gifoli has agreed to meet. Tomorrow morning at ten. He will send us the coordinates in due course."

"I will organize transport immediately for the men we agreed to."

I nod. "You'll attend to that other matter too?"

"Phillip has already sent me the details of the homeowners. I will have a house secured by the end of the day."

I climb out of the Merc and shut the door the same time Alessandro steps out of the SUV. "Did everything go okay?" I ask him when we are side by side.

He nods, fighting a yawn. "Frank is outside her sister's place."

"Good," I say though it does little to ease the tightness in my chest. I won't rest easy until Rowan and Sierra are safely hidden behind the towering walls of my Greenwich estate, far away from prying eyes. It pains me to have to leave them here for the moment, but I am putting things in motion to ensure they are protected. If I could conduct my business from Chicago, I would stake temporary roots here, but I can't.

"I still can't believe you have a son though you only need to look at the little guy to know he's yours," Alessandro says, showcasing a rare smile.

"That's what I'm afraid of," I admit. I told Frank and Alessandro what is going on last night as they are the only two men I trust to guard my son and his mother. Outside of my father and my sister, only Leo, Frank, Alessandro, and Ian—the backup nighttime guard Leo will shortly be putting on a plane—will be aware of my heir's existence. I'm not personally familiar with Ian, but Frank and Leo vouched for him—he's their cousin, on their mom's side—and that's good enough for me.

Telling anyone else is too risky.

Especially right now.

"Don't worry, boss. We will keep them safe."

I clamp a hand on his shoulder, nodding before I walk toward Sierra's front door.

The door swings open before I can knock, and Sierra appears in the doorway. Her hair is in a messy bun on top of her head, and her face is devoid of makeup, clearly highlighting the bruising shadows under her eyes and the worry lines on her brow. She obviously got as little sleep as I did last night. Her black yoga pants mold to her slim toned legs, and her top hangs off one shoulder, offering a glimpse of tantalizing skin. She's barefoot, and her toenails are painted an oxblood-red color. I don't have a foot fetish, but looking at her dainty manicured feet and her dark-red nails, I could easily develop one. I have a strange urge to suck on her tempting toes.

Sierra is effortlessly beautiful in a way most women aren't. She's not even trying. She has made zero effort on my behalf, and that only makes me appreciate her more. She is the most beautiful woman I've ever known, and that's not counting the inner beauty that radiates from her every pore.

Sierra is a good person, and I hate that I am dragging her into my world, but that decision was taken out of my hands years ago.

The moment she got pregnant, her fate was sealed.

I'm not the only one doing the checking out. Determined green eyes roam over every inch of my body as Sierra drinks me in. If she is disappointed I'm wearing a business suit and not casually attired, she doesn't show it. We haven't said one word yet, and she silently steps aside to let me enter. After she closes the door, I follow her into the kitchen. "Coffee?" she inquires, lifting one brow, and I nod. "Do you take cream and sugar?" I shake my head. "Black. Just like your soul. Got it," she adds with the merest hint of humor.

That raises a slight smile. Removing my suit jacket, I hang it on the back of one of the kitchen chairs. I take a seat at the dark wood table, letting my gaze wander around the homey room as I roll my sleeves to my elbows. Sierra has painted the kitchen cupboards a soothing pale blue, and it works well against the speckled marble countertops and the cream tiled floor. A myriad of colorful drawings adorns the buttery walls. Some I clearly recognize as Sierra's handiwork, but most are my son's. "I see Rowan inherited your artistic flare," I say as she sets a mug on the table in front of me.

"He loves art, and he's very talented. But he loves sports and nature and science, and he enjoys reading and playing games too. He's well-rounded." She claims a chair at the other end of the table, deliberately keeping her distance.

"I look forward to getting to know him."

"Is that really what you want?" she asks, running the tip of her finger along the rim of her mug.

I frown. "Of course. Why wouldn't I want to?"

"I imagine having a kid won't mesh easily with your lifestyle."

"It won't, but we'll make it work."

Her expression turns frosty. "We're not moving to New York." She drills me with a sharp look. "I'm not uprooting our lives to suit you. This is about doing what's best for Rowan, and you have a long way to go to convince me having you in his life is what is best for my son."

Her words piss me off. "I want to be a father to my son. Yes, the world I inhabit may not be ideal, but he will want for nothing. *You* will want for nothing, and I will ensure you are both safe."

"Look around," she says, waving her arm in the air. "Does it look like we want for anything?"

I prop my elbows on the table. "My son is lacking a father. I didn't think that required spelling out," I say through gritted teeth. "Don't push me, Sierra, because you won't like the way I push back."

A muscle clenches in her jaw as she glares at me. I see we're back to this. She was pleasant when I arrived, and I stupidly thought we could discuss this like grown-ups, but it seems she's determined to press every one of my buttons.

"How did you find out?" she demands, clasping her mug between both her hands. "You never answered me last night."

"Saskia didn't tell you?"

Her brow puckers. "Saskia? What's my sister got to do with it?"

"I was in town for a funeral, and I spotted Saskia on the sidewalk with Rowan. I pulled over to talk to her."

"Why?"

I lean back in my seat. Honestly, I have no clue why I got Alessandro to stop. Maybe it was gut instinct. Some sixth sense drawing me to my kid. I should tell Sierra that, but maybe it's time I pushed some buttons of my own. I smirk. "In case you've forgotten, I was close with your sister at one time. I wanted to say hi."

"You wanted to say hi to Saskia?" she repeats, her eyes darting all over my face.

"Is it a crime to say hello to an ex?" I smirk into my coffee as I bring the mug to my lips.

"She never mentioned you," she retorts, shrugging.

"That might have something to do with her slipping her business card in my pocket and asking me to call her to arrange a hookup."

Hurt shimmers in her eyes, quickly replaced with anger. "That sounds like Saskia. I can't imagine her husband being too pleased though. You should tread carefully."

I bark out a laugh, tapping my fingers on the table. "Felix Barretta doesn't scare me."

Shock splays across her face. "You know Saskia's husband?"

"I looked him up."

A scowl trips over her pretty face, and I decide to go on a fishing expedition to see what, if anything, Sierra knows.

"What's he like? What line of business is he in?"

"I don't know him very well. I'm not close to Saskia, and I don't spend much time with her or her husband. He travels a lot for work. He's some kind of business adviser."

I detect no trace of a lie on her face, which is interesting. I press on. "What about Serena and her husband? Are you close with them?"

A thunderous look washes over her face, and I stiffen. If Gifoli has done anything to Sierra, I will gut him without blinking.

"I'm close to Serena," she says, smothering her furious expression. "Rowan is only a year older than her son, Romeo, and they are the best of friends. She also has an eight-year-old daughter, Elisa."

"Why the murderous look?" I ask, draining the last of my coffee.

"It's nothing." Getting up, she grabs my mug to refill it. "I'm not close to Alfred. He's one of my father's best friends, and to this day, I have no clue why Serena married him. She's miserable as sin, and he's a lousy husband. He—" She cuts herself off, handing a full mug of coffee to me.

"He what?" I lift a brow as I blow on the steam rising from my cup.

"He's away a lot on business too." She averts her eyes as she plops back in her chair. That wasn't what she was going to say before she stopped herself. "And before you ask, he's into importing and exporting."

I almost spit my coffee out. Is that what we're calling it these days?

Narrowing her eyes suspiciously, she tilts her head to the side. "Why are you so interested in my sisters' husbands anyway?"

She seems clueless, and I want to keep it like that, so I reply in a way I know will set her off. I pin her with another smirk. "I'd think it was obvious why I was inquiring about Saskia's husband."

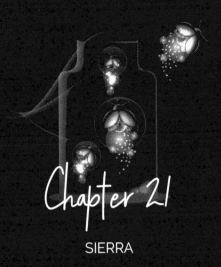

Chapter 21

SIERRA

MY BLOOD BOILS, and I know I shouldn't say it, but it's like my mouth is no longer connected to my brain. "Did you fuck her already, or are you waiting for the next time her husband goes out of town?"

I want to wipe the smug smile off his face as he stares at me while drumming his fingers on the table. I shouldn't care whether he fucks my sister or not. Ben is nothing to me but a sperm donor, and if I have any say, that's the way it will stay. I haven't changed my mind. I don't want him near Rowan.

Maybe Saskia lusting after him could work to my advantage. Maybe he'll get distracted by her and forget he has a son. "As a kid, I couldn't understand how you two were together, but I see it now. You two are a match made in heaven. Both narcissistic and cruel. You should get with her before she finds another fuck buddy."

There was a rumor floating around town last year that Saskia was cheating on Felix, and I didn't doubt it for a second. The only person Saskia is loyal to is our father. The rest of us are like chump change.

Folding my arms, I glare at him as he sits silently and arrogantly across the table. He's not reacting to my statement, so I don't know if I hit my mark. The longer he stares nonchalantly at me, the madder I get. If I had a gun, I wouldn't hesitate to plant a bullet between his smug brows in this moment.

After what seems like an eternity, he clears his throat and straightens up in his chair. The arrogance slides behind a neutral mask. "I came here to talk about my son, not your sister."

Spoken like a true politician. But I'm done with talk of my sister too. I just want to get this over and done with so I can get him out of my house. "What do you want, Ben? Because us relocating to New York is off the table."

"I agree it would be unsettling to move Rowan, so I'll let you stay here for now—on a few conditions."

"You'll *let* me?" I hiss. "How big of you." I barely resist the urge to flip him the bird.

Ignoring me, he continues as if I haven't spoken, and I grip the edge of my seat, grinding my teeth down to the molars. "One, Alessandro and Frank go with you everywhere, and I mean *everywhere*."

"Who is Frank?"

"Rowan's bodyguard. He's on duty outside Serena's house now."

I'm not surprised, and I don't disagree. I'm not naïve. I know if word got out that Ben had a son all kinds of degenerate scum would target me and Rowan. I won't jeopardize his safety, so if Ben wants to put protections in place, I won't argue. "Okay. What else?"

"I'm sending a guy over later to install a new alarm system with exterior cameras and lights. It took me ten seconds to disable your alarm last night." He drills me with a disapproving look, like it's my fault the salesman sold me a dud system.

"It's the standard system most families in the area have in their homes. How stupid of me to not realize it wasn't mafia proof." He looks surprised that I know. "You might have removed every trace of your mob connections from the internet, but I know you're part of the mafia. Why do you think I want to keep you from Rowan?"

He slams his fist down on the table. "For the last fucking time, Sierra, I am not a danger to my son!"

I jump up, knocking my chair over. "What you do for a living is a threat to my son! The people you associate with are a threat to my son! Your enemies are a threat to my son!" My tirade is interrupted by the vibration of my cell on the counter. With my chest heaving, I pick it up, swiping my finger across the screen. It's Dion, but I can't speak to him now, so I dismiss the call, tapping out a quick text telling him

I'll call him later.

"I will keep Rowan safe," Ben says in a clipped tone, glowering at my cell like it's done him a personal injustice. "I will keep you safe. We cannot change the fact he is my son. Whether I'm in his life or not, he is at risk, so get the fuck over yourself, Sierra, and sit the hell back down. I am trying to compromise, and you are making this harder than it needs to be."

A red layer spreads over my retinas, and I'm so enraged I feel like throwing something. "Go fuck yourself, Ben." I jab my finger in his direction. "You don't get to dictate to me in my own home, and you sure as fuck don't get to disrespect me. Your whores might be happy to be treated like shit, but I'm not."

"Goddamn it." He scrubs his hands down his face. "Why is everything so difficult with you?!" he shouts.

I like seeing him rattled. I like knowing I get to him in the way he gets to me. I'll take his anger over cold disdain any day, once he gets the point—I'm not like all his other women, and I'm no pushover. Straightening up my chair, I sit back down, calmly placing my hands in my lap. "I won't apologize for pushing you when it comes to the welfare of my son. Rowan is my priority. Not you and your hurt male pride."

His nostrils flare and his fingers twitch, like they long to curl around my neck again. Hell will freeze over before he puts his hands on me without invitation again. He bristles with anger as he glares at me, and I hit him with the same smug arrogance he showed me a few minutes ago.

I watch as he physically restrains himself from losing his shit, watching the anger retreat on his face, replaced with an emotionless look I'm getting used to seeing. His shoulders relax, and his voice is level when he speaks.

"My men will be living in one of the houses across the street. Frank and Alessandro will guard you during the day and whenever you step out of your house. Ian will watch over the house at night from their living room. My security expert will install panic buttons in each room here which will link to my men's house, and they will have access to the camera feeds as well. If you need them, you press one of those buttons, and they will be here in less than a minute."

"I don't understand." I glance out the window at the houses across the road. "None of my neighbors are selling."

"Everyone is open to selling for the right price. Leo is working on it. By nightfall, one of your neighbors will be gone, and I will own their house."

My jaw slackens, and my mouth hangs open. He bleeds confidence and arrogance, enough to make it happen. Looking at this version of Ben, it's so hard to reconcile him with the Ben of my youth. He is as far removed from that Ben as you can get. I wonder if there is any of the kindhearted bad boy with a chip on his shoulder left in him.

"Anything else?" I ask.

"No one can know I'm his father. Not yet. Not your family. Not the school. Not Rowan's *teacher*." He practically hisses the word. Dion is a sore spot. Good to know.

"I won't tell my *boyfriend*, but I'm not telling Rowan either. He's only five, and we can't ask him to keep such a big secret. Besides, I think he should get used to you as a friend first." He nods, and I release the breath I was holding. I was prepared for that to be our biggest argument, so I'm pleased he isn't fighting me on it.

Ben clasps his hands together on top of the table. "Has he ever asked about his dad? Where does he think he is?"

I chew on the inside of my mouth, squirming a little on my seat. "A month after he started preschool was the first time he asked me about his daddy," I explain. "I didn't want to lie to him, but I couldn't exactly tell him the truth either."

"Spit it out, Sierra." He drills me with an intense stare I feel all the way to the tips of my toes.

"I told him his daddy was someone I used to know but we had lost contact and I didn't know how to find you. I told him I was sure if his daddy knew about him that he would want to be in his life and that maybe at some time in the future, when he was older, he might get a chance to meet him."

"Were you ever going to tell me?" he asks, looking pained. "If I hadn't discovered the truth, would you have ever told me?"

I brace myself for this admission because there's no doubt this will infuriate Ben. "No. I didn't believe it was in Rowan's best interests, but I was planning on telling him when he was eighteen so he could make his own decision then."

His entire body is shaking with visible rage, and I'm betting he's back to wanting to throttle me again. He starts unrolling the sleeves of his shirt. "Two final things." His cold tone matches the icy look on his face as he dips his hand into the inside of his jacket. "I'm replacing your car with an armored SUV." He pulls a handgun out of his jacket pocket, setting it down on the table. My pulse spikes, and adrenaline instantly floods my body. "And I'm giving you this."

"I don't want it. I don't want a gun in the house with Rowan."

"You're taking it." He gnashes his teeth, and his expression brokers no argument. Standing, he snatches the gun up and walks around the table to me. "Find someplace safe to put it where Rowan can't find it but it's still within easy reach should you need it. Make sure you carry it in your purse or on your person anytime you step foot out of the bungalow." Taking my hand, he places the gun in my palm, curling my fingers around it.

It's lighter than it looks, but it still feels like a cold, dead weight in my hand. "I don't know anything about guns, and I have no desire to learn. Why are you assigning us bodyguards if I'm going to need to protect myself?" I put it down on the table, not wanting to touch it anymore.

"I have powerful enemies, Sierra, and it's smart to know how to defend yourself."

I exhale heavily. I hate this. My life was perfect. Everything was going great until my stupid sister had to go and mess everything up. "I know how to defend myself. I have taken self-defense classes for years."

"That might protect you against petty thieves and would-be rapists, but a trained mafia soldier would restrain you within seconds with ease." He drags a hand through his hair, messing up the perfectly coiffed strands. A few waves of dark hair fall across his brow, and it's sexy as hell.

I hate that I notice.

I hate even more that I like it.

My feelings for Ben are a clusterfuck of epic proportions. Which is something I need to unravel and put in a neat box labeled "my son's father" so I'm not tempted to put him into any other boxes.

"Alessandro will teach you how to use it," he says, putting his jacket on and buttoning it. He towers over me, like this force of nature that has just swept into my life, eviscerating everything in its path. I stand, not liking the feeling. "I'll drop by tomorrow to see Rowan," he adds. "I already told him I was a friend of Saskia's and that I knew you when you were younger, so we should stick to that story."

"We should stay here," I say because I don't want to risk being seen with him around the town.

"Agreed."

I nod, and awkward tension filters into the air.

He clears his throat, shoving his hands in his pants pockets. "I've seen your bank statements, so I know money isn't an issue, but I'm his father. I want to pay child support. I've instructed my personal accountant to make a deposit to your account next week. Going forward, a regular monthly deposit will be made."

Just as I was starting to lose my anger, it returns full force, slapping me in the face. "I don't want your dirty money!" I hiss, prodding my finger in his chest.

An amused grin spreads across his mouth, and I want to scream. "I run several successful legitimate businesses. I assure you my money is about as dirty as yours."

He has an answer for everything. It's infuriating. "You truly have no shame," I seethe. How dare he invade my privacy like this. He has no right. "Next, you'll be telling me you know my bra size."

His eyes lower to my chest, and I scowl, wanting to wrap my arms around myself to deprive him of the view. But I won't give him the satisfaction of letting him know how much he is getting to me either, so I don't move a muscle.

"You were definitely a B cup in Vegas, but I'm guessing you're a C cup now." He steps a little closer, and though my instinct is to fall back, I stand my ground, refusing to let this asshole intimidate me again. Bending down, he presses his warm mouth to my ear. "I would need to conduct a physical exam to make an accurate assessment."

I push him away, glaring at him. "You're a pig."

His lips pull up at the corners. "I don't remember you complaining in Vegas. In fact, I distinctly remember you begging me to suck harder on your nipples as I plowed my cock into your greedy pussy."

"Get out!" I bark, pointing at the door. "Just go."

He winks, and I invoke every shred of willpower I possess not to lunge at him and gouge out his eyeballs.

"Until tomorrow." He gives me a curt nod before exiting my kitchen, and I slump back in my chair, relieved he is gone but a little disappointed too.

Chapter 22

SIERRA

"Did you get all your shopping done?" Serena asks an hour later when I show up at her house to collect Rowan.

"Uh, yeah. Thanks." I hate lying to my sister, but it's safer if she doesn't know.

"The kids are in the movie room," she says as I enter the ornate lobby of her expansive home. "But I warned Rowan you were on your way."

Under the harsh glare of the bright hallway, the swelling on Serena's cheek is more obvious. The silk scarf tied around her neck has slipped a little, and the edge of the bruising is evident. "Are you sure you're okay?" I quietly ask as we pad down the corridor.

"I'm fine." She dismisses my concern like she has the couple other times I've noticed injuries on her face and body.

"You're not fine." Gently, I take her elbow, forcing her to stop. "I know Alfred is doing this. You don't have to say it for me to know the truth. You should leave him, Serena. I know you're not happy."

She wrenches her arm from my grip, snorting. "What the hell has happiness got to do with anything?"

"Happiness is a basic human right. You deserve to be happy."

"I am happy," she lies. "I adore my kids, and I get to be a stay-at-home mom. That's all I've ever wanted." If it's all she's ever wanted, I would like to know why she wasted years in college earning a business degree she clearly hated and why she worked for the accounting department of Lawson Pharma for eighteen months even though it clearly tore strips off her sanity.

Serena and I have grown super close since I got pregnant, but some days I still feel like I don't know her. Don't get me wrong. She's been a godsend. Mom, Serena, Pen, and Esme got me through my pregnancy and those tough first few months, and I'm very grateful. I love that Rowan is close to his cousins, and I enjoy our weekly meetups as much as he does.

But I don't get it. I don't get why Serena chose Alfred in the first place or why she stays with him when he treats her like dirt. The only positive is he is away a lot. "You are wealthy in your own right, and you could still be all those things without him."

"Sierra, I know you mean well, but just drop it." She stalks off, and I hurry after her.

"Why do you put up with it? Damn it, Serena." I tug on her arm, stopping her before she opens the door to the movie room. "You are worth more than this. You deserve more than this!"

"I don't have a choice!" she cries. Pain swims in her tired eyes. "You don't understand, Sierra."

"So, enlighten me."

Her mouth opens and closes before she pulls me into a hug. "He's my husband. I promised to love, honor, and obey him until the day I die, and that is what I will do."

I pull back, frustrated and pissed off on her behalf, but I know when to let an argument go. This is not one I can win, and I can't force her to make a decision just because I believe it's the right one. She has to reach that point herself. "I love you, and I'm always here for you, Serena. No matter what. If you ever want to tell me the truth or you ever need me, I'm here."

Tears prick her eyes as she folds her arms over her chest. "I know, Sierra, and it means a lot to me."

~~~

"Who is that?" Serena asks a few minutes later, pointing behind my head. I'm wrestling Rowan out the front door, trying to get him into the car before he totally goes crazy. Predictably, he doesn't want to leave yet, and he's currently putting up one hell of a fight.

"That's my new bodyguard," I confirm as Alessandro gets out of the car.

"Damn. Why couldn't our bodyguards have looked like that when we were horny teenagers?" she jokes.

"Because we were horny teenagers," I deadpan.

She looks at Alessandro, and their eyes meet. He nods respectfully in her direction but makes no move to come any closer. A faint blush stains her cheeks before she looks away.

Rowan quiets in my arms, turning his head to watch as Alessandro opens the back door for him.

"Is he one of Dad's guys?" Serena asks. "I don't recall seeing him before."

"No. He's someone I hired myself from a private security firm," I blurt, thinking up an excuse on the spot.

A fresh wave of tension tightens her shoulders. "Why? Has something happened?"

I set Rowan down on his feet, satisfied he has stopped fighting. He's too busy giving Alessandro the once-over to care that we're going anymore. "Nothing has happened. I guess I understand now why Father is so anal about protection. I have a child of my own, and I'd do anything to protect him. I just felt it was time we both had a bodyguard again, so I did something about it myself."

"I have my own bodyguard?" Rowan asks, his eyes popping wide.

"Yes." I tweak his nose, smiling as his eyes light up. "His name is Frank, and you will meet him back at our house."

"This is so cool!" He jumps up and down. "I have a bodyguard just like Romeo now!"

Serena and I trade smiles. "If I had known that's all it'd take, I'd have told him in the movie room and saved myself an ordeal." I had to practically drag Rowan away from his best friend.

"He's so cute." Serena stares adorably at her godson, and I pull her in for one last hug.

"I think so, but I'm probably biased."

Rowan is babbling away to an amused-looking Alessandro when

I climb behind the wheel. Alessandro tried to drive, at first, until I set him straight. He's my bodyguard, not my driver. He can protect me from the passenger seat while I retain some independence.

"Do you know Frank?" Rowan asks, as I wave to Serena before she closes the door.

"I do," Alessandro replies.

"Does he have drawings on his arms too?" Rowan inquires.

Alessandro's brow puckers, and I smile. "He means your tattoos."

"Eh, no. Frank doesn't have any ink on his arms."

"I have ink!" Rowan says, excitement bubbling in his tone. He strains against the straps of his car seat as he leans forward. "My mommy and me have lots and lots of ink and paints and clay and playdough in our art studio. You wanna see my art studio, Alesso?"

"His name is Alessandro," I explain, grinning.

"I know, Mom." Rowan rolls his eyes before eyeballing Alessandro. "But I like Alesso better. I'm gonna call you Alesso, Alesso."

I glance sideways at Alessandro, watching him fight a smile. I peer at my son in the mirror, smiling. "Alesso it is."

"LET ME GET this straight," Esme says later that night from her sprawled position on my couch. She gulps a mouthful of her red wine. "In less than twenty-four hours, Bennett Carver—"

"Mazzone," I correct, topping up Pen's nearly-empty glass.

"Whatever." Esme flaps her hands around. "In less than a day, he has managed to completely turn your world upside down. Bodyguards. Security cameras. Child support, new car on the way, and he's even got his men shacked up in the house across the street. He's an asshole, but I've got to hand it to him—he's a fucking fast worker. It's impressive."

"It's annoying." I slurp my wine as I flop down on the second couch alongside Pen.

"As usual, you're missing the point, Esme." Pen drills her with a look. Those two still fight like cats and dogs, but they would go to the ends of the Earth for one another if the chips were down. "Ben can't just show up here and railroad Sierra into doing what he wants."

"To be fair, he's trying to protect us, and he backed down on the

New York plan pretty fast." I tuck my knees underneath me.

"Now you're defending him?" Pen says, her tone dripping with incredulity.

"No. I'm…" I rub a tense spot between my brows. "I'm mad and confused and guilt-stricken and relieved and impressed and hurt and a million different things." I tilt my head to the side, eyeballing Pen. "It's a complicated situation. One part of me feels guilty that I kept Rowan from him. Especially when I see the lengths Ben is going to, to keep us safe. That part of my brain is questioning everything I've done."

"You did what you felt was right," Esme says, sitting up against the arm of the couch. "And you shouldn't feel guilty for that. You were protecting your son."

"You were terrified after what you discovered in New York, and you were right to be afraid. If I was in your shoes, I would have done exactly the same thing," Pen says.

"Everything is going to change now." I take another sip of my wine. "And I'm scared."

"Ben won't let anything happen to you or Rowan," Esme reassures me. "At least, in that regard, he hasn't let you down. Imagine how it would've felt if he had wanted nothing to do with Rowan?"

"That might have been better," Pen murmurs.

"I thought so at first," I agree. "But Ben is right. It wouldn't change the facts. Rowan is always going to be at risk because of the blood that flows through his veins."

"What's your new bodyguard like? Is he hot?" Esme waggles her brows.

"What has that got to do with anything?" Pen asks, rolling her eyes and muttering under her breath.

"She's virtually married to him now," Esme quips, and I almost choke on my wine. "It helps if he's easy on the eyes."

"He's definitely easy on the eyes."

"Oh my God." Esme spills some of her wine on the floor as she swings her legs around. "I know what you should do! You should seduce him! Imagine how fucking pissed Ben would be if you screwed one of his employees."

"Number one: I'm in a relationship and I don't cheat. Number two:

Ben would probably murder Alesso and me if we had sex. Number three: Alesso is loyal to Ben and fairly aloof. I would have zero success seducing him. And number four: We're not in high school anymore. Doing something so juvenile is beneath me."

Esme pouts, lifting her legs back onto the couch. "Well, that's no fun. I was hoping to live vicariously through you."

"Don't tell me you're going through a dry spell?" Pen inquires, crossing her feet at the ankles.

"We can't all be as lucky as you and find our soul mate in high school."

Pen tugs at her ears. "Sorry, I must be hearing things. What did you just say?"

Esme throws a cushion at Pen. "You heard me, and you also heard me the million times I apologized for ever doubting you and Eric." Esme smiles, but it's tinged with sadness. "I'm happy to admit I was wrong and you were right. I envy what you have, Pen. Marriage might not be in the cards for me, but I can see how happy you are. You love your husband and your kids, and you have the career too. You make it look easy, and I'm in awe of you." She turns to me. "And you too, Sierra. You made the right choices for you and your son, and you're a fucking amazing mother. No matter what happens with Ben, don't let him take any of that credit, because it's all on you."

"Don't sell yourself short, Esme," I reply, fighting a sudden wave of nostalgia. "I know we didn't talk for a few weeks after I found out I was pregnant, but I always knew your heart was in the right place. You have always had my back, and you came through for me when it counted."

"And you're going to be the most successful female lawyer Chicago has ever seen," Pen loyally adds. "Look at your amazing track record so far. You are the only attorney in your firm who has won every single case. That is freaking incredible, and you deserve it because you work damn hard."

"To us," Esme says, raising her glass.

"To us," we agree, joining in her toast.

"WHEN WILL HE get here?" Rowan asks the following day for the umpteenth time. I glance at the clock on the wall, fighting the anxiety clawing at my throat.

"Ben should be here any minute now," I tell him, wiping the kitchen counter down for the tenth time. I barely slept a wink again last night despite the alcohol sloshing through my veins. I've been antsy all morning, worried over how this is going to go down.

The bell chimes, and Rowan whoops, racing toward the door. Nausea swims up my throat, and my stomach is twisted into knots as I run after him, grabbing him before he reaches the door. "What did Mommy tell you about opening the door?"

"I am not to open the door on my own, but Mommy, this is different. Ben's not a stranger. He's my friend."

"Firecracker." I brush strands of his dark hair out of his eyes. "We don't even know for sure that it's Ben, which is why you must let Mommy check first."

He bobs his head, his eyes darting to the door with eagerness.

Butterflies swoop into my chest, and I offer up a silent prayer as I inspect the excited glee on my son's face. Please God, let this go okay for his sake. While I am still furious at the way Ben has treated me, I am determined to take the moral high ground and act civilized for Rowan's sake. Clutching my son's small warm hand, I peer out of my new peephole before opening the door to Ben.

Unlike me, he is the epitome of cool, calm, and collected as he stands on my porch looking hotter than any man has a right to look. He's ditched the suit for dark jeans, black loafers, and a fitted black shirt that molds to his impressive chest. Like yesterday, he has rolled the shirt sleeves up to his elbows, showcasing his strong tanned arms and a coating of sexy dark hair. A flashy black and silver Patek Philippe watch is strapped to his wrist. When he kneels in front of Rowan, the air swirls around him, blasting his spicy scent in my face. He smells as good as he looks, and I swear my ovaries swoon.

"Hey, Rowan," Ben says, smiling. "It's good to see you again." He lifts his clenched fist, and the second Rowan presses his much smaller knuckle against his father's, I almost choke on the messy ball of emotion lodged at the back of my throat. Rowan grins, and his blue eyes glow with happiness. Watching them up close like this, the resemblance is so uncanny it blows my mind. They are like carbon copies of one another, and cracks fissure the temporary walls I erected around my heart.

"You wanna see my art studio or see my bugs first?" Rowan asks, grabbing Ben's hand without hesitation.

Ben straightens up, keeping a firm hold of Rowan's hand as his glassy eyes meet mine. He looks how I feel, and I'm glad to see it. I'm glad to know that cold veneer he hides behind shields genuine emotion. Right now, he's feeling the magnitude of this moment as much as I am.

My heart is mincemeat behind my rib cage. A shredded mess barely sustaining my life force. My knees buckle, and I'm seconds away from losing all control.

"Why don't we start with the art room," Ben suggests, smiling down at his son. Rowan needs no further encouragement, dragging him forward. Unspoken words pass between Ben and I as Rowan tugs him into the house, chatting away, oblivious to the almost crippling emotion threatening to bring his parents to their knees.

"You go ahead," I croak, leaning against the wall in the hall. "I'll be right there."

Ben glances at me, opening his mouth like he wants to say something, but I shake my head, smiling as I fight tears, urging him to go with his son. He's used to containing his emotions, so I know he'll keep it together in a way I'm incapable of.

"I just need a minute," I mouth.

Leo exchanges some hushed words with Alesso before slipping quietly into the house. He tips his head in acknowledgment at me as he moves past, following Ben and Rowan. A strangled sob escapes my lips the second they turn the corner out of my sight, and I clamp a hand over my aching chest.

"Is everything okay?" Alesso asks, stepping into the hallway.

Tears stream down my face as I offer him a watery smile. I can barely speak over the lump in my throat. "I imagined this sometimes," I rasp in between choking sobs. "On rare occasions when I indulged stupid fantasies." I stare at him through blurry eyes, my chest heaving with raw emotion. "But nothing could've prepared me for seeing them together." My heart aches with a mixture of happiness and pain.

Watching Rowan with his father is indescribable. All thoughts of the kind of man Ben is fade from my mind. In this moment, he is just a father meeting his son for the first time, and I'm drowning in wave after wave of self-loathing. "How could I deprive my son of his father? How could I deny Ben all the precious moments he has missed?" I voice the questions out loud even though I'm talking to myself. Right now, I kind of hate myself despite the voice in my ear telling me my motives were pure and it was never my intention to hurt either one of them.

It doesn't exonerate me though. Like being Rowan's dad doesn't exonerate Ben of all the blood on his hands.

I'm a certifiable mess, and my head is anything but clear. My emotions veer like crazy, bouncing from one emotion to the next, as I grapple with what is right and what is wrong. And does it even matter now? It's not like Ben or I can change the past. The only thing that matters is how we move forward, and I'm determined to do that with my son as the sole priority.

I'm openly crying. That ugly snotty crying no one likes admitting to. But I don't care that Alesso can see. I'm beyond that point. Alesso looks like a deer caught in the headlights. He has no clue what to do with the blubbering female in front of him. A hysterical laugh cuts between the sobs as I watch his confusion.

Tentatively, he places his hand on my shoulder. "I know you had justifiable reasons, but you should know Ben is a good man, Sierra. He'll be a good father to Rowan."

It is not as simple as that, but I nod, unable to explain the confusion fogging my brain. Silent tears roll down my face as I peer into Alesso's concerned eyes. Out of the corner of my eye, I spot Leo lurking behind the wall that connects the living room to the hallway, and I wonder if he's been listening this whole time. Right now, I'm too emotional to care. I honestly didn't think I'd react like this, but it's no real surprise. My head has been in a tailspin since Friday night.

"Don't cry," Alesso adds, wiping my tears away with his thumbs. "You have nothing to fear."

I clutch his shoulders for support as he continues wiping the tears from under my eyes. "I *am* afraid," I whisper, staring into his warm brown eyes. I haven't even known Alesso forty-eight hours, but there is something solid and steady about him that makes me trust and confide in him. "I'm afraid of everything changing. Afraid of Rowan hating me when he finds out I kept his father from him. Afraid of Ben taking him from me. Afraid of nameless, faceless enemies wanting their pound of Mazzone flesh and coming after me and my son. Afraid that no matter what we do, there is no way to keep Rowan out of the mafia world. He'll be sucked in, whether we like it or not. I don't want that life for my son!"

"Ssh. Ssh" Alesso pushes a few stray strands of hair out of my face. "It will be okay. It will all work out. I promise."

I stare at him, wondering if he truly believes that. If *I* can believe it. His hand stalls on my cheek, and it's only now I realize how close we are pressed together and how inappropriate it is.

"What exactly is going on here?" Ben growls, and my eyes widen in alarm as I turn my head. Unrestrained rage shoots from his eyes like laser beams as he stares at Alesso. "Get the fuck away from her right now," he snaps, approaching like a tsunami hell-bent on destruction.

Chapter 23

BEN

I CAN BARELY see over the red rage blinding my eyes as I stalk toward Sierra and Alessandro. Wisely, he has stepped back, putting distance between them, but I saw enough. Jesus fucking Christ. Has she already cast a spell on him? I know she's desirable and easy to fall for, but it hasn't even been a day and a half, and she's already ensnared my most loyal soldier?

Rowan is in the bathroom, but he won't be long, so I make this quick. Grabbing Alessandro by the throat, I shove him up against the wall. He doesn't protest or fight, understanding he is in the wrong. "You are lucky my son is in the house, or I'd put a bullet through your skull."

"I'm sorry, boss. I was out of line, but it won't happen again."

Sierra tugs on my arm. "Let him go. It wasn't how it seemed. Alesso was only comforting me when I got overwhelmed."

"*Alesso?*" I bark, enraged she has a pet name for him already. I squeeze Alessandro's neck more firmly, enjoying the rasping sounds slipping involuntarily from his mouth.

Leo chuckles, and I whip my head around, glaring at him. I am in no mood for humor.

Sierra tugs on my arm again, and steam is practically billowing from her ears. Her cheeks are splotchy and her eyes are red-rimmed, confirming she has been crying. I tighten my hands around Alessandro's neck, and his eyes pop wide. "If you hurt her, I'll—"

The clicking of a weapon cuts me off mid-sentence as a gun is pressed to the back of my head. "We have approximately thirty seconds before Rowan barges out here," Sierra says. "Let him go or I'll pull the trigger. Trust me, asshole. I need little incentive."

My lips twitch as I fight a smile. She won't pull that trigger—we all know it—but I silently applaud her bravery. My little Firefly always had giant balls, and she loves nothing better than to champion the underdog. I release Alessandro, holding my hands up. Sierra removes the gun, and I turn around in time to see her open a lockbox in a cubby at the top of her hall tree and slip the gun back inside.

She fixes me with a furious expression I'm growing accustomed to. Funny thing is, my dick loves it when she gets mad, and her added feistiness only enhances the appeal. If she were to look down, she would see the evidence of my arousal straining the crotch of my jeans. She plants her hands on her hips, glowering at me, and I'm trying hard not to smirk.

I see so much of the little girl I adored in the woman who intrigues me, and I love that she has retained the essence of who she is. That growing up hasn't changed her too much. Yet there is an added layer to her fierceness that's new. Her momma bear instincts are driving her to fight hard for her son, and I respect her so much for that. It helps to know my son was in such capable hands. That he has not been denied love and protection during the years I was unaware of his existence.

"I don't understand how anyone can work for you with the way you treat people, and you really need to get your temper in check. I won't let Rowan near you if you don't learn to control yourself."

"It's cute you—"

She clamps her soft hand over my mouth, silencing me, and Leo's jaw drops. Alessandro is showing no emotion; most likely, he's afraid to even breathe in her direction now, which suits me just fine.

"I wasn't finished speaking." Her expression dares me to challenge her, and I can't resist. I lick her palm, laughing when she yanks her hand back with a grimace. "I just can't with you." She shakes her head, sending waves of smooth straight golden-blonde hair cascading over her shoulders.

My eyes glue to the long silky strands, and my fingers twitch with a craving to touch her. At least she has managed to deflect my anger, but I still don't know what the fuck was going on out here.

"As I was saying." Her eyes pin me in place. "Nothing inappropriate happened, but even if it did, it would be none of your business."

Placing one finger under her chin, I tilt her head back. "That's where you're wrong, Firefly. You are mine now, and my *soldati* know what will happen if they even look funny at you."

She scoffs, slapping my finger away and flapping her arms about. "I am not yours, you motherfucking—"

"Mommy!" Rowan's cute little voice commands everyone's attention. "You said a naughty word!"

My lips twitch as I lean back against the wall. "Yes, Sierra. That's a very naughty word."

She purses her lips as I smile. Giving my son my undivided attention, I add, "I think Mommy owes the naughty jar a dollar."

Rowan's brow furrows. "We don't have a naughty jar." Then his brow smooths out, and his eyes light up. "But we have a naughty step." Planting his hands on his hips, in a virtual mirror image of his mom a few minutes ago, he waggles his finger at Sierra. "You need a time-out, Mommy."

"Mommies don't get time-outs," Sierra says. "But nice try, Firecracker."

I press my mouth to her ear, speaking before engaging my brain. "I could put you over my lap and paddle your ass. I think that would be an appropriate punishment."

Two rose-colored dots bloom on her cheeks, only adding to her beauty. "You are incorrigible."

"And you're beautiful when you're embarrassed and when you're mad."

"Ben." Rowan tugs on the leg of my jeans. "Do you wanna see my garden now? I have bugs, and we have a vegetable garden and a fish pond!"

His eager tone does funny things to my insides, and I kneel so I'm at his level. "I really want to see that, but first I have something for you."

His trusting blue eyes light up. "What is it?"

173

I ruffle his hair, and emotion swells in my chest to the point of pain. "Wait here and I'll be right back."

Leo comes outside with me. "It wasn't intentional," he says, as we walk to the Merc. "Sierra got emotional when she saw you with Rowan, and Alessandro was only trying to comfort her."

"But?" I ask, hearing one, as I pop the trunk and remove the larger of the two boxes.

"They're the same age. She's beautiful. He lives like a monk. Now you've thrust them together, and they'll be spending a ton of time with each other." He shrugs.

"She is going to be my wife," I hiss, shoving the smaller box at his chest. "And if he can't keep his dick in his pants, I'll chop it off and solve the problem."

"Wow. She really has you all worked up."

I slam the trunk down with unnecessary force, hating he's right. I need to get a grip. I'm not acting like myself at all. "Shit." I rub a tense spot in my chest.

"If it helps, she appears to be struggling in the same way, and she seems somewhat remorseful."

I lean back against the car for a minute, not wanting to take too long when I know Rowan is waiting. "Being back in Chicago and being around Sierra again has brought a lot of memories and emotions to the surface. I've spent so long not thinking about my past, trying to forget about Vegas, and focusing on building the business and taking care of my father that I don't know how to deal with this. I'm not sure I'm equipped to handle the onslaught of things I'm feeling."

The first few years in New York I battled to hold on to the man I was until I realized I had to let him go or I wouldn't survive the cutthroat reality of my new world. Now, I'm wondering if I subconsciously maintained some of my previous persona, because it feels like I'm straddling a line between the man I was and the man I am now, and I have no clue which side I'll land on. It feels like I'm losing myself again, and that can't happen. There is too much resting on me, and I need to regain my control.

"It's okay to feel, Ben. You can feel and still be in control," Leo says, proving he knows me so well.

"Not in our line of work." I push off the car and walk toward the door. "I can't let my guard down. Not even for a woman I know I could love and a little boy I already do."

ROWAN LOVES HIS telescope and the new insect tank I bought him. We spend an hour in the garden before Sierra cooks an early dinner, and then I have to leave for my flight. Rowan hugs me when we are saying goodbye, bending another few bars of the steel cage surrounding my heart. Leaving was more difficult than I imagined, but I'm grateful I have the work week ahead of me. I plan to use the time to deal with everything that has happened and to get my errant emotions in check.

It's after nine when I arrive at my penthouse apartment in Manhattan with Ciro, my new bodyguard, in tow. He retreats to the apartment below, leaving Leo and me alone in my home office. "Do you think your little chat with Alessandro will work?" he asks as I pour a bourbon for me and a scotch for him.

"Alessandro is a good soldier with a promising future. He won't fuck it up."

"Maybe you should send Ciro to Chicago instead?" Leo suggests, swirling the amber-colored liquid in his glass before he takes a sip.

I stand facing the floor-to-ceiling windows, admiring the view of Central Park in the near distance. "Alessandro is the best. I want the best men watching my future wife and my son."

"When are you planning on breaking the news to Sierra?"

I turn around and take my seat behind the desk. "I'll let things settle for a few weeks before I broach the subject." Sierra has agreed I can visit with Rowan one day over the weekend. I plan to fly in and out on the same day because I'm too busy to leave New York for successive full weekends.

"Aside from you almost killing your best soldier, today went well," Leo says, crossing an ankle over his knee.

"It did." A smile graces my mouth. "He's an amazing kid."

"She's a good mother," he adds, and I nod.

"When will you tell Angelo and Natalia?"

"I'm going to spend Saturday in Greenwich. I'll ask Natalia to come by."

His Adam's apple bobs in his throat. "How is she?" he asks, avoiding eye contact.

"She's good."

He swings his gaze up, meeting my eyes.

"You would know if you talked to her more regularly."

He runs a hand over his five o'clock shadow. "We haven't had that kind of relationship since we were kids."

"I'm sure she would love to see you. You'll get your chance next month at Lawson's charity event. All five bosses will be there, and Natalia will be with Gino." My meeting with Gifoli went well, and it appears The Outfit has finally pulled their heads out of their asses and agreed to discuss the possibility of Chicago coming under The Commission's rule. Gifoli suggested the New York bosses attend the gala ball, and a formal meeting is taking place in the same hotel the following morning. It's an encouraging sign.

Leo scowls like he does anytime I mention Natalia's husband. "Great." He throws the rest of the scotch down his throat. "Something to look forward to."

THE NEXT FEW weeks are extremely busy, and I have little time to get lost in my head. Three days after Gino Accardi's visit to Tampa, the Russians attacked the Florida *famiglia* in a coordinated hit on their key bars, clubs, and restaurants, leaving a string of dead bodies and burned buildings in their wake. The only positive is Florida is firmly committed to The Commission now. They need our resources to rebuild and to provide protection.

The attack concerns me on a number of levels. It was well thought out and orchestrated, and there was no warning. They could have decimated the organization and taken the city, but they retreated, meaning it was only a first shot. They are planning something big, and we need to find out what.

Caltimore Holdings acquired a fifth top IT firm last week, and I attended daily meetings with the management team as we coordinated the transition, often running into the early hours of the morning. Add to that, we are preparing to break ground on one of the most prestigious luxury apartment blocks New York will ever see. Located on West 57th Street, overlooking Central Park, it will be the tallest building in the city, once completed, with one-hundred-and-eighty million-dollar condos, a five-star hotel, and a top department store on site.

I'm running on adrenaline, double espressos, and three hours of sleep a night, max. The only highlight of my weeks is my visits with Rowan and Sierra. I look forward to them like I haven't looked forward to anything in years. Hence why I'm already on a plane to Chicago, and it's only four twenty a.m. on Saturday morning. I have been alternating flight times and airports in an effort to hide my tracks. The last thing I want is the Russians discovering I'm making regular weekend trips to Chicago and figuring out the reason why.

I told Sierra I'd drop by at lunchtime, but I couldn't sleep and the need to see her and my son was greater, so I roused my pilot from his bed, and Leo, Ciro, and I headed to the airport to board my private jet. Ciro is dozing in the seat behind me with his earplugs in. My best friend and underboss is currently snoring, quite obnoxiously, in the chair across from me, ensuring I'll get no shut-eye before we touch down in Chicago.

Two hours later, I'm leaning my head against the window of the SUV, watching the sunrise as Alessandro drives. Ciro is beside me in the back. Leo is still snoring. From the front passenger seat this time. At least one of us managed to catch some decent sleep.

"You must have more patience than me, boss." Alessandro looks at me through the mirror as he lifts one shoulder in Leo's direction. "I'd have slit his throat on the plane."

Ciro harrumphs.

"The thought did cross my mind." I smile. "How have things been?" I ask even though it's not necessary. Alessandro sends me daily summary reports by email.

"Everything is fine. There have been no threats or persons of interest nosing around."

"What about that prick Lawson? Did he suspect anything when you and Frank attended dinner last week?"

Alessandro shakes his head. "He grilled us at the start, but it was the usual bullshit. He bought our story and didn't even look sideways at us after that."

Sierra told her family she hired the guys through a private security firm. I own such a firm—our protection services are more upscale than the shakedowns of the past—but I want nothing linking to New York, so I got Phillip to establish a new fake security company, and we sent official employee cards to Alessandro and Frank. Phillip is the best IT brain I have on my payroll, and I pay him way above market rate to secure his loyalty and his secrecy.

"Good."

"The man is a fucking asshole."

"He's a piece of work, all right. He hated my guts when I first dated Saskia. Told me bluntly I wasn't good enough for his daughter."

I eventually won him over. I'm not sure how, because I didn't give a fuck about her old man and things were never serious with her. If I wasn't in such a mess over Mom's death and being forced to leave college when I lost my scholarship, I doubt I would have ever dated anyone as high maintenance as Sierra's older sister.

They might share similar physical characteristics, but personality-wise, they are like night and day. Sierra is warm where Saskia is cold. Sierra is forgiving while Saskia bears grudges like no one I have ever known. Sierra always sees the positives and she delights in the world around her, while Saskia has a bitter outlook and never a kind word to say about anything or anyone.

While Sierra wastes no opportunity to bust my balls, things have been amicable these past three weeks, and we're settling into a comfortable routine. We spend time with our son together, and then she retreats, while she cooks us a meal, giving me quality time with Rowan alone.

I'm immensely rich, and I have grown to enjoy the finer things in life, but a simple meal shared in a small homey kitchen with my son and the woman I want as my wife has come to mean so much to me—more than anything my money can buy. Sierra has put her feelings aside so I can develop a relationship with my son in a comfortable environment. I'm under no illusions. I know she has done that for Rowan, but I appreciate it, and it only adds to my mounting respect for her.

If things were different, I could see myself falling head over heels for the mother of my child.

"Pull over," I say when I spot a woman unloading supplies from the back of a small van.

Alessandro parks behind the florist's van without question.

Ciro curls his hand around the door handle to get out. "Don't bother," I say, opening my door. "I won't be long, and there isn't a soul on the streets."

I'm smiling as I approach the woman in my jeans and sweater, hoping she doesn't notice the bags under my eyes and that my wallet and my legendary charisma will work its charm.

I climb back in the car a few minutes later with a massive bunch of flowers in my arms. Ciro continues looking out the window, and Alessandro says nothing, easing the car back out on the road and heading toward Elm Street.

Leo wakes up just as we round the bend toward Sierra's house. My heart spikes to coronary-inducing levels when I spot the unfamiliar Lincoln Navigator parked directly outside Sierra's house.

I know it's not one of ours.

"Call Ian," I snap, wondering why my soldier on night duty failed to inform us of a suspicious car parked outside my future wife's house. "And if he's asleep on the job, I'll make it permanent."

I pull my Glock out as Alessandro parks in front of the Navigator, readying myself to run in there when he turns sheepishly toward me, rubbing the back of his neck. "It's her boyfriend's car," he quietly says.

"What is it doing parked outside her house?" My voice is calm, betraying no hint of the storm brewing inside me.

"I don't know for sure, boss, but it's been here since last night, so I'm assuming it means—"

"Why wasn't I told about this?" I snap. There has been no mention of any home visits from the teacher in my email reports, and I assumed it meant Sierra had kicked him to the curb.

"The guy was vetted and passed," Leo reminds me.

"I still need to know when he's in the house with my son!" I bark, wringing my hands and wishing it was Dion Stewart's neck. I warned Sierra I wouldn't tolerate any man trying to take my place, and I am ready to charge in there and slaughter him in her bed, consequences be damned.

"Oh shit."

Leo's tone pulls me from my head, and I watch with rising anger as the front door of Sierra's house opens and she appears with the douche.

His brown hair is sticking up in every direction, like he was just dragged through a bush. Either that or he hasn't owned a comb in years. His jeans are hanging loosely off his hips, like he dressed in a hurry. Blood pounds in my skull when he leans in and kisses her. Grabbing her face in his hands, he angles his head and deepens the kiss, and that's the moment I lose control of the tenuous hold on my emotions.

I've seen enough.

That asshole is dead.

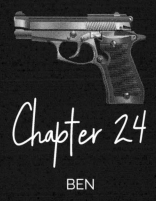

Chapter 24

BEN

I AM OUT of the car before I've processed the movement, racing toward the kissing couple, with my gun in hand. My shoes crunch on the gravel in Sierra's driveway, and her eyes pop open, widening in horror as she spots me advancing.

She has no time to warn Dion before I grab a fistful of his shirt and yank him back, away from her. Tossing him to the ground, I hover over him, pressing the muzzle of my gun to his brow. The front door closes with a soft snick as Sierra screams. The grinding of gravel underfoot signals my men have arrived, but I don't look up, keeping my gaze trained on the douche. Sierra is pleading with Alessandro, but she fails to understand they act on my instructions, not hers. Neither of them will intervene unless I give them permission.

I stare into Dion Stewart's petrified brown eyes, wondering what the hell Sierra sees in this sniveling idiot. "Do you know who I am?" I ask, pressing the gun harder into his brow.

"No. And I don't know who you think I am or what's going on, but it's clearly a case of mistaken identity."

"Did you fuck her?" I hiss.

"What?" His Adam's apple jumps in his throat as his brows knit together in confusion.

"Did. You. Put. Your. Cock. In. Sierra." I say it slow in case he's hard of hearing or understanding.

"Don't answer him, Dion," Sierra yells, amid sounds of thrashing behind me. "Let him go, Ben. He has nothing to do with this, and you have no right to ask him that. I can fuck whoever I want," she adds.

Curling my finger around the trigger, I press the gun harder into his forehead. I continue staring into the eyes of the coward underneath me while I respond. "I don't think so, Firefly." I bark out a harsh laugh. "You. Are. Mine. Go on. I dare you to deny it." I would love an excuse to blow this fucker's brains to smithereens.

"Ben, please." Her voice is lower, calmer, but I can still detect the hysterical undertone. "Let Dion go home, and we'll talk about this. Think of Rowan. He'll be awake shortly, and he can't see this."

That is the only thing she could say that would bring me out of the murderous rage clouding my judgment. I tuck the gun back in the waistband of my jeans and fist a hand in the guy's shirt, pulling him to his feet.

He shoves me away as Sierra races toward him. She stops a couple of feet from him because she knows if he lays another finger on her all bets are off. He stands in front of her, shielding her from me, and it's comical he thinks he can protect her when he almost pissed his pants a minute ago. "Call the cops, Sierra," he says, glaring at me.

"Someone found their balls," Leo says, sauntering to my side.

"A little too late," I reply, folding my arms and pinning Dion with a deadly look.

"If you leave, we won't tell anyone about this," he blusters. "We don't want any trouble. This is a quiet neighborhood."

"Who does this schmuck think he is?" Leo says to me.

My eyes find Sierra's. "Set him straight or I will."

"Dion. It's okay," she says, walking around him so they are face to face. "I know him. He's an asshole, but he won't hurt me or Rowan."

"What the hell is going on here, Sierra?" Confusion is drawn all over his face, and I'm glad Sierra managed to follow at least one of my instructions. The guy clearly doesn't know who I am.

"Ben is an old family friend," Sierra lies. "His bark is worse than his bite." Her eyes flit to mine, and I can tell even she's not buying the bullshit she's peddling.

"I'm not leaving you here with him," the teacher says, and I'm officially done.

Yanking him by the shirt again, I bring his face right up to mine. "I'm done playing nice. Here's the score. Sierra is my future wife, so whatever the fuck you think you have with her is over. You're finished. Walk away now or you won't walk away at all."

"What. The. Actual. Fuck?" Sierra shrieks, pulling on my arm. "You are insane. Like clinically insane. I am *not* marrying you."

"You are and you will. It's not up for discussion."

"The hell it isn't. You can't make me."

I tilt my head to the side. "Watch me."

"I'm calling the cops," the douche says, right before he headbutts me.

Pain rattles in my skull, but I don't let go of him. He cusses, blinking, realizing how stupid that move was. "You really shouldn't have done that." I flash him a lethal smile before tossing him to Leo. "Get rid of the trash, and remind him to keep his mouth shut while you're at it."

"My pleasure, boss."

Dion takes a swing at Leo, and Leo pops him square on the nose, leveling him with a second powerful punch that knocks him out cold.

Sierra screams, instantly slapping her hands over her mouth before she wakes Rowan.

Ciro helps Leo carry the unconscious teacher to his car while I wait for Sierra to let rip. Her small fists pound into my chest. "You're a prick. I hate you. I fucking hate you." She continues beating her fists on my chest even as I pick her up and carry her inside the house. "You can't just kill him! Someone will notice he's missing, and I'm probably the first place they will come looking. How the hell is that protecting us?"

"No one said anything about killing him," I reply, clamping my hand down on her butt as I walk to her bedroom.

I close the door and throw her down on the crumpled bed, straddling her hips and pinning her in place. She beats at my chest again, bucking her hips and trying to throw me off, but I'm much stronger and I've got at least sixty pounds on her. When I've had enough of her pitiful attempts to hurt me, I grab her wrists, pulling her arms up over her head as I lean down into her face. "That's enough," I grunt, feeling my dick thicken as my body acknowledges the way we are strategically aligned. "If you want to blame someone, blame yourself. I warned you not to bring any man into this house. I told you what would happen if anyone tried to take my place."

"He wasn't taking your place, you psycho!" She wriggles underneath me, and all the blood in my body rushes to my cock. "Rowan doesn't know we're dating. Dion comes over after Rowan is asleep, and he always leaves before he wakes up."

"I don't care." I thrust my groin against hers. "That is the last time that man is in this house. The last time his cock goes anywhere near your pussy." I rock my hips again and graze my teeth along the column of her neck. "If you need to be fucked, I will fuck you."

"Get off me!" She wriggles again, and the instant her pussy makes contact with my straining erection, we both groan. She is only wearing light cotton pajama pants and I can feel her heat through the thin material. Dusting a slew of openmouthed kisses along her neck, I nip at her earlobe as we grind against one another. "Stop!" she hisses, biting my neck hard. "I don't want this."

"Liar," I whisper in her ear as my hand closes over one breast through her flimsy pajama top. Her nipple is standing at attention, and she arches her back when I flick the taut peak. "Your body betrays you."

"That's just a physiological reaction to you sitting on my pussy and kissing my neck. It's nothing more than a natural physical response. I still loathe you with every part of my being," she pants, fighting her obvious attraction to me.

Having Sierra hate me is good. It means there is little risk of love growing between us. I *need* her to hate me, and everything I have said and done has been designed to achieve that goal. So why do her words feel like someone is sliding a knife slowly and methodically straight through my heart?

Shaking off my unhelpful thoughts, I smirk right in her face because I know how much my smirks irritate her. "Hate-fucking happens to be one of my favorites, so spew your vitriol, Firefly. All it does is turn me the fuck on."

I slam my lips down hard on hers, devouring her mouth with wild abandon, channeling all the pent-up rage churning inside me. She tries to resist, for all of two seconds, before she succumbs to our mutual lust, kissing me back with the same anger and toxicity flowing through my veins. I bite and suck on her lips, thrusting my tongue into her mouth as we battle for supremacy, like vipers competing for the lethal kill.

We brutalize each other, our mouths fighting for control, bodies grinding against one another, and I'm primed to explode. I don't know how long it goes on, only I'm dangerously close to the edge, so damn near losing all control. Her hands delve into my hair, and she tugs hard, yanking my head back. We are both panting and glaring at one another, and it's glorious.

I haven't been this turned on in years.

Not since Vegas.

"You don't have to like me to fuck me," I rasp. "You've just proven that point."

Her eyes narrow to slits, and I wait for her to sling her next shot. "I agree. You could be any man sitting on top of me and my body would respond the same way." Her eyes glimmer mischievously. "Dion sat right there a half hour ago, only we were naked and he was sliding his cock in and out of my pussy, and I fucking loved it."

"You're really starting to piss me off, Firefly." I knead her breast and shove my dick into her pussy through our clothes. "This pussy is mine and mine alone."

"You are insane if you think I'm agreeing to that."

I sit upright, still straddling her hips but keeping my hands away from her tempting body. "You will agree or I will slaughter any man who touches you in cold blood."

"You wouldn't." Her face pales.

"I would and I wouldn't advise you to test me." I climb off her body, needing to get out of here before Rowan wakes. I don't want him to see me like this—when I'm angry and sexually frustrated and quite likely to throttle his mother if she keeps this shit up. I'll grab a few hours' sleep across the road and come back when I've regained my composure.

"So, I'm expected to break up with my boyfriend and only have hate sex with you while you get up to who knows what in New York, and you seriously think I'll be okay with that?"

I adjust my hard-on behind my jeans. "I don't care what you think. All that matters is that pussy remains mine. What or who I do in my spare time is no business of yours."

I haven't fucked a woman in weeks. Not since I came to Chicago for the funeral. And the only woman starring in my dreams is the vengeful vixen glowering at me on the bed. Her messy blonde hair is strewn across the sheets like the rays of the sun, and she's magnificent. No one holds a candle to her, and I have zero interest in calling any of my usual fuck buddies.

It's safe to say Sierra Lawson has ruined me for all others. I've known it since Vegas, but I could continue the charade while she wasn't a part of my life. Now, she is a part of my past, my present, and my future and the only woman I have any interest in fucking. Not that she will ever hear those words leave these lips.

She props up on her elbows, glaring at me. "I won't accept double standards, and I'm not agreeing to fuck you. We share a son. We are co-parents, and that is the extent of our relationship."

"We can do this the easy way or the hard way, Firefly." I shrug. "I have no moral indecision when it comes to killing anyone you take to your bed, but can you say the same? Can you live with yourself if you continue this nonsense with that man and he ends up dead? We both know he is not worthy of you, so do us all a favor and stay away from him."

Remembering I need her to continue hating me, I leave her with one final parting blow. "If I'm not mistaken, Saskia's husband is out of town this weekend. I think I'll pay her a little visit." I harden my features and plant my mask firmly on my face, ignoring the hurt brimming in her eyes. "I'll return to visit with Rowan at the original agreed time." I walk out without giving her a backward glance, and she doesn't verbally retaliate, my parting shot delivering the message, loud and clear.

"Stay with Sierra," I tell Alessandro when I exit the house. "And make sure Frank goes with you if they leave the house. I'll be back later."

Alessandro throws Leo the keys to the SUV, and I climb into the front while he slides behind the wheel. Ciro gets in the back. "Where to?"

"Drive around to the back road and park at the rear of my house." He looks at me like I'm nuts. "Just do it."

"You're the boss."

We drive in silence around the corner and park behind the back wall that borders the house.

"What do you want to do with them?" Leo asks, casting a glance in the back seat.

The flowers are still propped up on the floor, against the side of the door. I have no idea what possessed me to buy her flowers. I've got to learn to manage my impulse control before I ruin everything. Presenting Sierra with flowers would have only given her the wrong impression. "Throw them in the trash," I instruct, climbing out.

I'm punching in the code on the back door when my cell vibrates in my pocket. Pulling it out, I grimace.

"What's up?" Leo asks, coming up behind me.

"Could this day get any worse?" I show him my screen.

Briefly, I consider not answering, but that will only infuriate him more, so I push the answer button as I stroll through the door and into the garden. "Saverio. What can I do for you?"

Chapter 25

SIERRA

I FIDGET WITH the full skirt of my silver and gold ballgown as I attempt to tune my sister's irritating voice out. Father insisted we travel to the gala event as a family, so I'm currently sequestered in a limo with my parents, Serena and Alfred, and Felix and Saskia. Our bodyguards are traveling in two armored vehicles. One in front of us and one behind us.

As usual, Saskia is monopolizing the conversation. She just loves the sound of her own voice. They only picked me up fifteen minutes ago, and I already want to bail. It would've been good to have Dion with me tonight, but I broke things off with him the Monday after that disastrous weekend.

I'm pissed Ben forced my hand, but the truth is, the writing was on the wall with my relationship even before Ben reentered my life. Initially, when Ben reappeared, terrorizing me that first night, he sent me racing straight into the safety of Dion's arms. I tried to convince myself settling for safe and secure was the right choice, but it didn't last long.

You will have to kill me before I'd admit this to anyone, even my besties, but Ben's cold gaze, cruel words, rough touch, and brutal dominance has excited me like never before. Don't get me wrong— he still scares the shit out of me and I haven't forgotten he's a cold-blooded killer, but I've turned into one of those idiots in romance books: the ones who get off on possessive alpha men who know how to work a woman's body better than she knows it herself.

I'm determined to fight this madness, and it's one of the reasons I have gone to great lengths to avoid him these past three weekends. He has already proven I can trust him with Rowan, so I have made myself scarce when he's shown up and kept our interactions to the bare minimum.

Saskia throws back her head, laughing as Felix fills her glass with more Cristal Champagne. She smiles at her husband, and I can't help wondering if her good mood has anything to do with Ben. I don't know if he carried out his threat, but even the thought of it hurts so much.

I've got to stop nurturing stupid fantasies when it comes to that man. He has never been mine, and he never will be, and that's a good thing, right?

"Here." Serena tops off my glass from beside me. "You look like you could use this."

"I have a feeling I'm going to need a lot more than a couple of glasses of champagne to survive this night."

Father holds this ball every October in support of one of my mom's charities—the recipient is rotated annually. Mom is on the board of several charities, and she spends her days volunteering and offering practical support, so she isn't just a sponsor like a lot of wealthy women.

Mom was the inspiration behind my decision to work with The Dream Catcher Foundation. It's a local anti-trafficking support center, and I man the phones one night a month with Esme. Pen tags along sometimes when Eric is at home to watch the kids. I also donate on a monthly basis as they are almost entirely reliant on donations to survive.

Esme and I worked tirelessly with a small team from the foundation a couple of years ago to lobby local politicians to update the TVPA legislation.

What happened in Vegas troubled me for a long time, and after Rowan was born, I decided to do something practical about it. Human trafficking—and sex trafficking—is a massive global problem, and it's something I feel strongly and passionately about. Maybe, returning to the fold won't be such a bad thing if I can convince Father to make The Dream Catcher Foundation the annual recipient one time. These galas are attended by the richest and most powerful men in Chicago, and they always raise millions for the chosen charity. The Dream Catcher Foundation could do a lot with a sizable donation.

Tonight is important to Mom, and she's the main reason I'm here. It's been years since I attended one of these balls, thanks to my single-mother status, but Father seems to be in a forgiving mood lately.

That doesn't make me suspicious at all.

"You aren't mistaken," Serena murmurs in my ear. "Tonight holds extra importance because Father has invited some powerful men, from out of state, to attend."

"I'm surprised he insisted I be here. Isn't he worried I'll open my mouth and disgrace him?" I reply, sipping my champagne as I watch Saskia laughing with our parents and Felix while casting a surreptitious glance our way.

Serena and Saskia had a big falling-out a few years ago, and they aren't close anymore. I bet Saskia hates the bond I have with Serena now. In her bitchy head, she probably thinks I orchestrated the entire situation just to reel Serena to my side, but she couldn't be more mistaken. As much as I dislike Saskia, I would never, could never, deliberately harm her. She is still my flesh and blood—even if there is little about her I can relate to or respect.

"It's a good thing you are here. It means you are officially back in the family, and that gives me peace of mind. I know you are passionate about things, but I suggest you keep your opinions to yourself and toe the line tonight. If you do anything to cause a scene, Father will blow a gasket."

"Don't worry," I murmur, taking a healthy mouthful of bubbles. "I have no desire to ruffle any feathers. I have enough stress in my life as it is right now."

She looks funny at me. "Is there something I should know?"

I want to confide in Serena so badly, but I'm afraid she might tell Alfred and he would tell my father and then everyone would find out and it'll turn into an epic shit show. I want to avoid that, at all costs, so I have no choice but to keep the truth to myself. "It's nothing. Work has been super busy, and we have a new receptionist. She's ditzy as fuck, and she keeps making mistakes." That's not a lie. I'm the only acupuncturist at the center, and I'm booked out solid for the next three months. I'm having to turn down clients, which I hate. The manager is pushing for me to go full-time, but I won't sacrifice my time with Rowan. If I wanted to work full-time, I wouldn't have applied for a part-time position.

"We're here," Father announces, and I quickly finish my champagne. "It's important we put on a united front tonight," he adds, eyeballing me on purpose. "I want this event to go off without a hitch, and that means being charming and hospitable to all our guests." He's drilling a hole in my skull, and I know his little speech is all for me.

"Don't worry, Father. I won't embarrass you. I know how important tonight is to Mom."

Saskia mutters something under her breath as the limo pulls up in front of the hotel entrance, but I ignore her. That's the best way to handle my sister. It infuriates her when she doesn't get attention. Pretending she doesn't exist has always been my greatest weapon.

Alesso is waiting outside when my door is opened, and I gratefully accept his hand, struggling to get out of the car without stumbling.

I made the mistake of going dress shopping with Mom, and she coerced me into wearing this Christian Dior gown. It's beautiful and a real showstopper with the golden mesh outer layer over a silver bodice and very full skirt. Clusters of beads and glittering diamonds in the shape of butterflies are strategically arranged over the length of the gown in a mix of silver and gold. The sweetheart neckline and corset-style top make the most of my cleavage. The makeup artist Mom sent to my house dusted my décolletage with a light coating of shimmer, and I'm wearing a trowelful of makeup, but she did a great job of making it appear natural. My hair is pulled into an elegant chignon, and I know I look good.

I just don't buy into all the falseness, and I know I'll need to keep a fake smile plastered on my face all night as spiteful women lie with their compliments while the men at their sides barely contain their leering looks. The bullshit is tiresome, yet it's for a good cause. I'll just have to keep reminding myself of that.

Alesso is dressed in an Armani tux, and he looks devilishly

handsome as he offers me his arm. He is my official "date" for the night. Father wouldn't let me attend on my own. I knew if I didn't find someone, he would foist some horrible pervert on me. He wasn't pleased I was bringing my bodyguard as my date, but I guess Mom sweet-talked him into agreeing.

Alesso almost passed out when I mentioned it to him until I told him the alternative was letting my father appoint my date for the event. That or asking Dion to do me a favor. It seems Ben quickly agreed to the arrangement after that.

"You look beautiful," he says as we follow my family along the red carpet.

"You clean up very nice yourself," I say, smiling and nodding as we pass members of the hotel staff. "On a scale of one to ten, how pissed is your boss?" I ask, fighting a smug smile. Considering how crazy Ben went that time in my hallway, I'm surprised he didn't make Frank escort me tonight.

"You'll find out soon enough," Alesso murmurs as we walk across the marble lobby toward the main ballroom.

My strappy gold Dior heels make a clicking noise as we advance. "What do you mean?" I ask, smiling at the two men standing guard outside the ballroom as we pass by.

"Ben will be here." He throws it out so casually, and I almost trip over my dress with the shock.

"What?" I cry. "Why would he be here?"

"It's business," he replies, taking my elbow and steering me toward the large circular table at the top of the room in front of the podium.

Ben must be one of the powerful out-of-state men Serena referred to. But why would my father invite him? As far as I know, Ben doesn't have any pharmaceutical business interests or any connections to my father. From what I remember, Father wasn't fond of Saskia's boyfriend.

Thoughts of my sister has all the blood draining from my face.

Is she responsible for this? Did she maneuver things so her lover could be here?

Flaunting her lover in front of her unsuspecting husband's eyes would be right up Saskia's alley. Perhaps this is Ben's way of paying me back for ignoring him.

"Business or pleasure?" I hiss, the bite in my tone clear, as Alesso holds out a chair for me.

He shrugs, like he knows nothing, and I inwardly seethe as he claims the seat on my left.

A waiter magically appears at our table, looming over my parents, holding a bottle of champagne in one hand. I lift my hand, waving to capture his attention. Father scowls at me, but he can't say anything as he's conversing with a short man with a rotund belly and a bad comb-over. I've met him before, but I can't recall his name. He's on the board of Lawson Pharma and a big suck-up.

The waiter fills my glass to the halfway point, and I encourage him to keep going. Alesso declines, filling his glass with water. Without asking, he fills a second glass, purposely sliding it to me. "You should pace yourself."

"You should mind your own business," I retort, taking a healthy glug of my champagne.

"Did something happen on the way through the lobby?" Serena asks, frowning as she slides into the seat on my right.

"No. Why would anything be wrong?"

"You have a murderous look on your face, and you're clutching that glass like it's somebody's neck."

I bark out a soft laugh because she is so close to the mark. "I'm just trying to talk myself off a ledge. You know what I'm like. I'm practically allergic to these types of events."

Things only go from bad to worse as the room quickly fills. My parents, Saskia, Felix, and Alfred are busy greeting guests while Serena and I talk in hushed voices at the table. Champagne sloshes through my veins, helping to relax me, but I don't want to get drunk and end up disgracing myself. I'm a mom, and that role is the most important thing to me. I never want to do anything to let Rowan down. So, I drink water, deciding to take Alesso's advice and pace myself.

Father claps his hands, looking proud as punch, as he fixes a wide smile on his face, moving away from our table to greet someone. The look on Saskia's face tells me all I need to know, and I swivel in my chair, watching a large group approach this side of the room.

A distinguished-looking man leads the charge, escorting a knockout Sophia Loren look-alike on his arm. The woman has long dark hair, styled into glossy curls, and killer curves that make her gorgeous fitted red dress look molded to her body like a second skin. Piercing blue eyes and full lips painted in a similar shade of red complete her look. She wears a diamond choker and matching bracelet, and she screams sophistication in an effortless way.

I'm so entranced by the unfamiliar woman that I don't see Ben until he is a few feet away, holding a chair out at the table right alongside ours. A painful pressure sits on my chest as a gorgeous brunette slides onto the chair, beaming up at him like he hung the moon. My claws come out, and I want to gouge her eyes from her eye sockets so she can't look at him like that and slice her lips from her face so she can't smile adoringly at him.

I know her face. I recognize it from some of the photos of Ben on the internet. "Who is she?" I ask under my breath.

Alesso shoots me a strained look. "I probably shouldn't say."

My eyes bore into his. "I didn't ask you to tell me who she is to him. I merely asked for her name. Are you that afraid of your boss you won't tell me?"

He runs a finger along the collar of his shirt. "Her name is Chantel LaCroix."

My brows climb to my hairline. "Any relation to Judge LaCroix?" Judge LaCroix is the chief judge of the New York State Court of Appeals. The judge is on my radar because he has a name for being particularly lenient in granting appeals tied to sex trafficking cases and rumored mob hits.

He scrubs a hand over his chin, and I roll my eyes. "For God's sake, stop being a pussy and tell me. If the asshole gives you a hard time, I'll tell him I googled it."

"She's his daughter," he replies just as Ben's gaze finds mine. His smug smile is in place, like he wore it especially for me.

"Bennett Mazzone. I couldn't believe it when Daddy said you would be in attendance," Saskia says, materializing in front of my baby daddy, acting like she didn't run into him in Glencoe six weeks ago. Her gaze leisurely roams his body. "My, my. Haven't you grown up."

Chantel clears her throat, but Saskia ignores her, placing her hand on Ben's arm. Blood boils in my veins, and I grip the sides of my chair, digging my nails into the velvet padding.

"Saskia, darling," Ben says, taking her hand and raising it to his mouth. "It's always a pleasure, and I could say the same to you. You look amazing." He tilts his head ever so slightly, his eyes meeting mine and holding as he presses his lips against my sister's knuckles.

Red-hot fury washes over me, and it's a struggle to remain in my seat, but I won't give that asshole the satisfaction of knowing he is getting to me.

Instead, I smile sweetly at him as I stretch my arm along the back of Alesso's chair, leaning into his side and pressing my mouth to his ear. "Drink up, Alesso. I have a feeling you might need a little liquid courage."

A muscle ticks in Ben's jaw as he slowly lowers Saskia's hand, keeping his gaze trained on me even as Saskia babbles away in his ear.

Alesso flinches when my lips brush against his cheek. "Relax," I whisper. "You're my date. We need to make it look real." I sweep my fingers along the curve of his defined jawline while I maintain eye contact with Ben.

His hands clench at his sides, and his look screams a warning.

Well, guess what, asshole? You started this by parading your fuck buddy on your arm and then blatantly flirting with my sister. Don't issue a challenge if you don't want me to rise to the bait.

Two can play this game.

Suddenly, I don't think this ball is going to be quite as tiresome as I imagined.

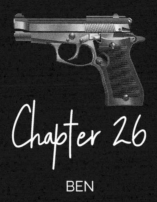

Chapter 26

BEN

"**Y**OU PROMISED THIS would be fun," Chantel whines for the umpteenth time, and if she doesn't put a sock in it, I will shove her annoying ass in a car and send her on a plane back to New York. I thought bringing her would be a good idea. That it would help me to keep my hands and my thoughts off Sierra, but it has backfired in a major way.

"I promised no such thing," I reply, sipping from my glass of Perrier. "You know how these events go. Don't pretend otherwise."

She gulps a large mouthful of red wine before turning to face me. "I thought after months of you giving me the cold shoulder this would be as much about pleasure as business, but you're ignoring me, and no one ignores Chantel LaCroix," she snipes.

Leo coughs to smother his snort of hilarity, and I grit my teeth. Chantel is getting on my very last nerve. Add Sierra's blatant flirtation with Alessandro to the mix, and I am wound tight at a time when I need to remain focused.

The recent Vegas situation has everyone on edge, and we're wondering what the Russians have planned for their next move. Having all five New York bosses plus their consiglieres and underbosses here, along with strong representation from The Outfit, is risky. We all know this presents the Russians with the perfect opportunity to strike, so everyone is on high alert.

We considered pulling out of the gala, but we can't afford to insult The Outfit when negotiations are at such a delicate stage. So, we arrived with a large entourage and a plan to get in and out of Chicago without giving the Russians an opening to attack. The ballroom and the hotel are heavily protected with *soldati*, and we are all armed, but no one can afford to drop their guard.

Especially me.

So, I need female drama like a hole in the head. "I'm not keeping you here, Chantel. Feel free to leave any time you want."

"Father won't be happy to hear how you're mistreating me."

Her arrogant tone rubs me the wrong way. She's crazy if she thinks she has any power in this situation. My lips curl into an amused grin. I fucked Chantel to get to her father, but I don't need her anymore. We have a thick file on the corrupt judge that will keep him in line now. She has outlived her usefulness, and it's time to cut her from my life. She's a decent lay, and she usually knows how to keep her mouth shut at society events, so that's why I kept her on speed dial. But I did not sign up for this shit, and I have no interest in fucking her anymore.

This ends tonight.

I won't be seeing her again, and I'll be deleting her number.

"Do I look like I give a fuck?" I dump more red wine in her glass, moving it in front of her. "Drink up and keep your mouth shut, or I'll be the one having a quiet word in Daddy's ear."

Fire spits from her eyes as she glares at me, but she doesn't retaliate, so I count that as a win. She takes another healthy gulp of wine, and I know it won't be long until she's drunk and ready to pass out.

I thought her presence would infuriate Sierra, but she doesn't seem to care. She's too busy flirting with Alessandro to notice. Glancing over at the top table, my lips pull into a tight line when I discover Sierra draped all over her bodyguard like a blanket. She's laughing at something Alessandro said while running her hands up and down his arms. To outsiders, she looks smitten, and I am slowly losing control of my temper. That woman pushes my buttons to the extreme, and she is playing with fire.

Alessandro is also treading a very fine line right now. His stiff body language tells me he's uncomfortable, but he's not putting her in her place, letting her paw at him and press kisses to his cheek. Fuck this shit. I can't even drown my sorrows in bourbon, because I need to keep my wits about me.

"She's stunning," Natalia whispers in my ear, her eyes glued to the adjoining table.

"Stop looking at her. You're making it obvious."

She laughs, and her blue eyes sparkle with mirth. "I hate to break it to you, brother dearest, but you haven't taken your eyes off Sierra all night. *I'm* not the one making it obvious."

I know she is right, and I hate it. I hate that my eyes latch on to her of their own volition. I hate that I can't go five seconds without thinking about her.

I can't let Sierra distract me.

Not now, not ever.

But I see the way the men in this room are watching her, and I don't like it one little bit. I know she is purposely drooling over Alessandro to rile me up, and I'm liable to snap before the night is out.

"Sierra and Alessandro seem close," Natalia says with a wicked gleam in her eye. "They are close in age too, no?"

"Natalia," I hiss. "Quit pissing me off."

She laughs. "Don't spoil my fun, Benny. I have never seen you like this over any woman. Ever. I thought your heart had shriveled up and died, but she is bringing you back to life. Now you just need to get your head out of your ass before you fuck it up and lose her."

I sigh, ignoring her. If I try to deny it, she will only protest. I know when I can't win an argument and when I'm better off keeping my mouth shut. I wish time would fast-forward so this night could be done. But someone up there is determined to make me suffer.

The band starts, and Sierra grabs Alessandro, dragging him to the dance floor. He doesn't even glance in my direction as they rush past. The little coward. I'm going to string him up by his balls and enjoy inflicting pain with my knife.

"Dance with me." Natalia tugs on my arm the same time Chantel does.

I stand, offering my sister my hand. "It would be my pleasure." This way I can avoid dancing with my date while keeping a close eye on Sierra and my disobedient soldier.

Two birds, one stone.

"You look stunning tonight," I tell her as I guide us out into the middle of the dance floor. It's true. Natalia is a striking woman, and in that red dress, she is garnering as much attention as Sierra. Like my baby momma, she is also more than the sum of her looks. Natalia is intelligent and compassionate with a great sense of humor.

I lucked out on the sibling front, for sure.

Natalia was the one who got me through those dark early days, and I appreciated it because she was grieving and she could have easily resented me when our father claimed me purely so I could replace the brother she had just lost. But she never held it against me. Instead, she helped make things bearable, and we forged an instant bond.

I love my sister, and I would burn the world down for her.

I position us directly beside the other couple, and my skin ripples with rage as I watch my future wife circle her arms tightly around my soldier's neck. Alessandro bristles, finally making eye contact with me. He doesn't cower under my dark glare, but he forgets I know him. His body is as stiff as a brick, his dancing mechanical, despite Sierra's best efforts to get him to loosen up.

"Thank you, Benny. You are always so gracious." Natalia kisses my cheek before angling her head in Sierra's direction. "She looks like an angel," she adds, as we sway to the music.

"Don't let that beautiful innocent exterior fool you. Right now, she's the devil incarnate," I say, tightening my hold on my sister's waist as I watch Sierra press her lips dangerously close to Alessandro's mouth. If she kisses him, I will rip her from his arms, toss her over my shoulder, and drag her to my room to give her a physical reminder of who she belongs to—consequences be damned.

"I saw her sneaking glimpses at you during dinner," Natalia murmurs. "She looked like she wanted to murder you half the time."

"Good. That's exactly how I prefer it."

"The rest of the time she looked equal parts hurt and besotted." Her blue eyes pin mine in place. "Don't destroy her, Benny. Let your heart feel." Her hand sweeps along my cheek. "Would it be so bad to let yourself love her?"

"You know it would," I say in a clipped tone. "It's not going to happen. Whatever fantasy you've conjured up is all in your head." My grip tightens on her waist.

"Ease up there, tiger," Natalia says. "If you keep it up, you'll leave bruises, and the last thing I want is Gino leveling more accusations at me."

Retracting my gaze from Sierra, I focus on my sister's beautiful face. "Is there something I should know?" I search over her shoulder for her husband. If he has hurt her, I will level him. I don't care what kind of political maelstrom it would cause within The Commission. No one hurts my loved ones and lives to tell the tale.

"It's nothing." She attempts to deflect it, probably because she spots the murderous intent on my face.

"Don't lie to me. Either tell me or I'll ask Gino myself."

Her chest heaves. "It's nothing new."

Understanding dawns on me. "This is about Leo."

She nods, and her eyes dart to the side. I twirl us around so I'm facing the other direction, my gaze meeting Leo's. He's dancing with Georgia Lawson, but he's barely paying any attention to my future mother-in-law, staring wistfully in Natalia's direction.

It seems I'm not the only man being painfully obvious tonight.

"He's in love with you," I quietly say.

"I know," she whispers. Her eyes lose a bit of their shine as sadness washes over her features.

I won't ask if she returns his feelings, because it's irrelevant. She is married to Gino Accardi, stepmother to his twin sons, and death is the only way of escaping her reality. "Are you unhappy? Do you want me to have a word with him?" Wives are respected in the New York *famiglia*. There is no obligation on any man to love his wife, or even to remain faithful to her, but there is an expectation of respect and kindness.

"I'm not unhappy, per se." Natalia grips my shoulders more firmly. "He treats me well, and he loves me, in his own way, but he's not *in* love with me, and I'm not in love with him."

"You know this is the way of our world. You know it better than me. You have grown up understanding the reality of being a daughter within the *famiglia*."

"Do you think that makes it any easier to accept? I know it was hard for you growing up ignorant of the truth. I saw how you struggled when Father first brought you to New York and you were initiated. But sometimes I think you were lucky, Benny. You got to live a real life. To make your own choices. And while I know this wasn't what you wanted at first, you have forged your own path in this world, and you get to make your own decisions. You still have control, which is something I have never had."

"I didn't know you felt like that," I admit, ashamed I never stopped to consider what it must have been like for Natalia.

"What was the point in articulating it? It wouldn't have changed anything. I have always known I was destined to marry for the *famiglia*. I have always known it wouldn't be my choice." Her eyes briefly find Leo's again, and I hurt for my sister and my friend. Breath rattles in her chest as she places her palm right over my heart.

"At least I am still breathing, and your heart still beats. Unlike Mateo." Pain shimmers in her eyes, like it does anytime she mentions our brother. I never got to meet him, but Natalia grew up with him, and by all accounts, they were close. "We are alive, and we are fortunate in a lot of ways." She smiles, all trace of sadness vanishing from her face. "Excuse my selfishness. I don't indulge often. I prefer to focus on the positives. Dwelling on the what-ifs is pointless. You need to tell Leo that. He needs to move forward with his life. He should be married by now."

I don't tell her he refuses to marry because, deep down, my sister knows. This is the most honest conversation we have had about her and my best friend. The closest she has come to confirming she feels the same way he does. But it makes no difference. They can't be together, and that's not changing any time soon.

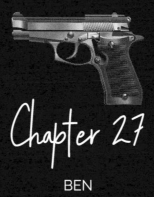

Chapter 27

BEN

"I WANT TO talk to her," Natalia says, bluntly changing the subject, as she gestures in Sierra's direction.

"Absolutely not." I don't trust Natalia not to say something she shouldn't to Sierra. She is giddy over the prospect of a sister-in-law, and she can't wait to meet Rowan. The old man is eagerly anticipating meeting his grandson too, and I will have to arrange a visit soon. Angelo's days are numbered, and I don't want to deprive him of the opportunity to meet Rowan. I will need to start pushing Sierra to make our engagement official, to agree on a time to tell Rowan the truth, and then they will move into my Greenwich property. I don't care how much she fights me over it. It's happening, whether she approves or not.

I glance at the couple still dancing beside us, scowling as I watch Alessandro twirl Sierra around the floor. Her head is thrown back, her cheeks are flushed, her eyes excited, and she's laughing like she's having the time of her life.

"You don't control me, Benny," Natalia says, sliding out of my arms and making a beeline for Sierra.

I curse under my breath.

What is it with the women in my life?

None of them listen to a damn word I say.

I walk after her, glaring at Alessandro as I approach. Natalia has projected herself in between the couple, and her arm is extended toward Sierra. "I'm Natalia. Ben's sister. But please don't hold that against me." She grins, and I work hard to mask my irritation.

"Commiserations," Sierra says. "I don't know how you put up with his grumpy ass."

Natalia laughs. "It's challenging, but don't let this hard exterior fool you." She grabs me, snuggling into my side. "He's quite the softie underneath."

"Nat!" I snap. Good God. I think every woman in this room has been sent to test me tonight. I drag a hand through my hair, desperately needing a drink.

"I once thought the same thing," Sierra says. A nostalgic expression splays across her face, matching her whimsical tone. "But that man doesn't exist anymore," she softly adds. "At least not for me."

Natalia slaps my arm, scowling at me. "Bennett! What have you done to this girl?"

"Nothing she hasn't enjoyed." I flash my trademark smirk as I recall the time in Sierra's bedroom. She has ignored me ever since, which has equally annoyed and pleased me. Sierra keeping her distance is a good thing, especially considering I have repeated that morning, on her bed, in my mind, on a continuous loop in the intervening weeks.

Sierra is dangerous for my sanity.

She has infected my brain and infiltrated my body and every day is a battle to stay away from her.

"Said the sadist to his latest victim," Sierra scoffs.

Natalia bursts out laughing. "I already love her." She darts in, wrapping Sierra in a hug, whispering something in her ear. Out of the corner of my eye, I spot Chantel heading this way, just as Gino arrives to claim his wife. He doesn't know anything about Sierra or Rowan— Nat gave me her word she would keep it a secret, and I trust her—and he's frowning at the two women hugging.

"Dance with Chantel," I hiss at Alessandro, moving in front of Sierra as Gino wraps his arm around his wife, spinning her away.

"I'm not dancing with you," Sierra pouts, stepping back.

"Don't make a scene." I place my hands on her hips, reeling her in to my body. "I don't think your father would appreciate it."

"My father is an asshole." She sets her hands lightly on my shoulders. "But you're an even bigger one."

A laugh rips from my mouth before I can stop it. "I got the memo,

Firefly. You don't need to remind me every chance you get."

"I do when you choose to parade your fuck buddies in front of my face." Her pretty mouth twists into a scowl as she watches Alessandro steer Chantel over to the other side of the dance floor. Chantel is drunk, swaying a little unsteadily on her feet while shooting daggers in my direction.

Ah, so Chantel *has* gotten to her. I frown as another thought pops in my head, my mind occupied with self-doubt for a split-second. Maybe it's because she doesn't want *Alesso* anywhere near Chantel.

"If you want me to stop saying it, maybe try not being an asshole for five seconds," she says, moving her hips in time to the music.

"Your father has made being an asshole a career choice, so why shouldn't I?"

"You seriously want to emulate that man?" She arches a brow, and I instinctively pull her closer. "I don't remember him being impressed with you or in any way pleasant to you, and now you want to be just like him?"

"I never said that." I twirl her around, admiring the view. Her dress fans out around her as she spins, her body swaying elegantly, like a dancer on top of a music box. "But sometimes being an asshole is the only way to achieve certain results."

I spin her back around and she collapses against my chest. Instead of pushing her away, like I know I should, my arms tighten around her lower back, and I hold her close. Her delicate floral scent wraps around me, and I wish I could steal her away. Someplace where it's only the two of us and no interruptions. The things I want to do to her should be outlawed.

She peers up at me, shielding nothing, and my heart pounds at the naked vulnerability on display. God, she is so beautiful it makes my heart ache. "Is there any of the old Ben left in here?" she whispers, sliding her hand up my chest, resting it on my heart. Unlike when Natalia did it, my heart speeds up, beating furiously against the wall of my chest, almost as if it recognizes her touch and is straining toward it.

"That man is gone," I tell her, and I'm grateful for the reminder. I can't be the Ben of her memories. Not if I want to keep her and our son safe. Removing her hands, I take a step back though it kills me to put distance between us. "And you should know better than to waste your time on childish hopes."

I expect her to lash out, but she hasn't shaken the mantle of vulnerability yet. The fact she is being so honest with me now only adds to my guilt. She shakes her head, visibly gulping. "You're right, I should." Her face drops, and I hate I'm the cause of her misery, even if I know it has to be this way. "It's not like I ever meant anything to you. Even now, you only tolerate me because of who I am to Rowan."

She couldn't be more wrong, but I don't correct her. I say nothing, hiding my feelings behind my usual mask. Over her head, I spot Accardi motioning for me. He's wearing his serious expression, which means something must have happened. "If you'll excuse me. I'm needed elsewhere." I turn to walk away but stop, glancing over my shoulder. She's hurting, and it's my fault. I want to give her at least one truth. "You are breathtaking tonight. You steal all the air from my lungs every time I look at you."

I don't wait for a reply or to see her expression, walking off before I do something idiotic like profess undying love. Instead, I leave her standing there, looking hurt and confused.

I find Alessandro before I join the other dons. He is struggling to hold Chantel upright, and her eyes are barely open. She is more drunk than I thought, and I'm disgusted. I would never have brought her here if I realized she no longer knew how to conduct herself in polite society. She's a disgrace and an embarrassment. I need her gone.

"Take her up to her room," I say, sliding her key card in his pocket.

"Bennett," she slurs, making a grab for me. "I love you so much. Why are you so cruel to me?"

Someone is definitely testing me tonight. "Get her out of here with the minimal amount of attention," I tell Alessandro, "and I might forgive your earlier transgressions." He nods. "Ask Sierra's father to get one of his men to keep an eye on her," I add, "but don't take long. Hurry back."

I stalk off, heading toward Accardi. "What's up?"

"We have a situation we need to handle," he says. "Follow me."

We exit the ballroom, taking a left down a long winding corridor, passing the male and female restrooms and a few other smaller convention rooms, until we reach a dead end. One of Accardi's soldiers stands guard at a door on the right, and he steps aside to let us enter. I follow Gino down a flight of stairs into a dark basement room. The other three bosses are there, circling two men tied to chairs. One of the men is bleeding from the nose and has a split lip, and the second can barely see out of his swollen left eye.

"Bratva," I supply, noting the distinct markings on their necks.

"We found them sniffing around outside," DiPietro says, kicking the legs of one of the chairs. The man with the swollen eye takes a tumble to the cold hard ground with a thud.

"They are saying jack shit, but we've doubled the perimeter guards," Maltese confirms as I pull my knife from the sheath on my calf.

Pressing my knife against the second man's throat, I yank his head back. "Who sent you and why?"

He spits in my face, saying something that sounds like "mudak." I punch him in the face, and his nose gushes more blood. I land a few well-placed blows to his gut, and he grunts in pain as his head drops.

"We don't have time for this," DiPietro says, his usual impatience coming to the fore. "Just kill them."

"No." I wipe the spittle off my face with my handkerchief. "I want to interrogate them. Ask Gifoli for a place to transport them to, and assign a couple of our men to watch them." I don't like the idea of Russians hanging around Chicago. I doubt these two are here alone. "I'll make my excuses shortly and head there to handle it myself."

I stuff the soiled handkerchief in the man's mouth before lifting his shirt. I slice a deep line across his gut, just under his navel, careful not to get any blood on my Prada tuxedo. His screams are muffled by the handkerchief, but tears leak involuntarily from his eyes, and pain is etched upon his face. "That wound will slowly bleed out, and it will eventually kill you if not treated. Perhaps it will incentivize you to talk. Tell me what I want to know, and I'll let you live," I lie.

The others nod, and we leave the basement in the care of a few of our best men. Noticing a few blood spatters on my hands, I stop by the men's restroom to wash up.

When I emerge, I find a blonde waiting for me. But it's not the blonde who occupies my every waking thought.

"Hello, Ben," Saskia says, pushing off the wall and sauntering toward me. Her green silk dress leaves little to the imagination, and while it's clearly expensive and she has spared no effort with her appearance tonight, she looks cheap and tacky in comparison to the vision that is Sierra.

Sierra trumps Saskia in every regard.

"I've been looking for an opportunity to get you alone all night," she purrs, pressing herself up against me. I spotted her looking in my direction a few times, but for the most part, she didn't look my way. Saskia is smart enough to not draw attention while her husband and her father are in the vicinity. But I knew she would attempt an ambush

SIOBHAN DAVIS

at some point. Whiskey fumes fan over my face as she leans in close, and I realize she's quite inebriated. Her eyes are a little bloodshot, her skin flushed.

I step sideways, removing her hands from my body. "I don't understand why."

She bats her eyelashes, sidling up to me again. "Don't be coy. I know you still want me the way I still want you."

She's persistent.

I'll give her that.

But she's about as appealing as a deadly rattlesnake.

"I have no interest in you, Saskia," I truthfully admit. I haven't forgotten she called the mother of my child a slut and my son a bastard. I also haven't forgotten how mean she was to Sierra when she was a kid.

She titters like I've said something amusing. "You don't have to worry about being seen or heard. Felix is with Alfredo and my father, and they are discussing some important business with your friends." Her hand slides down the gap between our bodies, aiming for my crotch.

I grip her wrist before her fingers touch my cock. "You appear to be hard of hearing, so I'll make this easy for you. I didn't want to fuck you when we were dating, and I don't want to fuck you now. Is that blunt enough for you?"

She tilts her head to the side, smiling up at me, and I wonder if she has more than just alcohol pumping through her veins. "I know what you're up to. You want to make me beg, but I don't beg any man, Ben. Not even you."

Wow. She is truly a piece of work.

Before I can push her away, she slams me against the wall and slants her mouth against mine. A sharp gasp claims my attention, and I lock eyes with Sierra over Saskia's shoulder. Tears roll silently down her face before she turns around and takes off, heading in the direction of the lobby.

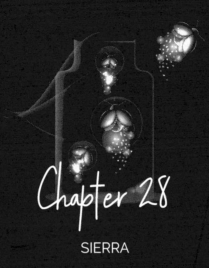

Chapter 28

SIERRA

I RACE THROUGH the entrance doors and down the stairs with no clue where I am going. All I know is I need to get out of here. I can't erase the image of Ben kissing Saskia from my brain, and the pain spearing my chest is almost unbearable. I'm thirteen years old again, hiding in the shadows, watching my older sister kiss the guy I'm in love with, and my heart is aching for him, screaming at him to notice me, yet he still doesn't see me.

Ben is stomping all over my heart except this time it's worse because he is purposely choosing her over me.

I shouldn't care.

He's a monster, and I know I can do better. I've seen what he is capable of, and I should want nothing to do with him.

But I can't lie to myself anymore.

I'm still in love with him.

I think I probably always have been, and I'm slowly accepting that loving a man like Ben means loving all parts of him.

I'm no better than I was as a kid. I'm still pining after a guy who will never be mine. The difference is, I'm a grown-up now. I'm a mother. I know better than to waste my time loving someone who will never love me back.

Sobs wrack my chest as my feet hit the sidewalk, and I dash along the side of the imperial gray stone building, my dress floating around me as I run with no direction. Piercing pain pokes holes in my chest as tears roll down my face, and I can hardly breathe over the intense internal agony ripping me apart on the inside.

It hurts. God, it hurts. So fucking badly.

"Sierra!" Ben shouts after me, his deep voice piercing the air.

I don't stop, running aimlessly, needing to get away from him. I don't want him to see me like this. He can't see how pitiful and stupidly naïve I am, so I push my legs faster, fleeing from him. But my voluminous dress restricts my movements, and he has longer legs, so it doesn't take him long to catch me.

"Sierra. Stop." He takes my arm, forcing me back against the wall. I hang my head, unable to look at him. "What the hell do you think you're doing running outside by yourself? Has nothing I've said these past few months registered with you?" I can tell he's working hard not to shout at me. "It's not safe, Sierra. Especially tonight."

I ignore him, looking at my feet, wishing I could click my fingers and magic myself back home. I want nothing more than to be curling in a ball under my comforter in bed, crying until I expunge my anguish.

I hate the power Ben has over me.

I hate I'm the one granting him that power.

I hate that I love him even more.

"Look at me," he commands, but I ignore him, clamping my lips shut to keep my pain trapped inside.

"Firefly, please." His voice is softer, his tone concerned, and it takes me back in time.

I'M TRYING NOT to cry, but the deep gash in my shin burns like I shoved my leg into a furnace instead of falling out of the tree, ripping the skin on a branch on the way down. I'm limping around the kitchen, leaving a trail of blood on Mom's pristine white tiled floor as I search for the first aid kit. I know she keeps one in here, but I can't find it.

"If it isn't my favorite girl," a deep voice says, startling me, and I jump, a shrill squeak fleeing my mouth before I can stop it. Bracing my hands on the kitchen counter, I silently pray that Ben turns around.

I don't want him to see me crying like a sissy. He'll never see me as a woman if I keep giving him reminders I'm a kid.

"What happened?" he asks, concern underscoring his tone. "Why are you bleeding?"

"It's nothing," I lie, quickly swiping my tears away. "You should go back to Saskia. She's probably looking for you."

I feel him step up behind me, heat rolling off his body in waves. Butterflies run amok in my stomach, and my limbs tremble, like they always do in his presence. "Firefly. Look at me."

"I'm okay, Ben."

"I'd like to see that for myself." He squeezes my shoulder, very lightly, and it's brief, but it's everything.

"Please, Firefly. Turn around and let me see."

"Sierra." Ben's rich timbre pulls me out of the past. His finger presses under my chin, tipping my face up. His piercing blue eyes strip me bare, and he sees everything I have tried so hard to keep from him. From myself too. But I'm too heartsick now to shield the truth. "Please don't cry." He wipes his thumbs along the moisture collecting on my cheeks.

"Don't touch me," I say, but my tone lacks heat. I try to latch on to my anger because I know it's there somewhere, simmering under the surface, but all I can find is sadness.

"Come here. Let me hold you."

A spark of anger flares inside me. "I don't want your pity, Ben. Go back to my sister. I'm sure you only have a short window to fuck Saskia before her husband starts looking for her."

"It's not what it looked like," he says, looking completely unruffled, and that pisses me off.

"You kissed her! I saw you. Don't even attempt to deny it."

He steps closer, pressing his body flush against mine as he peers deep into my eyes. "*She* kissed *me*."

My nostrils twitch as pain roars through me, transforming my sadness, fueling me with liquid rage. I push him back until there's some distance between us. "That's just semantics, Ben."

His large palms grip my face, and a muscle pops in his jaw as he stares at me. "It's not semantics. She cornered me and kissed me. You arrived just at that moment before I could push her away."

I attempt to wrest my face from his hands, but he holds me firmly, refusing to let me go. "Quit with the bullshit, Ben. I know you've been fucking around with her, and it's not like I have any claim on you. You are free to screw whoever you want. It's no skin off my back if you have shit taste in women."

I'm expecting one of his legendary smirks, but he surprises me, maintaining a solemn expression. "I haven't touched Saskia in years, Sierra, and I never fucked her."

Hope is a fickle beast, but he's there, lying low, ready to throw a party. "But you said—"

"I was pissed, and I said it to annoy you, but I didn't go to Saskia when I left your bedroom that day. I went to my house and slept for a few hours until I was calm enough to return to you and our son."

"What about Chantel?" I hiss her name like it's poison, and I hate myself for being so transparent. But my emotions are raw, powering through me and taking control in place of logic and self-preservation.

"She means nothing."

"Did you fuck her?"

He shakes his head. "I haven't fucked her in months."

"So why is she here?"

He sighs, releasing my cheeks, and I instantly miss his touch. He scrubs his hands down his face, looking left and right. "We need to get back inside."

I cross my arms over my chest. Oh no. He's not deflecting. "Answer me. Why is she here?"

"You want the truth?"

"Always," I whisper.

He takes my hand, lacing his fingers through mine. A flurry of shivers whips up my arm at his touch, and I curl my hand around his, not wanting to let go. "I needed her to distract me from you."

My brow puckers. "I don't understand."

He mutters under his breath, and conflict rages on his face. He moves closer again, lifting his free hand to my face. His fingers sweep across my cheek, igniting flames in their wake. "I'm trying to stay away from you, Firefly, but you make it so difficult."

"Why do you want to stay away from me? Why are you fighting this?" His words tell me he feels the connection between us too. That I'm not the only one confused and struggling to make sense of it all.

He cups one side of my face. "I'm trying to keep you safe, but I'm not as strong as I thought." He presses his forehead to mine and his minty breath washes over my face. I rest my hand on his waist, pulling him closer. Our bodies are flush, our heads touching, and it would take nothing to kiss him, but I won't be the one to make that move. I don't know what's going on here, and I won't line myself up for another rejection.

"Sierra," he whispers, peering deep into my eyes. Torment is etched upon his face, as clear as day, and I want to wipe it away. My eyes drift to his mouth, and my breath stutters in my chest as unbridled longing surges through my veins. I want to kiss him so badly. But I'm still hurting over Saskia, and I can't offer myself up to him like a lamb to the slaughter no matter how much I wish to throw caution to the wind.

Kiss me.

His eyes lower to my lips, and I stop breathing. Butterflies are careening around my chest, and my heart is beating to a wild new reckless beat. Do it, Ben. Take charge. Take the decision out of my hands.

Kiss me.

Indecision races across his face, and I don't think either one of us is breathing. He lifts his eyes, finding mine again, and we stare at one another for a few intense moments. It feels like my heart is about to burst through my rib cage and take flight. Longing coats my body in a fine layer of need, and I'm silently urging him to man up when he moves his face in closer, his lips aiming toward my mouth.

My heart is doing cartwheels and my palms are sweaty as I close my eyes and tip my chin up in expectation.

His lips brush the corner of my mouth before gliding to my cheek, and disappointment is heavy in my limbs as I silently scream in frustration. Damping down my disappointment, because I don't want to indulge it and end up crying in front of him again, I choose to take my thrills where I can get them, savoring the feel of him pressed up against me. He's all solid muscle and powerful restraint, and I want to ingest the safety and protection of having him this close. To cocoon myself in him and indulge my inner teenage self.

"I don't want to hurt you, but I can't love you either," he whispers. "To love you is to place you at even greater risk, and I won't do that."

My eyes pop open as he pulls his head back. We stare at one another, and there is so much unspoken between us. "What exactly are you saying, Ben?"

"I'm saying there is no one else, Firefly." He squeezes my hand, and I cling to his touch, our fingers still intertwined. "I don't want Chantel. I don't want Saskia." His eyes drill into mine, and I have stopped breathing. "The only woman I want is you, but—"

"Boss," Alesso shouts, the sound of approaching footfalls heralding his arrival. He's panting like he's just run a marathon. "I've been looking everywhere for you both." He stops, taking in our close stance, clearing his throat. He looks a little sheepish. "I'm sorry to interrupt, but you're needed. It's an emergency."

Ben removes his fingers from mine, and I want to cry. I glare at Alesso—he has the worst timing known to mankind.

"Take Sierra home, and I want you on guard inside the house tonight."

I open my mouth to ask what's going on, but Ben levels me with a serious expression. "Don't fight me on this. I won't negotiate when it comes to your safety and Rowan's safety."

I nod, not willing to compromise on our safety either. "Okay."

In a surprising move, he pulls me into his arms, pressing my head to his chest. One large hand holds my head in place while his other arm wraps around my back. He rests his chin on my hair, and I circle my arms around his toned waist, closing my eyes and siphoning his warmth. A profound sense of contentment settles deep in my bones as he holds me without speaking. His action speaks volumes, and that hopeful beast springs to life again, whispering promises of what may come. After a couple of minutes, he lets me go, planting a chaste kiss to my brow. "Stay with Alessandro. He will keep you safe."

Without another word, he walks off, leaving me almost as confused as when he found me.

Chapter 29

SIERRA

Ben shows up early the following morning to see Rowan. I had nurtured silly notions he might appear in my bedroom at some point during the night, but, after a fretful night with little sleep, I woke to a cold bed and a fragile heart. I don't know if he meant any of the things he said to me last night or if he just said them to console me in the heat of the moment.

"Ben!" Rowan screams in excitement when he sees him, racing across the living room, charging straight into his arms. My heart soars as I watch them embracing. I've denied myself this these past few weeks, and I'm as emotional as I was the first time Ben showed up here. I can't deny how much Rowan has grown to love him. He looks forward to these weekend visits so much it's almost impossible to get him to sleep the night before Ben is due to visit. Today's visit is unexpected. Ben wasn't sure if he could find time to see him, but I'm glad he has made the effort.

"Hey, buddy." Ben closes his eyes, lifting our son easily in his arms as he stands. "I missed you." He nuzzles his nose into his hair, holding Rowan close.

"I missed you too," Rowan says, wriggling in his arms. Ben plants his feet on the ground, smiling. "Guess what?" Rowan tugs on his hand, leading him out toward the bedrooms. "I saw a shooting star!"

he squeals.

Rowan is addicted to the telescope Ben bought him, and he's obsessed with stars and planets. He now wants to be an astronau when he grows up; however, his aspirations tend to alternate quite regularly, so I don't know how long it will last. I took him to the Adler Planetarium a couple of weeks ago, and he loved it.

"That's amazing. I wish I had been here to see it with you."

A pang pierces my chest cavity. I can only imagine how hard it must be for him being away from Rowan for most of the week. It's not only the big things he's missing out on but the little mundane things of everyday life.

"If you have time, you could participate in *Skywatch Weekly?*" I suggest. "It's something the Adler Planetarium does," I explain, answering his unspoken question. "There is a weekly episode on YouTube every Thursday, and they make it interesting for the kids with fun facts and weekly challenges and suggesting things they can look out for, for themselves, in the intervening week. Rowan loves it, and I'm learning stuff I never knew."

"Oh yes! Please come over for the show, Ben!" Rowan jumps up and down, bubbling with excitement. "It's awesome. Mommy makes popcorn, and we write down the weekly challenge every week after the show is over."

Shit. I walk to my son, crouching down. "Sweetheart. Ben lives in New York, so he wouldn't be able to come to our house, but he could watch it at his house, and then we could video call him after to talk about it?"

"Aw." His little face drops, and my heart hurts.

"Hey." Ben kneels on the other side of Rowan. "The show sounds awesome, and I would love to watch it. And maybe sometimes I might be able to watch it here with you, if that's okay with your mommy."

Rowan turns to me, his cute face expectant.

"That would be fine with me."

Ben and I exchange a look, and my heart pounds in my chest with the intense way he's staring at me. Ben always has this way of looking at me that feels like he really sees me. Like he can dive through my outer layer and see what lies beneath.

And why does he have to be so gorgeous and so irresistible? He hasn't shaved, and the five o'clock shadow on his face only adds to his sexiness, but it's his eyes that always get me. They are a stunning blue, with a silvery sheen that makes them pop, and I could stare into his eyes all day long.

I want nothing more than to lean over and kiss him, but he's not mine to kiss, and he probably won't ever be. He may have feelings for me, but it's clear from the things he said that he won't allow it to go any further. Or maybe he did just say those things to calm me down and I'm imagining feelings that don't exist. I've been seesawing back and forth all night trying to figure it out, but there is no point torturing myself because it's not going to happen. My head agrees it's the most logical approach.

After all, this is about Rowan.

Not me and his father.

But try telling that to my lovesick heart.

"Yay!" Rowan flings his arms around me, almost knocking me off balance, as Ben straightens up. "Thanks, Mom. I love you."

"I love you too, Firecracker." I dot kisses all over his adorable face. "So, so much."

Ben offers me his hand when Rowan lets go, helping to pull me to my feet. I swear his eyes look glassy for a split-second, but it could be my overactive imagination at work again.

"I want to show you my picture. I drawed the universe." Rowan tugs on Ben's hand, and I smile, nodding my consent. They wander off, and I put on my boots, needing some fresh air. My head is a little sore after all the champagne last night, and I could use a cold breeze to blast the cobwebs from my skull.

"Are we heading out?" Alesso asks, grabbing his coat from the coatrack in the hall.

"I need a walk." It's well into October, and it's decidedly chilly, so I button up my coat and wrap my scarf around my neck.

Alesso disappears, to update Ben, no doubt, returning a minute later. "Come on."

We step outside and walk toward the park in amicable silence, at first. The park is deserted this early on a Sunday morning, and I welcome the peace and serenity as we walk the most popular trail through the woods.

"I'm sorry I interrupted last night," Alesso says, pushing some stray branches aside for me.

"It's fine. It was most likely for the best."

"Ben would probably kill me if he heard me say this, but he has feelings for you. I've seen the way he looks at you when he thinks no one is watching, and Leo said everyone saw it in Vegas."

I'm pretty sure Vegas was just lust for Ben. I laugh. "Vegas meant nothing to him, Alesso. He couldn't wait to get rid of me the next day." Although, it's probably come to mean more to him retrospectively if his commitment to spending time with Rowan is any indication.

"He deliberately pushed you away, Sierra." Alesso shoves his hands in his pockets as a gust of wind slams into us. "He doesn't get attached on purpose, but it's more than that. He hasn't been interested in any woman the way I see he is interested in you. He has never let any female get close to him. You are the only exception, and I think you scare him a lot. It's dangerous for men in his position to care about others, and he's paranoid about keeping you both safe."

"I get that, and his fear is palpable. I don't know much about the way your world works, and I'm not sure I ever want to know, but I know enough. It's dangerous. Being associated with him is dangerous, but it's not like we can change the situation. Rowan is his flesh and blood, and I could never keep him away from his son. Not now I see how they are with one another."

"It's beautiful," Alesso agrees as we step out of the forest onto the path at the back of the park. "You and Rowan are changing him, and he might not see it, but he needs that." Alesso gently takes my arm, and his features soften. "I think you do too." He smiles. "I see the way you look at him as well, and I'm rooting for you guys."

I gulp over the messy ball of emotion clogging my throat, but I don't respond because I'm not sure how to.

"Don't give up on him," he adds, letting go of my arm. "I know he's an ass at the best of times, but be patient. He's a good man."

"You seem so sure of that, yet I've seen him angry at you a lot."

Alesso grins as we stroll side by side around the far side of the park. "That's only because he's struggling to control his emotions around you, and he's jealous." He narrows his eyes, pinning me with a chastising look. "You were a brat last night. You deliberately goaded him."

I hold my head up, meeting his gaze with one of my own. "I refuse to apologize. He deserved it for bringing that woman on purpose to piss me off."

Alesso chuckles. "I admire a woman who fights back, but next time, find someone else to use against him. I know Ben is a good man, but he's a dangerous man too, and we can only push him so far. His loyalty to me has been tested a few times in recent months, and I'd rather not push him to the edge. I value breathing."

I can't tell if he's joking or serious, and I decide to change the topic because I don't want to discuss that side of Ben. Plus, Alesso isn't often talkative, and I want to take advantage of his present openness. "How did you end up in this life anyway?"

He grimaces. "It's not a pleasant story."

"It won't make me think any less of you," I say, sensing that might hold him back.

He shakes his head. "I know that. I just meant...ah, I suppose it doesn't matter." He wets his lips before he starts explaining. "I didn't have the best childhood. My mom was a junkie who sold her body for drug money. I never knew my dad. I don't know if my mom even knew who he was. A john, most likely. Or maybe it was her disgusting pimp." He shrugs, like it's no biggie, but his body betrays him. His shoulders are stiff, his muscles tense, jaw locked. Telling me this is hard for him, and I'm guessing he doesn't share his story often. That he trusts me means a lot. I briefly squeeze his hand in reassurance, urging him to continue.

"Mom was washed out by the time I was fifteen," he continues, as we head toward the entrance to the park. "And that's when she came up with the bright idea to pimp me out. I took off the night two johns showed up looking for a good time with me. I fought the bastards, trashed the place, and left. I never went back." His chest heaves, and he averts his eyes, grappling with inner demons I can't see.

I wait him out, realizing again how fortunate I was to grow up with a mom who loved me and in a rich family where everything I needed was given to me. Except for my father's love, but it seems almost petty to feel neglected when there are people like Ben and Alesso who grew up with so little. Father may not have wanted me, but he provided for me.

"I lived on the streets for a while, barely existing." His Adam's apple jumps in his throat, and he looks dead ahead as he speaks. "Then I got into street fighting, and I found a way to use all the pent-up anger and frustration inside me for something positive. I made a name for myself. Got enough money to get a crappy studio, but I didn't care. I had a roof over my head and food in my belly and a reason to live. One night, a bunch of jealous idiots jumped me in an alley after a fight. I fought them, but there were six of them and only one of me, and I was beat after my match. I didn't realize Ben was there, and he saw the whole thing. His men killed the guys, and he took me to his place. Fixed me up with a doctor. Forced me to stay in bed and heal."

We walk out through the gates as a couple I know approaches. We greet them before letting them pass. I'm sure my neighbors are wondering what's going on with all the strange men coming and going from my house, but they are too polite to inquire.

"What happened next?" I ask, glancing at Alesso.

"Ben talked to me. He told me his story and how he saw a lot of himself in me. He gave me a choice. Explained about *la famiglia* and the life of a soldier. He asked me if I wanted to be initiated and trained, and I didn't have to think long before accepting."

"And you clearly have some Italian blood flowing in your veins," I say, in a nod to his name. "Which must have helped." The mafia research I uncovered on the web suggested you have to be of Italian descent to be initiated.

Alesso steps aside to let a little girl on a bike pass us. Her mom is jogging behind her, and she waves as she runs past. "Actually, as far as I'm aware, I'm not Italian. My mother just liked the name Alessandro." He shrugs, and I wonder if his father was Italian, because it's not just his name. He has that look about him too with his Roman nose, dark hair, and brown eyes.

"It didn't matter, anyway," he continues. "Every crime family has their own rules, and while you usually have to be of Italian descent, Ben didn't give a crap. He has drastically altered the way things run. He has modernized the *famiglia*, and a lot of the soldiers are men hired through his private security firm. Not everyone has Italian roots though anyone without it won't ascend any higher in the ranks."

"Does that bother you?"

He shakes his head. "I like what I do. It was a great honor when Ben chose me as his personal bodyguard and again when he asked me to guard you. It demonstrates trust and loyalty. The same trust and loyalty I have for him." Alesso halts on the sidewalk across from my house, stepping in front of me. "Ben saved me, and I would die for that man. He has my allegiance for life, as do you and Rowan. I would take a bullet before I'd let any of you get hurt."

I throw myself at him, hugging him tight. "I know you would, and I appreciate it so much."

Of course, Ben would choose that moment to step out of my house. His eyes find us almost instantly, and I pull back at the instant scowl that furrows his brow. I curse under my breath and let Alesso go. The one time I'm not trying to purposely annoy Ben through his bodyguard, and he has to see. Typical.

I skip across the road as Ben makes his way toward the familiar black Merc. Three men step out of the car, and Ciro opens the back door for Ben. Leo is not around today, which is strange, as Ben rarely seems to go anywhere without him.

"You're leaving already?" I ask when I step up on the curb.

"I have a business meeting to attend."

"I was hoping we could talk."

"It will have to wait." He's all businesslike, and his cold mantle is firmly back in place.

Hurt shuttles through me. I don't know why I'm surprised. This is the usual pattern with Ben. "Suit yourself." I stalk toward the house, irritated I'm wearing my emotions on my sleeve again.

"Sierra." Gravel crunches noisily as he steps up behind me. I stop, but I don't turn around. His mouth brushes my cheek, sending shivers cascading across my skin. "Things are particularly tense right now. Please don't take any unnecessary risks. I will call or text you about Thursday." His fingers dance fleetingly in my hair. "Be safe."

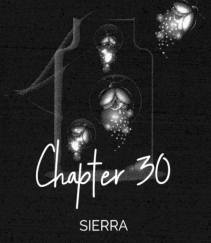

Chapter 30

SIERRA

IT'S THE WEDNESDAY after the charity ball, and the only time Ben has reached out to me is via text. It was a brief message, confirming he will watch the *Skywatch Weekly* episode tomorrow and FaceTime with Rowan after. There was no mention of us, and I don't push the issue. Now that I've had time to reflect on it, I think Ben is right. There can be no future for us as a couple. Things are complicated enough as it is, and the last thing I need is to be more submerged in his criminal world. So, I lock up my heart and store the key in a mental lockbox.

A knock on my door surprises me, and I glance at the clock on the wall. I'm at work, and not expecting Dee, my next client, for another forty-five minutes. I penciled a free hour in today so I could catch up on paperwork and update my records in our patient system.

Opening the door, I find Alesso wearing a lopsided grin and holding two paper cups. He's been hanging around inside the building all week, much to the manager's consternation. I don't know what's going on in the big bad mafia world, but tensions appear to be running high, and Alesso and Frank have been extra vigilant. The guys are all sharing rotations at night so Ian can guard Rowan with Frank during the day.

I'm pissed Ben left on Sunday without filling me in. If things are bad enough Rowan needs two bodyguards while he's at school, then I should have been informed. I was tempted to call him and raise hell, but I would rather wait until I have calmed down and talk face to face. Ben has dragged me and Rowan into this life, whether we chose it or not, and it's about time I understood it better. I don't want or need all the gory details—just enough to understand the risks more clearly.

"Green tea," Alesso says, thrusting one of the cups at me.

"Let me guess. Another peace offering from Lucille?"

Our new receptionist still hasn't gotten the hang of our computer system, and she has messed up a ton of shit in her few weeks here. Last week, she accidentally wiped out the records for ten of my current clients. Hence why I'm manually adding their records back into the system. Lucille offered to do it, but I don't trust her. So, she has resorted to other means of making it up to me. I told her she didn't need to buy me tea every day, but she seems insistent.

"Yep." He waves his coffee cup at me. "And it seems I'm on the apology list too. This is my third free coffee this week."

"What'd she do to you?" I ask, setting the cup down beside my printer.

"Nothing. I guess she sees me as an extension of you." He grins, and I like the easygoing nature of our relationship. I thought he might be embarrassed after telling me his story, but he seems almost relieved to have shared it, and an additional barrier has lowered between us.

Now, I just need to work on loosening Frank up. He's as tight-lipped as they come but very mannerly and respectful. He's sweet with Rowan, even though I can tell he's a little uncomfortable around young kids. The most important thing is, Rowan likes him, and he has taken to having a bodyguard like a duck to water.

"She wants to get in your pants," I tell him, smirking. And why wouldn't she? Alesso is hot with his dark hair, dark eyes, and ripped body, and I've seen her drooling over his tattoos. He arches a brow, like it's unheard of for a woman to lust after him. "Why do you look surprised? You can't tell me women aren't throwing themselves at you. You certainly got your fair share of admiring glances last weekend."

"I don't have time for women," he says, sounding too much like his boss.

"You don't have time for them, or you don't like them?" I inquire, leaning against the doorway. "Are you batting for the other team and you neglected to mention it?" I probe with a teasing smile. "Because I gotta say, the idea of you being into men gets me hot." I have watched some gay porn, and it seriously gets my juices going. There is just something about two men fucking that gets me all worked up.

"I'm not into men." He rushes to reassure me. "I like women. I fuck women. But that's all I'm interested in."

I push on. "Lucille is pretty."

"Don't you have work to do?" he grunts, and I giggle. He's right though. I'm procrastinating because I freaking hate admin tasks.

"You should ask her out. She's a terrible receptionist, but she seems like a sweet girl."

"Go. Work," Alesso says before drinking his coffee and pulling the door shut.

I'm chuckling as I plonk down in my chair, hauling my mail in front of me as I pop my AirPods in and crank up "Sad Song" by We the Kings. I'll sort my mail first and then attack the mountainous pile of files propped beside my desktop PC. I play "Sad Song" and "Without You" by The Kid LAROI on a loop, as they are feeding my mood today. I'm so engrossed in my work and immersed in the lyrics I forget all about my tea, only remembering it when it's too cold to drink.

I'm singing away when the door to my room bursts open without warning. I swivel on my chair, and all the blood drains from my face as I lock eyes with the stranger standing in my doorway. The man is wearing faded black slacks, a black leather jacket, and a black turtleneck that barely fits around his wide neck, looking like an extra in a dodgy B-movie from the seventies. His cropped black hair is shorn tight to his head, and there's an ugly scar running along one cheek, which gives me awful flashbacks of that night in the basement in Vegas with Scarface Salerno.

Behind him, Alesso is slumped on the floor in the hallway, and my pulse throbs wildly in my neck as fear races through my veins. I can't tell if he's passed out or dead. Panic jumps up and bites me as the man narrows beady eyes on me, cursing in a foreign tongue as he shuts the door and cracks his knuckles. His nostrils twitch, and his mouth pulls into a snarl as he rakes his gaze over me.

I'm momentarily frozen as we stare at one another, but the instant he moves a foot forward, I jump up, stumbling against my chair and almost losing my balance as I step away from him. Ripping out my AirPods, I discard them on the floor. "Stay back!" I shriek, raising my palms while my eyes flit to my purse at the far end of the desk. The gun Ben gave me is in there, and if I can get to it, I might be able to defend myself. Alesso and I have gone to the gun range a couple of times, and I know the basics.

"This would be much easier if you were sleeping," he says, advancing with a menacing snarl. He has an accent. Clearly European, and I'm guessing he might be Russian. "Come with me now, and I won't hurt anyone else," he adds, as if I can believe a word that comes out of his mouth.

As if I would willingly go anywhere with him.

I lunge for my purse, and he jumps me from behind. Grabbing my wrist, he digs his nails into my sensitive flesh before twisting. His other hand comes to my mouth, stifling my scream of pain. My purse plummets to the floor, and potent terror whittles through me when he drops my aching wrist and his meaty hand grips my hip. His front is pressed against my back, and a deep shudder works its way through me. Bile travels up my throat, and I know I need to do something before all hope is lost.

I shove my elbow back, meeting soft flesh, but it doesn't dislodge him, so I bite down hard on his hand, sinking my teeth into his callused flesh. A muffled roar is quickly followed by a slew of cursing as he yanks his hand back on instinct. Reaching around me, I grab his junk and squeeze it, hoping I don't puke, while I simultaneously stomp down hard on his foot.

He staggers back with a loud roar, and I seize the opportunity, dropping to my knees and sliding under the desk to grab my purse. My fingers have just reached it when I'm yanked back by my hair. I scream as stinging pain rips across my scalp.

"*Suka*," he hisses, dragging me out one-handed by my ponytail. Pain dances across my head as I thrash about, trying to pry his hand away. Lifting me by my hair, he throws me face-first against the wall. My face slams into the framed certificate, which takes a place of pride on the wall, and the sharp edge of the wooden frame pierces my cheekbone, drawing blood. A throbbing sensation radiates across my face, but I barely feel it over the adrenaline pumping through my body and the blood thrumming through my ears. I slump to the ground, automatically cradling my sore cheek, my fingertips coming away bloody.

He comes at me again, cupping his crotch with one hand. I kick his shin, and he stumbles. Leaning forward, I push him hard, and he takes a tumble. I crawl away, scrambling to my feet as I race to my desk for my gun, but he's on his feet fast. His hands wrap around my neck from behind as he shoves me forward. The edge of my desk presses into my stomach as I claw at his arms, struggling to draw enough oxygen into my lungs.

I'm going to die.

That's the only thought going through my mind as he grips my throat tighter. My hands wander haphazardly around my desk, looking for something I can use as a weapon, latching on to the silver letter opener under some papers. He hasn't noticed. He's too busy squeezing the life from my body, so he doesn't see me lift it and drag the sharp point swiftly across his hand.

He yells, stumbling back, as blood pours from the wound.

I don't hesitate.

I don't stop to think.

It's kill or be killed.

Adrenaline, instinct, and the will to survive drive me forward, and I do what needs to be done.

Launching myself at him, I bury the letter opener in the side of his neck, shoving it to the hilt. It goes in a lot easier than I imagined. Blood sprays from the wound, hitting me in the face, and I know I have hit an artery.

His eyes pop wide as he staggers back, his legs going out from under him. He collapses flat on his back on the carpeted floor, making a strange gurgling sound. Blood leaks from his neck and spills from his mouth as I stand frozen in place, my entire body trembling as I hold a shaky hand over my lips. I see the moment the light dies in his eyes, and his body stops twitching.

Oh my God. I killed him. I just killed a man.

It seems like barely any time has passed, but time has lost all meaning as I stand rooted to the spot, numb with shock. I stare at the dead man with my letter opener stuck in his neck, shaking uncontrollably until I push through the fog in my brain and spring into action.

Rowan!

What if they have gone after him too? I know this is no random attack. Ben was worried this week for a reason, and it's obvious this is connected. The dead guy must be Russian, and whatever beef he had with them still exists. I curse myself for not demanding Ben tell me more, and I make a silent promise to get answers from him.

But it can wait. Right now, I need to make sure our son is safe.

Racing out to the hall, I drop to my knees beside Alesso. I'm panting heavily as I press a finger to the pulse in his neck, emitting a cry of relief when I feel the steady vibration under his skin. I look up, grateful Wednesdays are usually quiet at the center and that it's the manager's day off.

Dragging Alesso into my room by his feet, I lock the door, praying to every deity known to mankind that he wakes up soon. I need him. Flinging papers off my desk, I find my cell and dial Frank's number with shaky hands. He answers immediately and I almost cry in relief. "Where's Rowan?" I shout. "Is he safe? Do you have eyes on him right now?"

"He's in class." I hear the confusion and concern in his tone. "He's safe. I'm looking at him right now. What's going on, Sierra? Where's Alessandro?"

"I don't have time to explain. I just need you to take Rowan out of class right now and drive him to my parents' house." I'm not risking going home. If they know where I work, they know where I live. Dad has a security firm on speed dial, and the house is like Fort Knox. It's the safest place I can think of. "I was attacked, but I'm okay. They drugged Alesso, but he has a pulse. I'm going to call Ben now, but I need you to keep our son safe. Please, Frank. Don't let anything happen to him."

"I will protect your son with my life, Sierra. I promise you that. Ian is here, and we won't let anyone harm him. Call Ben and hold tight until he sends reinforcements. Call me back if you need me."

I hang up without a goodbye, instantly pressing Ben's number. I have never called him before, and I don't know how easy he is to get a hold of. All our arrangements are usually done by text or prearranged the previous week. My heart is racing like a Formula 1 car as the phone rings and rings. Eventually, just before it disconnects, he picks up.

"Sierra. Is everything okay?" he asks before I have said a word.

Brief relief rushes through me when I hear his voice. In a garbled tone, I tell him what has happened.

"Are you hurt?"

"I'm fine." It's not really a lie even if my wrist is hurting, my cheek stings, and my throat feels scraped raw.

"It's going to be okay. I promise," he says in a calm voice that offers much-needed reassurance. "Do you have your gun on you?"

I nod until I remember he can't see me. "Yes. I have it."

"Get it. Keep the door locked and your gun pointed at it. Fire at anyone who enters unannounced. I am going to send men to you, and I'll contact Frank."

"If they get to Rowan, I—"

"No one is touching our son," he growls, and I hear movement in the background. His breath sounds uneven, like he might be running. Muffled conversation filters down the line as he talks to someone I can't hear. "Leo is talking to Frank," he confirms. "They are in the car en route to your parents' house. No one appears to be following them."

Air whooshes out of my mouth in grateful relief. "If anything happens to him, Ben, I will die," I sob, as tears spill out of my eyes and down my cheeks.

"Sierra. Listen to me. Rowan is safe. No one is getting past Frank and Ian. I need you to stay calm, sweetheart, until I can get help to you. Can you do that for me, Firefly?"

I nod again. "What about the dead guy?" I whisper.

"I'll handle it. Just focus on protecting yourself until Alessandro wakes or my men arrive."

A sob rips from my mouth, and I feel so cold. I think it's delayed shock. "Okay," I whisper, wishing he was here and not miles away in New York.

"Sierra," he says in a gentle tone. "You did good. You did real good, sweetheart, and you are going to be fine. So is Rowan." I don't know if he believes it or he's just saying it to stop me from losing my shit. "I am coming to take care of you. I will be there as soon as I can, and I will keep you both safe. I promise."

"Hurry," I whisper before hanging up.

Chapter 31

BEN

"THAT'S ORGANIZED. THE helicopter will be waiting for us at the airport," Leo confirms, placing his cell on the walnut table situated between us. Leaning back in the seat of the private jet, I swirl the bourbon in my glass, but I can barely stomach drinking it. I am sick with worry even though I know Sierra and Rowan are safe at her dad's place.

I got my personal plane in the air in record time, and we should arrive at the Lawson estate in less than an hour, but it'll still be almost three hours in total from the time of my call with Sierra before I reach her and Rowan. That is three hours too long. I don't know what I was thinking leaving them there after the Russians were poking around last weekend. I should have insisted they return to New York with me, but I let my reluctance to have Sierra close impair my judgment.

Never again.

I will just have to learn to control myself around her because there is no way I'm leaving my family in Chicago after this.

"Are you sure we can trust Joseph Lawson?" Leo asks, sipping slowly on his scotch. "I know you don't like him."

"I don't have to like him to trust him in this scenario, and it was my only option." It would have taken me too long to get my own crew to Chicago. I needed someone to get Sierra out of her place of work

ASAP because I didn't know if the Russians had more men outside. "This whole thing is fishy. I know the Russians are getting more organized—their successful attack on Vegas proves that—so why send in only one guy?" Lawson called me after his men picked up Sierra and Alessandro to confirm there were no other assailants found. He also arranged for removal and disposal of the dead body.

"The guy could've gone rogue."

I nod slowly. "Perhaps, but it's not their latest MO." The Bratva were notoriously disorganized until a few years ago when they started getting their shit together. They are definitely more structured now and a much bigger threat considering their numbers across the US rival ours. They snuck up on Vegas and snatched the territory right out of Salerno's hands. No one noticed anything was amiss until it was too late.

However, that doesn't mean they are a well-oiled machine and they don't still have a few loose cannons running around with their own agenda. Maybe the guy planned to take my girl and use her to gain an in with the Bratva leaders or he needed to make amends for something and she was his meal ticket? Or he was acting on orders but instructed to keep it below the radar? I don't know, and I won't rest until I find out.

"At least they don't seem to know about Rowan," Leo says.

Air expels from my mouth, and I rub the tight pain in my chest. "Thank God they haven't discovered my son; otherwise, they would have gone for him instead."

"Or targeted both of them at once, like they did with the Vegas attack," Leo says, accepting the sandwich from the flight attendant when she materializes at our side.

I dismiss her with a wave of my hand. I couldn't force a morsel down my throat right now. She offers the sandwich to Ciro who is seated in the seat behind Leo, and he accepts it with a grunt. I'm not enjoying having a new bodyguard, but I can't fault Ciro's professionalism. He's damn good at his job, but he's a surly bastard, and I miss Alessandro's easygoing manner.

I refocus on Leo. "It's not adding up, and I'd like to know how they got to Alessandro and why they only drugged him." Most mafioso would have used a silencer and put a bullet in his skull.

"He's going to be so pissed when he wakes," Leo says in between mouthfuls of his sandwich.

I nod because I have no doubt Alessandro will see this as a personal failure, and he will beat himself up over it. But that is the least of his concerns. This shouldn't have fucking happened on his watch, and I want answers as to how he let himself be drugged. Maybe I made a mistake assigning Alessandro to guard Sierra. Maybe he's having as much trouble as I am staying focused around her. The thought does nothing to quell the murderous intent swirling in my gut.

"What are you planning on doing when we get there?" he adds, stuffing the rest of his sandwich in his mouth.

"Getting my family the fuck out of Chicago," I snap. My patience is in limited supply, and I have no time for stupid questions.

"Woah." Leo holds up one hand. "I know you're mad. I'm furious too, but I'm trying to help. We'll find the bastards and make them pay."

"I never should have left them in Chicago. I should have taken them to Greenwich last weekend—even if I had to drag Sierra kicking and screaming."

"It's not your fault." Leo leans forward, uncapping a bottle of water. "You got the intel from those Russian scum on Saturday night, and we took care of their base. You couldn't have known there were more of them hanging around or that someone went rogue. He must have spotted you with Sierra outside the hotel and decided to target her."

"I am going to find every last one of those scumbags and hang them by their entrails until they bleed out." I crack my knuckles as a red haze coats my eyes. "No one fucks with my girl and gets away with it."

Leo's lips twitch.

"What?"

"It's just nice to hear you acknowledging it."

I realize what I said. "Stop. I don't have time for this now." I scrub my hands down my face, stifling a yawn. I have barely had any sleep the past few days, working around the clock with Gifoli and The Outfit to hunt down the rest of the Russians, to ensure the city was safe. I would have stayed in Chicago if I didn't have pressing business in New York. It's a miracle I'm even able to stand, but the need to protect my family is driving me forward. I just want to take Sierra and Rowan and hole up in my house for a few days.

Leo wisely drops the subject. "You'll have to admit the truth to Lawson, if he hasn't already guessed."

I unbutton the top button of my shirt and loosen my tie—I feel like it's choking me today. "I know. He was peppering me with questions on the phone, and I told him we'd speak when I arrive. I messaged Sierra, telling her to say nothing. She has been through enough trauma today without being the one to break the news to her father. I want to be there with her when her family finds out."

Her father has always been a prick to her, and I don't want him mouthing off at Sierra when I'm not there to protect her. I have no clue how Joseph Lawson will react when he discovers I am Rowan's father. He was civil and respectful to me at the gala event, with no hint of the derision he used to hold for me in evidence, but the man is a master manipulator, and who's to say it wasn't all an act? Gifoli would have told him who I am, and he isn't stupid. He has provided a service to The Outfit for long enough to know how things happen in mafia circles. He would know to disrespect me places a target on his head and his family by default. So, he could have been playing an expected part.

"He's a conniving cunt," Leo says, gulping back water. "He will try to use this to his advantage."

"He can try, but I'm not the same man he remembers. He can't shout insults or push me around like he once tried to. I have little love for the man, and Sierra doesn't either. Only the fact he is Rowan's grandfather will protect him."

The plane lands, and we hop on board the helicopter, staying silent as we travel toward the Lawson family estate. I didn't mention we would be landing on his front lawn when I spoke to Joseph, but if he's got a problem with it, I'll be glad to take all my pent-up aggression out on his face.

We arrive fifteen minutes later, jumping out of the helicopter when the pilot confirms it is safe and racing across the lawn toward the open front door. A bunch of expensive cars are parked outside, confirming the rest of the Lawson family is here.

This should be fun.

I cannot wait to wipe the smug expression off Saskia's face for good—to finally put her in her place. She will be spitting blood when she discovers I am Rowan's father, and that's not even the full extent of it.

"Bennett." Joseph Lawson slaps me on the back as he greets me at the front door. "Thanks for coming." He nods at Leo and Ciro, stepping aside to let us inside. "Everyone is in the family room," he says, ushering us into the house.

Leo looks around with his eyes out on stalks, and I get it. The house is impressive, but I always thought it was stuffy with its polished marble floors, glistening chandeliers, ornate furniture, expensive oil paintings, and the pillars and columns that give it an ancient European vibe. My Greenwich home couldn't be more different with its comfortable furniture and modern aesthetics, but it feels like more of a home than this place.

"Ben!" Sierra jumps up the second I enter the room, and we

rush toward one another. She throws herself at me, and my arms automatically lock around her trembling body. "I'm so glad you're here."

"I wouldn't be anywhere else." Being extra careful, I tilt her head up so I can get a proper look at her. I frown when I spot the raised gash on her left cheek. The wound has been cleaned and someone applied ointment, but I wonder if it might need stitches. The thought of her beautiful face being permanently marked doesn't sit well with me. "You said you weren't hurt." I drill her with a look as I gingerly lift her bandaged right hand and glare at the faint bruising forming around her neck.

"I'm okay," she says. "It's not broken."

Anger plows through me at an unprecedented rate, and I wish I could resurrect the bastard who did this to her and kill him slowly and painfully so he understands what happens to any man who dares to hurt my woman. But Sierra needs me to be strong and supportive, so I hide my anger and the sense of helplessness I feel and concentrate on being the man she needs me to be. I hug her closer, careful not to squeeze too tight in case she is hurting anyplace else. I just want to get her home and get her checked out by my doctor to ensure there is no permanent damage.

"What the fuck is going on here?" Saskia barks, and my eyes scan the room for the first time.

I didn't notice anyone else when I first arrived. My eyes latched on to Sierra, and she was all I saw.

"Saskia, please watch your language," Georgia Lawson says, approaching me with a smile. "Forgive our eldest daughter, Bennett. It's good to see you again so soon although I wish it were under different circumstances."

Judging by Saskia's reaction and the quizzical expressions on everyone else's faces, it appears Lawson obeyed my instruction to keep my impending arrival a secret. I knew if he announced I was en route Sierra would be fielding questions alone. It's good to know Lawson respects my commands, but I still don't trust him.

Georgia's troubled eyes move to her youngest daughter. She is clearly concerned. Sierra is still pressed against my body, her slim arms wrapped around me, and I dare anyone to pry her from me.

"Where is Rowan?" I ask, my eyes dancing over everyone else and not seeing him. Gifoli is here with Serena, but I don't see their kids in the room either. Felix is here too, with his arm flung possessively over a scowling Saskia. He was pretty standoffish with me last weekend, and I'm guessing he is familiar with our history. If he knew I had no interest in his wife, either years ago or now, maybe he would loosen up. Though I doubt it. Being married to Saskia is akin to wearing a permanent chastity belt—she has his balls locked up securely in every sense of the word.

"Ben!" A familiar cute voice screams from someplace behind me, and I turn Sierra and me as one, watching our son racing across the room toward us. A dark-haired girl and boy stand in the doorway, eyeing me with curiosity, and I'm guessing they are the Gifoli sister and brother.

"Hey there, buddy," I say, the knots in my chest easing when he reaches me. Bending down, I lift him up with one arm, holding both of them close to me.

"Mommy. Ben is here, and it's not even the weekend." Rowan grins, leaning across my chest to kiss Sierra on the lips, and it's the sweetest thing ever. My heart swells, and I think I'm already a lost cause when it comes to these two.

"Oh my God," Serena exclaims, and I look over at her. Her gaze bounces from me to Rowan, and I can tell she has made the connection. Her eyes are bugging out of her head, and shock is splayed across her face.

"Don't say—" Sierra starts to speak, to warn Serena not to say anything in front of Rowan, I'm guessing, when she is rudely cut off by the bitch I once dated.

"No fucking way! *You're* Rowan's father?" Saskia yells, pushing her husband away and stalking toward us.

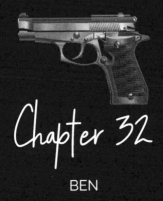

Chapter 32

BEN

Sɪᴇʀʀᴀ ᴀɴᴅ I look at Rowan at the same time, and his adorable little face is scrunched in confusion.

Fuck Saskia.

I didn't want to do this today. I was going to ask Sierra if we could tell him soon but only once they were settled in my home, *their* home, and Rowan was ready to hear the news.

But, of course, Saskia has to try to make this about her.

Sierra pulls away from me, straightening up to confront her sister, but I'm not letting her get far. I reposition us so we are standing side by side, holding Rowan on my hip on one side and circling my arm around Sierra on the other. We present a united front as a clearly angry Saskia storms right up to us. I watch our son carefully, holding him tighter while I press a kiss to his cheek. "It's okay, Rowan," I whisper in his ear. "We will explain everything soon."

He looks into my eyes, and I want to murder Saskia when I see the lost look on his face. He doesn't know what is going on, and he is scared and confused.

"Yes, Ben is Rowan's father," Sierra says through gritted teeth as Saskia comes to a halt in front of her. If it wasn't obvious before that Saskia is jealous of her little sister, it is painfully obvious now. "And that is something we wanted to tell Rowan together, privately, when the time is right. I can tolerate you being nasty to me, but you will not hurt Rowan. Why does everything always have to be about you?"

"Because this *is* about me!" she shouts, and I rub Rowan's back as he flinches in my arms.

I want to get him out of here before he is even more traumatized. "This has nothing to do with you," I coldly tell her. "And lower your voice. You're upsetting our son."

She waves one bony finger in my direction, and her nostrils flare as steam practically billows from her ears. The skin on her forehead and across her cheekbones is stretched so tight it looks like it might split. Anyone contemplating cosmetic surgery should take one look at Saskia Barretta's face and reconsider. "Sierra has always wanted everything I had, and that includes you!" she screeches, ignoring my warning and shrieking like a banshee.

"You were never good enough for him," Sierra says, and although her voice is calm, I can tell she's angry and ready to explode. "And you couldn't have been too heartbroken if you married Felix six months later."

"That was—"

"That's enough, Saskia," Joseph Lawson cuts in, pinning his eldest daughter with a ferocious look, before he turns to her husband. "Control your wife before she says something she regrets."

A loud slap rings out around the room, and my head whips back to Sierra. She's cupping her injured cheek with her hand, and Saskia's slap has reopened the cut. Blood trickles down her face, startling Rowan.

"Mommy!" he cries, stretching his arms out, reaching for her.

Quietly, I hand Rowan to Sierra and spin around, grabbing Saskia by the neck. Everything I have been keeping locked up inside ruptures as I tilt her head back and glare at her. My voice is low but deadly and dripping in menace because I want her to get the message loud and clear. "If you ever touch my fiancée again, I will kill you. The same thing goes for my son." I tighten my grip around her neck as I notice Joseph Lawson restraining an enraged Felix Barretta, whispering something in his ear.

"Ben." Sierra places her hand on my lower back. "Rowan is frightened," she quietly adds, and I hear her underlying warning.

That is the only thing she could say to force me to back down. Reluctantly, I let Saskia go, shoving her back at her husband as Lawson releases him. I look down, and my heart hurts when I see Rowan with his face buried in Sierra's shoulder, sobbing uncontrollably. His small arms and legs are wrapped around her, and his little body heaves.

I'm glad he is facing away so he didn't see me almost strangling his aunt. I need to rein in my anger for my son's sake. I want to be the one to console him, but I'm not sure he wants me anywhere near him right now. He is scared and confused, and Sierra is his comfort blanket, so I need to let her look after him while I deal with everything else.

Fuck that bitch Saskia. This is all her fault. I swing bloodthirsty eyes in her direction, wishing I could teach her a lesson. She is lucky, because I'm pretty sure my son just saved her life.

I lower my voice so little ears can't hear. "Just so we're clear, Saskia, I never cared about you. I'd just lost my mom and my college dreams when we met. I was lost, and you plucked me up like I was some project. A fixer-upper. If I hadn't been broken, I never would have lasted longer than one date because you remain, to this day, the most selfish self-absorbed cruel evil bitch to ever walk the planet." I rake my gaze up and down her body in a deliberately derisory fashion. "I walked away from you that day, and I never gave you a second thought." It's the truth. She wasn't in any way memorable, and I never wondered about her over the years like I wondered about Sierra.

"Sierra is worth a million of you," I continue, sliding my arm around Sierra's waist again. "And she is going to be my wife." Technically, I haven't asked Sierra yet, but—like she'd say—that's only semantics. It's going to happen and soon if I have my way. "That has absolutely nothing to do with you and everything to do with her being the most amazing woman, the most incredible mother, and the woman I choose to be by my side."

"She tricked you!" Saskia cries, swiping at the angry tears rolling down her face. "That's the only explanation that makes sense," she adds, proving she is clearly delusional and suffering from hearing loss. Everything I just said went in one ear and out the next. There is no speaking to the witch.

Felix eyes me coldly, as if this is my fault. What a pussy. Saskia must be walking rings around him if he can't see what is staring him in the face. He needs to man up and put that stupid bitch in a muzzle where she belongs.

"Remove your wife from the room before she embarrasses herself further," Lawson says, drilling Saskia with a look I can't decipher. Felix throws a belligerent Saskia over his shoulder, and she's crying and screaming abuse as they exit the room.

241

"I apologize," Lawson says to me, sidling up to his wife and wrapping his arm around her so they are almost mirroring our position. "Saskia has a dramatic side we could never quite stamp out."

Sierra rolls her eyes, but she says nothing, focusing on Rowan as she smooths a hand up and down his back and whispers soothing words in his ear.

Lawson puffs out his chest, preening like a peacock. "It would have been nice to do things the traditional way, but I'm willing to overlook it considering you are finally willing to make an honest woman of Sierra."

Pompous ass.

Sierra opens her mouth to speak, but I silence her with a subtle shake of my head. I want her to let me handle this while she comforts our son. "I might not have been there for them at the start, but I'm here now, and I'm going nowhere. Sierra and Rowan are my responsibility, and I will take care of them." Swallowing the surge of internal fear that has risen to the fore, I say, "I will love and protect both of them until the day I die."

Georgia Lawson holds a hand over her mouth as her eyes turn glassy. "This is wonderful news," she adds a few seconds later when she has composed herself. "Just wonderful."

I'm half-expecting Sierra to jump in and confirm nothing is settled, but she's either as anxious as me to get out of here, more worried about Rowan, or just shell-shocked after the day from hell and too tired to protest.

Serena steps in front of us, beaming with genuine happiness. Sierra mentioned they had grown closer over the years and that Serena helped her a lot when Rowan was a baby. I'm glad she has one selfless sister she can rely on. Gifoli is nowhere to be seen, so I figure he took his kids out of the room when Saskia started throwing a hissy fit. "I'm so happy for you, Sierra. You too, Ben." Her eyes soften when she looks at Rowan. "This is the best news for Rowan." Leaning in, she kisses the back of his dark head. "He's such a beautiful boy and such a happy child."

"He is," I say, pride suffusing my tone. "And that is all due to Sierra. She has loved and cared for him in a way I appreciate, adore, and can only envy."

Not that I'm envious of my child or begrudge him his happy childhood. It's more that he has caused me to reflect on my own unhappy childhood lately, and I've been a little melancholy. I have also found myself looking back at my childhood with a slightly different lens, remembering the happy times I shared with Mom, before everything turned to shit, because it wasn't all bad even though most of the dark memories have snuffed out the happy ones.

Rowan has stopped crying now, and while he is still cradled in Sierra's arms, his head is angled, and he's watching me closely.

"You hanging in there, buddy?" I ask, concern overriding every other emotion.

He nods, and I see the same turmoil on his face. We need to get out of here so we can get him settled and talk to him. I don't want him going to sleep upset or worried. I lock eyes with Sierra. "We should go."

"There is no rush," Lawson says. "We have plenty of room and the means to protect you. Besides, your man is still out cold."

"Not anymore," Leo says, appearing in the doorway with a drowsy-looking Alessandro. I didn't even notice Leo had slipped out of the room. Ciro is positioned by the door, wearing his usual dour expression, his arms folded across his bulky chest. Frank and Ian hang back in the hallway, and I spot the duffel bags at their feet.

I had messaged Frank when we were in the air to pack a bag for Sierra and Rowan. I can send my movers to pack up and ship the rest of their things, but I didn't want to organize that without talking to Sierra. She will most likely argue. Though I don't want to force her hand, she *will* be moving to Greenwich with me. There is no way I'm leaving her here in Chicago while the Russians pose such a huge threat.

"I want to go," Sierra says, surprising me. "I'm grateful for all your help today." Her eyes flit between her parents. "Both of you, but I need to think of what's best for Rowan, and right now, that is being with Ben." I shouldn't be surprised she is placing his needs, and his safety, above her own because I've seen her do that time and time again.

"Of course, darling." Georgia Lawson walks over to us, circling her arms around Sierra and pressing a kiss to her brow and Rowan's. She pats my arm. "Take care of my daughter and my grandson."

"I will guard them with my life."

"See that you do," Lawson says, coming up alongside his wife. "I know you are keen to get away, so I won't hold you up, but you and I need to meet. We have a few things to discuss. Perhaps I can come visit once Sierra and Rowan are settled."

I nod even though I want to rip him a new one. He's more

concerned with getting answers and finding out how this will work to his advantage than ensuring his flesh and blood are safe. I won't be letting him come anywhere near my Greenwich home. Its existence is a heavily guarded secret for a reason. As far as the Lawsons are concerned, they will be told Sierra and Rowan are staying at my New York penthouse, and Lawson can come to my office at the Caltimore Holdings building if he wants to talk.

"Call me," Serena says, hugging her sister.

"I promise I will." Sierra holds Rowan tightly against her upper torso as I usher them out of the room.

"Are you okay?" I ask Alessandro, working hard not to punch him for his stupidity. Hauling him over the coals can wait but not for long. I want to find out how this happened so I can punish those responsible.

"I'm fine," he slurs, as Leo props him up. "Are you okay?" He fixes Sierra with worried eyes.

She nods. "I'm good. We can talk when the drugs are fully out of your system. You should sleep," she adds because she's a much nicer person than me.

"Good. Let's get the fuck out of here," I tell everyone.

Frank takes a hold of Alessandro's other arm, and between him and his brother, they walk him out. Ian and Ciro silently follow them.

"Where are we going?" Sierra quietly asks as we walk along the hallway, trailing my men. I still have my arm around her while she's holding Rowan.

"To my home in Greenwich, Connecticut," I whisper in her ear.

"Okay."

I glance at her with arched brows, thinking it can't be that easy.

"Don't look so surprised. You know I always prioritize Rowan's needs, and right now, getting out of Chicago is what's best." A violent shudder works through her, and her body trembles against my side. She is scared too. That much is obvious, and no one would blame her after the ordeal she endured today. I never want her to be in a position like that ever again.

"I couldn't agree more." I hold my family close as I walk them out the front door, eager to escape Chicago as fast as humanly possible.

Chapter 33

BEN

ROWAN IS FAST asleep in Sierra's arms as we exit the elevator, entering the hallway of my penthouse apartment in Manhattan. It's too late to travel to Greenwich tonight, so we will sleep here, and I will drive with them to Connecticut tomorrow.

"Where can I put him?" Sierra whispers, stifling a yawn as we step into my open-plan living space.

"Follow me," I whisper, gesturing to Alessandro and Leo to take a seat on one of the couches. I need to have a word with them before they retire to their apartments for the night. I already excused Ciro, and he went directly to his apartment without question.

Owning the building means I was able to reserve the top five floors for my personal use before the realtor sold the rest of the development a few years ago. We have our own elevator and rear entrance from the parking lot so we maintain complete privacy. The rules are clear— no one entertains guests unless they have been previously approved. Safety is key, and it's important we don't give our enemies easy access to attack us. It's one of the reasons why I have never brought a woman here or to my house. Why I always met my fuck buddies at hotels. It's also one of the reasons why I had a small pool of women to call on when I needed sex. Trust is difficult when you're in my line of work.

Guarding my reputation is also of paramount importance, and all my soldiers represent me through their actions and their words, so I expect them to be above reproach. Alessandro and Leo have their own apartments, and we have a bunch of guest apartments that are rotated among other soldiers as the need arises. Sometimes, visiting members of *la famiglia* stay here.

Sierra follows me up the stairs to the second level where the three bedrooms are. I open the door to the middle bedroom and stride across the room, peeling the comforter back so she can lay our son down. He barely stirs, exhausted from the day. We haven't had a chance to talk to him yet because it was too noisy in the helicopter and he fell asleep almost instantly when we were on the plane, but it will be the first thing we attend to in the morning.

Sierra removes his sneakers and carefully maneuvers his hoodie off, leaving him in his long-sleeved shirt and sweatpants. She tucks the covers over him, as he snuggles down into the bed, before pressing a soft kiss to his cheek. I lean down, softly brushing his dark hair away from his forehead, before kissing his warm skin. My hand curls around Sierra's as we stand beside the bed, staring silently at our son as he sleeps. The steady rise and fall of his chest is comforting because I know how close I could have come to losing both of them today.

We walk hand in hand out of the bedroom, and I love that Sierra is leaning on me instead of pushing me away. I don't know what the future holds for us, but tonight, she needs me, and I want to be there for her.

"The doc is here," Leo tells me when our feet hit the lower level. "I put him in your study."

"Can I get you something to eat or drink?" Alessandro asks, looking more alert. He slept the entire plane journey and the car ride here, so I'm hoping it means most of the drugs have left his system by now.

"Order food," I say when Sierra's stomach rumbles. I doubt she has eaten much all day. I know I haven't, and I'm suddenly ravenous. "And I want the doc to check you out when he's finished with Sierra," I add.

"Sure thing, boss."

Placing my hand on Sierra's lower back, I guide her across the full length of my living area toward my study.

"Your apartment is beautiful," she says, drinking everything in as we walk.

I had an interior decorator design and furnish the place. It's largely monochrome with the odd splash of color on a painting or a rug or the cushions on the couch. The space is more clinical and less homey than my house, but that's on purpose. I stay in the city during the week to be near work, and my apartment is mainly a place to rest my head at night. I don't even eat here most nights, choosing to dine out instead. I wanted something stylish yet practical, and it suits my needs perfectly.

"I'm betting the view is stunning in daylight," she adds, staring at the successive floor-to-ceiling windows that run the full length of the apartment at this level.

"It is," I admit, steering her over to the right, to where my study is enclosed behind the large white and gray kitchen. "If it's not too cold in the morning, we can eat breakfast on the terrace."

I also want to show Rowan the rooftop terrace because you can see for miles across the city and I have something up there he will be excited to see. If he hadn't fallen asleep, I would have taken him up there tonight to watch the stars through my new telescope. I purchased it and one for the Greenwich house after our conversation last Sunday. I had hoped one day to watch the *Skywatch Weekly* show with my son in person, and it seems like I will now get my wish much earlier than anticipated.

We enter my study, and I make introductions, staying with Sierra as my personal doctor attends to her injuries. Using steady, skillful fingers, he applies a line of small paper stitches to the gash in her cheek and examines her wrist, to double-check it's not broken, before wrapping it in a soft brace. With deliberate tenderness, he probes her bruised throat for permanent damage. Sierra winces, confirming her neck is sore, and I stuff my clenched fists in my pocket. I attempt to cage the fury swirling through my veins because I don't want to spook Sierra, but it's not easy.

I will murder any asshole who dares to lay a finger on her without stopping to think about it.

No one is hurting her again on my watch.

I make my other request, expecting Sierra to vehemently argue with me, but she agrees to the procedure. I take her palm in mine, letting her squeeze my fingers until it feels like there is no blood circulating in my hand while the doc inserts the chip in her upper arm. "We need to implant one in Rowan too," I add, kissing her cheek as the doc wipes her arm with rubbing alcohol and applies a soft circular bandage.

"Can you do that while he's asleep?" Sierra inquires.

"I could inject a mild sedative first," the doc suggests, "to ensure he doesn't wake and then perform the procedure."

Sierra's brow's knit together. "I don't like the idea of giving him a sedative." I'm not surprised to hear that, given what Sierra does for a living. She looks up at me. "Could we wait and do it another time, when he's awake?"

I don't want to delay implanting the tracking device in our son, because it's added protection, but I don't like the idea of injecting him with a sedative either. "Could you come back in the morning?" I ask the doc.

"Of course. I am at your disposal." I'm glad to hear it. I pay him a massive retainer and huge on-call fees so he's immediately available to me.

I call Alessandro in next, and Sierra leaves to check on Rowan. I wait as the doc examines him and asks him a few questions. He takes a blood sample for testing, but he's unsure if there will be any evidence of the drug left in his blood stream. His guess is Alessandro's coffee was spiked with Rohypnol, which can be fatal if too strong of a dose is administered. Sierra mentioned she believed her tea had been drugged, and I'm so fucking glad she didn't drink it. If the dose Alessandro was given knocked him out for hours, who is to tell what it might have done to my Firefly. She could have been killed.

Our food has arrived by the time the doc leaves, so we sit at the dining table and chow down. No one speaks. All of us are too hungry to do anything but eat.

After, we move over to the seated area, and I pull Sierra down on the leather couch alongside me, circling my arm around her shoulder and tucking her into my side. Leo and Alessandro sit on the couch opposite us, the latter sitting stiffly, looking rigid with stress.

"How did this happen?" I ask, working hard to keep my tone neutral.

"They must have gotten to the new receptionist," Alessandro says. "She has been buying us drinks all week, so I didn't suspect anything."

"I'm glad I forgot about my tea," Sierra says, placing her small hand on my thigh while she snuggles in close to me.

"What do you know about her?" I ask, peering into her tired green eyes.

"Not a lot. The manager hired her. She's a few years younger than me. Degree educated. She was having a hard time getting the hang of the job, but now I'm wondering if that's because she was a plant with no skills suitable to the position."

"I will have Phillip pull up everything we can on her. Your father said she wasn't in the building when he arrived, so she's most likely on the run already."

"What about the manager?" Leo asks. "And other staff members? She might not have been acting alone."

"She's a stickler for the rules and completely honest," Sierra explains. "There is no way she is involved with the Russian mafia. The other therapists have all worked at the center for years, and I doubt they are involved either. There were only two other therapists, me, and Lucille in the building yesterday."

"We will check them all out," Leo says.

"I want the receptionist found. Alive," I add.

At least for now.

If I find out she conspired to drug my fiancée, I can't guarantee her survival. I'm enraged and itching to make someone else pay.

Sierra stiffens against me, and I know she wouldn't be down for that plan. "I want to talk to her myself," I say.

"I'm very sorry, Sierra," Alessandro says.

"It's not your fault." She is quick to reassure him, and a surge of jealousy slaps me in the face. I know Sierra isn't interested in Alessandro like that. They are friends, and I'm being ridiculous. I know I'm acting like a moody possessive teenager, but I can't help how I feel.

She is mine.

Mine.

"It's my job to protect you, and accepting drinks from strangers is sloppy," he tells her. "I know better."

"You do." I drill him with a look, but I don't rip him a new one. Not in front of Sierra. He nods, understanding fully that he messed up.

Sierra yawns, and I press a kiss into her hair while maintaining eye contact with Alessandro. "It's been a long day. Get some rest. We'll talk more tomorrow."

Both guys stand.

"I want a quick word, Leo," I say, hauling Sierra to her feet. Leo flops back on the couch while Alessandro walks to the elevator. Gently, I palm Sierra's uninjured cheek. "Alessandro put your bag in my room already, but if you'd prefer to stay with Rowan or in the other bedroom, that's your choice."

She places one hand on my chest, staring me straight in the eye. "I don't want to be alone tonight."

Thank fuck for that because I need to keep her close. To remind myself she's safe. I nearly lost her today, and it's put a lot of things into perspective for me. I brush my lips against hers, uncaring that Leo is here. "I will be up in a few minutes."

"Good night, Leo," she says, clamping a hand over her mouth to stifle another yawn as she walks off.

"I'm glad you're okay," Leo says, and she smiles before grabbing hold of the glass bannisters. "See you in the morning," he adds, and she nods. I watch her walk up the stairs and disappear into my room before I reclaim my seat.

A shuddering breath escapes my mouth as I lean forward on my elbows, running one hand through my hair.

"You look beat," Leo says.

"I am," I truthfully admit. Lack of sleep is catching up to me. "It's been one hell of a day."

"What time do you want to head out tomorrow?"

"Before lunch to beat the traffic, but it will depend on when Rowan and Sierra wake. I don't want to rush either of them. They've had a traumatic day."

"I'll ensure everything is ready to go, and I'll touch base with Phillip first thing."

I already called my IT guru when we were en route to Chicago and got him to pull up the employee listing for the center. I knew someone who worked there was involved, so Phillip is already looking into everyone. "Call him now and ask him to prioritize Lucille. We need to find her." Hopefully, Phillip will have background information tomorrow so we can narrow her whereabouts down.

"Consider it done, boss."

"One other thing. I need you to accelerate finding a property for Saverio and Anais."

He nods. "I'll consider it a priority. Until then, why don't we move them to the west wing of the house?"

The last place I wanted to take Salerno and his daughter was my house, my own personal refuge, but he called in his favor, and I had no choice. He was badly injured in the attack on Vegas and lucky he got out of there with his life. As far as we know, the Russians are still after them. As long as Salerno is alive, their hold on Vegas is not guaranteed, so the threat to his life is considerable. I couldn't turn him away in his time of need, so Leo drove him, Anais, and a couple of their soldiers—all with blindfolds on—to Greenwich in the dead of night. All the staff has been sworn to secrecy so no one reveals the location.

I had put them in the east wing so Angelo could keep an eye on them while I'm not there during the week, but housing Sierra and Rowan with them is not a good idea. There is no love lost between her and Salerno, and I want him nowhere near my future wife. I haven't forgotten how much he wanted her.

Having them in my house is not ideal—at all—and it was only meant to be temporary while Salerno healed and we identified a secure house to move them to. Their remaining men are scattered across a few different safe houses, and the plan is to find one large property where they can all regroup and we can plan retaliation.

Now my priorities have changed, and I need to get them out of my house ASAP. Until then, I want them kept far away from Sierra and Rowan. If she knew they were there, she would resist moving in, and I can't let them fuck this up for me.

"Ask Natalia to make it happen." I called my sister earlier, and she immediately dropped everything to go to my house. I had a list of things I wanted her to set up for me, and she didn't hesitate to offer her help.

Leo sees himself out, and I grab a few bottles of water from the refrigerator before switching off the lights and heading upstairs. I set one bottle down on the bedside table in Rowan's room, kissing his brow and watching his breathing for a few minutes to reassure myself he is okay, before I pad out of the room and into the master suite.

Sierra is already in bed, but she's not sleeping. She is sitting upright against the headrest tapping out a message on her phone. "Is everything okay?" I ask, tugging my shirt from my pants.

"I'm just updating Esme and Pen. The news is all over Glencoe, and they were worried about me."

"Don't tell them about the Greenwich house," I say, perching on the side of the bed beside her as I unbutton my shirt.

She frowns. "Why not?"

"I don't want anyone to know you and Rowan are there. As far as family and friends are concerned, you are both living here. Until we figure this out, keeping our location a secret is critical. Besides, no one knows where my house is. I have gone to great lengths to keep it hidden, and I'd like to keep it that way." I remove my shoes and socks, digging my toes into the soft plush gray carpet.

"How bad is this, Ben? And please don't lie to me."

I take her hand in mine when she sets her phone on the bed. "I won't lie to you, Sierra. I will tell you anything you need to know, but is this really what you want to discuss now?" I tuck her hair behind her ear. "I'm not deflecting. You've been through a lot today. Let's just sleep, and when you and Rowan are settled into the house tomorrow, we can talk."

She nods slowly. "I thought I could keep myself removed from what you do, but I realize now how stupid and naïve that was."

"I understand, and honestly, I would rather you didn't know too much, but shielding you by keeping you in the dark was a foolish plan. You don't need to know everything, but you need to know enough to understand the risks. Maybe if I had told you about the Russian threat and what has happened in Vegas, you might have been more suspicious, and you might have guessed what Lucille was up to."

"It's doubtful," she says, "but knowledge is power, and I can't protect myself and Rowan if I don't know the basics."

"I agree."

She smiles. "Look how far we have come."

I lean in and kiss her, just because I feel like it. This kiss is tender, unlike any kiss we have shared before, but I can't be rough with her today. Not after the things she has endured. "Hold that thought," I whisper over her lips. "I need to grab a shower." I stand, battling a yawn.

"Esme and Pen are going to my house tomorrow to pack up more of our stuff," she says, her eyes widening as I remove my dress shirt. Her eyes follow a path from my shoulders, down over my chest, and along my abs. Two rosy dots stain her cheeks as her eyes latch on to the line of dark hair leading into my pants and the obvious swelling of my cock behind my zipper.

It's on the tip of my tongue to say something dirty, but I won't make tonight about sex. Clearing my throat, I fight a smirk as she whips her head up to my face, her cheeks staining a darker shade of red. "Just let me know when they are ready, and I'll send a van to pick everything up," I say.

"I'm not packing up everything," she supplies. "And I'm not saying this is a permanent arrangement either."

"Whatever you say." I let my smirk loose. She can act delusional if she wants. I'll give her that tonight.

She purses her lips and narrows her eyes. "I thought you were taking a shower."

"In a rush to get rid of me now?" I ask, removing my belt and unbuttoning my pants. I let them fall to my feet, enjoying the shocked gasp that escapes her lush lips.

"I'm tired," she blurts, working hard to avoid ogling me as I finish removing my pants, standing before her in tight black boxers that do nothing to hide my semi.

"I won't be long," I say, shoving my boxers down my legs before taking them off and scooping up my clothes.

A red flush creeps up her neck and onto her face as I walk off, flashing my bare ass at her. I would love nothing more than to bury myself balls deep inside her tonight, but I won't push her into anything until she is fully in control of her faculties and I know she wants me as much as I want her.

All I know with surety is that I'm done fighting my feelings for her. I can't deny it any longer, and after today, I don't want to. I nearly lost her, and it has put a lot of things into perspective for me. Allowing myself to go there might make me weak, but I no longer have a choice.

Sierra might believe my suggestion of marriage is one of convenience, but I'm about to show her that is very far from the truth.

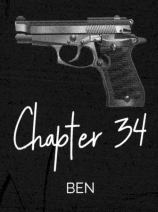

Chapter 34

BEN

I TAKE THE quickest shower known to mankind, careful not to get my hair wet, and I brush my teeth before pulling on sleep pants and exiting the bathroom. I usually sleep in the nude, but I don't trust myself to get into bed naked with Sierra. My lust for her is at an all-time high. Combined with the fact I haven't gotten laid in months, I doubt I could stop my dick from driving inside her. I don't want her thinking I would take advantage of the situation.

When we fuck, I want it to be consensual and because we can't keep our hands off one another.

Sierra is lying on her back in the bed, staring up at the ceiling. The only illumination in the room is from the lamps on the bedside tables by my king-sized bed. Rolling back the thick comforter, I climb into the bed, moving closer to her but still maintaining a distance. Today has been stressful, and while I don't like reminding her, I need to ensure she is okay. I cough, and she tilts her head in my direction. "You killed someone today. I know that's a big deal. How are you coping?" I vividly recall my first kill and remember how it had a profound effect on me.

"Honestly?" She stares me dead in the eye. "I'm glad I killed that fucker. He would've killed me and not lost any sleep over it, so I'm going to do the same."

That is most likely true. The man was a member of the Bratva and probably an experienced killer. I know from personal experience how it becomes routine after a while. But Sierra is an innocent, and it may come back to haunt her. I hope it doesn't because that bastard deserved to die, and she's probably done the world a favor by wiping him from existence.

She turns onto her side, and her blonde hair cascades around her face like a golden halo. She doesn't have a scrap of makeup on, and she looks beautiful. Even the line of paper stitches on her cheek can't detract from her natural beauty.

"What?" she whispers, noticing my singular attention.

"I don't think you realize how truly beautiful you are." I touch my fingers to her uninjured cheek. "You are gorgeous, Sierra. Inside and out."

She takes my hand, bringing it to her lips. Fiery tingles zip up and down my arm when she sweeps her lips across my knuckles. "I used to dream about you saying that to me."

I chuckle. "That doesn't shock or surprise me. I knew you had a little crush on me, Firefly."

"Trust me, there was nothing *little* about it." She takes my hand, holding it to her chest. She's wearing a silk and lace black camisole sleep top, that does nothing to disguise the creamy swell of her breasts, over matching black silk pants. Her heart thuds powerfully underneath our conjoined hands, and the strong rhythm reminds me of how resilient she is. She fought and killed a man today. I don't know a lot of men, let alone women, who would have fought and won in her situation.

She stares deep into my eyes, and I could stare at her stunning face all day long. But it's the raw emotion shimmering in her eyes that has snared my attention, and I couldn't look away even if I wanted to.

"I've heard it said that your life flashes before your eyes in a near-death situation," she adds, her voice quaking a little. "But that didn't happen to me. I was too busy fighting to survive. It was only afterwards, when I knew Rowan was safe and you were on your way, that it hit me like that." Her chest heaves, and she lowers my arm to my side. I move closer, placing one hand lightly on her hip, drawing her nearer.

We maintain eye contact the entire time, and I don't interrupt or coax her into continuing, happy to wait patiently for her to explain. "I realized if I had died today I would have regrets. Things I hadn't said to you that need to be said." She lifts her hand, tracing her fingers along the stubble on my chin and cheeks. Tears well in her eyes as she looks at me. "I'm sorry I kept Rowan from you, Ben. I see how amazing you are with him and how much he already loves you, and I hate that I deprived you of that."

I open my mouth to speak, but she silences me with a few well-placed fingers. "I'm not finished."

I smile, gently rubbing her hip through her pajama pants.

"I don't regret the decision I made. I did what I thought was right for my son. *Our* son. You scared me that day, Ben. What I saw in that basement dungeon scared me. I didn't want that for Rowan. I still don't, but I see now what I didn't back then. It was always inevitable, and I've made my peace with it now. Continuing to fight fate is a waste of energy, and after today, I'm done trying. To exist in this world, I need to find a way to fit in, and that is what I will do. I don't regret the decisions I made, but that doesn't mean they sat easy with me. Because they didn't, Ben."

I don't doubt it's the truth because it radiates from her like a beacon. "I thought of you every single day. It was hard not to, when I saw so much of you in Rowan, especially as he got older. And I carried the guilt of depriving you of one another around with me the entire time. I don't want you to think it was easy to deny you your son because it wasn't, even if I didn't regret my decision because it was the only decision."

I nod because I get it. I do. And I don't blame her for it anymore.

"The other thing I don't regret is that night in Vegas." Her eyes burn with a mixture of emotion. "How could I when it has given us the most precious gift?" A single tear rolls down her face. "He's a miracle. Our miracle. Every time I look at Rowan and I see parts of you and parts of me, I marvel at the wonder that is human nature."

More tears roll down her face as she cups my cheek. "I want you to know how much that night meant to me. It was the most erotic, intimate moment of my life. I have never felt as close to another soul as I did to you that night, Ben. When I look back now, I think it was obvious we were creating a new life because I *felt* it." Her hand leaves my face, moving to her heart and then her stomach. "I felt it in here and here. I know that sounds crazy, but that night was magical. I have never been like that with anyone else. Never felt the things I felt that night. I have never been as free and uninhibited to just let myself explore and feel like I did with you that night, and I can never regret it, despite how cold you were to me the next day. That night, I realized my crush wasn't just a crush. It never had been."

She lets that statement hang there for me to draw my own, obvious, conclusions. I open my mouth to speak again because I can't let that go unacknowledged, but she shakes her head, urging me to remain silent.

"I know you didn't feel the same way, and that's okay. I don't have any expectations when it comes to us, Ben. I know you want to marry me as the best way to protect me and Rowan, and I'm not going to fight you on it. I will do whatever it takes to keep Rowan safe, and I know you will too." She wipes her tears away, softly smiling. "I just wanted you to know that," she quietly adds, her voice barely louder than a whisper.

Slowly, I lower my head, my eyes dropping to her lips so she knows my intent and can stop it. She doesn't though, sighing instead when my mouth meets hers. I kiss her softly. More softly than I have ever kissed anyone. More softly than I thought I was capable of. I pour everything I'm feeling into the kiss while holding my potent lust back because lust has no place in this kiss.

She kisses me without hesitation, and the hope that has been lying dormant in my chest these past few weeks surges to the surface, buoyed by her words and her reaction. But she's been through an ordeal today, and a part of me understands that could be influencing her behavior. Reluctantly, I pull my lips back, hauling her body in flush to mine, holding her close as I dot kisses into her hair. My heart thumps to a new beat as I hold her tight, savoring the feel of her in my arms. Reveling in how right it feels.

I have never let myself get vulnerable with any woman, but Sierra gave me her truth, and I owe her mine in return. Clearing my throat, I ease out of our embrace because I want to look her in the eye when I tell her this. "I was angry when I first discovered the truth. So fucking angry and hurt, but I understand now, and I don't blame you or harbor any ill will toward you for making the decisions you have made."

Keeping one hand on her hip, I run my free hand through her silky hair. "I know you did what you did for Rowan, and it was the right call. He's amazing, Firefly. Such a happy, well-rounded kid. And yes, I know some of that is his personality, but a lot of it is thanks to you. You have always put him first. You show him unconditional love. You support him and keep him safe without clipping his wings. You are willing to sacrifice your own happiness for his. You did what my mother was never strong enough to do, and I could never hold that against you." I cup her face in my hands. "Stop feeling guilty. Forgive yourself because I have already forgiven you."

She chokes on a sob as I bring my lips to hers again, dusting light kisses along her mouth and her cheeks and her jawline.

"Do you really mean that?" she asks, as I press a kiss to the corner of her mouth. Her eyes glisten with unshed tears and naked emotion.

"I do." I stop kissing her, holding a hand to her back, drawing her close again. "There's more." Her hopeful gaze encourages me to continue. "I didn't mean a word of what I said to you the morning after our night together in Vegas." I don't really remember what I said, just that I was cold and cruel on purpose, saying the things I needed to say that would keep her away. "I deliberately pushed you away, Firefly, because I didn't want this life for you. You deserve so much more than what I can offer." A pang of guilt spreads across my chest.

"What about Saskia? Did you mean what you said at the house earlier?"

"Every word." I draw soothing circles on her back with my fingers. "Saskia means nothing to me. She never has."

"Then why did you date her?"

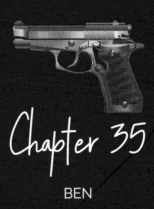

Chapter 35

I'D PREFER NOT to talk about her sister when I finally have Sierra back in my bed, but she needs to hear this. I see the vulnerability in her eyes, the doubt that still lingers there, and it needs to end now.

"I met Saskia two months after my mother OD'd," I explain. She rests her hands on my bare chest, and the warmth of her skin seeps deep into my bones, comforting me. "I was in a really bad place. I felt responsible for Mom's death because I had left for college and I didn't look back. I didn't know how bad things had gotten because I hadn't been home in over a year. If I had been there or visited more often, I might've prevented it."

"I don't know the full history, but she made her own choices, Ben. Her death isn't on you."

"I know that now, but at the time, it felt like I'd failed her. Like I ruined her life by existing and then I abandoned her. She died, and then I got kicked out of college for beating up a guy on my football team. The jerk was mouthing off about my mom, and I lost it. Beat him so bad he ended up at the hospital. My grades had slipped, and I knew I was going to lose my scholarship, so it was inevitable anyway. That was two weeks before I met Saskia. I was sleeping on Terry's couch. I had nowhere else to go. Nothing to do. Things were looking bleak."

"Who is Terry?"

"Terry Scott was one of Mom's old boyfriends. The only decent guy she dated. After they broke up, he looked out for me. He was the only role model I had in my life. He died a couple months back. That was the funeral I was attending the day I ran into Saskia and Rowan."

"I'm sorry."

"Me too. He was a good guy, and I had lost touch with him." I owed him more than biannual phone calls. Terry was a bit of a loner, and he never reached out to me, so I excused my lack of effort by claiming it was two-fold, but the truth is, I should have come back to Chicago to check up on him. I didn't even know he was sick. I might have been able to do something to help.

"You're a busy man, and friendships take work. It's one of the reasons why Esme and Pen are my only two friends. I didn't have time to cultivate more."

Because she sacrificed her friendships for Rowan.

I don't have any such noble excuse.

Anyway, we are getting off track. "The point is, Saskia came along at a time when I had nobody and nothing. I was drowning, and she threw me a life jacket. I put up with her shit because it was better than being alone. She helped me to get a job at a local bar, furnished the small studio apartment I rented, and she lavished me with gifts." My hand stalls on her back. "It wasn't my finest moment, and I'm not proud of myself. I was little more than a glorified prostitute. Without the sex," I add, reminding her I never fucked her sister.

"Don't say that. You were grieving and lost, and she most likely took advantage of that."

"I don't know what she got out of it, but by the end, I could hardly tolerate her. That final night, after the things she said to you, I knew I was done. I broke things off with her, and the sense of relief was enormous."

"Is that why you disappeared?"

"Not really."

She arches a brow while fighting another yawn. Her natural curiosity battles exhaustion, but I know this isn't the time for that conversation.

"It coincided with my real father showing up, but that's a long story and one best kept for tomorrow." I kiss the tip of her nose. "The most important thing you need to realize now is that I never had feelings for Saskia. I never felt even an ounce of what I feel for you."

"What do you feel for me?" Her eyes probe mine, looking for deceit, no doubt, but she won't find it.

"That night in Vegas meant the world to me too, Firefly. I felt those same things you felt. No other experience has ever come close to it." I gulp over the messy lump, wondering if I should admit this, but I've come this far, so I might as well go whole hog. "For six years, I have wrestled with my feelings for you. I pushed you away that day to keep you safe, but you always lived up here." I tap my temple. "And here." I tap my heart. "It's like you burrowed your way in and took up residence. I could never get you out. I have been tempted to look you up so many times, but I always reined myself in. I didn't want to be a selfish prick, but now I can't stop myself. It's too late."

Tears roll down her face again, but she's smiling.

It's a pivotal moment in our relationship.

Neither of us needs to vocalize it to feel the winds have changed. Fate has altered, and our axis has tilted. Whether it's for the better or not is yet to be determined, but we both know there is no going back. There is a certain serenity in accepting it. In trusting fate to take over and guide us along the right path.

If Leo was privy to my thoughts right now, he would never let me live it down.

"This isn't just about Rowan, Sierra." I cup her face firmly. "This isn't just a marriage of convenience." I draw a brave breath, preparing to say words I have only ever spoken to my sister. "I—"

"Mommy!" A shrill cry slices through the air, cutting me off.

"Rowan!" Sierra jumps up as Rowan's crying escalates.

I hop out of bed, rushing out of the room after her, trailing her into Rowan's bedroom. He is sitting up in the bed, sheets tangled around his little body, and his cheeks are soaked with tears.

"What's wrong?" Sierra asks, racing to him.

"I had a bad dream," he sobs, flinging himself at her as she sits on the side of the bed, alongside him. "Can I sleep with you?"

I crouch down beside Sierra, touching her arm. "You can stay here, and I can go back to my room, if you want."

Rowan lifts his little face, and the sight of his tearstained eyes guts me. I want to eradicate his heartache and remove every trace of worry from his life. "I want to sleep beside Ben too," he mumbles into his mom's neck.

"We can all sleep in my room," I rush to assure him. "That bed is the biggest."

He nods, and Sierra stands with him in her arms. I move back to the master bedroom and pull back the covers.

Rowan crawls into the bed without hesitation, and Sierra and I lie on either side of him. We pull the covers up, turning on our sides so we are facing one another, with our son in the middle. My heart is racing so fast it feels like it might burst from my chest.

Sierra has her arms around Rowan from behind, and she's pressing kisses into his hair. I want to touch him, to comfort him, too, but I don't want to startle him or upset him any more than he's already upset.

"Sleep, Firecracker," Sierra murmurs into his hair. "You're safe now."

He closes his eyes, and I don't take mine off him. His features are so perfect yet so small and fragile looking at the same time. An outpouring of love swells my chest, and I will do everything in my power to keep him innocent and safe. I want him to grow up loved and cherished and ignorant of the world I live in for as long as possible.

I want him to have dreams and goals and to feel like he can achieve anything he sets his heart to. I never want him to suffer disappointment or fear or regret, but I know that's just wishful thinking. Experiencing those things is part of growing up, but I want to shield him from everything in a way I was denied.

I want him to be a kid. To be free of burden for as long as possible.

"Ben," he whispers, and his eyes pop open.

"Yes, buddy?" I whisper even though there's no need because Sierra is still awake too.

His big blue eyes are trusting and hopeful as they stare into mine. "Are you my daddy?"

I can scarcely speak over the messy ball of emotion stuck in my throat. "Yes, Rowan," I croak. "I am your daddy."

"Forever and ever?" he asks, and Sierra clasps a shaky hand over her mouth as tears roll down her face.

"Forever and ever, buddy." I smile at him as my heart tries to beat a path out of my chest. "I promise I will never leave you or Mommy. And I know we have lots of things to catch up on, but we will have fun doing that."

He sniffs, and I stiffen. "Daddy?" he whispers, and I can't hold my emotions inside anymore. Tears well in my eyes, and I purposely avoid looking at Sierra because I will break down if I do. He wiggles closer, and the second his soft little hand presses on my chest, I wrap my arms around him without hesitation. He melts in my arms, no trace of fear or anxiety tensing his little body. "I love you," he whispers against my chest.

"I love you too," I tell him, closing my eyes and pressing my nose into his hair. "I love you so much."

Mommy too.

I want to say that out loud, because I was interrupted before I got to tell Sierra, but now isn't the right moment. This is about Rowan, and Sierra understands. She moves closer, snuggling against Rowan's back as he snuggles into my chest. I place my arm around them, and I fall asleep feeling more content than I have ever felt in my life.

Chapter 36

SIERRA

"OH MY GOD, Ben. This place is magnificent," I say, poking my head out the window of the SUV as Leo drives us along the sweeping driveway leading to Ben's exquisite Connecticut estate. Majestic trees line the wide smooth driveway as we advance, and the massive gardens are well-maintained with an abundance of shrubs and flowerbeds, but there are no colorful displays this time of year. The air is biting as it flows through the window, but I welcome the stinging freshness as it zings across my face. It makes me feel alive, and there is a lot to be said for that today.

The driveway seems to go on forever until gradually an expansive two-story property comes into view up ahead. It's on a circular plot within the sprawling estate, with various entrances. A line of tall trees forms a border around the house, granting privacy, while the vast use of glass offers plenty of light, I'm guessing. I thought my parents' lavish mansion was excessive, but this modern build puts their traditional three-story property to shame.

Ben confirmed his main home is on a five-acre site in an area known as The Golden Triangle in Greenwich, Connecticut. Lots of wealthy people have homes here and many are regular commuters to the city. The property is surrounded on all sides by a large whitewashed wall, and I spied several cameras mounted above the barbed wire fencing on top. The humongous wooden gates are only accessible via a code, and several armed guards man the entryway. A separate house near the front of the property houses a full security team. Ben explained they patrol the grounds twenty-four-seven, and no one can get in or out without their approval.

It's clear Ben takes security very seriously, and I can't deny the sense of relief I felt driving through the gates a couple of minutes ago.

It took just under an hour to drive here from New York, and Rowan was as excited as I've ever seen him. He has accepted the news about Ben better than I expected. If he was older, I assume he would have lots of questions. But he seems happy with the news—thrilled even—and he has fully embraced it, readily calling Ben Daddy this morning at breakfast in front of Leo and Alesso with no qualms. The guys were delighted for Ben, I could tell. Ben seems to be in a permanent state of shock, but he looks happier, more rested, and less stressed than I've seen him in recent weeks.

The events of yesterday seem almost like a dream to me now; however, the threat is all too real. And I haven't forgotten Ben promised to give me answers either. I will get us settled in our new home, and when Rowan is asleep tonight, I'll be cornering his daddy and asking my questions.

Something changed in our relationship last night. Like some invisible wall came crashing down, and I trust him to tell me the truth. I think he was going to tell me he loved me, or maybe I'm reading too much into things. Although he did tell me our night together was special to him too and that he's also had a hard time forgetting about me. His admission did funny things to my insides. Hope is no longer a fickle beast. He's a confident larger-than-life presence, waiting expectantly in the wings for things to develop.

My head and my heart are a mess, and the only thing I know with certainty is that I want to be here. Ben makes me feel safe. Being away from Chicago makes me feel safe. And I need that now more than anything—even if it means everything is changing.

"Look, Mommy!" Rowan screams, almost leaping out the window as he points at an enclosed playground on the vast lawn to our right. My eyes pop wide as I skim over the various slides, swings, and climbing frames, large tree house, and the miniature obstacle course.

"I took the liberty of installing it when I first found out about Rowan," Ben explains, noticing my expression. "This house is my safe haven, so I don't go out in the town or socialize with any of my neighbors. My staff does the shopping, and they have all signed NDAs. No one knows I live here, and I intend to keep it that way."

"Daddy! Daddy!" Rowan throws himself into Ben's arms. "I want to play in the tree house!"

Ben chuckles, ruffling his hair. "You need to see your new room first, and I have some other things to show you as well. But we'll visit the playground later."

I'm only half-listening to their conversation, mulling over his previous words. "That means we can't leave either, I assume?"

"It's not safe."

I look out the window, my excitement dimming a little. The surroundings might be beautiful, but it's still a prison.

"Hey." Ben touches my arm. "I know it will be hard for you, but I have tried to ensure you have everything you need so you don't feel too isolated."

"What about Rowan's schooling?"

"When things have quieted down, we can consider enrolling him in the local private school. Until then, I thought we could hire a tutor?"

I'm not comfortable at the idea of Rowan spending an extended period of time cooped up here without kids his own age to play with, but this is about safety first, so I nod.

"Natalia is lining up some options. I asked her to show you the applicants, and I can organize interviews with those you deem suitable?"

"Natalia is here?" I'm pretty sure Ben said she lived in the city with her husband and stepsons.

He nods. "I called her yesterday and asked her to help get things set up for you. I want you both to be as comfortable as possible."

Warmth spreads across my chest at his thoughtfulness. He is trying so hard, and I appreciate it so much. I lean in and press a kiss to his cheek, trying not to be obvious when I inhale the familiar delicious spicy scent of his cologne. "Thank you."

Leo swings the car around to the front of the house, parking to the side of an ornate water feature. A few steps lead up to a large paved area in front of the main entrance. Natalia and an elderly man in a wheelchair wait in the doorway. "Is that your father?" I whisper in Ben's ear as Alesso opens the back door, lifting Rowan out.

"That is Angelo Mazzone," Ben confirms.

Nerves fire at me from all angles, and I smooth a hand over my silk blouse, trying to rub out the wrinkles. "If I'd known I was meeting your father, I would have made more of an effort." I'm wearing skinny jeans with ballet flats, a silk blouse, and a cashmere cardigan.

"He won't even notice what you're wearing when he gets a look at your stunning face." Ben squeezes my hand. "Besides, you look beautiful no matter what you wear." He rubs the back of his neck, looking a tad anxious. "I, ah, should have mentioned he lives here."

I arch a brow because that's the first I'm hearing about it. Ben has been notoriously quiet on the subject of his dad. "He's sick. Dying. He has stage-four lung cancer."

My face pales. "I'm so sorry."

He shrugs. "He's been ill for years with different ailments, and then he was diagnosed with cancer eighteen months ago. His condition has deteriorated a lot these past few months. He doesn't have much longer left to live."

"You should have said something."

"I know." He sighs, dragging a hand through his hair. "I had every intention of asking you to come here for a weekend soon. I have always wanted him to meet you and Rowan before it was too late."

"He knows about us?"

"Of course. I told him and Natalia as soon as I found out," he says, keeping a hold of my hand as he slides out of the car.

Rowan is clinging to Alesso's back while Frank retrieves our bags from the trunk. Thankfully, Ben left Ciro in the city. That guy is always grumpy and unfriendly. I don't like being around him. Ian has come with us, because Ben wants him to train with the security detail at the house, while Frank and Alesso will continue to be our permanent bodyguards. It seems unnecessary now if all we will be doing is hanging around the house and grounds. There are enough guards on the property to keep us safe, but this is one area I am happy to leave to Ben's expertise. If he wants Frank and Alesso around, I'm not going to argue.

Ben takes Rowan from Alesso, letting our son crawl onto his back as I cling to his hand. Then we walk as a family toward his father and sister.

Natalia rushes forward to meet us when we get closer. "I'm so glad you are safe." She bundles me into her arms. "I was freaking out when Ben told me what had happened." She keeps me at arm's length, studying the wound on my cheek and the clear bruising on my neck with a frown. "Does it hurt?"

I shake my head. "I barely feel it."

"Daddy," Rowan says. "Who is that pretty lady?"

"Oh my." Natalia's eyes fill up as she looks at Rowan. His chin is resting on Ben's shoulder as he peers curiously at his aunt.

I slip my hand from Ben's as he pulls Rowan around to his front. "This is your Auntie Natalia," he says. "Natalia. This is my son, Rowan."

Pride suffuses his tone and stretches across his face, and I find myself tearing up again. When Rowan asked Ben if he was his daddy last night, I could barely contain myself. It was one of the most emotional moments of my life, and I cried silent tears of joy watching them hugging. Nothing could have prepared me for the tsunami of emotion I feel every time I watch father and son together.

Seeing them together is beautiful.

Visualizing our lives together as a family is beautiful even if it's scary too because so much is hanging in the air.

"I'm really happy to meet you, Rowan," Natalia says, choking back tears. "You look so much like your daddy." She glances briefly at me. "And you're every bit as beautiful as your mommy."

"I think you're beautiful," Rowan says. "A princess, just like my mom."

Natalia laughs, swiping tears away. "Oh, you're most definitely your father's son." She clasps Ben's hand and mine at the same time. "He's so precious."

A gentle whirring sound captures all our attention at once, and we turn as one toward the man wheeling toward us. His clothes hang off his skeletal frame, and his arms look like they might break as he pushes the wheels of his chair with feeble strength. A thick gray-and-blue-plaid blanket rests at his waist, covering his legs. His breath puffs out in wheezy spurts as he comes to a stop in front of us. Ben kneels, bringing Rowan with him. "This is your Grandpa Angelo, Rowan."

"Hello, young man." Angelo extends a shaky arm, clasping bony fingers around Rowan's hand. "I've been looking forward to meeting you for weeks."

"Hi." Rowan's voice is meek as he clings shyly to his dad. He has never seen anyone in a wheelchair or anyone this sick before.

"Come sit." Angelo pats his knee.

"Papa." Natalia shakes her head, but Angelo raises a hand.

"Stop fussing." A rattling sound erupts from his chest, and I'm questioning the wisdom of letting Rowan sit on his lap when an older woman, with her graying hair pinned into an austere bun, rushes out of the house. She's wearing blue scrubs and carrying what looks like an oxygen tank. "Quick, Rowan," Angelo wheezes. "Give your *nonno* a hug before Nurse Ratchet locks me away in my dungeon."

Rowan looks petrified now, so Ben keeps a hold of him, leaning across and whispering in his ear. Rowan doesn't sit on Angelo's lap, but he gives him a quick hug from the safety of Ben's arms.

"He's a good boy," Angelo says, beaming with pride. His gray pallor seems to warm a little under his shaky smile.

"Unlike some." The nurse glares at Angelo. "What have I told you about exerting yourself?"

"It's my fault," Natalia says. "I got excited and left him at the door."

"Relax." Angelo waves his hands in the air, pushing the nurse away as she tries to fit an oxygen mask around his face. "I'm not dead yet, and I wanted to see my grandson."

"Let's go inside," Ben says. "It's cold out."

"Not before I say hello to my future daughter-in-law," Angelo says, wheezing heavily. The nurse tries to put the mask on him again, but he slaps her hands away.

I can see where Ben gets his stubborn streak from.

"I'll make you a deal," I say, crouching down so we're eye level. "You put your mask on, and I'll stop by your room after I get Rowan settled so we can get acquainted."

His cold, trembling hands grasp mine. "Don't go making deals with the devil. They'll only land you in trouble." He says it with a smile, and it's hard to look at this frail, sickly man and remember he was once a fearsome mafia don. Angelo keeps a hold of my hands, ignoring my deal as he looks up at his son. "She's even more beautiful than you said." He lets go of my hands to point a finger at Ben. "Don't go messing it up."

"Inside, Angelo." The nurse pins him with a "don't mess with me" look that's impressive.

Ben takes my hand as Angelo finally allows the nurse to fit the oxygen mask over his mouth. Natalia pulls the blanket up over his shoulders before pushing her father inside the house.

"Ready to see your new home?" Ben asks, just before we step over the threshold.

The moment feels huge. Like I'm not just crossing the threshold into a house but a new life. Ignoring the butterflies in my chest, I squeeze Ben's hand and smile as I take a step forward. "Lead the way."

Chapter 37

SIERRA

"THIS IS THE east wing of the house," Ben explains as we step behind tall double mahogany doors into an enclosed section of his property. He just gave us a fifty-cent tour of the main living spaces including the large kitchen and breakfast room, homey living room, family dining room, expansive sunroom, indoor pool and gym, movie theater, game room, and bar. He also has a formal ballroom, but it's never been used since he doesn't invite guests here. There are two offices, both on this side of the house, and he told me I'm welcome to use Angelo's office as he doesn't use it anymore.

My eyes almost bugged out of my head when he showed me the large library. It's like something you see in the movies with tall shelving and row upon row of neatly stacked books. Several desks are dotted around the large room, but I favor the seated area in front of the roaring open fire, and I can already picture myself sprawled across the fabric couch with a blanket covering me as I savor my latest romance book. I will definitely make good use of the space.

Ben explained he is renovating the west wing, and it is off-limits for now.

"My master suite is on this level, and I had the adjoining bedroom prepared for Rowan. Angelo's quarters are on this side of the house too but at the opposite end of the hallway," he adds, keeping his hand on my lower back as he steers me through a bright living room. "This is our own living room," he explains as Rowan races ahead of us into the hallway. Ben pushes a door open on my right. "You have a small kitchen if you need it for drinks or snacks. My staff caters all meals though you are welcome to cook yourself if you want."

"What about upstairs?" I ask, as we haven't been up there yet and I assumed that is where our bedrooms would be. This place is ginormous and about twice the size of my parents' palatial home.

"I rarely use the upstairs space," he says, shrugging. "There are more bedrooms and bathrooms up there and staff quarters for those who live in."

We step out into the hallway, and he points at an elevator on the right. "You can go exploring any time you like. The elevator also goes to the roof garden."

"Your home is really impressive."

"I hired one of the best New York architects to design this place, and it took years to build. I wanted to ensure it met all my current and future needs." His eyes drill into mine. "And it's not *my* home. It's *ours*." My heart speeds up at his words and the intensity in his gaze.

"Mommy!" Rowan's screams almost burst my eardrums.

Ben chuckles. "I think he discovered the playroom."

I walk quickly beside Ben, almost keeling over when I step foot in the large rectangular room filled to the brim with toys and games. Rowan is currently jumping up and down in the ball pit, and I have never seen him so excited. The entire area on that side of the room has Velcro walls, and the ball pit is a corner pool surrounded by floor trampolines that are full of foam blocks. Ropes hang overhead to flip from above, and one of the Velcro walls is a rock climbing wall.

I am already imagining having to drag him kicking and screaming from this room most nights.

"This is awesome!" he shouts, throwing a few balls around the room.

Three bicycles are propped against the far wall, and I walk toward them, running the tips of my fingers along the shiny metal. "Wow. You really thought of everything." I beam at Ben.

He shrugs, shoving his hands deep into the pockets of his jeans. "I tried. There are some nice cycling paths around the property and a couple of decent walking trails through the woods at the back. I don't want you to feel like you're stuck indoors."

If snow hits next month, we might have little choice. Winters here can be as brutal as Chicago, so I'm not hedging my bets. "I appreciate the effort you have put in," I say, touching his arm. "Thank you. It will make the transition easier."

"You haven't seen the best room yet," he adds, lacing his fingers in mine.

"Rowan," he calls out, jerking his head to the side. "I've got another surprise. Come on."

Rowan doesn't need any encouragement, tumbling out of the ball pit and racing toward us like a tornado.

Ben chuckles again. "I love how excited he is."

"You might not be saying that later when we can't get him to bed," I tease.

"I don't mind." He tugs me out of the room after Rowan. Our son is sprinting along the hallway toward the next door. "This is all new to me, and I'm loving every second of it."

"You were always good with kids," I admit, remembering how he was with me.

"Now you're making me feel old and a little creeped out, Firefly," he teases, waggling his brows.

"It should probably feel weird, but I barely even remember there's an age gap between us," I truthfully reply.

"I agree." He leans down and kisses me. "Though I try to forget you were barely out of diapers when I was losing my virginity." He flashes me a grin, and I whack him in the chest.

"Don't be gross unless you're telling me you lost it when you were like eleven," I say, quickly doing the math in my head.

"Mommy!" Rowan comes barreling out of a door just up ahead, his cheeks flushed red and his eyes out on stalks. He grabs my hand. "Mommy! You have to see this."

I let him drag me into the room, and all the air leaves my lungs in a rush. Tears stab my eyes as I glance around the large, airy, bright, well-equipped art studio. Canvases of all sizes are propped on easels and against the walls. Shelves groan with paints, pencils, and all types of art supplies. He even has a pottery wheel and clay oven installed.

"That door leads to a dark room," Ben says, pointing at a door at the far end of the room. "And the box outside holds some cameras and equipment. I know you probably have your own, but—"

I cut him off with my lips as I throw myself at him. My arms wind around his neck as I press a succession of kisses to his mouth. I'm half-laughing, half-crying, when I pull back, and my smile is so wide it threatens to split my face in two. "How did you do all this?" I cry. "When? How? It's too much. I—" I slap a hand over my chest, and I'm feeling too much. My heart is fit to burst.

"Don't get mad," he says. "But I started remodeling a week after I found out about Rowan."

I place my hands on his chest, stretching up to kiss him again. "I'm not mad. Not in the slightest. Ben, this is incredible. No one has ever done so much for me and Rowan. I just…I don't have words to describe how I'm feeling. How grateful I am."

His arms slide around my waist, and he reels me in close. "I want you to be happy here, Firefly." He rubs his nose against mine. "I want you to be happy with me."

"I am, Ben." It's overwhelming and a lot to take in, but I'm not lying. To have Rowan squealing with joy and me feeling every wonderful emotion under the sun after the day we had yesterday is all due to Ben.

The last of my reservations flitter away.

Everything is going to work out.

I feel it in my bones.

"Good." His mouth lands on mine, soft and adoring, and I melt against him as he kisses me with more tenderness than I thought him capable of.

"Ugh. That's gross, Daddy."

We break apart and look down at our son. Rowan's nose is scrunched in disgust, and a giggle bursts from my lips. Ben grins, crouching down so he's at Rowan's level. "Trust me, buddy. Kissing your mom is far from gross."

"I'm never kissing girls." He crosses his arms over his chest, still looking disgusted.

Ben scoops him up, tickling him. "Famous last words, Firecracker."

BEN TAKES ROWAN outside to the playground after the doc injects his tracking device. He was supposed to come to the apartment this morning, but there was some emergency that delayed him. Rowan hates needles, and he cried a little, so Ben took him up to the tree house afterward to distract him. Next on the agenda is a rooftop trip to show Rowan the telescope.

I stayed behind to unpack our things. Ben automatically assumed I'd be sharing his master suite, and I didn't correct him. Butterflies scatter in my tummy at the thought of sharing a bed with him on a permanent basis. I know he'll be spending his weeks in the city, but he has already promised to come home on nights when he doesn't have to work late.

Ben had to practically drag Rowan from his superhero-themed room, and I'm hoping his love of his new bedroom might mean he's happy to go to bed at his usual time tonight. Routine is important, and I intend to stick to ours here even if I have no work to go to and Rowan won't have school until we have hired a private tutor.

I wander in the direction Ben told me, rapping a few times on the door to the room at the very end of the hallway.

"Come in," a female voice calls out, and I step into Angelo's bedroom as the nurse is fixing pillows behind his head. Ben's father is sitting up in an elevated hospital bed with a few wires hooked up to machines. The room is spacious, and it has a seated living area at the far end with a lit open fire, some messy bookshelves, and a massive widescreen TV.

"*Bella signora.* Come." Angelo points at the chair by his bed, smiling at me.

"You can stay for an hour, but Mr. Mazzone needs to sleep after that," the nurse says, stepping aside for me. She thrusts out her hand. "I'm Ruthie, by the way."

I shake her hand. "Sierra. Nice to meet you."

"There are refreshments in the refrigerator if you like," she says, "or help yourself to coffee." She gestures toward a counter with a coffee station, a kettle, a small refrigerator, and a sink. "Press this button if you need me," she adds, pointing at a large blue button affixed to the side of Angelo's bed. "I'll just be in my room next door."

"I'm good, but thank you." I take a seat as Ruthie slips out of the room.

"It's no wonder that woman never married," Angelo says, his chest wheezing. "She would nag any man into the grave."

I smile even though I probably shouldn't. "She's just doing her job, and from the looks of it, you are making it difficult for her."

"Everyone loves a challenge." He winks, and I shake my head. He's incorrigible.

"Something tells me you were a tyrant in your day," I tease, folding my hands in my lap.

"I was," he freely admits with no hint of shame. He eyeballs me with a steeliness I missed earlier. "I was a cold-blooded killer, but I needed to be. Things were different in my day." I nod because I'm not sure how else to respond to that. "So much has changed. Some for the good. Some for the bad. But my Bennett has done good. I know he didn't want this life, but he didn't shirk his responsibilities, and he is making his mark in a way Mateo never could have."

"Mateo?" I inquire because I don't know who that is.

"My eldest son. My firstborn. He was my legitimate heir until he was gunned down by those bastard Bratva fourteen years ago."

It can't be a coincidence it's around the time Ben disappeared from Chicago, but I don't press Angelo on it. I'd prefer to hear that part of the story from Ben. It's no wonder the Italians hate the Russians. It seems they have a lot to answer for, but it could be retaliation for equally heinous acts initiated by the Italians.

"I'm sorry for your loss," I say.

He reaches out for my hand. "I lost my Mateo only six months after I lost my wife, Rosa. Those were dark times."

His cold palm trembles against mine. "And Rosa was Natalia's mother too?" He nods. I probably shouldn't ask this, but he seems open and much easier to talk to than I imagined. "So you were married to Rosa when you conceived Ben with Jillian Carver?"

His lips tug up in a smile. "If you had asked me that question twenty years ago, I probably would've had you killed for your audacity."

Okay. I take my previous sentiment back. I don't know if he's joking, but something tells me he's not. A chill whistles up my spine.

He chuckles before breaking into a coughing fit. I move to press the button, but he shakes his head, pointing a bony finger at the jug of water by his bed. I pour him a glass, sticking one of the oversized straws in it before holding it to his lips and helping him to drink. When he is done, he pushes my hand away, and I set the glass back on the table.

"You should have seen your face." He engages in another little chuckle before a more solemn expression plays on his face. "I loved my Rosa, but her role was to be my wife and to sire me an heir. I was away a lot on business, and a man has needs. I enjoyed several dalliances, and I kept permanent whores from time to time." He shrugs like it's no biggie. "All the bosses did."

Wow. Like that makes it okay. I can't even begin to process that or all the ways it is unfair and morally wrong. How can you claim to love your wife while constantly cheating on her? Rosa probably knew about it and had to ignore it. It was the way things were done then. I make a mental note to add it to my list of questions for Ben.

He told me previously he would be faithful to me, and I need to ensure he knows it's a nonnegotiable condition before we let our relationship progress any further. Infidelity is a deal-breaker for me. I won't tolerate cheating. Heck, I won't tolerate him even looking sideways at another woman. I've spent years lusting after Ben, and now I've got him, I intend to keep him. He is mine, as I am his, and I won't entertain any more gold-diggers like Chantel LaCroix. Ugh, even thinking of that woman makes my blood boil.

I don't know how those poor mafia women put up with it. If I was Rosa, I would have cut his dick off while he was sleeping.

"Do you have other children?" I ask, genuinely curious.

"Not that I'm aware of, and I spent time looking. Natalia and Ben are my only surviving children."

I'm connecting the dots in my head. "You went looking because you needed to find someone to run the business after Mateo was killed."

"I knew about Ben from the start," he says, surprising me. "His mother came to me when she was pregnant. I gave her some money and told her to go away, but I had someone watching over him from the shadows."

Shock splays across my face. I know how Ben grew up, and I'm indignant on his behalf. I rip my hand back and scowl at the sick man on the bed.

"You think I'm an evil prick for ignoring my own flesh and blood."

"That's a polite way of putting it," I hiss.

"I did it to protect him."

"Bullshit," I blurt.

He smiles, and I'm beginning to think he's legit crazy. "If my enemies knew I had a bastard, they would've targeted him too. I kept away to protect him."

"Until you needed him." I sit up straighter. "Do you know the kind of things he had to endure growing up?" Even I'm not privy to all the facts, but I know enough to understand he had it rough.

"His childhood made him the man he is today."

I'm growing madder by the minute. "There are so many things wrong with that. He suffered so much, and he didn't need to!"

"You are right, but I cannot change time, nor would it have

mattered. Back then, things were different."

"I don't know how Ben can even stand to look at you." I don't conceal my disgust. How could you knowingly turn your back on your own flesh and blood? There is nothing he could say that will ever make me understand how he neglected Ben.

"*Bella, bella.*" His blue eyes drill into mine. "I like that you are angry for my Bennett. I like that you speak your mind and you stand up for what you believe is right. I don't disagree with you. I did not do right by my son, and he spent years hating me. He probably still does, and I would not resent him for his feelings or expect him to love me."

"Yet he takes care of you. He took control of your business and has made it even more successful."

"Because he is a good man. A better man than me, and he respects responsibility and *la famiglia*."

"Answer me one thing." I sit up straighter in my chair. "Do you regret it? Wish you had treated him better?"

"I do." Sincerity bleeds from his tone, and the edge slices off my anger. "He deserved better."

"Have you changed that much, or are you telling me what I want to hear?"

He shifts in the bed, and a grimace spreads across his mouth. The rattling wheezy sound in his chest deepens, and I grab the glass of water again, helping him to take small sips from the straw.

He pats my hand when he is finished, and the spluttering quiets down. "I am old, *Bella*. I am dying. That forces a man to reevaluate the things he has done. The things he wishes he hadn't done. It changes a man, but above everything, Bennett has altered my views. He had a vision of a different future. One he has nurtured into existence, and he has shown me there is a better way. I can die in peace knowing my family is in safe hands." His eyelids flutter as he fights sleep, but he pushes on.

Clasping my hand in his weak one, he stares me directly in the eye. "Knowing my son has found a woman worthy of his love also gives me peace of mind. Bennett needs you. He will claim otherwise, but you are the missing piece he didn't even know he was searching for."

Chapter 38

SIERRA

"HOW DID YOUR talk with Angelo go?" Ben asks me later that night, as we walk side by side along one of the trails in the woods on the grounds of his estate. Rowan is fast asleep, not even lasting through one page of his book. I think Ben was disappointed he didn't get to read to him, but there will be plenty of nights for that. Rowan was exhausted from an action-packed day, and he got to stay up later tonight to watch *Skywatch Weekly*. We watched it from the roof, via Ben's laptop, and Rowan's clear delight at watching it with his daddy almost induced a fresh wave of tears. My hormonal outbursts are getting embarrassing at this stage.

"It was…interesting. Enlightening. Infuriating," I admit.

Spotlights embedded in the beige stone path light the way as we stroll. The night air is brisk, but we are wrapped up warm in heavy coats, thick scarves, and leather boots.

"That sounds about right," Ben grins. "Angelo is an infuriating bastard at the best of times."

"You don't call him Dad?" I inquire, having noticed this previously. Although, now I've met the man and heard some of the backstory, it makes sense. I would be reluctant to call that man Dad too if I was in Ben's shoes.

Ben sighs, pulling the collar of his black woolen coat up around his neck as we walk. "Our relationship is complicated."

"He told me about Mateo. He also said you have made your mark in a way Mateo never could."

Ben quirks a brow, looking at me with respect and surprise. "He said that?" I nod. "Hmm." His tongue darts out, wetting his lips, and he looks pensive for a few moments before he breaks the silence. "He must like you already. He rarely talks about Mateo. Even to Natalia."

"It must have been hard for her when he died."

"It was, but she never let it get in the way of our relationship. She welcomed me with open arms."

"You love her."

"I do. Very much. Outside of Leo, she's my closest friend."

"I like her a lot, and I'm glad she's here."

"She will stay for a week to help you settle in." He pushes a branch away, clearing a path for me. "I have to return to the city on Sunday night."

I detect the guilt in his tone. "It's okay, Ben. I know you have to work."

Tugging on my arm, he pulls me to a stop. "For the first time ever, I have a reason to stay, and I don't want to return to the city. I will try and wrap things up early one or two nights and either drive or fly here."

"That would be great, but I don't want to add to your stress. I want to make your life easier," I say, holding my gloved hand to his face.

"You already do. I'm so happy you are both here."

I'm loving how he is opening up to me. This Ben is the one I remember from my childhood, and it's encouraging to know he hasn't lost that side of himself. I'm not naïve though. I know he is a different man now. That there is a dark side to him as well. I'm determined to love all sides of him. To understand fully what makes him tick now.

I'm ready to embrace everything that comes with being with him because living my life without Ben in it is no longer an option. For either Rowan or me. I'm committing to him now with everything that entails.

The wind picks up, and we hurry back to the house, settling side by side on the couch in front of the roaring fire in our private living room. Ben swirls expensive bourbon in his glass while I sip a glass of fruity red wine. "You wanted to talk, so talk. I'm an open book," he says, sliding his arm around my shoulders.

I have so many questions, but starting from the beginning seems the most logical route. "How did you come to leave Chicago? It was after Mateo died, right?"

Ben bobs his head. "I was leaving the bar where I worked one night when I was accosted by a few men. They forced me at gunpoint into a car, and I was driven to a house in Greenhaven, Rye, on the very outskirts of New York. It's not too far from here, actually." He takes a mouthful of his bourbon while I wait for him to continue.

"They took me to Angelo's house. That was the first time I met him. He explained he was my father, that he was the don of one of the five New York Italian mafia families, and his eldest son, Mateo, had just been murdered. He told me, point-blank, that I was needed to fulfill my duty as his sole remaining heir."

"He strikes me as the type of man who doesn't hold back." I turn in his arms, placing my hand on his chest. Heat warms my palm even through his sweater. "That must have been one hell of a shock."

"I thought he was joking at first until I googled it. It was only fourteen years ago, but even then, no one gave a rat's ass what was said online. It was one of the first things I convinced Angelo to let me do after I got over my initial shock and resistance."

I'm not surprised to learn Ben is behind the lack of information on the internet, and I suspect his interest in the tech industry stems from his desire to control all that is said about him and his business. "Did you have to initiate or did you get a pass because you were older?"

He smirks, and I swat his chest. "Don't make fun of me! You successfully wiped all information from the web, so I'm forced to rely on romance novels for my intel."

"I like hearing that," he says, and I roll my eyes.

His expression turns more somber. "I had to initiate, the very next night. I did it under duress, but I wasn't stupid. I knew I had no choice. To deny him meant death. I initiated and spent a few years training and working as a soldier."

"Have you killed a lot of men?" I don't want an actual number, but I won't shy away from the truth.

"I suppose that depends on your definition of 'a lot.' But, yes, I have killed men. Tortured them. Stole from them. I've done a lot of shit I didn't want to do, but I had no choice then. I knew the only way I could change things was by doing the dirty work, proving I deserved my place, working my butt off to earn it and the respect of the men and the other families, and when I took power six years ago, I began my program of changes."

I take a gulp of my wine before setting it down and turning fully around so I'm facing him. "Tell me about it. I want to know. I remember how shocked and impressed I was when I visited the Caltimore Holdings building. It was not at all what I expected."

Ben's face comes alive as he tells me what he's been doing during the years of our separation. "Tradition is very important to the Italian mafia. To most mafia organizations, actually. But the whole structure needed modernization. RICO laws have made it tough to continue doing business the same way, if you want to stay out of jail. So, I have focused on legitimizing as much of the business as possible, placing huge focus on developing our construction companies, transforming our clubs and casinos into high-end establishments catering to powerful VIPs, networking with the right people in industry, government, and the judicial system, and buying up strategic IT firms."

"I read about that and formed my own assumptions, but I'd like to hear it from you. What exactly is your interest in technology?"

"First, IT is a very good investment in the current climate. But it also gives us a means of elevating core traditional businesses."

I wasn't expecting him to say that, and I'm not quite sure what he means. "I don't understand."

He puts his glass down, facing me. His entire face exudes passion, and I can tell he genuinely loves what he does. "Racketeering and extortion were how a lot of mafia organizations were built, but the days of sending thugs in suits to shake up bar owners, restaurateurs, and local store owners are gone. Now we offer protection against online fraud, and our customers pay a monthly retainer to avail of those services. Of course, our tech companies also provide regular services to clients, and we have a division that focuses on internal business—investigative work and keeping shit off the net."

I mull over my other questions. "So, you don't sell drugs or guns or sex?"

"Not guns, but we still sell drugs and sex."

I grimace, and nausea swirls in my gut. "Please tell me you aren't involved in sex trafficking."

"I'm not. None of the New York families are."

I breathe a sigh of relief. "Thank God." He cocks his head to one side, curiosity clear in his gaze. "I took an interest in it after what happened in Vegas. I volunteer at a local support center—or I guess I did," I add, realizing I will have to call the manager and let her know I am no longer available.

"When things settle down, I am sure you can find another center locally or find other ways to help. It's something I feel strongly about too."

I can tell he means that, and it reassures me. "So, if you're not involved in trafficking, what kind of sex do you sell?" Bile swirls in my mouth as I remember that seedy club I visited with Tony when I was pregnant.

Ben takes my hands in his. "High-end sexual services through our network of casinos and clubs. It's not like that place you stumbled on in Queens. I got rid of all those shitholes. All our clubs are upmarket, and we only cater to the rich and powerful. We don't have dealers or hookers on streets anymore. We supply high-quality drugs to VIP member clientele who frequent our clubs and casinos. We also use those establishments to wash money. We have a team of women who service our clients either by prior private appointment or at one of our sex clubs."

He laughs at the look of shock on my face, and my cheeks heat. "Are you really that shocked?"

"I hadn't given it much thought. I see you wearing your designer suit, and sometimes it's hard to remember you're not a regular businessman." On some of the occasions Ben visited Rowan, he had come straight from the office. The sight of him in a suit is enough to set my ovaries on fire. Seriously. The man is a bona fide sex god when dressed in a suit. I squeeze my legs together, ignoring the sudden ache pulsing between my thighs.

"I'm a regular businessman, most of the time. And, to be honest, a lot of 'regular' businessmen, with no mafia ties or connections, are more corrupt than me or any of the other dons. You'd be surprised." A funny look crosses over his face, but before I can probe him on it, he continues talking.

"My mom was a hooker, and I saw the shit she had to put up with from pimps and johns. I make sure our girls are treated well and with respect. That's why we have a waiting list a mile long for vacancies. We only hire the best women, and they are carefully vetted, as are the clients. A bodyguard accompanies every one of our girls on private dates, and security is tight at all the clubs. The girls are well paid, attend regular beauty appointments, and have medical checkups every month."

A horrid thought enters my mind, and I spew the words out. "Do you fuck those girls?"

"Never." He pulls me onto his lap. "I don't fuck employees. It's a hard and fast rule that is part of the employment terms and conditions for all staff who works at our clubs. Similarly, staff is not permitted to take drugs, and we run regular drug tests. I run a clean establishment. I have HR departments and teams of people who ensure everything we do is the same as any other professional company."

"Wow. You really have made a lot of changes."

"It doesn't stop there. We have a couple of private security firms, and our soldiers make up ninety percent of the employee body. They still undergo initiation. That's one tradition I will never be able to change. But they attend initial training in one of our high-tech training facilities, and then they move to the security firms to pay their dues." He chuckles. "I have to laugh when I see some of our guys on camera working charity events and doing security at concerts and gigs and movie premieres."

"You have infiltrated every part of society." A shiver runs up my spine with that acknowledgment.

"Yes." He tweaks my nose. "And it's all legit and above board." His hand lands on my thigh, and I jump at the unexpected contact. "Do you have any more questions?" he asks, brushing my hair aside and nuzzling my neck. "Or can we retire to bed?" His voice drops a couple of octaves, and the gruff husky tone does funny things to my insides. He drops a slew of drugging kisses up and down my neck, and I'm having trouble breathing.

"Just one." I press on his shoulders, urging him to stop. I can't think clearly when he is touching me, and this is serious. I have already given him my heart, but before I give him my body again—before I hand him control of my pleasure—I need to know I can trust him. That he will be faithful to me.

He must sense that because he stops kissing my neck and straightens up, eyeballing me. "Shoot."

"I want to be with you. I want to have a real relationship, but that will only happen if you are faithful to me. Other women are a deal-breaker, Ben."

He cups my face in his palms, peering deep into my eyes. "You are the only woman for me, Sierra. Since Vegas, it has only been you." His gaze probes mine. "This might surprise you, but I have not been in a relationship since I left Chicago."

That does surprise me. "But what about those women in pictures with you on the web? What about Chantel?" I want to get it all off my chest so that we can move forward with a clean slate.

"None of those women were my girlfriends. It was only ever sex."

"And they knew you were only using them for sex?"

"Yes. I was always up front though it didn't stop some of them from thinking they could sink their claws in me. They used me too, Firefly. Being on my arm at key society events helped to elevate their status in those circles."

I have been raised in a similar world, and I understand that's how things happen, but it still sickens my stomach. I'm not sure what my expression betrays, but it encourages Ben to go further.

"None of them meant anything to me." He brushes his thumb along my lower lip. "None of them stood a chance at ever claiming my heart because I had already given it to you that night in Vegas."

"You did?" Disbelief radiates in my tone.

"I did." He nods, leaning in to press a brief kiss on my lips. "I didn't know I'd lost it that night, but it became obvious over time when I couldn't get you out of my head. Reconnecting with you confirmed everything I had been denying." My heart is jumping in my chest at the intense way he's looking at me. "I love you, Sierra. You are the only woman for me. Now and forever."

I can barely speak over the emotional lump in my throat. "I love you too," I whisper, fighting tears. "I always have."

He kisses me again, much harder this time, and I fall into him, wrapping my arms securely around his neck as I squirm on his lap.

"And to answer your initial question, yes," he says, trailing his lips down my neck. "I will be faithful to you. Always." Lifting his head, he peers deep into my eyes. "You can trust me. I will never cheat on you. I could never do that to you, and I have no interest in any other woman, now or ever. You are the only woman I desire in my bed and in my life."

His words sink bone-deep, heart-deep, reassuring me and helping to remove the last vestiges of doubt. "Thank you. I needed to hear that."

"Any other questions?" he asks, flashing me his signature smirk. "Or can we dispense with talking and move this to the bedroom?" He tugs on my earlobe with his teeth, making me shiver all over.

"I think that's enough questions for now," I pant.

"Thank fuck." He jerks his hips forward, pressing his growing erection against the side of my thigh. "I have spent what seems like an eternity dying to have you back in my bed." His hands wind through my hair, and he tilts my head back, staring at me with a dark intensity that both exhilarates and terrifies me.

"To sleep or…?" I leave my question open-ended on purpose, even if we both know what will happen when we get to the master suite.

His hand casually roams the left side of my body. "That is totally up to you," he purrs, as his fingers brush against the edge of my breast.

"Oh God," I moan as heat floods my core.

"I want to drive my cock inside your tight pussy," he growls in my ear as his hand reaches my thigh. "I want to fuck this insatiable need for you out of my system, only to begin all over again, because there is no quenching my thirst when it comes to you."

His hand slides between my thighs, and he rubs my pussy through my jeans. "But I can wait if you need more time. We can do other things."

The friction heightens every nerve ending in that part of my body, and I rock against him, needing his touch more than I need air to breathe. "Take me," I whisper, locking eyes with him. "Take me and do with me whatever you please. I am yours to command." I wouldn't dream of uttering those words to any other man. I have never given anyone else permission to dominate me in the bedroom. But the most intense sexual pleasure I've ever had was my night in Vegas with Ben when I willingly handed sole control to him. I have dreamed of a repeat performance plenty of times. Fingered myself to sleep many nights in bed dreaming of his touch and his cock, and both are being offered to me on a platter now.

Only a fool would say no.

"Fuck, yes." He even makes that sound sexy.

I shriek when he stands abruptly, throwing me over his shoulder and slapping my ass hard. "Buckle up, Firefly, because I'm about to give you the ride of your life."

Chapter 39

SIERRA

"STAND THERE," BEN says, positioning me over by the small seating area in his bedroom. Nerves prickle my skin, but they're the good kind. After locking the door, he hooks his cell up to his sound system. "Naughty Girl" by Beyoncé fills the room, but he's set the volume low so it's not too loud. He flops down into one of the velvet tub chairs in front of me, spreading his thighs and smirking. "Strip for me, Firefly. Nice and slow. I want to take my time drinking in every inch of your gorgeous body before I devour you with my fingers, my tongue, and my cock."

"Holy shit." I squeeze my legs together as a gush of liquid warmth floods my panties.

His brows climb to his hairline in question as I stand rooted to the spot. "Is there a problem?" he asks, and I shake my head, snapping out of it and raising trembling fingers to the hem of my sweater. I pull it over my head, dropping it to the ground. Heat flares from his eyes as he stares hungrily at me, his gaze dipping to my breasts. My nipples pebble behind my white and pink lacy bra, and adrenaline courses through my veins, flicking a switch inside me. His ravenous stare is the confidence boost I need to do this. Moving my body to the sultry beats of the song, I sashay my hips, mouthing the lyrics as I lean forward at the waist, offering him a glimpse of my cleavage under my flimsy camisole.

Turning around, I shake my ass while tilting my head back, letting my hair cascade down my back as I dance. The music loosens my tense muscles, and I let it sweep me up in its hypnotic beat, banishing any lingering doubts or nerves. Easing my camisole up my body, I slide it off and toss it aside as I continue swaying my body in sync with the music.

"Turn around," he grunts, and I bite my lip as I slowly spin around.

I pop the button on my jeans, deliberately licking my lips as I zone in on the noticeable bulge in his jeans.

He's enjoying this, and that spurs me on.

Dropping to the floor, I quickly remove my socks and shimmy my skinny jeans over my hips and down my legs. It's not as easy to do that part sexily, but Ben doesn't seem to mind. His eyes are like laser beams on my skin as I reveal more and more flesh. Kicking my jeans away, I crawl closer to him, using his legs to pull myself upright.

The buttons on his jeans are undone, and he has his hand stuffed into his boxers, stroking himself. The outline of his long thick hard cock behind the black cotton is enough to send me orbiting into heaven. Liquid lust coils in my belly at the thought of ripping those boxers away and impaling myself on his monster cock. I whimper while my hands roam freely over my body, and his heated gaze tracks my every move.

Sultry tones bounce off the wall as the song changes. Ben jerks himself off as I slowly slide my bra straps down my arms. Pushing my breasts together, I lean closer, dangling them in his face.

"You're playing with fire, sweetheart," he groans, his eyes glued to my chest.

I undo the front clasp and let my bra float to the floor, brushing my bare tits against his face as I hook my thumbs in my panties.

"Fuck," he hisses as his tongue darts out, licking one of my nipples.

It's as if there's a direct line from my tits to my pussy, and I convulse with longing as he lavishes attention on my nipples, sucking, tugging, and nipping my taut peaks with his teeth and his tongue.

That's it.

I'm done waiting.

The show is officially over.

I need him inside me right now.

I hurriedly remove my panties and kneel between his legs, reaching for his jeans, when he shakes his head.

"Nuh-uh, Firefly. This is *my* show." He chuckles at the clear frustration on my face. "Stand."

I do as I'm told, and my skin is on fire when he grips my hips, pulling me close. He buries his face in my bare pussy, and the most embarrassing moan escapes my lips. He sniffs before parting my pussy lips with his thumbs, exposing me to him. I hold on to his shoulders because it feels like my legs could go out from under me.

"So fucking sweet," he says, keeping me open while he licks a line up and down my slit.

"Oh my God. Ben. Please." My pussy quakes with need, pulsing and clenching with potent desire.

"So fucking sexy," he adds, plunging his tongue inside my tight inner walls.

I gasp, gripping his shoulders tighter as he ravishes me with his tongue. I can only close my eyes and hold on for the ride.

Without warning, he pulls away a few minutes later, and I cry out in exasperation.

"Patience, Firefly," he says, standing and removing his jeans, sweater, and T-shirt. Saliva pools in my mouth as I inspect every glorious inch of him. He's even more ripped than I remember. His chest seems broader. His abs more defined. His biceps bulkier.

I might be drooling.

And creaming my panties—if I had any on!

He chuckles, and I drag my gaze from his sexy body to his even sexier face. A growl rips from the back of my throat at the familiar smug expression on his face. Roughly, he grabs the nape of my neck, pulling my mouth to his for a soul-crushing kiss that goes on and on. I press myself against him, rubbing against his erection through his boxers and clawing at the warm flesh of his back. If I could climb him, I would—I'm that horny.

He sucks on my lower lip, and I melt against him. Every part of my body is on fire, and only Ben can quench the flames. "The things you do to me should be outlawed, Firefly," he says, biting down hard on my neck. "I want to eat you alive. I want to bury my cock so deep inside you I can never pull it out."

"That sounds painful," I pant, arching my neck to grant him greater access as he continues to bite and suck on my sensitive flesh. He's careful to keep his touching below the still tender part of my upper throat. "But surprisingly tempting. I need you, Ben. Please."

He slaps my ass, and I yelp at the unexpected contact.

"No begging, Firefly." He winds my hair around one of his hands, tilting my head back a little. "My queen never begs."

He brushes his lips against mine fleetingly. "Get on the bed, on all fours, and wait for me."

His laughter follows me as I race across the room to the bed, getting into position. I hear him walking to his dresser and pulling things out of a drawer. My pussy clenches in anticipation. I am so turned on I could implode. Clothing rustles, and out of the corner of my eye, I spy his boxers flying a few feet away. I moan when the bed dips behind me, knowing his cock will be inside me soon.

"Sit up," he says, coming up behind me.

I kneel, leaning back against his chest. "Trust me?" he whispers across my ear and his warm breath fans over my face.

"Yes," I rasp.

He slips a blindfold down over my eyes before pulling my hands behind my back. "Is your wrist still sore?" he asks, gently touching my injured hand.

"Only a little." It's not broken or sprained, just bruised.

"I'm going to bind your hands with a silk tie, but I won't tighten them."

I nod as butterflies run riot in my chest. This is new, and I fucking love it. The only sound in the room is our joint rapid breathing as he loosely ties my hands. "Is that okay?" he asks.

"It's fine." I'm panting like a dog in heat as the anticipation rises and rises.

The bed shifts, and I'm more conscious of his movements without the use of my sight or my hands. He stands in front of me on the bed, and heat rolls off his body in waves. "Open wide, baby," he commands, and I obey. "Suck," he says before shoving his throbbing cock in my mouth. He holds my shoulders to keep me steady as I work him over with my lips and my tongue. He thrusts into my mouth in sync with my movements and not being able to see what I'm doing or touch him only elevates my desire to new, dizzy heights.

"That's enough," he says, yanking his cock from my mouth with a pop, a few minutes later. "Resume your first position."

He's so bossy, but I love it.

The bed moves as he jumps onto the floor, and I let my head flop to the comforter. He crawls up behind me, parting my legs wider, and my desire leaks from my pussy, trickling down my thighs. He slides one finger inside me, and I cry out as my pussy grips his digit like the hungry slut she is. "Goddamn, Sierra. You are so fucking wet and so tight."

"Ben, puh—"

I scream as he slaps my ass hard.

"Baby, shush. Let's not wake Rowan. I have big plans for you tonight, and we need time," he says, massaging my stinging cheek. "Now what did I tell you about begging? Hmm."

"Ben, I—"

I muffle my scream in the comforter this time as his hand whacks my other ass cheek.

"Naughty, Firefly," he purrs, rubbing my ass with his large warm palms.

I say nothing, playing the dutiful part he wants.

"Good girl." He presses a soft kiss to each ass cheek before diving to my pussy and plundering my channel with his skillful tongue.

The noises coming out of my mouth as he eats me from behind are not human. Stars spin behind my blindfold, and I'm awash with sensation as he devours me like he will die if he doesn't consume me. His fingers move around to the front of my pussy, and he rubs my clit in time with the thrusts of his tongue. My climax builds fast until I'm shattering into dust particles, my entire body elevating from this plane of existence. I can feel nothing, see nothing, taste nothing, but the most intense orgasm as it lays claim to my body, rendering me nothing but a mass of quivering cells and nerve endings.

"Fuck, Sierra. You slay me," he says before he slams inside me without any advance warning. I can only hold on for the ride as he pivots his hips and drills into me like a madman. His sheathed cock strokes my inner walls as he rams in and out of me, his fingers digging into my hips when he pulls my ass up higher and spreads my legs a little wider, giving him greater access.

Another orgasm builds as he works my body like a pro. Suddenly, my hands fall loose at my sides as he removes the silk tie and then the blindfold. He flips me over, stretching my thighs wide as he climbs over me. Propping himself up on his hands, he hovers over my heaving body. "I want to see your face when I come." He dips his head, crashing his lips to mine as he guides his erection back inside me. "I love you," he whispers in my ear as I wrap my legs around his waist.

"I love you too, Ben. So much."

We kiss and touch and fuck, climbing the ascent together, and nothing has ever felt as right as being connected to this man. Sex has never been this good for me, and he elicits responses from my body I didn't know I was capable of.

"Come for me, Firefly. I need you to come first," he demands, pinching my clit hard as he rocks into me. A sheen of sweat rolls down his chest, and his face is flushed. My hair is a mess of tangled knots around my head as I arch my back, preparing for rocket launch. Ben pinches my clit a second time, and I scream as my release hits me full force.

Ben cusses under his breath and then he's shouting out his release as he comes powerfully. He collapses on the bed beside me, instantly pulling me into his embrace. "I will never get enough of you. Being inside you is like heaven. And watching you come is a thing of beauty."

I rub his arm, dotting kisses against his clammy chest. "Sex with you is out of this world," I agree.

"Good." He grins, leaning over me as he sweeps damp knotty strands of hair out of my face. "Because I'm not finished with you tonight. Not by a long shot."

I smile as he crawls back over me, feeling his cock hardening again. "Do your worst because I'm nowhere near finished with you either, Ben."

Those are the last words spoken in a very long time.

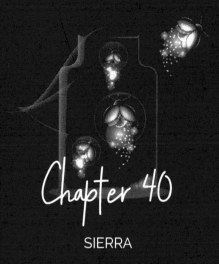

Chapter 40

SIERRA

"PEOPLE LEGITIMATELY SIGN up for this?" Angelo asks as he lies before me on the flattened hospital bed in his room.

I position the last needle in place, gently wiggling it until I feel the resistance under his skin. "Can you feel that?"

"Yes. It's weird. Like a pulsing pressure."

I laugh, pulling off my plastic gloves. "That is one of the most powerful points on the body for nausea. That you can feel it is a good thing." I place my gloves on the counter before dimming the lights. "And to answer your previous question, yes, people willingly sign up for acupuncture. It's very popular. A lot of my clients are women who either need help with fertility issues or support combatting pregnancy sickness."

"You think this will work for me?"

"Let's hope so," Natalia says, appearing in the doorway.

"Get out," Angelo hisses, clearly embarrassed to be seen like this.

"Stop with your bitching and whining," Natalia says, handing me the blanket I asked her to fetch. "And I'm going." She kisses his clammy brow. "I hope it works. I hate seeing you so sick."

Since Ben left for the city on Sunday, Angelo's condition has taken another turn for the worse. He can't keep anything down, and if this continues, he will need to have a feeding tube inserted. I know he doesn't want that, so I offered to help.

I'm glad I had the foresight to ask Esme and Pen to pack up my work supplies. Pen ran by the center to collect everything after I emailed the manager my resignation letter. I don't know if she is suspicious that I resigned without giving notice at the same time her new receptionist disappeared, but I have to trust my dad and Ben cleaned up the mess and she is none the wiser.

Anyway, it's good I have my things so I can do this for Angelo. Acupuncture can assist with a wide range of conditions, but it's especially helpful with nausea. I might not like the man much, but I won't stand by and watch someone suffer when I can do something about it. He *is* Ben's father and Rowan's grandfather after all.

I place the blanket over his body, being careful not to dislodge any of the needles. Lighting the diffuser, I let the exotic scents swirl around the room before pulling up one of my most popular playlists with my clients on my cellphone. The oriental orchestral piece is meant to be soothing and serene to help the patient relax. I find a lot of my clients actually fall asleep during the session, which is always a good sign.

"I'm going to leave you here for thirty to forty minutes," I tell Angelo, patting his arm as the music starts. "Press the button if you need help, and Ruthie will call me. Empty your mind, close your eyes, and try to relax," I add, spotting the wariness on his face. I'm not surprised he is doubting the process. He's old school, no matter how much he spouts about changing with the times. The fact he is willing to try this tells me how badly he wants to avoid the feeding tube.

"I can't believe you got the old bastard to do that," Natalia says after we have exited the room and shut the door. I notice she refers to her father as "the old bastard" a lot, even to his face, but it's said with affection. It's evident she has a very different relationship with Angelo than Ben.

"I had to coax and distract him a lot," I admit, as we walk toward the playroom.

"I've never had acupuncture," she says as we step inside Rowan's domain.

"I can do a session with you before you leave, if you like," I offer.

Rowan is currently bouncing on one of the trampolines, singing to himself, without a care in the world. Apart from asking when he will see his cousin Romeo again and when his daddy is returning, he seems quite content.

Alesso looks up from his spot on the floor, across the large room, nodding by way of greeting.

"Hi, Mom!" Rowan waves as he bounces on the trampoline, his hair lifting from his head with the motion. "Hi, Auntie Natalia!"

I wave at him, and Natalia blows him a kiss. "Hello, little charmer."

I grab some waters from the small refrigerator in the room before taking a seat alongside Natalia on the couch. "I would like a session," Natalia says. "If it's not too much trouble."

I snort out a laugh. "Have you not been watching me go slowly insane?"

"You like to keep busy," she surmises, smiling as she watches Rowan.

"Doesn't everyone?"

"I envy you," she says, twisting her head to look at me. Glancing in Alesso's direction, she lowers her voice so he can't hear. "You got to choose what you did with your life. And Ben won't curtail you either. Once this threat is dealt with, he will support you with whatever you wish to do."

"And your husband doesn't?"

She runs her tongue along her plump lips. "It's not that he deliberately stops me from doing what I want to do. It's more the perception. Mafia wives usually don't work."

"I don't see what the big deal is," I say, uncapping my water. "Why can't you work? We're not living in the Dark Ages."

"Gino says it's for protection. A way to keep the wives safe, whereas I believe it's more about control."

"Isn't Ben changing things though?"

"He is, but that's within the Mazzone *famiglia*. Yes, some of the other families have adopted some of his new ways, but the manner in which women are treated in this world is still significantly lacking."

"I'm sorry. That sucks."

"It does." She sighs, tossing her long glossy dark hair over her shoulders. "I had to drop out of college when I married Gino. I only got to go in the first place because Ben convinced the old bastard to postpone my wedding until I was twenty-one and to let me attend NYU."

"So, your wedding was an arranged marriage?" I had wondered when I saw them at the charity ball in Chicago. Her husband looks a good bit older than her, and while it could have been by choice, I had a sense it wasn't.

"I was promised to another man before I was even born," she admits, and I can't keep the shock from my face.

"I can't even imagine what that must be like."

"Like a life sentence. I grew up knowing I was destined to marry this man and that I wouldn't be allowed to date anyone else. I was expected to be a virgin on my wedding night while my fiancé was entitled to fuck as many women as he liked, both before and after our marriage. It disgusts me." She swallows a few mouthfuls of water, but it does nothing to disperse the angry set of her mouth. "I fought my parents nonstop over it. Begged them to let me out of it."

"And did they?"

A bitter laugh escapes her mouth. "No, but fate intervened. Gino Accardi's wife died when his twins were only three. He needed a new wife to take care of them, and I was desperate to be promised to anyone but the man I was promised to." A shudder works its way through her, and I want to ask why, but I sense it's not something she wishes to share. At least not now. "The old bastard worked his magic, getting me out of the earlier arrangement, and within a few months, I was married to Gino and taking care of his boys. I had to drop out of college midway through junior year."

"Can't you go back now the boys are older? Or complete it online or by night classes?"

"It's a possibility. When the boys start high school next year, I intend to convince Gino to let me complete my degree. Then I'll work on him about med school."

"If I can do anything to help, let me know."

She squeezes my hand. "Thank you. I will." The frustration and anger disappear from her face, replaced with a softer look. "I am so glad you and Ben reconnected. The difference in him is incredible. He—"

"Sorry to interrupt, ladies," a deep voice says, startling both of us.

"Leo. What are you doing here?" I ask, getting up. I glance into the hallway behind him, hope bubbling in my chest.

"I had to collect some documents for the boss, and he asked me to drop these off."

I can't be disappointed Ben isn't with him when he produces a massive bunch of flowers and a smaller box from behind his back. His smile is genuine as he hands them to me. Leo seems to have thawed to me recently, and I'm glad. I know he is Ben's best friend, as well as his trusted number two, so it's important we get along. However, I can't say I know the man, and there is still a distance between us I would like to eliminate someday soon.

I can't keep the grin off my face as I bury my nose in the fragrant flowers, setting the box down on my knees.

"Wow. I never thought I'd see this day." Natalia smiles. "Who knew my brother was such a closet romantic?"

"I think that's supposed to be a secret," Leo says, staring at Natalia with a look that can only be described as longing.

Interesting.

I thought I caught him looking at her when she was dancing with Ben at the ball, but I didn't pay much attention to it. I wonder what the story is there. Surreptitiously, I watch the two of them over the enormous bunch of flowers on my lap.

"Of course." Natalia's smile fades out. "God forbid any made man outwardly shows love and affection toward his wife."

A frown appears on Leo's face, and he opens his mouth to say something when Rowan notices him, cutting him off before he can form a word.

"Leo!" Rowan shouts, bouncing off the trampoline, and almost face-planting on the ground. He races toward Ben's right-hand man in his socks. "Is my daddy here?"

"Daddy's at work, buddy. Sorry," he says, ruffling his hair. He crouches down to his level when Rowan pouts. "He told me to tell you he'll be home on Friday for Halloween, and he asked me to give you this." He hands Rowan a large paper bag of candy, and his eyes pop wide.

"Hand the candy here, Firecracker." I set my flowers down on the floor by the couch, stretching my arm out. If I don't take the bag from Rowan now, he will throw a hissy fit.

"But, Mom!" he protests, pouting.

"You can have some now, just not the whole bag." I don't want to rain on Ben's parade, not when he's being super sweet and thoughtful, but a small bag of candy would suffice, and I'll need to tell him that for future reference.

"I'd better get back," Leo says, straightening up. "Ben is waiting on these." He waves a handful of folders in the air.

"Okay. Thanks for stopping by."

Leo jerks his head in Alesso's direction, and he gets up, following Leo out of the room.

Natalia is lost in thought while I dispense a small portion of candy into a bowl for Rowan. Rowan returns to the trampoline, emptying the candy onto it as he lies flat on his tummy, munching away.

"I don't mean to pry, but did anything ever happen between you and Leo?" I ask, as I open the box he gave me.

"Why do you ask?" she inquires, as I peel back the lid of the box, unable to stop the grin spreading across my face when I see the six lush red-velvet, and peanut-butter-truffle, cupcakes.

"I see the way he looks at you," I say, offering her the box.

"At one time, I entertained thoughts of him and me, but it could never be." She lifts a cupcake out. "What's this?" she asks, extracting a folded sheet of paper on the bottom of the box.

I set my cupcake down, unfolding the paper and reading the email Ben forwarded to the local bakery with tears in my eyes. "Oh my God. I can't believe he did this."

She leans over my shoulder reading it. "Damn, Benny has it bad." She squeezes my shoulder. "It must be love if he's gone to this much trouble to ensure you got your favorite cupcakes."

"I can't believe he emailed the old bakery in Glencoe and got the exact recipe for the cupcakes I like. To even remember my favorite cupcakes is enough to have me swooning." I take a quick selfie with the flowers and the cupcakes and send it to Ben with a loving note.

He is so getting laid when he comes home Friday.

She swipes a stray tear from my eye, and I hate the sad wistful shroud that veils her beautiful face. "You are so lucky, Sierra. Both of you are. Love is so precious, especially in this world. Protect it with everything you've got."

"Don't worry. I plan to."

NATALIA LEFT FOR the city today, and I already miss her. I'm missing Ben so much too. We spent every spare minute together last weekend, and when he left Sunday night, it was as if I was missing a limb.

Thoughts of his hands all over my body—and the hours upon hours of catching up we spent in the bedroom—have me flushing all over. Which is most inappropriate, given I'm cycling with Rowan around the grounds of the house.

There is an icy chill in the air, and I wouldn't be surprised if it was snowing by my birthday.

"Who's that?" Rowan shouts as he cycles alongside me.

I frown, looking around and not seeing anyone. "Who do you mean?"

"I saw a girl in that window." His bicycle wobbles as he points at a room on our left.

I reach out to steady his handlebars before he takes a tumble. "Are you sure?"

He vigorously nods his head. "She was staring at me."

Huh. "Stop here for a sec," I say, helping him down from his bike.

We walk over to the window, pressing our noses to the glass, peering inside. This is the west wing of the house. The side getting renovated. Though I don't see any evidence of that as I examine the stunning living room inside. It's a warm inviting room with a patterned rug, soft comfortable couches, colorful cushions, artwork on the walls, and a modern cream stone fireplace with a large shiny mirror hanging over it. The space is empty of life though, so if there was a girl there, she's long gone.

"It was probably one of the staff," I tell Rowan. "Come on. I'll race you to the tree house."

That night, I review the tutor files Natalia left for me, shooting Ben an email when I have it shortlisted to three applicants. He replies almost immediately, confirming he will arrange interviews for this Saturday. He is as anxious as I am that Rowan doesn't miss out on classes for too long. After I shut my laptop down, I head to my studio to work on my new painting before retreating to bed alone. As I snuggle under the covers, stretching my hand across the bed to the cold empty space

Ben usually occupies, I comfort myself with the knowledge he will be home tomorrow.

"BE CAREFUL," I shout after Rowan as he climbs the ladder to the tree house the following day. The tree house is, hands down, his favorite part of the playground.

"Don't worry," Alesso says. "I'll stay with him." I smile as I watch him climb up behind Rowan into the large enclosed wooden structure. Rowan adores Alesso, and I'm tempted to suggest Frank and Alesso swap assignments. Don't get me wrong, Frank is a nice guy, just a little more reserved and harder to get to know than Alessandro. It's a moot point at the moment, anyway, considering Frank left for the city early yesterday. There was an emergency, and Ben needed him. I told him he should keep Frank in New York. The guys are just hanging around the house, bored out of their skulls most of the time. With the number of bodyguards on the grounds, having both Alesso and Frank watching us is excessive.

I decided to bring my easel and canvas outside today to paint. It's not quite as cold as recent days, and this will probably be my last chance to paint outdoors for a while, if the weather forecasts are to be believed.

I'm lost in my painting, immersed in my own colorful world, so I don't hear the footsteps approaching until the last few seconds.

My eyes pop wide as a gorgeous girl with long dark-blonde hair walks up to me. I put my paintbrush down, grabbing a wipe to scrub the dried paint off my hands. "Hello," I say, regarding her warily as she comes to a stop beside me.

She stares at my painting. "Interesting," she drawls, sounding like it's anything but.

She sounds American, but there is a hint of an accent to her voice, and my guard goes up. I glance over at the tree house, wondering if I should call out for Alesso. He and Rowan must be lying on the bean bags, playing a game, as I don't even see the tops of their heads.

"Do you work for Ben?" I ask, even as I note she's not wearing the uniform the rest of the staff wear.

She barks out a derisory laugh. "Hardly."

Alarm bells ring in my ears. Who the hell is this girl, and where did she come from? I wouldn't put it past the Russians to use women to do their dirty work, and I'm immediately suspicious. I take a couple of steps back from her. "Who are you?" I ask in a sharper tone.

She twirls a lock of her hair as she fixes me with a smug smile. "Didn't Bennett tell you?"

All the tiny hairs lift on the back of my neck. "Tell me what?"

She closes the space between us, lifting her chin and pinning me with a haughty expression. "I'm Anais. I'm Bennett's fiancée."

Chapter 41

BEN

SOMETHING IS WRONG with Sierra, and I can't figure out what it is or how it happened. We only spoke this morning on the phone, and everything seemed fine. Maybe I've gotten greedy, but I'd expected a much warmer welcome than the frosty one I received. Scrubbing a hand down my face, I sigh. Honestly, I could do without this shit. It's been the week from hell, and I don't need the additional stress. I'm reminded of one of the reasons why I've avoided relationships for most of my adult life.

Women are complex creatures, and I rarely have the patience to deal with them.

But this is Firefly.

I love her.

I *adore* her.

If she's upset, *I'm* upset.

If something is wrong, I want to know what it is so I can fix it.

I long to pull her aside and demand to know what the issue is, but I don't want to put a damper on Rowan's little Halloween party. Sierra has gone to a huge amount of effort to make it special for him so he doesn't miss trick or treating. She has transformed his playroom with long painted sheets of ghosts, skeletons, witches, and goblins. Fake cobwebs hang in streams across the ceilings, and she covered all the lights in the room with sheer red sheets, casting a bloody haze over the room. The side table holds bowls of candy, chips, and drinks.

Sierra is dressed like an angel, in a costume she made for herself, complete with white and silver wings stuck to her back. She's a vision of innocence. One I wouldn't mind corrupting. Rowan is wearing a store-bought Batman costume, and funnily enough, I picked up a devil costume from a place in the city on my way home today.

The angel and the devil. It really couldn't be more apt. It wouldn't be as funny if we had planned it, but we didn't. My decision was a spur-of-the-moment thing.

Leo scowls at me, and I smirk at the sight of him in the too tight Thor costume. It was the only size they had left in the store, and I couldn't resist. Every so often he adjusts the suit in the crotch area, muttering under his breath, and I can't help laughing. Alessandro is some kind of ancient gladiator, resplendent with a fake sword and plastic headpiece, and he's taking it in stride. Even Angelo entered into the spirit of things, dressing as Charlie Chaplin. Ruthie is a USO nurse. Most everyone is in good spirits, feeding off Rowan's excitement.

Sierra is an amazing mother. Rowan is so blessed to have her as his mom, and I can't wait to make her my wife. Whatever has happened, I won't let it come between us. I'll cut her some slack, even if I want to put her over my lap and spank her bare ass every time she glowers in my direction. I asked Alessandro what is going on when I first arrived and noticed her attitude, but he's as in the dark as I am. That didn't give me the warm fuzzies.

What the hell is going on with my most trusted solider? He seems distracted, and that concerns me. He should know if something happened. Perhaps I should have left Frank here and sent Alessandro to Philly instead.

There is no point pondering it now. I can't do anything about this until I talk to Sierra. So, I do what she does. I plaster a happy smile on my face as we bob for apples, share candy, and watch *Casper* in our home theater.

After tucking a sleepy Rowan into bed, I strip out of my costume, changing into jeans and a long-sleeved Henley, before hunting down my woman. I don't have to search far. She is pacing in front of the fire in our living room, looking like she's ready to shred the world to pieces.

Or maybe just me.

She has removed the angel wings, but she's still wearing the white and silver dress, and I long to tear it from her body and do all manner of devilish things to her. Her head whips up when I close the door to the hallway, giving us complete privacy. Alessandro has already retreated to his room, wanting to stay out of the line of fire, I'm sure. Though there will be no avoiding it if I find out he is at fault in any way.

Her eyes narrow, and her hands ball into fists at her side, and I'm pretty sure sexy times are off the table right now.

"What is going on, Firefly?" I ask, approaching hesitantly. I love Sierra's feisty momma-bear side, but the look she is currently giving me is on a whole other level, and honestly, I'm a little afraid.

"You tell me," she snarls, shoving at my shoulders when I stop in front of her.

"I have no clue what the issue is, but if you tell me what's troubling you, I will fix it."

She harrumphs, and I can almost see the steam billowing from her ears. "Why is there another woman, a *girl*, living in this house, and why does she claim to be your fiancée?" she spits, looking like she wants to rip my throat out.

Oh. Fuck.

"Calm down, Firefly. It's not whatever you are thinking."

And that was definitely the wrong thing to say.

"Calm down!" she yells. "Don't you dare tell me to calm down. You fucking lied to me! You told me you were getting renovations done in the west wing when this whole time you've been hiding your other woman in there! Do you have any idea how much it hurt to be accosted by her outside when I had no clue who she was? Yet she appeared to know exactly who I am. How is that? Huh? How does your other woman know about me when I didn't know of *her* existence?"

I would like to know the answer to that question too. Anais shouldn't know anything about Sierra or Rowan, and heads will roll for this. I am going to throttle Alessandro. Where the fuck was he when this was going down? "There is no other woman," I say, working hard to hold on to my calm demeanor. This is bullshit, and she should know it. What else do I need to do to prove to Sierra that she is the only woman for me?

"Don't fucking lie to me, asshole!" She shoves my shoulders again, and I'm getting mad. "I saw her! I spoke to her. Anais just loved telling me how she was your fiancée." She slaps a hand across her chest. "Her! Not me!"

"She's the liar," I snap, rubbing a tense spot between my brows. "She—"

"Was any of it real? Or were your professions of love just a ruse to get me back underneath you?"

That's it. The tenuous hold on my brittle emotions snaps, and I lose it. "You know it is fucking real!" I roar. "And if you'd stop acting like a brat for five seconds and let me explain, you'd realize that!"

Her nostrils flare, and she beats her fists against my chest. "Fuck you, Ben. Fuck you and your condescending cheating ass. I'm out of here tomorrow. I'm taking Rowan, and you can stay the fuck away from both of us."

She moves to walk away, and I grab her arm. "Like hell you are." Sweeping her legs out from under her, I toss her over my shoulder.

"Let me down, you fucking asshole." She beats on my back, but I barely feel it.

I slap her ass firmly as I stride out of the double doors and into the wide hallway. "I'm not letting you down until you've seen reason. This bullshit ends right now."

She proceeds to fight, thrash, and pummel her fists against my back as I storm across the length of my house toward the west wing. I continue to spank her naughty ass even though it only enrages her more.

Well, I'm fucking pissed too.

Finding an exposed part of my shoulder, she sinks her teeth into my skin, drawing blood. My cock hardens behind my zipper, and I'm a crazy mix of rage and lust as I shove through the doors to the other wing, relieved to find Salerno alone in the living room.

He looks up from his tablet, sending me an amused grin as he watches Sierra wriggle and fight on my shoulder.

I slap her ass one final time. "I'm letting you down, but if you don't behave, I'll tie you up and shove a gag in your mouth," I threaten.

"I'd like to see you try, asshole," she spits.

Salerno chuckles. "What do we have here?"

I haven't told Saverio about Sierra or Rowan because I wanted him nowhere near them. I just said I had guests staying for a while to keep him over on his side of the house. The deal was they were to remain inside, within the west wing, and to stay away from the windows.

Something his little bitch of a daughter had an issue obeying.

The instant I met her, I felt relieved the Russians attacked Vegas and Salerno needed to use his favor to secure protection and safety.

I hadn't given much thought to the favor over the years, especially the longer it went on and he hadn't called it in. I would have found some way out of it, if he had used it to try to force my hand into a marriage arrangement, because, the second I met Anais, I knew there was no way I could stomach living a fake life with the spoiled Salerno *principessa*. It's clear Saverio has indulged her every whim, and it's done her no favors. Even if his reputation and his territory weren't in tatters, he would struggle to get anyone to agree to a match unless they went into it blind.

I wonder if that is why no marriage agreement is already in place. Something that is strange for a girl who is nearly eighteen.

Sierra stiffens in my arms, and I'm guessing Saverio's voice has triggered something in her memory. "It's okay," I assure her, sliding her down my body. "He's here as my guest." She turns in my arms to face him. "He isn't a threat to you," I add. I would kill him before I'd let him come anywhere near Sierra.

"Ms. Lawson. Now this is a surprise," Saverio says, putting his tablet down.

"Not a pleasant one, I assure you," Sierra says, still holding on to her anger.

I'm quite happy to let her unleash the rest of her fury in his direction. His daughter is the one who started this, after all.

Though I didn't help by concealing their presence here. I should have fessed up after she arrived, but things were going so well, and I didn't want to fuck things up. My motives weren't entirely selfish though. I also didn't want her to feel unsafe in her new home, and I know Salerno's presence here would've spooked her—understandably so.

We are negotiating on a property on Salerno's behalf right now, and they should be moving out in a matter of days. I thought I could get rid of them before Sierra even realized they were here.

Guess I've only made it worse, and now she'll be back to doubting me again. All the progress we have made will be undone.

Great.

"We need to talk," I tell him, ushering Sierra to the couch across from where Saverio is sitting. I push her down, clamping my arm around her shoulders to keep her in place. "Sierra is my fiancée," I explain, placing my hand over her lips when she opens her mouth to disagree. "And she lives here now with our five-year-old son."

Shock splays across his face. "You have a son?" He looks between her and me before emitting a bellowing laugh. "Vegas!" He slaps a hand on his thigh, chuckling. "You conceived in Vegas, and I caught the moment on tape."

I make a mental note to come back to that as Sierra sends daggers in Salerno's direction at the reminder.

"That's not important right now. What is important is that your daughter is running around my property spewing filthy lies when I specifically told you to keep her indoors."

"Ah. I see." He grins, and I want to riddle his face with bullets.

I remove my hand from Sierra's face, pinning her with a cautionary look. "This is no laughing matter, Saverio. Please explain why your daughter is saying she is my fiancée when we both know that is not true."

He leans forward, clasping his hands on his knees. The overhead light shines directly on his scarred, pockmarked face, and Sierra flinches against me. I squeeze her tightly, reassuring her she is safe. "You are aware, Ms. Lawson, that Ben owed me a favor from that night."

She nods tersely.

"I had been proposing a marriage agreement between Anais and Bennett for some time before that night. Angelo was open to discussing it, but it was clear Ben wasn't interested, and he's not like most made men. I knew he wouldn't be forced into it, so I was prepared to let it drop. Then you entered the mix, and things got interesting." He leers at her, letting his gaze drag down her body, and I see red.

"Show my future wife some respect, or you and I have a big problem, Saverio," I bark.

He holds up his hands. "I apologize. I mean no disrespect. You are a lucky man, Ben. She is even more exquisite than I remember."

"And you're even more of a disgusting pig than I remember," Sierra unhelpfully supplies.

All hint of humor fades from his face, and this is going downhill fast. "Sierra means no disrespect," I say, clasping my hand over her mouth again. "But she is understandably upset and angry. Anais had no right to say the things she said."

"She didn't, and I will have words with her," he agrees, and some of the tension leaves my body.

"Why does she believe she is going to marry Ben?" Sierra asks, folding her arms and leveling a dark glare in Salerno's direction.

"That is my fault. I had intended on using the favor I was owed to marry her to Ben, but I was holding back until Anais came of age. I was certain once he took one look at her, his reservations would fade away and he would be happy to agree to it."

I fix him with a sharp look. "No offense intended, but your daughter pales into insignificance next to my Firefly." I want to add that Anais is fucking ugly on the inside, but insulting the man while he's still living in my home—a home where my son lives—is not wise. Saverio has killed men for less. "Sierra is the only woman I have ever loved. The only woman I would ever marry." I risk pressing my lips to her temple, and I feel her relax a smidgeon against me.

"I will ensure Anais is aware of that." It's obvious now that Salerno hadn't set her straight when they moved here. He was still clinging to the hope I would fall at her feet and agree to marry her, even though he has already called in his favor. I don't blame him for holding out hope, even if it was futile. His empire has collapsed, and while The Commission is planning a counterattack to regain control of Vegas, a suitable marriage arrangement would go a long way toward restoring his reputation.

"See that she does," Sierra says. "Because I won't tolerate being spoken to like that in my own home."

I inwardly breathe a sigh of relief at her words. I'm sure I'll be in the doghouse for a while, but no permanent damage has been inflicted. I will grovel, as needed, until she forgives me.

"I'm sorry for any pain it might have caused you," he says, and I can tell Sierra is surprised at his response. Salerno isn't always a murdering sleazebag. He shows glimmers of humanity from time to time.

Saverio was shocked to see how ill Angelo is. I've managed to successfully hide that intel from most people. The Commission is aware of his condition, and I'm sure most of the other families suspect, because he hasn't been seen in public for over a year, but I trust Salerno to keep the secret. He knows I have gone above and beyond our favor to help him in his time of need, and I know he won't forget that in a hurry.

His daughter is another matter entirely. I don't trust Anais, and she needs to be dealt with. "I want to find out how Anais knew about Sierra."

He nods. "Agreed, but I suggest I talk to her alone. She will be more pliable without an audience."

I don't argue because I'm not sure I won't strangle the bitch if I'm in the same room as her right now. "I want that to happen tonight, and I want answers."

"You will get them," he assures me, so I move on to the next important topic.

"About that tape," I say before we conclude our conversation. "I would like it back."

He frowns. "You don't already have it?" His gaze swings to Sierra. "I thought Tony was your bodyguard?"

"Tony?" Disbelief laces Sierra's tone as she sits upright. "What has this got to do with my old bodyguard?"

His features soften a little, and I instinctively pull Sierra closer. "He showed up a few months after that night, demanding we hand over the tape. I threw him out, but he broke into my office a few nights later and stole it, along with my laptop. He hacked into our system and wiped all traces of the video from our servers. I assumed he had sent it to you."

Sierra flops back on the couch, looking at me with shell-shocked eyes. "I told him everything when I discovered I was pregnant, but I had no idea he would go to Vegas to retrieve the video." She worries her teeth between her lower lip, and concern fills her face. "I wonder why he never sent it to me or why he never made contact with me again?"

I have a fairly good idea why, and as my eyes meet Salerno's knowing gaze, I see the truth.

"He probably destroyed all the evidence rather than risk having it fall into the wrong hands," Saverio says, confirming they didn't find it when they caught up to him.

Maybe I should say something, but the knowledge that Tony is dead, at Salerno's hand, will not keep the peace, and it will only hurt Sierra. Maybe I'm wrong to let her believe Tony is out there somewhere living a full life, but I don't see how revealing the truth benefits anyone.

Tony died protecting Sierra's honor, and I owe him a debt I can never repay.

But I can do this for him.

I can let him live on in Sierra's memory instead of admitting the truth and watching her blame herself for his actions. I didn't know the man, but I heard enough to know he was a decent, honorable, loyal man, and he wouldn't want Sierra knowing the truth.

So, I say nothing, bidding Saverio goodbye, as I lead Sierra back to the sanctity of our private rooms.

Chapter 42

SIERRA

MY THOUGHTS VEER all over the place as I lie in bed with my back to Ben. I'm so pissed at him for lying to me. How could he let me stay here knowing that disgusting man and his equally obnoxious daughter were sharing the same floor space? Okay, I know I'm probably overreacting a little. This place is ginormous, and we have armed men protecting us, but it didn't stop that conniving bitch from confronting me outside.

"I want her gone," I say, knowing instinctively that Ben isn't sleeping. "I want both of them gone." I've had time to think about the conversation since we left the west wing, and I know Scarface Salerno had something to do with Tony disappearing. I don't want to contemplate the thought he is in a shallow grave somewhere, but that's what those guys do. Tony broke into his office and stole from him. There is no way Salerno would have let that pass. There is a slim chance Tony got away before they caught up to him, and maybe I should cling to that hope, but I promised myself I would stop being delusional when it came to this life.

My heart is heavy, and I'm doubting everything again. The thought that Tony might have died doing something to protect me slays me on the inside. What I wouldn't give for one more day with him so I could tell him how much he meant to me. How much I value everything he did to protect me after Vegas. I owe him a debt I can never repay.

"I will have them moved to a hotel first thing in the morning," Ben says, without hesitation, and that goes some way toward reassuring me.

But he is still in the doghouse. I'm not forgiving him that easily. "Thank you."

"Firefly, I—"

"I'm tired, Ben. I don't want to talk or fight anymore."

"Fine," he huffs, and the sheets rustle as he turns on his side, facing the other way.

I hate that we're fighting, and that Anais is the cause of it, but he needs to realize he can't keep lying to me.

Things are no less tense the following morning. My sleep was fitful, as was Ben's, and he looks as miserable as I feel. I retreat to my studio to paint while he takes Rowan outside to the playground.

We meet, just before lunch, to interview the three shortlisted tutors. I discount the first two women immediately when I see how they are looking at Ben, stopping both interviews after five minutes when it is clear they are more interested in my fiancé than my son's education.

I breathe a sigh of relief when the older gentleman with the salt-and-pepper hair takes a seat on the couch across from us. Mr. Spielberg is a distant relation of the famous movie director, and he has made a career out of tutoring kids on movie sets. He recently returned home to the area, and he has been looking for new work. He has glowing references, he is respectful and articulate, and he emits good vibes. I warm to him instantly, as does Ben, and Rowan seems to like him when we bring him in to say hi. He is gentle and patient with Rowan and appears to enjoy his exuberant personality.

After he is gone, Rowan comes with me to paint while Ben heads to his study to email the man an offer of employment.

Dinner is a tense affair, not that Rowan seems to notice. He practically carries the conversation. Ben insists on bathing him, and as I stand just outside Rowan's bedroom door forty minutes later, listening to Ben reading Roald Dahl, I notice the strain cording his shoulders and the worry lines etched in his brow.

Stepping away, I walk to the living room to wait for him. I hate this, and I don't want him returning to the city tomorrow with things so awful between us. We need to talk about it. To try to find a way to move forward that is acceptable to both of us.

I pour Ben a bourbon when I hear him quietly closing Rowan's bedroom door, bringing my wine and his drink to the coffee table and setting them down. I sit on the couch, waiting until he shows his face.

"We need to talk," we say in unison, and it helps to ease the stress, a little.

"I poured you a drink," I say, holding it out to him.

"Thanks. I need it." He takes a healthy mouthful before sinking on the couch beside me. He puts his glass on the table, and his thigh brushes against mine as he unfolds something in his hand. He smooths out the creases in the paper, spreading the faded drawing on his lap.

My heart jumps in my chest. "You still have it."

"It's one of my most precious gifts," he admits, lacing his fingers in mine. I cling to his hand, savoring his warmth. "Like the woman who drew it." His blue eyes find my green ones. "I'm sorry, Firefly. I know you are angry at me and you have every right to be. I hate hurting you. Hurting you hurts me too."

"I appreciate and accept your apology, but how can I trust you if you continue lying to me, Ben?"

"Sweetheart." He places the drawing on the table, taking both my hands in his as he swivels on the couch. I twist around so we are facing one another. "I want to be honest with you, but it's not always going to be possible. I hear how shitty that sounds, but let me explain." His eyes probe mine and I urge him to continue. "There will always be secrets in my world. Things I can't tell you because to do so places you at risk. That is not an excuse to keep things from you. It's the cold hard truth." He squeezes my hand. "As my wife, you will be a target. My job is to keep you safe. Part of that means ensuring you are not exposed to information that could jeopardize your well-being."

"I understand that, to a point, Ben. But there have to be exceptions. I have to know enough to be vigilant, and to be able to protect myself, and you can't keep things from me that I *need* to know." I peer deep into his eyes. "I needed to know Salerno was here. I needed to know about Anais."

"I know, and I was wrong to keep it from you. At first, it was because I knew you wouldn't come here if you knew the truth, and I had to protect you. I don't think you understand the sheer terror I felt when you called me that day. My only concern was getting you and Rowan out of Chicago to safety."

"I don't understand why you couldn't have just moved Anais and Salerno to a hotel before we arrived. You were able to do it within a few hours this morning." I was delighted to see them being driven away just before lunch. Good riddance.

"The situation is extremely dangerous with the Russians right now. They have control of Vegas, and it was a bloody battle. Salerno was injured, defeated, and putting them in a hotel would have been too risky."

"Yet you moved them to one now."

"I did that for you."

"Are you saying they are at risk?" I don't like the man or his daughter, but I don't want to be responsible for their deaths either.

"Yes, but my team is working around the clock to close the deal on their new property, and I put more of my soldiers on protection duty."

"I feel bad now."

He tucks a piece of my hair behind my ears. "Don't. You are my priority. You and Rowan. And they will be okay for a couple of days."

"Did you find out how Anais knew about me?"

His face hardens. "The little bitch followed us that night we walked in the woods. She eavesdropped on our conversation and put things together. Rather than confronting her father, she decided to try and chase you off."

"How old is she?"

"Seventeen."

"Wow. She's vicious for someone so young."

"A lot of the women brought up in our circles are. It's a conundrum. Most seem to be either wholly innocent or spitefully evil. There doesn't appear to be much middle ground."

"I'm not sure that's true or fair. Natalia isn't like that."

"You're right. She isn't, and I shouldn't generalize."

"You are being very conciliatory tonight," I admit, extracting one of my hands from his so I can raise my glass of wine to my lips.

"I don't like fighting with you, and I don't want to let things fester between us. Today was shitty, and that's not how I want to start our relationship."

"Me either."

"Am I forgiven?" he asks, arching a brow.

"Are you going to keep lying to me about things I need to know?"

He cups one side of my face. "Sierra. I will be as honest with you as I can. I promise to give you the information you need to be vigilant and to be cognizant of anything you need to know that impacts you personally."

"Okay."

Air whooshes out of his mouth in grateful relief, and a layer of stress seems to lift from his shoulders. "I didn't think you would forgive me so easily."

"There is nothing easy about it, Ben, but I don't believe in holding grudges or withholding forgiveness. Grudges are poisonous and difficult to weed out once they have set in. You have apologized and promised not to do this again, so I would be in the wrong to cling to my anger, to fail to forgive you. That is not how I want our relationship to be."

He kisses the corner of my mouth. "Every day, you amaze me more. Every day, you make me want to be a better man." He kisses the other corner of my mouth. "I know I'm not worthy of you, Firefly. I know I have fucked up, that I will likely fuck up again, but I promise to continue trying to be the man you deserve. I have spent my life alone. My work has been my wife. This is all new to me, but I am trying."

"I know you are, and I love you for that." Alesso, Natalia, and Angelo have all remarked on the changes they see in Ben, and I see it myself. When he is with me, he has lowered a lot of his guards. That harsh, cold exterior has cracked wide-open, and he's showing me the man he is underneath. The man I always knew he could be.

But I can't expect miracles.

And I know he can't change the man he is now.

Loving Ben means loving all parts of him. I have already accepted that. Now it's time to fully embrace what that means.

Chapter 43

SIERRA

"IN THE INTEREST of transparency, and so you know I'm sincere, let me update you on a few things," Ben says.

I smile, finally relaxing, because he is making the effort, and I cannot ask for more than that. "I'm listening."

"The Russians have been at war with us for years, but in recent times, they appear to be getting their act together. They coordinated an attack on Vegas, one of our strongholds, and yanked it out of Salerno's hands with no warning."

"How is that even possible?"

"He was betrayed by his underboss. Gambini sold Salerno out."

"Why? Isn't loyalty and honor at the core of everything the mafia is about?"

"Gambini has some Russian blood, on his mother's side. It was distant but enough for the Russians to reach out to him with an offer he couldn't refuse."

"Wow. I'm betting that pissed Salerno off." I sit up straight. "Wait! He was in Vegas that night, wasn't he? He was the big brute of a guy with the scary eyes."

"That's him. He's lording over things in Vegas now. Thinking he's King Big Dick. I can't wait to wipe the smug smile off his face."

"You're going to war with the Russians?" I surmise, as nausea swells in my gut.

"We have no choice. We can't lose Vegas. This is the very reason The Commission was reestablished. We need to show a united front or else The Commission is only a smokescreen to hide behind. If the Russians see that, they will keep attacking."

He drags a hand through his hair, and I see the stark worry on his features. "Turn around," I demand, spreading my legs wide. He settles between my thighs without question, his back to my chest. "You're so tense," I supply when my hands land on his rigid shoulders.

"I've got a lot on my plate right now. We received word of an imminent attack on Philly, so we've sent men there. We are all on edge waiting for it to happen. I'm also frustrated that we have no leads on Lucille. I need to find that bitch to eliminate the threat against you and Rowan. And to top it off, The Outfit is stalling now."

"Why? I thought you said they were on board and ready to join The Commission?" At least, I'm pretty sure that's what he told me the last time we talked about Chicago.

"So did we. But it's that bastard DeLuca throwing a wrench in the works again."

"That's the big mysterious boss man who lives in Sicily?"

"Yeah, and it seems he's as opposed to The Commission as he was the last time around."

"How much damage will it cause if they don't join?"

"Chicago is the second biggest Italian mafia territory in the US. If they back out, it might force others to reconsider. We can't have them on the outside. Especially not now." Frustration seeps from his tone. "I can't fathom it. The Russian threat is real, and they aren't our only enemies. If it's known The Outfit is an isolated unit, they are likely to be attacked, so it makes no sense. They should want to unite. I don't understand what is holding DeLuca back."

I knead the tight muscles of his shoulders and upper back, wanting to erase the strain in his tissues.

"Fuck, that feels so good. Your hands are magic."

"I can give you a massage or do some acupuncture, if you like? It would help."

"A massage sounds wonderful." He hops up, pinning me with a heated look that makes his intentions perfectly clear. "You can take care of me, and then I'm taking care of you." He swoops in, scooping me up into his arms, and I giggle.

"You won't hear any complaints from me!"

"YOU ARE SPOILING me," I say as Ben holds out a chair for me. I have missed him so much this week. Rowan has too. And I'm glad he made it back last night for my birthday weekend. I can't believe he has gone to this much trouble or that he pulled it off right under my nose.

The rooftop has been transformed, and it's like a magical fantasy land. An enclosed marquee and several freestanding heaters keep the space warm. Copious bunches of flowers surround the circular table in the middle of the area, scenting the room beautifully. The table is set with crisp linens and the most expensive silverware. A large candelabra sends flickering light against the sides of the marquee, giving the entire setting an old-school romantic feel.

"It's your birthday, and I love spoiling you." He kisses my cheek. "I've a lot of lost time to make up for."

I love this romantic side to my man. Things are better than ever between us since we cleared the air last weekend. He calls every day to speak to me and Rowan, and he has made a big effort to tell me about his day, letting me know what is going on in his world. Flowers have arrived daily, along with more cupcakes, and if he keeps this up, I will have enough to open a florist shop.

I'm glad we resolved things and that our relationship is back on track. Ben explained there was one other thing he was keeping from me but he needed to have a conversation with someone else first. He promised he would update me as soon as he could. I'm curious as to what it is, but I'm placing my trust in him, so I've put it out of my mind for now.

My long red silk gown swishes against my body as I sit, and I'm glad I took his instructions to dress up seriously. Natalia arrived unexpectedly this afternoon, and she helped to style my hair in smooth glossy waves and to apply a full face of makeup that looks subtle despite how heavy it feels. She is babysitting Rowan while we are indulging ourselves on the roof. Not that there is a need for it as Alesso would have been happy to read him his bedtime story. I think Natalia wants to visit more often now Angelo's days are numbered, and I can understand that.

Ben pours two glasses of Cristal Champagne, handing one to me before he takes his seat. "To us," he says.

I clink my glass against his. "To the future."

We chat casually over a sumptuous dinner handed to us by a few of his trusted staff, sneaking kisses in between courses and more glasses of champagne.

"Oh my God." I rub a hand over my belly. "I'm not sure I can fit dessert in. If I eat any more, I might burst."

"We can share," he says, handing one of the plates back to the waitress. "That will be all, Miranda. We would like privacy now." He slides the plate of decadent chocolate cake in between us, as his staff slips out of the marquee, leaving us entirely alone.

"Open," he says, raising a forkful of cake to my mouth.

I let him slip the delicious cake into my mouth, groaning as my tastebuds explode with the rich, spicy, chocolatey goodness. "Damn, that's good," I say, when I've finished eating, fluttering my eyelashes at him. "Almost as good as sex."

"That had better be a joke," he growls, fidgeting in his seat.

I lean in, brushing my chocolate-coated lips against his mouth. "You know it is." Warmth creeps up my neck, plopping onto my cheeks, as I recall our nocturnal activities last night.

Sex with Ben just keeps getting better and better, and I'm insatiable for him. Did I mention how fuckable he looks in his black Prada tux? Or how edible he is with that sexy layer of scruff on his face and his dark hair tumbling in silky waves over his brow, demanding to be touched? "On that note," I add, rubbing my hand up and down his thigh over his pants. "Why don't we skip the cake, and you can have me for dessert?"

"Hold that thought," he says, suddenly looking nervous. His chair scrapes as he pushes it back before dropping to one knee in front of me.

My mouth turns dry, and my heart jackhammers furiously in my chest. Oh my God. Butterflies scatter in my tummy as adrenaline courses through my veins.

He pops open a box, displaying the most perfect platinum engagement ring. The center diamond is circular, encased by a curved band of glistening emeralds shaped like a flower, and while it isn't huge, it's not small either. It's pretty and delicate and exactly what I would choose for myself.

"I realized recently that I went about things all wrong," Ben says, peering up at me. He is shielding nothing, and emotion radiates from his every pore. "You are so beautiful and so precious to me, and you deserve to have everything you have ever dreamed about, starting with choice." His Adam's apple bobs in his throat.

"I never want to assume anything, especially when it comes to something as important as our marriage." He takes the ring out of the box. "I love you, Firefly. I love you more than I can express. You have this innate light that fills the world with glorious sunshine. No one is immune. You touch every person with your goodness and your big heart, and I am honored to share the most precious little boy with you. More than that, for some reason, you have deemed me worthy of a role in your life, and I promise to never take that for granted. I promise to honor, worship, protect, and cherish you in this life and the next."

He clears his throat, looking more scared than I have ever seen him. "Don't cry, baby," he says, wiping tears from my cheeks.

"I didn't realize I was," I choke out. "But I assure you these are happy tears."

That seems to bolster his courage. "I love you, and I love Rowan, and I would be honored if you agreed to be my wife. Marry me, Firefly. Because you want to spend your life with me and you want us to be a family." He pauses for a moment, and his chest heaves with potent emotion. "Marry me for love not necessity."

"Yes, Ben!" I fling my arms around him. "Yes, I will marry you. Nothing would make me happier."

He pulls me to my feet, lifting me up and swinging me around. "I love you." He peppers my face with kisses, and my heart is so full it feels like I'm soaring through the sky. "And I don't want to wait," he adds, placing my feet back on the ground. He slides the ring on my finger, and it's a perfect fit. "It seems like I've waited forever to call you my wife."

"I know the feeling," I agree, snuggling into his embrace. "I've dreamed of this moment since I was thirteen."

"What about Thanksgiving?" he asks. "Could we pull it off by then?"

It's only a little over three weeks away, but it's doable. "If we keep it small, we can."

He frowns, as if he hadn't thought about that. "I don't want to deprive you of anything. If you want a big society wedding, we can wait."

I quirk a brow. "I thought you knew me?" I tease, running my hands up his suit jacket, enjoying the solidity of his chest under my palms.

"I do, Firefly." He kisses the tip of my nose, smirking because he loves that he got his way. "Thanksgiving it is."

Chapter 44

BEN

"I THOUGHT THE next time we'd see my family was at our wedding," Sierra says, as we sit in the back seat of the SUV en route to the funeral in Glencoe. Leo is driving, and we have Alessandro with us. Ciro and three of my other soldiers are following in another armored vehicle. I'm not taking any chances, and if I'd had my way, I would have attended Felix Barretta's funeral alone. However, Joseph Lawson wouldn't hear of it.

Funny how he's happy to forget his youngest daughter exists when it suits him. Yet when it comes to presenting a united front at his son-in-law's funeral, he won't hear of Sierra sitting it out. He's lucky he didn't request we bring Rowan as I would have torn into him for even suggesting it. Rowan is at the house with Natalia and over twenty bodyguards, yet I still want to wrap things up here as fast as possible to get back to him.

Lawson is a snake. He's been badgering me for a meeting these past couple of weeks, and he hasn't once asked how Sierra and Rowan are.

I do need to meet with him.

To find out why Sierra is in the dark about his mafia connections, but I have had more pressing matters to deal with, and I also didn't want to meet him until I had dug up everything I can on him. Phillip is working on his file, but right now, everything we are finding is surface level, and that has me on edge.

Why would Lawson keep this knowledge from Sierra? Clearly Serena and Saskia are in the know, so why not his youngest? Does he hate her so much he doesn't want her to know anything about his business affairs, or is there more to it? And why hasn't Serena said anything to Sierra? They are close. Serena and Georgia are the only family members who check in with Sierra every few days, so I don't understand how her mom and her sister have kept this from her.

Something is pricking my subconscious, and I'm trying to figure out what before I tell my fiancée the truth about her family's mob connections.

"I know," I agree when Sierra stares at me expectantly, waiting for an answer. "This has come out of the blue." I have my arm around her while I keep watch out the window as the familiar landscape passes by.

"Why would anyone murder a business consultant in broad daylight?" she murmurs, pursing her lips. I can almost see the wheels of suspicion churning in her mind. The more her mind is opened to the ways of my world, the more skeptical she becomes. It's a good thing though, even if I hate that she is now questioning everything.

Leo catches my eye through the mirror, and I feel the weight of his disapproval.

He has let go of his initial reservations about Sierra. Being around her, seeing how she is with Rowan, and how she handled herself when she was attacked earned his trust and his respect. He also notices how much happier I am with her and my son in my life, and I know he's thrilled for me.

Leo doesn't understand why I won't just tell Sierra about her family, and explain who Felix really was. I hadn't wanted to give her half-truths, and I was waiting until I was privy to all the facts, but Barretta's death changes things. I can't drag this out any longer. She deserves to know, and I'm hoping to find an opportunity to corner Lawson today and get the truth out of him once and for all. Phillip can keep digging, and I can always go at Lawson again if my intel uncovers anything of importance.

"You need to tell her," Leo says in a hushed voice, as we hang back outside the church while Sierra talks to her family. I want to check out the grounds and the attendees and scan the area for threats before we go inside for the ceremony.

Alessandro is with my fiancée, standing back to give her privacy but still close enough to protect her. I ripped him a new one for Anais, and he knows he's on shaky ground with me now. I made it clear, in no uncertain terms, that he needs to get his act together and deal with whatever is distracting him from fulfilling his duties to the best of his ability.

"I know, and I plan to after we get home." I can't tell Sierra right now because she is liable to flip. I didn't have much time for Barretta, and I'm not overly religious, but I do believe a funeral is a time for respect.

"Why would the Russians take out the consigliere heir and not the consigliere? Hell, why didn't they go after Gifoli?" Leo poses questions I have already asked myself.

"Thomas Barretta and Alfredo Gifoli are better protected and harder to get at. If the Russians wanted to send a message, they have achieved their goal."

"Let's hope The Outfit gets the message then," he adds, pushing off the car as Sierra looks over her shoulder, seeking me out.

"If this doesn't convince them, nothing will," I say.

My men form a solid line behind us as I join my fiancée and her family.

"Oh, Ben!" Saskia sobs, throwing herself at me. "I'm so glad you are here." Crocodile tears stream down her face, and her lower lip wobbles. She is putting on one hell of a performance, but it's not hard to tell it's completely insincere.

Sierra pulls me back just as I move to sidestep her sister. "I know you're upset, Saskia, but Ben is my fiancé. He's not yours to touch anymore. I'm very sorry for your loss, but you can't fling yourself at him like that."

Round one to my feisty Firefly. I slide my arm around her shoulders, tucking her into my side while I smother my amused grin.

Saskia scowls, and it's remarkable how fast her tears have dried and her lips have stopped trembling. "Don't be such a bitch! My husband is dead! And you're not married to Ben yet."

"Our wedding day can't get here soon enough as far as I'm concerned," I say because she seems to have trouble absorbing the truth.

"Saskia." Joseph Lawson's voice rings out loud and clear, the warning obvious.

"Sweetheart." Georgia circles her arm around Saskia. "We should take our seats. The ceremony is about to begin."

Saskia nods, sobbing as she resumes the mourning widow mask, allowing her mother to guide her inside.

"Bennett. Good of you to come," Lawson says, looking behind me. "Is there anyone else from New York here with you?"

You have got to be kidding me. Did he really expect the other New York bosses to attend when there are Russians running rings around The Outfit right now? If Thomas Barretta, the current consigliere, had been murdered, rules would have dictated they attend, but we are talking about his successor, and it doesn't warrant more than representation.

"It's just me. I trust that is sufficient." I'm careful not to say too much until I have fully explained things to Sierra. As it is, she is watching our interaction with a curious frown.

His lips pull into a tight line. He does not like that. Who the fuck does he think he is?

"We should go in," he says, puffing out his chest. "After you."

The funeral is the usual solemn affair, and we go through the motions.

Saskia puts on an Oscar-worthy performance at the graveside, sobbing and crying as she clings to Thomas Barretta. From the carefully controlled expression on his face, I'm guessing he's buying it about as much as we are.

"She makes me sick," Sierra whispers. "She didn't stop looking at you throughout the entire ceremony, and now she expects us to believe this farce? She never seemed to care much about Felix." She snuggles in closer to me as the priest brings things to a close. "I wouldn't be surprised if she hired a hitman to get rid of him so she could make a play for you."

"Saskia is a lot of things, but even I don't think she would take it that far." I hold Sierra's hand out, running my thumb over the ring I put on her finger. "This speaks volumes."

"To most people, yes. But Saskia is not most people."

"She's coming over here," I murmur.

"Grant me patience." Sierra sighs, turning to face Saskia and Thomas.

"I'm sorry for your loss," I tell Barretta, shaking his hand. Up close, I can see the man is severely grieving.

"Thank you for coming."

"Yes, thank you for coming," Saskia says, ignoring the fact Sierra is nestled into my left side as she pushes herself up against me, sobbing into my neck.

Thomas pulls her back. "Get a hold of yourself," he hisses.

Saskia shucks out of his arm. "You don't get to tell me what to do."

She preens in my direction, and I wonder if she has finally snapped because this is erratic, even for her. Appearances always mattered to Saskia, and she's drawing attention to herself in a way that isn't favorable. You can't go around disrespecting the fiancée of a don or potentially causing any ill will between two mafia families. Thomas understands that, yet Saskia fails to understand she no longer serves a purpose. She never gave Felix a child, so any protection she enjoyed as his wife is erased with his death.

"Hey." Pen and Esme appear at the perfect time. Sierra is close to lunging at her sister, and I really wouldn't blame her. Saskia is way out of line. "Are you okay?" Pen asks, giving Sierra a quick hug.

"Yes," Sierra says through gritted teeth.

"We have missed you." Esme hugs Sierra next. "Let me see the ring," she adds, almost wrenching Sierra's arm from its socket as she tugs on her hand. "Oh my God," she shrieks. "It's gorgeous and it's so you!" She thumps my forearm, and I bite back my irritation. "Way to go, Ben."

This is only my second time meeting both women, but I can already tell I won't be a big fan of Esme. Penelope is a sweetheart, but I'm still trying to work out what Sierra and Esme have in common.

"Hmph," Saskia scoffs, glancing briefly at the ring. "I didn't take you for a cheapskate, Ben."

Sierra's hands ball into fists at her side. "Ben knows I'm not some self-obsessed drama queen who needs a big flashy diamond to impress society bitches. He designed something he knew I would love, and that is worth far more than that gaudy rock on your finger."

"Jealousy is very unbecoming on you," Saskia retorts, folding her arms in such a way that the rings on her finger are front and center.

Sierra's laugh is mocking. "Do you even hear yourself? You have the nerve to accuse me of jealousy when you are throwing yourself at my fiancé at your husband's funeral. You can't even respect Felix in death."

I pull Sierra back as Saskia lunges at her. Thank fuck most of the mourners have already left, and it's mostly family and close friends left.

"That's enough, Saskia," I snap, keeping Sierra shielded with my body as Thomas drags Saskia back. "I don't know what delusions you're suffering from, but they *are* delusions. I love Sierra, and I am marrying her in two weeks. Get that through your thick skull or you can forget about attending."

"You think I want to come to your pathetic excuse of a wedding?" she says, her voice laced with scorn.

Out of the corner of my eye, I spy Joseph Lawson approaching with a thunderous face.

"Well, that solves a dilemma," Sierra hisses. "Consider yourself uninvited."

"He won't marry you," she says. "He—"

Lawson clamps his hand over her mouth, glaring at her as he passes her off to her mother. "Take Saskia back to the house, and call Dr. Fleming. The stress of the past few days has obviously taken its toll." He turns to Barretta. "Please accept my apologies for my daughters' behavior." Lawson glowers at Sierra, as if this is all her fault, and my blood boils as my fists beg to connect with his face.

Barretta's face is cold as he snaps a terse nod before walking away. I can tell he wants to say more, but this isn't the time or the place.

"Mr. Barretta," Sierra calls out after him. He stops and turns around. "I'm so very sorry for your loss, and I apologize if my behavior upset you. I didn't mean any disrespect. Felix was always courteous to me and Rowan."

"*You* don't need to apologize," he says, driving his point home. "You were just defending yourself." He walks off, without saying another word, leaving tense silence behind him.

Lawson looks fit to kill someone, but I can't work out if it's Saskia, Sierra, or Barretta.

"Control that woman!" he snaps at me, and I level him with a dark look.

"Say that again and we have a problem." My voice is calm though I am far from calm on the inside. It appears Lawson needs reminding of his place. I turn to Alessandro. "Take two of the men and return to the car with Sierra. We're leaving." There is no way I'm going back to the Lawson house now, and I already know Sierra is happy with this plan.

Esme and Pen loop their arms through Sierra's as they walk off, followed by my men.

Leo steps up beside me while Ciro and the other soldier hang back. Lawson returns my glare with one of his own, and his lack of respect grates on my nerves. I don't care if this imbecile is going to be my father-in-law; he doesn't get to disrespect me like this. I glance around, ensuring there is no one else at the graveyard, before I grab him by the throat and shove him up against a tree. "You need to remember who you're speaking to, Joseph."

He barely breaks a sweat as I squeeze his throat, and I'm wondering how many times this has happened to him. I let him go, shoving his shoulders. "We are going to be family, but that doesn't mean I will tolerate you disrespecting me. The same goes for Sierra and Rowan."

"I have respect for you. A lot of it, actually," he says, smoothing down the front of his jacket and pushing me out of his way. "You have impressed me with how far you have come, Ben, and how much you have achieved since you dated Saskia, but I won't be pushed around by you or anyone else."

At least now I know where Saskia gets her delusional side from.

"Why doesn't Sierra know you wash cash for The Outfit? That her sisters are married to made men?"

"That is none of your business."

I put myself up in his face, enjoying the fact I tower over him by at least four inches. "Sierra *is* my business, and she has a right to know."

"So tell her." He shrugs. "I'm not stopping you."

"If you're hiding something, I will find it. You can count on that."

His amused grin rubs me the wrong way. If he wasn't Sierra's father and Rowan's grandfather, I'd throw him in the empty grave beside Felix Barretta and bury him alive.

"You think you're so clever, *Bennett*, but you're not. With the right mentorship, you could be. Your arrogance will either be the making of you or your downfall."

I've had enough of this condescending prick. If I stay here much longer, nothing will save him, so I turn around and walk away before I say, or do, something I'll regret.

"I'd take the back roads, if I were you," he calls out after us. "I've heard there are Russians rampaging through town." His callous laughter follows me all the way from the graveyard, out past the church, sending pangs of unease slithering up my spine.

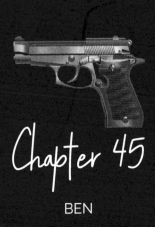

Chapter 45

BEN

"HOW THE HELL did you grow up in that house and not want to murder your father in cold blood every day?" I ask, as I slide in the back seat beside Sierra.

"Who says I didn't?" She rubs circles on the back of my hand, and it's unbelievably soothing. "Most days it was a toss-up between who I hated more. My father or Saskia. You didn't honestly think she plucked her attitude from thin air?"

Leo glides the car out onto the road, and the second SUV trails close behind. "Should I take the back roads?" he asks, glancing at me through the mirror.

I shake my head. "Stick to the main roads. If anyone targets us, they will be more reluctant to attack with civilians nearby." I drill him with a look, and he understands I'm saying this purely for Sierra's benefit. If the Russians want to attack us, they won't give a flying fuck which road we are on or how many civilians are nearby. Unlike us, they don't care about innocent bystanders and they must think they are above RICO laws.

"We shouldn't have come," Sierra says, rubbing her temples. "I hate I let her get to me."

"Your sister has serious mental issues," Leo says, and he's not joking.

"Tell me something I don't know," Sierra replies, as we round the bend.

"I don't understand how your father favors her so much. She's the most troublesome in the family," I say.

"He doesn't see it like that. He can't see any fault in her. He loves that she works for the family business, and she sucks up to him any chance she gets."

"Yet she embarrasses him in public," Alessandro says, glancing over his shoulder from the passenger seat.

"That's a recent development," Sierra says, looking thoughtful. "She never used to be like that."

"Who'd have daughters?" Leo quips. "They are nothing but trouble. You're lucky you have a son." He waggles his brows at me through the mirror.

A smirk tilts my lips as I sit back and let Sierra handle it.

"I think there must be something wrong with my hearing," she says, sitting up straighter. "Because I could not have heard that misogynistic comment coming from Leo, of all people. Shocker right there."

Leo grins, and I know he said that on purpose to get a rise out of her. It's his way of trying to distract her and lighten the mood.

"Well, I—"

A loud bang cuts him off mid-sentence, and I turn around in time to see the vehicle behind us careen off the road before rolling over a few times. Smoke billows from the SUV as it screeches to a halt, upside down.

Fuck.

Leo puts the pedal to the metal as Alessandro pulls a gun out from under the passenger seat.

"Baby, get down." I shove Sierra to the floor, lifting the seat to get at our supplies. We didn't come unprepared. We knew there was a possibility the Russians would come after us today.

"Is it the Russians?" she asks.

"I assume so," I say in a calm voice as I distribute Kevlar vests. "Put that on, and then cover yourself with this blanket, and stay down until I tell you it's safe to get up." I hand the red-and-blue-plaid blanket to Sierra.

"Take the next left," I instruct Leo. The only advantage we have is my knowledge of the area. We are very close to where I grew up, and if we can't shake them off, I know a few places we can hide.

I help Sierra put her vest on as Leo takes the next left, heading away from the busy main road up ahead. Sierra screams as a succession of loud thumps hits the rear window. "It's okay," I assure her. "It's bulletproof glass." Leo and I exchange wary expressions through the mirror as Alessandro leans out the side window, firing back.

Yes, this is an armored car, but it's not my usual car, which has the thickest bulletproof glass that was built specifically to stop all bullets. Most non-custom armored vehicles are less secure, so I cannot say with absolute certainty that they can't breach the glass. However, panicking my fiancée at a time when I need her to maintain a cool head won't help. I press a hard kiss to her lips, clutching the back of Alessandro's seat to steady myself as Leo zigzags across the road. "Trust me. We will keep you safe."

She nods, working hard to keep her terror at bay.

"No matter what you hear, just stay under the blanket until one of us gives you the all-clear," I tell her.

"I will." She reaches out, taking my wrist. "Be careful."

"Don't worry about us. We know how to handle ourselves." It's a false assurance because she's just witnessed my four soldiers getting tossed around in their car back there. I don't know if any of them survived, but I can't worry about my men now. Protecting Sierra and getting us the fuck out of Chicago is my sole priority.

She covers her body and her head with the blanket, and I strap my vest on and remove the rifles from the secret stowage compartment under the back seat. I hand a rifle to Alessandro as Leo races up back streets, weaving around parked cars and the odd civilian we meet. Flattening my back against the back of Leo's chair, I press the button to lower the window and lean out, indiscriminately firing my weapon. Alessandro and I continue shooting at the SUV chasing us, ducking and diving as they retaliate. Bullets bounce off the rear window, some embedding in the metallic panels of the car.

"Aim for the tires," I say to Alessandro. "On my count."

He nods, and I count down from three. "One!" I shout, and we both lean out our windows at the same time aiming for the front two tires. Alessandro's shot goes wide when the vehicle swerves to avoid it, narrowly missing hitting the car parked at the curb, but my shot meets its target, and the front left wheel explodes, sending the car spinning out of control. Alessandro and I plow bullets into their SUV in a relentless stream of firepower. A massive explosion evokes a whimper from Sierra, from under the blanket, and I watch with grim satisfaction as the Russians' car bursts into flames.

Kneeling on the floor, I slowly retract the blanket. "It's okay, baby. They're gone. You're—"

"Stay down!" Leo roars, and I throw myself over Sierra as the right-hand side back window shatters, raining glass on top of us. I curl around Sierra as bits of glass embed in the back of my head and my neck while Leo accelerates ahead.

"Shit," Alessandro shouts. "Another SUV has just appeared from a side street." If I hadn't bent down to attend to Sierra, I'd be dead, but there is no time to dwell on what-ifs. We need to get off the fucking road before they force us off it.

"Get us out of here, Leo," I bellow, lifting my head and taking a quick peek to gauge my surroundings.

Alessandro fires at the new SUV, now chasing us from behind, while I form a plan. We're exposed with the open window, and I don't like our odds. We need an alternate option, and I think I have one. "Take the next left. Then a sharp right," I instruct Leo. "At the T-junction, take the right, and it brings you straight into a wooded area. Park and we'll take it on foot from there."

Leo follows my instructions as I resume shooting at the SUV. "We need to create a distraction so we can get away," I shout at Alessandro. "Aim for the gas tank on that red Chevy." I jerk my head at the vehicle haphazardly parked at the curb. The back end is jutting out, too far onto the road, and it will suit as a temporary obstacle.

"Got it, boss," he says as I continue trading gunfire with the Russians.

He fires at the Chevy, pumping bullets into the gas tank until it detonates, shooting flames and debris in all directions. The brakes on the Russians' SUV screeches as they battle to stop before barreling into the flames.

It won't hold them for long, but it'll be long enough for us to get to the warehouse.

We ditch our SUV at the corner of the woods, fleeing on foot around the perimeter of the forest. Sierra races beside me, with determination on her face, while Leo and Alessandro protect us from behind. Thank fuck, she had ballet flats in her bag because running in her heels or her bare feet would have held us up.

I breathe a sigh of relief when the old warehouse comes into view, around the bend. I haven't been back here in years, and I couldn't be sure it was still standing.

"In here," I shout, racing for the side door. The warehouse is freshly painted, and the roof looks new, so it appears it is still serving the same purpose. Reaching up, I run my hand along the corrugated ledge, silently rejoicing when my fingers curl around the key.

"What is this place?" Sierra asks while Leo and Alessandro keep watch for any sign of people following us.

"You remember I told you about Terry?"

"The guy who was like a father figure to you?"

The door opens, and I bundle her inside, closing it firmly as soon as Leo and Alessandro are inside. "Yeah, Terry was a member of a local MC. This is their safe house. When I was a kid, he showed me this place. Told me if I was ever in trouble to come here and hide. It's wired with triggers, so someone already knows we are here. We just need to wait it out until someone shows up."

"What if the Russians show up?" Sierra says, looking around the large space with trepidation. Apart from a few tables and chairs, and a heap of boxes and crates stacked along various parts of the wall, the place is empty, and I can see how it looks like we will be sitting ducks.

"They won't find us." I grin, striding toward the middle of the space, tugging her along with me. "Stay here." Dropping to my knees, I push a chair aside and crawl under the long table. I spread my fingers along the floor, feeling for the latch. They all watch me like I'm crazy, but they're not doubting me when I push down on the floor in the right spot and a door pops up. "Come on."

"What the hell is this place?" Sierra whispers, crawling toward me.

"It's a secret room in the floor. No one will find us here unless they know to look for it. Alessandro, pull that chair back into place after you, and pull this door shut firmly, making sure the edges are seamless," I instruct, extracting my cell and switching the flashlight on.

"I got it, boss. Get Sierra to safety." I walk in front of Sierra down the steps, feeling her close to my back as we descend lower into the hidden space below. When my feet hit the bottom, I feel around for the light switch and turn it on, illuminating the space. They have had work done since I was last here. The space is cleaned out, and there is a couch, a table and chairs, and a small refrigerator and pantry. A side door leads to a toilet.

"There's no cell service," Leo says, claiming a seat at the table while he frowns at his phone.

"I didn't expect there to be," I say, flopping down on the couch as Alessandro appears.

"This is pretty fucking cool." Alessandro looks around with appreciation in his eyes.

"So, what now?" Sierra asks, taking some waters from the refrigerator.

"Now, we wait for help to show up."

Chapter 46

BEN

"HOW DO YOU know they will help us?" Sierra asks, handing me a water.

"Terry was family, and I used to hang out with them here some nights. I expect at least some of the members will still remember me."

"Okay," she quietly says, before adding, "I'm going to use the bathroom."

We are silent until she closes the door.

"Will they know of your reputation now?" Leo asks in a low tone, raising one brow, and I get what he's asking.

"I assume so. But they're friendlies. They have no reason to fear us or us them."

"Let's hope they get to us before the Russians," Alessandro says.

"The Russians won't find us down here. It's a sweet setup," Leo says.

"They won't find us," I agree. "This is a well-guarded secret. The MC have hidden from the authorities and rival gangs several times over the years, and no one found out about it. Unless they saw us come in here, we're safe."

"What is going on, Ben?" Alessandro asks, taking a seat at the table. "This whole situation reeks."

"I agree. Something is not adding up, and I won't rest until I find out what."

"I'm scared," Sierra whispers a little while later as we sit patiently on the couch waiting for someone to rescue us. We had all held our breaths as footsteps explored the warehouse a short while ago, the creaking floorboards betraying enemy presence. But it's been silent for the past fifteen minutes, and I'm pretty sure the Russians are gone. Like I said, they wouldn't find us unless they knew to look down here. Sierra's head is on my shoulder, and I have my arm wrapped around her, running my fingers up and down her arm. She's like a brick in my embrace, tense and scared, even if she's not outwardly showing it.

"Don't be. I'm not going to let anything happen to you."

"What about Rowan? What if something has happened to him?"

"Firefly." I tilt her face up. "Rowan is safe at home. Our property is well-protected, and my soldiers know to take him to the safe room if there is any threat. Natalia will make sure nothing happens to him." I press a kiss into her hair. "Why don't you try sleeping. We could be waiting a while."

"I can't sleep. I'm too wound up."

"Try." I say, pressing her head into my lap.

She falls asleep five minutes later, and I stare at her, watching small puffs of air seep from her slightly parted lips as she sleeps. She is so beautiful it hurts to look at her sometimes. In sleep, she looks even younger, and I have a burning need to protect her from all the evils of this world. I know she has chosen a life with me. That she agreed to marry me of her own volition when she said yes to my proposal, but I still carry guilt for bringing her and my son into this life. I *don't* want this for her, yet I'm far too selfish to ever let her go.

"You look like a creeper," Leo says, not lifting his head from the crossword puzzle he's doing. He found a bunch of old newspapers, and he and Alessandro are keeping themselves occupied doing crossword puzzles.

"You have that scary intense look on your face again," Alessandro adds.

"What scary intense look?" I whisper, not wanting to wake my Sleeping Beauty.

"The one you wear when anyone looks funny at Sierra or says anything nasty to her."

"It's your 'I'm gonna rip out your insides and hang you by your entrails' expression," Leo adds, briefly lifting his head to smirk at me.

"Assholes," I murmur, flipping my finger up, as the floorboards creak overhead again. A flash of brief light filters down the stairs, alerting us to imminent company.

Leo and Alessandro are instantly alert, whipping out their guns and moving to the bottom of the stairs.

"Sierra," I whisper in her ear, gently shaking her shoulders. "Wake up, baby."

I place my hand over her mouth when her eyes blink open, cautioning her to keep quiet.

Heavy feet thud down the stairs as I stand, pulling Sierra with me, keeping her shielded behind me, and raise my weapon.

A skinny man with long dark hair pulled back in a ponytail appears in front of us. His brow puckers as he drinks us in, rubbing his scraggly beard. I peer at him more closely, a grin spreading across my face as I recognize him. "Pillow?" I exclaim, stepping forward, taking Sierra with me but keeping her firmly behind my back.

He startles, staring at me in confusion for a few seconds before a light goes off in his eyes.

"Benny? Benny Carver?" He guffaws. "Or it's Mazzone now, I hear." He looks at our guns. "Don't be pointing those weapons at me, boys."

I nod at the guys, and they put their guns down the same time I slide mine in the band of my black slacks. I pull Sierra to my side, taking her hand in mine. "It's good to see you, old man, though I hardly recognized you." I turn to my friends. "Pillow here used to carry a lot more meat, especially around his middle. The guys loved teasing him he was soft and cuddly like a pillow."

"Motherfucking assholes can't call me that now," Pillow says, reaching forward and clasping me in a hug. "It's good to see you, Benny boy." He claps me on the back. "Terry was very proud of all you've accomplished."

"I didn't see you at the funeral," I say.

"I was out of the country at the time. Terrible business, that." He shakes his head, sighing heavily.

"I didn't even know he was sick. I hadn't kept in regular contact with him those past few years when I should have."

Confusion, mixed with concern, crosses his face. "Terry wasn't sick, boy. I thought you knew that."

"What do you mean?"

"Why don't I tell you when we get in the van. I assume you need a lift someplace?"

"The airport," I say, quickly introducing the others.

"Did you spot anyone lurking around outside?" I ask, as we climb the steps back into the warehouse.

"If you mean those ugly Russian fuckers, we took care of that problem for you." He tosses a grin over his shoulder. "The guys are cleaning up as we speak."

I don't ask for specifics because I don't trust Pillow not to give us the warts and all account, and Sierra doesn't need to hear that. She's been traumatized enough today, even if she appears to be holding it together fine.

"I owe you," I say, hauling myself into the back of the large white van behind Sierra. It's parked right outside the warehouse, facing the other way, blocking the view from anyone who might be looking. Nightfall is creeping in, and it's dusky out. Alessandro takes shotgun while Pillow slides behind the wheel. I keep my arm around Sierra on the hard wooden bench, sitting up close to the front seats so I can talk to Pillow as we drive toward the airport. Leo claims a seat on the bench across from us.

"You're family, Benny boy. You don't owe us anything."

"All the same," I say, handing him my business card. "If you or any of the MC ever need my help, you only have to ask."

"Appreciate it, man." He tucks it into a pocket in his leather cut.

"Did you happen to hear anything about an SUV accident just outside town?" I ask, wondering what happened to my soldiers.

"They were your guys?" Pillow eyeballs me through the mirror. I nod. "I heard two are dead and two have been taken to the hospital."

"Shit," Leo mutters, already tapping away on his cell. "I'll handle it," he adds.

"What was it you want to tell me about Terry?" I ask Pillow, holding Sierra close as we shuffle back and forth over bumpy terrain.

"We're among friends here, I assume," he says, looking at me through the mirror.

"Of course. You can speak freely."

"I expected you would know, but it's obvious you don't. Terry was a made man, Benny. He was a soldier for The Outfit and our main point of contact for years. We sell guns and drugs on their behalf."

That revelation almost knocks me over. I had no idea. Maybe if I had visited him after I left, after I became involved in this world, it would have been noticeable or he would have confided in me, but I had no clue. "I didn't know. He never told me."

"He wasn't sick, Benny. Someone wanted Terry taken out, and we believe it was The Outfit."

Shock races through me. "Why would they want to take out one of their own? What had he done?" I know the reasons why soldiers are killed, but Terry was one of the most loyal, most honorable men I know, and I can't imagine him betraying the organization.

"Something went down around the time you left. He wouldn't tell us. Said it was safer we didn't know, but he lived in fear. He was a hermit after you left Chicago. Staying in his house except when he had to work or do a job."

"That explains why he rarely answered my calls in those early days, and when I did get talking to him, he usually had little to say." I press my palm to my brow, consumed with guilt. "I should have pushed him harder. Done more for him." It was a shitty way to pay him back for everything he did for me.

"He knew you cared for him, Benny. He knew it was you who paid the mortgage on his house. Did you know he left it to you?"

I shake my head. I didn't know that.

"Someone burned it to the ground a few days after his funeral."

I didn't know that either. I had only just discovered Rowan, so I was preoccupied.

"He told me he left a box for you. It might be stretching things, but I wondered if whoever torched his house did it to destroy that box."

"In our world, things are rarely a stretch." Damn it. I need to find out who handled his legal affairs and ask them why no one made contact with me. If it was important enough, maybe he left the box with his lawyer.

"I don't have any proof," Pillow says, entering the ramp that leads to the highway. "But word on the street is The Outfit took him out for something he had done years ago."

"That makes no sense," I say. "Unless they only became aware of his actions recently."

"All I know is he lived every day in fear. I asked him about it once, a few years later. I asked him why he was living in fear instead of confronting it head-on because that was the kind of man he was. He told me it wasn't just about him. That he needed to stay alive to ensure you never came back to Chicago."

All the blood drains from my face, and I feel every pair of eyes on me. "This was about me?"

"Let's just say I don't think it's a coincidence you returned to Chicago when you did."

"You think someone killed him to lure me back?" I ask, continuing his train of thought.

He shrugs, peering at me through the mirror. "I could be wrong, and I have nothing to back it up, but I don't believe in coincidences."

"Neither do I." I've known for some time that something is fishy. That things weren't adding up. But I would never have put Terry in the middle of it. If he was killed because of something he did to protect me, then I owe it to him, as much as myself and my family, to get to the bottom of this.

I'm fucked if anyone else is going to die on my watch.

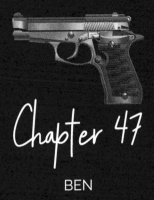

Chapter 47

BEN

"TELL ME THIS is some sick joke," Sierra says. She is dressed in silk pajamas, wearing a line in the carpet as she paces back and forth in our bedroom.

"I wish I could." I pull on sweatpants and a plain white T-shirt. We only got home a little over an hour ago, and Rowan was already asleep. After eating the pasta Natalia heated up for us, we grabbed a quick shower together. I thought Sierra would be too tired to talk or to fuck, but she pounced on me in the shower, and I screwed her against the wall, needing to feel our connection after the day from hell.

Then I sat her down and told her everything I know about her family and their connections to The Outfit.

She stops pacing, sinking to her knees on the floor. "I'm shocked, but there's another part of me that isn't," she admits. "I've always known my father was an evil piece of shit, so finding out he's laundering money for the mafia and that his hands are dirty, most likely bloody too, isn't that big of a surprise."

I sit cross-legged in front of her, taking her hands in mine. "Did you have any inkling?"

She shakes her head, sending waves of damp hair tumbling over her shoulders. "I grew up knowing my father was a very wealthy businessman. Bodyguards and drivers were the norm. I didn't stop to question it even if I thought some of the men he introduced me to at parties and balls were shady motherfuckers. Father never discussed business in front of me, and neither of my sisters ever said anything."

Pain slashes across her face, and her eyes well up. "Why wouldn't my mom or Serena tell me any of this? That's the part that has shocked me the most."

"I can only surmise your father dictated they keep it a secret."

Tears roll down her face, and my heart hurts for her. I gather her onto my lap, snaking my arms around her. "Don't cry, Firefly. They don't deserve your tears."

"It hurts, Ben," she croaks, rubbing a hand across her chest. "Everything I thought I knew was a lie. I thought I could trust Mom and Serena, but they have lied to me for years. How could they do that to me? *Why* would they do that? Is my value so little to my family that they would keep this from me?"

"I don't know, baby." I press a hard kiss to her temple. "I wanted to get to the full truth so I could explain it all to you, but I didn't want to keep this a secret any longer. You deserve answers."

"Thank you for telling me." She swipes at her tears and stands. "And I do need answers. I feel like such a fool. Everyone in Glencoe must be laughing at me."

I stand, reeling her into my arms. "It's not common knowledge what your father does. To most, he is the legitimate businessman he appears to be."

"But Serena and Saskia are married to powerful mafia men! Surely people know who *Alfredo* is?" She spits out his real name as her fury surges to the surface.

"Again, only those who mix in those circles would be aware of Gifoli's position. It's not like we go broadcasting it. And if others, outside our circles, suspect, they know better than to talk about it. Especially to Gifoli's sister-in-law."

"At least I know why Felix was targeted now. It didn't make sense before, but it does now."

"It's not unusual to target important heirs, and he must've gotten sloppy to let them catch him in an unguarded moment in public."

Her eyes pop wide. "So much makes sense now," she murmurs, tapping her fingers off her bottom lip. "Neither of my sisters are in love with their husbands, and it's no wonder when they were both clearly in arranged marriages." Air expels from her mouth. "At least, I dodged that bullet."

"I think you getting pregnant with Rowan saved you from that fate."

She shrugs. "My father hates me. I doubt he would have married me off anyway."

I tuck her damp hair behind her ears. "Baby, that wouldn't have come into it. Your father is a cold disloyal prick. If he had found a way to forge a connection through you, he would have taken it. I'm sure of it."

"Then I guess I have something else to thank you for." She stands on her tiptoes to press a fleeting kiss to my mouth. "But I'm done second-guessing things. I need to hear the truth. I'm calling Serena," she says, shucking out of my arms. "I'd prefer to have the conversation face to face, but wild horses couldn't drag me back to Chicago after today. If I never step foot in the place again, I'd die happy."

I know she doesn't really mean that. She loves her little house and has made tons of happy memories there with Rowan, but I understand where she is coming from.

I retreat to my study to call Phillip while Sierra calls her sister. "I need you to prioritize the Lawson case," I tell him when he picks up on the third ring. "And I need you to do something else for me." I explain about Terry, his supposed affiliation with The Outfit, the suspicion over his death, and the fact he apparently bequeathed his house and some mystery box to me. "Both things are urgent. I need intel ASAP."

"I will work around the clock, Mr. Mazzone, I promise."

I make a mental note to double Phillip's annual bonus. The guy never tells me no. He mustn't have much of a life because he willingly drops everything when I need him. Or he's just that good of an employee he makes the sacrifice without question. "Thank you, Phillip. Good night."

I hang up, walking to our private living room to pour us some drinks while I wait for Sierra to finish talking to her sister and her mom.

"I've changed my mind about the wedding," she says, a few minutes later, storming into the room. My heart falters in my chest, and I'm not sure what expression she sees on my face, but it's enough to have her rushing to reassure me. "I still want to marry you," she blurts, coming around the couch. "But I don't want my family there. I just want it to be us, Rowan, Angelo and Natalia, Leo and Alesso, and Esme and Pen." Snatching her glass of wine, she drains half of it in one go.

I swirl the dregs of my bourbon in my glass, watching her quietly seethe. She flops down beside me, bristling with rage. "Do you want to talk about it?"

"I've made up my mind," she says, turning her head to face me. "I don't want them at our wedding. I mean it. I'm not going to change my mind."

That wasn't what I meant, but I go with the flow. "Whatever you want, Firefly." I brush my fingers along her cheek, over the faint mark left behind by the stitches. The doc says it should fully heal in time, and I hope it does. I don't want her to have any permanent reminders of that day.

"I'm so mad I could spit."

I circle my arm around her, pulling her close. "What did they say?"

"That they were protecting me!" she hisses before narrowing her eyes at me. "If I ever hear that excuse again, from anyone, I'm liable to commit murder."

"Noted." I finish my drink and set the empty glass on the end table.

She heaves out a sigh. "You were right. Father didn't want me to know anything, but Serena said she has harbored huge guilt over all the lies she has had to tell. She said she came close to fessing up so many times, but she put herself in my shoes, and she wouldn't want to know." Her hands clench into balls, and I curl my hand around one of hers, gently unfurling her tense fingers. "She said she hated she had no choice. But she failed to realize in keeping it a secret she was doing the same to me! She could've mentioned a little and asked me if I wanted to know more. At least I wouldn't have been completely ignorant of the truth then."

She slumps against me. "Mom wasn't apologetic at all. She told me if she had the chance to do it again she would still conceal the truth from me because I have had a better life not knowing." Angry tears fill her eyes as she looks at me. "I get wanting to protect your child. I would die for Rowan, and I don't want him to know about this life yet. But he must be told when he is eighteen, if he hasn't figured it out before then. I couldn't lie to him about something this big. Mom doesn't seem to realize how betrayed I feel. I could never do that to my son."

I am surprised she doesn't ask me about initiation and Rowan's future life, and I can only guess her distress has clouded her mind. It is something we will need to discuss at some point but not now. We have had enough of the heavy for one day.

I wasn't given a choice with this life, and I won't do that to my son. I never expected to have an heir, assuming one of Natalia's stepsons, or any child she may have with Gino, would carry the Mazzone name and keep our legacy alive, but things have changed. I hope to have more children with Sierra, and they will have the right to decide what they want to do with their lives. I won't stop them if they want to join *la famiglia*, but I won't force them if they choose to have nothing to do with this life.

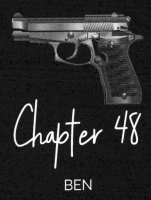

Chapter 48

BEN

A FEW DAYS pass and I'm getting more and more impatient for new intel. I peer out the window of my office at Caltimore Holdings as I wait for Phillip to arrive to debrief me. I can't shake the sense something is lingering outside my peripheral mind. That something obvious is staring me in the face and I'm missing it.

In positive news, we held the Bratva at bay when they attacked Philly two nights ago, slaughtering their men, leaving the dregs to slink off with their tails between their legs. We needed that win to send a powerful message to our allies within The Commission, to the Russians, and to all our enemies.

Yet still The Outfit is reticent. I tap my fingers on my desk. Why is that?

"Come in," I call out, as a sharp rap sounds on my door.

Phillip hurries into the room, carrying a few files. My secretary closes the door behind him, and I press the 'do not disturb' button on my desktop phone.

I meet him at the large table in my office, the one I usually conduct my meetings at. He dumps the files on the table, before we claim our usual seats. "What do you have for me?" I ask, placing my arms on the table.

Clearing his throat, he pushes his glasses up the bridge of his nose.

"I have completed my background check on Terry Scott, and it was as you assumed. He was a soldier for The Outfit. Initiated when he was seventeen. His death *was* covered up. The real autopsy results were hidden, but they hadn't been properly deleted from the ME's system, so I was able to access the report." He slides it across the table to me, and I skim over the neatly typed sheets of paper.

"He died of multiple gunshot wounds. There was no evidence of any cancer," he adds.

"What about the house and his will?"

"The attorney who handled his affairs mysteriously vanished a couple of days after Terry's house went up in flames. His business and his home were packed up, and I can't find a trace of him or his family anywhere."

"Someone helped him to disappear," I say, setting the report down and trying to make sense of it in my head. What was Terry concealing from The Outfit that was so important to hide? Was it about me? Could this be the reason why The Outfit is stalling? It seems like a far reach, but I'm ruling nothing out now. "What else did you discover?"

"Several people I talked to confirmed Terry did leave a box for you, but no one knows where it is now."

"I think we have to presume the attorney took it with him or it burned down with the house."

"Those were my conclusions too, Mr. Mazzone."

"What about Lawson?"

He squirms a little in his seat, and his nose scrunches. "I have exhausted every avenue over the past few weeks I have been working on his case, and I have hit a dead end. Johnny too," he adds, referencing one of my PIs who has been working closely with Phillip on the Lawson file. "It's like the man didn't exist before he married Georgia Lawson."

Lawson Pharma is a multibillion-dollar corporation, and it's not unthinkable that Joseph Lawson uses his internal tech resources to control what information is in the public domain. It's what I do. However, you will find details of my past on the web, and I have spoken about my mother in interviews and at relevant charity events. I have hidden the mafia part of my persona to protect myself and *la famiglia*, but I haven't attempted to erase my past in the way Lawson has done. To wipe all trace of his background proves he is hiding something.

But what?

I scrub a hand over my jaw, more troubled than I'd like to admit.

"There is one thing I find especially odd," Phillip says while he gathers up his files. I urge him to continue with my eyes as Leo knocks on the door and slips into the room.

Phillip glances uneasily at my underboss, like he does every time Leo is in proximity. I find it comical that Phillip is more afraid of my number two than me, but it's not surprising. I've spent years hiding my dark persona behind a corporate veneer, so most people suspect nothing. Leo isn't as skilled at hiding his true self, nor does he care to. He is mostly polite around the office, but the majority of my employees give him a wide berth. He has this way of cutting a person down with one look, without even realizing he's doing it, and it scares most people away.

"You can speak freely in front of Leo," I say, eager to get this done now. If Leo is here, it means the girl is ready for me.

"I find it strange that the man changed his name when he got married. It's usually the other way around."

"That is a little odd," I agree because I have pondered the same thing. "But Lawson is a name that carries considerable weight around Illinois, and he knew he would one day be running Lawson Pharma. I can understand his logic, to a point."

"A man like Joseph Lawson doesn't strike me as the type of man to readily give up anything or the kind of man who would bow to his wife's name in place of his own, even though you raise valid points," Leo says, lounging against the door frame. "I agree with Phillip. It's more than odd."

"He wants to keep his name a secret," I surmise as prickles of awareness dance over my skin. I look at Phillip, standing the same time he does. "His name must be on his marriage certificate."

"That's the other odd thing. I can't find any record of their marriage, and there is no certificate on file anywhere."

We are onto something. I know it.

"I will ask my fiancée," I say. "She might know where they keep it." It's a long shot, considering Sierra's family kept so much from her, but Serena might know if Sierra doesn't. Things are still frosty between them, but it won't last forever. "Thank you, Phillip. That will be all," I say, grabbing my jacket off the back of the chair behind my desk.

He leaves as I slide my arms into my sleeves. I eyeball Leo. "We have her?"

He nods. "She's terrified. Cried nonstop the whole trip from Montana, apparently."

One of my PIs came through, and he found Lucille hiding out on a godforsaken ranch in Montana. It's the second good piece of news this week. "Let's hope that means she is ready to reveal all." I don't torture or kill women, but Lucille was complicit in the attack on Sierra, and if she won't speak freely, I will inflict pain until she tells me what I need to know, and I won't lose any sleep over it.

"HERE'S THE DEAL," I say, pulling over a chair and placing it in front of the quivering woman. I told my men to take Lucille to the dungeon we use to house guests on purpose. I want to scare the living daylights out of her so she will readily give up what she knows. Her feet and wrists are bound to the chair she's sitting on, and the frigid temperature has raised obvious goose bumps on her arms. The less than welcoming surroundings combined with the way her wild eyes keep darting to the torture tools lined up on the table beside me lead me to believe I've accomplished my aim.

Removing my jacket, I hang it off the back of the chair, deliberately letting her see the gun holster on my waist. "This can be easy or hard," I continue, rolling the sleeves of my shirt to my elbows. "I don't enjoy hurting women, but I will make an exception in your case, if necessary." I drill her with a menacing look, and tears stream down her face while a trickle of urine flows down her legs. "You see, Sierra Lawson is my fiancée, and you helped the men who tried to kill her."

"I didn't know they were going to do that!" she shrieks. "Daddy said they wouldn't hurt her, I swear! I really like Sierra. She is the only one who took the time to explain things to me at the center."

"Your father made you do this?"

She nods, and her eyes dart to the torture tray again.

"What's his name?"

She gulps, and more tears leak from her eyes. "What are you going to do to him if I tell you?" she cries.

"Your father doesn't seem to care about your predicament, so why should you care what happens to him?" I deadpan, deliberately palming my gun.

"He's still my father," she whimpers.

I remove my gun from its holster, and terror skates across her face. "Don't hurt me. Please don't hurt me! I didn't have a choice."

I rest my gun on my thigh, and she audibly gulps before spewing her guts. "They were going to kill my dad if I didn't do this. They made me apply for the job with a fake résumé, and they told me to wait for further instructions. Then they gave me stuff to put in Alesso's coffee and Sierra's tea, and they…they kidnapped me. Please. I didn't want any of this," she sobs. Snot coats her nose, and she's a hot mess.

"His name," I repeat, and she gives up the fight.

"Jasper Ford," she mumbles, and I nod at Leo. He leaves the room to place the call to Phillip while I try to figure this out.

Lucille joined the center three weeks before the attack, which means the Russians knew about Sierra before the gala event. If they were planning to take her to get at me, why didn't they go after Rowan because they must have known about him too if they had been watching her. Or was this something to do with Sierra and unconnected to me? My brain spins ideas without any answers, and I'm growing more frustrated at my inability to connect the dots. What the fuck am I missing?

"Who are *they*?" I ask because I don't want to assume anything.

"The mafia. My father told me they were after him because he owed them money."

"I need more than that," I growl. My patience is stretched thin.

"The man my father brought me to meet was from Chicago though he did speak some words in a foreign language."

"Russian?"

She shrugs.

"Or Italian?" I add, going with a hunch.

She shrugs again. "Maybe. I don't know. I'm not exactly advanced in Languages 101."

Her flippant comment enrages me. Reaching out, I grab her around the throat. My gun slides to the floor with a thump. "Do you think this is a fucking laughing matter?" I snap, snarling at her.

She shakes her head, trembling and crying and peeing herself again.

I let her go, and her hysterical cries bounce off the walls, grating on my nerves, but I force myself to calm down. Taking my gun, I secure it in my holster and try to summon patience. She is scared, and it's obvious she's a pawn in a game she doesn't understand. Sierra liked Lucille, and she wouldn't want me to hurt her, so I slam a lid on my temper and force my tone to a more pleasant one. "I'm going to show you some photos, and I'd like you to tell me if you recognize any of these men. Okay?"

She sniffs, and her lower lip wobbles. My new temporary

bodyguard, Nario—a man Leo suggested—shifts behind her, looking bored with this, and I almost miss Ciro's grumpy face. Nario is one of our most brutal soldiers, and he's bloodthirsty. Leo has had to rein him in a few times with close calls. We thought he would be a good fit to take over until Ciro gets out of the hospital because he is vicious, so he'll protect me well, but I thought I could teach him a lesson too. To show him there is more to this business than killing. Yet I can already tell he's a lost cause and I should probably cut him loose.

Extracting my cell, I run with my hunch, opening a file on Chicago and The Outfit, scrolling to the images. I kneel beside her, and she flinches, her cries getting louder again. "Calm down," I say. "I'm not going to hurt you. I'm just going to show you these men, and you let me know if any of them are the man you met with your father."

I scroll through them one at a time, growing more disheartened as we move through the photos and there is no flash of recognition.

"Wait!" she screeches. "Go back to the previous picture."

I swipe left, and my breath catches in my throat as I stare at the familiar face. "Him," she says. "That's the man who told me to do it."

"Are you absolutely sure?" I ask as Leo returns to the room.

"One hundred percent. That's him. That's the man who tried to kill Sierra."

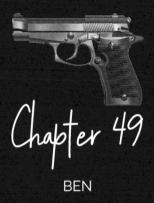

Chapter 49

BEN

I SIP MY bourbon, looking at my watch for the umpteenth time since the plane took off, wondering why the flight from New York to Chicago feels like it's taking forever instead of the usual two hours. My foot taps anxiously on the floor, and I'm strung as tight as a cello.

I spoke to Sierra before we boarded the plane to reassure myself she and Rowan were okay. I wanted to tell her my discovery, but I don't want to freak her out either. Leo spoke with Ian and Alessandro, so they know to be on their guard. I'm probably overreacting, but this has shaken me to my core.

"If you are right, this changes everything," Leo says, propping his elbows on the table.

"I know, but it's the most logical conclusion. I can't believe he's been under our nose this entire time." I bark out a laugh. "You've got to hand it to him. It's a stroke of genius." I don't have all the missing pieces, and I know the other four dons are a little skeptical of my reasoning, but they didn't stop me from confronting Lawson.

"Why the fuck would he try to kidnap or kill his own daughter?" Leo asks.

"I don't know, but I'm damn well going to find out." Fury simmers underneath my skin, and I can't fathom how I'm supposed to tell Sierra this. There is little love lost between them, but he is still her father. This will devastate her.

If my assumptions are correct, I can't kill Lawson despite how much my hands long to feel his blood coating my skin. Accardi made me promise not to touch him, and this is one tradition I can't ignore.

For now.

At last, the pilot tells us to buckle up for landing, and I finish my drink, mapping out how to play this in my head.

However, I didn't factor on a welcoming committee waiting for us on the tarmac.

"How the hell did he know we were coming?" Leo hisses in my ear as we step out of the plane right into an ambush. Three blacked-out SUVs are idling before us, and twelve armed men point guns at our chests.

"We have a mole," I murmur, and the realization does not reassure me. My thoughts instantly flicker to Sierra and Rowan, and I'm regretting not going home first and moving them someplace. I have a real bad feeling about this now.

"Mr. Mazzone." A surly guy with a shaved head and a mean expression steps toward me. "You're to come with me."

"On whose authority?" I ask.

"Mr. Lawson's," he replies, prodding me in the chest with his gun. "I will need all your weapons." He jerks his head sideways. "Same goes for your men."

I nod at my guys, letting them know it's okay to relinquish their weapons. We can't exactly have a shootout on the airfield with cameras around, and we are outnumbered two to one. Besides, Lawson clearly has an agenda, and he won't risk that by killing my men and enraging me.

I follow Brutus to a sleek black Mercedes waiting behind the last SUV. He opens the back door, and I slide into the seat where my soon-to-be father-in-law is waiting for me. Gifoli is in the passenger seat, and he turns around, palming the gun on his hip. "Don't try anything,

Mazzone. I won't hesitate to put a bullet in your skull. Unlike the armored glass, the privacy screen isn't bulletproof." I guess The Outfit's regard for traditions has truly flown out the window. He holds out his hand. "Cell phone."

Removing my cell from my inside jacket pocket, I hand it over without argument.

Lawson clicks his fingers, and the privacy screen whirs into place as the driver reverses the car. Outside, my men are being herded into the three different SUVs. He turns to me, pinning me with hazel eyes that are more green today, reminding me of my beloved. "Bennett. How good of you to come to me. Saved me any more theatrics."

I wet my lips, schooling my face into a neutral line. "Theatrics do run in your family, Lawson, and I'm not talking about my fiancée." I shove my hands between my thighs to avoid the almost insurmountable urge to strangle the bastard beside me. "Or should I call you DeLuca now?"

He slowly claps his hands, grinning, and I want to slam his head against the window repeatedly until his brain leaks from his skull. "It's about time, Bennett. It took you long enough to figure it out. What gave me away in the end?"

"We caught up with Lucille, and she identified you. I pieced the rest together myself."

"I knew I should have shot that bitch after I fucked her."

"How long have you been colluding with the Russians?"

"We began negotiations at the start of the year."

"I don't know how they do things in Sicily, but in the US, consorting with the enemy is an immediate death sentence."

He pulls two cigars out of a tin in the center console, offering me one. I shake my head, uncaring if he feels slighted. "I am well aware of how they do things in the US, my boy. I have lived here most of my life."

"Why conceal your identity? Why have everyone believe you were leading through Gifoli from your seat in Sicily?"

"Why do any of us make any decisions?" he says, flicking open an old silver lighter. "For power and control."

"How have you managed to keep this a secret for so long?" I won't show any admiration for the man because there is nothing I admire about him, but what he has achieved is no easy feat.

"By containing the knowledge of my true identity to a small handful of trusted people." He lights his cigar, bringing it to his lips and inhaling.

"It's why you took Georgia's name when you married her." I bark out a laugh as something occurs to me, and he eyes me curiously. "You dangled the truth in front of us. If I'm not mistaken, Joseph is the English version of Giuseppe. I bet you got a real kick out of that."

"I did." He smirks, continuing to puff on his cigar. "You all think you're so clever in New York. That The Outfit is second to your organization, but you are wrong." A muscle clenches in his jaw. "Chicago is the true seat of power, and I am the Italian mafioso's true natural leader. The Commission will answer to me, not the other way around."

That power trip has clearly gone to his head. He might have fooled us all these years, but his business is inferior to ours. We have increased our *soldati* numbers two-fold in the past five years, and our net worth has quadrupled. DeLuca has been so busy patting himself on the back for pulling the wool over our eyes that he has missed the memo. Things are moving forward, and if The Outfit doesn't catch up, they will soon be obsolete. In his twisted head, he might believe he holds all the cards, but he is the one who needs us more. "The Commission will never answer to you. All that you will achieve is a bloody internal war. Is that what you want? To see your men slaughtered? Your city ravaged? Your power in tatters?"

"Ben, Ben, Ben." He shakes his head. "I thought you were the insightful one."

I visualize slamming his face into the window this time with my hands around his neck, squeezing every last bit of oxygen from his lungs.

"Of course, they won't answer to me. Those smug bastards think they are above everyone. No, the only way we can do this is to get rid of them."

"*We?* You can't seriously be suggesting what I think you're suggesting." Disbelief radiates from my tone.

The car heads down the ramp, onto the highway, and I wonder where he is taking me.

"Don't pretend you haven't been on the ultimate power trip these past few years, Bennett. Own your achievements, son."

Bile floods my mouth, and I bite hard on my cheek to ignore the urge to retaliate. "I know what I've achieved and what is still left to achieve. Killing the rest of the New York *famiglia* is not on my agenda."

"I know you are loyal. It is our way, but think about it." He finishes his cigar, leaving the butt in the ashtray, and grips my arm. "Together, you and I will be a formidable force. We will reorganize The Commission, and I will rule La Cosa Nostra as don, and you will be our underboss."

I'm guessing Gifoli isn't listening in on the conversation unless DeLuca is lying and he plans to use me to get the other dons out of the way and then dispose of me. I wouldn't put it past him. "You are crazy if you think anyone would commit their allegiance to you after wiping out The Commission."

"That's where you come in. Your powers of persuasion are legendary, and I've already struck a deal with the Bratva. In exchange for gifting them a couple of key territories, we will sign a peace treaty. That is what I offer my fellow Italian Americans. Peace and prosperity."

"You were behind the attacks on Vegas and Philly," I surmise.

"I designed the strategy and helped the Russians with execution. See how easy it was to run rings around The Commission?"

Either he's suffering from amnesia or he's deliberately ignoring the Bratva's failure to take Philly this week.

"And they have the nerve to call themselves the leaders of La Cosa Nostra." He tut-tuts. "They are a disgrace." He slams his hand down on the arm rest. "An abomination."

"I won't do it," I tell him. "I won't betray my family."

He chuckles, and I'm two seconds from throttling him with my bare hands.

"I know you won't, which is why I arranged for the right incentive." He pulls a small TV screen down from the ceiling, and every muscle in my body strains with fear and rage as the image flickers to life.

Sierra is slumped on the floor of a dirty van, lying motionless with her eyes closed. Around her, eight men converse and laugh while eyeing her with dark intent.

My hands are around Giuseppe's throat before I've processed the motion. Spittle flies from my mouth as I squeeze his neck, wanting to snuff out the amused look in his eyes. "You better pray she is just unconscious because I will burn your fucking world down if you have hurt her or my son!" I roar.

The muzzle of a gun presses into the side of my skull. "Release the boss now, Mazzone, or I'll fucking shoot," Gifoli says, digging the weapon in tighter. I didn't even hear the privacy screen lowering or sense him leaning into the back.

DeLuca shoves me away when I let him go, and Gifoli keeps his gun trained on me. "Let's make one thing clear here, Bennett. You are no longer in charge—of anything," DeLuca hisses. "I call the shots, and you will do as I say, or I will order my men to shoot her." He jabs his finger at the screen, and pain slices across my chest as I watch my fiancée lying motionless on the floor, surrounded by hungry vultures. "Of course, I'll let them have their way with her first. They can fuck her, cut her, piss on her for all I care."

"If they so much as touch a hair on her head, I will kill you," I calmly say.

"They are under clear instructions not to touch her, but I can change that at any moment, Bennett."

"Where is my son?" I growl.

"He is at your home, sleeping off the effects of the gas we pumped through the air-conditioning system."

"You bastard." I lunge for him, and Gifoli presses the muzzle to my forehead this time.

"I believe that accolade is more fitting for you and your son," DeLuca says, lighting a second cigar. "Let's not make Rowan an orphan."

Peering closer at the screen, I curse when I see a familiar face among DeLuca's men. "That double-crossing asshole." I've been wondering how the hell DeLuca managed to get to Sierra when there is no way in and out of my house without meeting a barrage of bullets. Leo's cousin has betrayed us. "How long has Ian been working for you?" I grit out.

"I recruited him when you brought him to Chicago," he replies, sending a cloud of cedar-scented smoke into the air. "It was remarkably easy," he adds. "He harbors a lot of resentment toward Leo and Frank and their father. You really need to look after your people better, and I'd take a long hard look at your security procedures. It was way too easy to infiltrate your inner circle."

Touché, asshole.

"How long have you known Rowan is my son?" I demand to know.

"I discovered that information the same day you did," he replies, startling me. He barks out a laugh. "It's ironic your heir was sitting right under my nose this entire time. You know, I never thought Sierra would amount to much, but I welcomed her back to the family when she gave birth to a boy." He puffs on his cigar as the car turns down a winding side road. "I thought he might be my only chance for an heir considering Saskia and Felix couldn't conceive and Serena had only birthed a daughter. But then Gifoli came through," he adds, grinning at his current underboss. "When Romeo was born, I had no need for Rowan anymore, so I removed my protection."

Intense pressure sits on my chest, and I'm like a volcano, boiling under the surface, ready to explode.

He clamps his hand down on my shoulder. "If I had known he was your son, I would have treated him differently, but that is neither here nor there now. I have ensured your son was kept out of this once it was clear he was your flesh and blood, and I assure you no harm will come to him."

"Pity you didn't afford your daughter the same courtesy," I hiss. "You don't need to use Sierra. I will agree to your crazy plan. Let her go, and I give you my word I will do whatever you want."

"Don't insult me," he snaps. "And need I remind you I am calling the shots?"

The car slows down as we approach a large white building with Lawson Pharma in big gold lettering on the front.

"You will agree to my plan, and in exchange, I will let Sierra live. Not in the US, though. Saskia wouldn't tolerate that."

"What the fuck does that annoying bitch have to do with anything?"

He punches me in the face, and blood trickles out of my nose. "If I hear you speak about Saskia in such a derisory tone again, I will instruct my men to inflict the next punch on Sierra."

I used to think Sierra's dad was a cold-hearted bastard, but that front concealed his true nature. He is cold because he does not feel emotion. He has obsessions, possessions—like his need for ultimate power, and his weird fixation with his eldest daughter—but he's an unfeeling monster because he is a psychopath. It's painfully clear now there is no reasoning with the man. Everything I say or do from this point on will either save Sierra or kill her. I won't take any chances with her life, so I will play this game the way he expects.

I grind my teeth to the molars but say nothing, knowing he will continue because he loves the sound of his own voice.

The car glides to a halt at the back of the building in front of a small painted door.

"You were always meant to be with Saskia until that meddlesome Terry Scott fucked things up. You do know he killed your brother, Mateo. Right?"

My jaw slackens, and I can't mask my shock in time. "What? Why?"

"It seems Terry overhead Gifoli on the phone to me planning a path for your future. He must not have liked what he heard because he concocted a scheme to take out your brother, knowing Angelo would come looking for you. It was all done to snatch you from me, just when I was ready to make my move."

A muscle pops in my jaw, as I struggle to deal with that bombshell. If it's true—and that's a big if—why would Terry send me running from the hands of one mafioso to another? Unless he saw Angelo Mazzone as the lesser of two evils? Given the bizarre turn in this conversation, I've got to agree with my late friend.

"We got rid of Felix to pave the way for this to happen," he continues, confirming he conspired with Saskia to kill her husband. Sierra wasn't far off the mark with her comment that day at the graveside. "Poor Saskia can't bear children, and she's been tormented these past few years, but she will love Rowan like he is her own child because she loves you and Rowan shares your DNA."

Rowan also shares Sierra's DNA, but I don't articulate that point for fear he'll carry out his threat and hurt her. I work hard to keep the shock from my face, presenting a neutral front while my entire world is crumbling around me. "What exactly are you saying?" I ask as the driver steps out of the car.

"I will ensure my men keep their hands off Sierra and let her live a comfortable existence in Europe after you marry Saskia and she adopts Rowan."

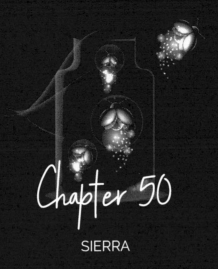

Chapter 50

SIERRA

MY ARMS ACHE, my body is exhausted, and my head feels fuzzy as I slowly come to. My eyes repeatedly flicker open and shut as darkness tries to drag me back under. Fighting the lure of unconsciousness, I force my heavy eyelids to open in the dusky room. It's a small enclosed space with bare brick walls, a low ceiling, and an uncovered floor. Apart from an old, stained toilet and a rickety wooden chair propped in one corner, the windowless room is empty. The thick steel door ensures I won't be getting out of here anytime soon. Fear crawls up my spine, and I shiver all over.

Panic sluices through my veins when I move my frigid limbs and something cold and sharp digs into my wrists. I look up, and my pulse throbs wildly in my neck as I peruse the steel manacles that bind my wrists to the exposed stone wall, keeping my arms raised above my head.

I'm slumped on my side against the wall, so I attempt to straighten up, biting back a whimper when the manacles dig into my sensitive flesh. As my eyes adjust to the lack of light, my gaze roams over the unfamiliar surroundings while I trawl my foggy brain for answers.

Rowan!

My panic elevates a thousand notches and my breath oozes out in anguished spurts. The last thing I remember is the bodyguards swarming the house, advising us of a security alert as they rushed us through the hallways, toward the safe room. Then a misty veil descended from the ceiling, and everyone started dropping like flies. My very last memory is holding Rowan to my chest as I struggled to stay awake.

Terror has a vise grip on my heart at the thought he could be chained in another cold, dank, dark room. "Help," I croak, struggling to get to my feet. Standing isn't an easy feat with my arms chained over my head. "Somebody, please help me." I know any person who comes to my aid is no savior, but I need to draw attention to myself in the hope I can find out what has happened to Rowan.

Smothering my painful cries, as the manacles tear into the delicate flesh of my wrists, I struggle to my feet, banging my knee off the hard wall in the process. Pain shoots through my leg, and I slouch against the wall, feeling weak and useless. My head pounds like someone is hammering on my skull from the inside, and my eyes sting. Whatever gas was used to knock us unconscious is still lingering in my system. "Hey, asshole," I shout when my pleas for help rouse no one. "I'm awake, motherfucker. Show yourself, you freaking coward!"

My spine stiffens when the door groans before slamming inward. A guy with cropped strawberry-blond hair steps into the room, flashing me a mouthful of crooked teeth. He's dressed head to toe in black, and he has a gun belt strapped around his waist, a Glock perched on his toned hip. "Watch your mouth, bitch," he says, striding toward me. "Or I'll shut it for you." He grips my chin, pinching my flesh with dirty nails. His stale breath fans across my face, and bile travels up my throat.

"Where is my son?"

"Who said you could ask questions?" He digs his nails in farther. "You're our prisoner. We get to ask the questions, not the other way around."

"Z." Another man steps into the space. "Back off." His deep voice is abrasive, but he carries an air of authority.

"I don't take orders from you," Z says, releasing my chin before plastering his disgusting form against my body. He's taller than me, so my face is pressed up against his chest, making breathing difficult. Sweat and the stench of cigarette smoke clings to his black top, and I gag.

Suddenly, he is yanked back without warning, and I gulp in lungsful of air.

"The boss was clear. No touching her," the new guy says.

"I was just laying down the ground rules," Z says, folding his arms. Although he has his back to me now, I hear the petulant pout in his tone.

"Where is my son?" I repeat, looking at the tall, broad-shouldered man with reddish-brown hair.

"He's not here," the newcomer says. "Our instructions were to take you and you alone. We didn't go near your son."

I burst out crying as relief thunders through me though it's short-lived. While I'm relieved Rowan isn't here, that doesn't mean he is unharmed. Who knows what the aftereffects of the gas might have done to a child, and poor Angelo! His lungs are already under attack from cancer, and he might not have survived.

"I've got this," the taller man says, and Z storms out of the room, clearly not happy.

"I'm B," he supplies. "Let me give you some advice. Cooperate and this will be easier on you. If you disobey us, I will have no choice but to leave you chained up, cold, and hungry."

"Who are you?" I ask because neither of the two men sounded Russian. Unless it's not the Bratva who took me?

"I've got it from here," another man says, entering the room carrying a small tray.

"Ian?" I frown as I stare at him, struggling to understand what is going on.

"I brought you some dinner, Sierra. You should eat."

"You fucking traitor!" I hiss as I connect the dots. Only an insider could have gained access to the internal air-conditioning system to render us unconscious. Ian must have created some emergency to get all the bodyguards into the house so he could disarm them in one fell swoop. "You did this!" I can't say I know the man well because he was mainly our nighttime guard in Chicago, and he worked with the main security detail at the house when we moved to Greenwich. Anytime he was around, he tended to keep to himself.

"It's nothing personal, Sierra. Just business." He stares at B. "Why are you still here?"

B gives him a terse nod, glancing at me briefly, before walking out of the room. My eyes trail him out into the dark hallway, spotting more steel doors on either side of the narrow space. He trudges up a small set of stairs at the end of the corridor, which looks like the only way out of this basement area. It doesn't present much chance of escape.

"Why?" I ask as Ian places the tray on the floor a few feet away. "Why did you do this?"

"I was just following orders," he says, unlocking one of my manacled wrists.

"Whose orders?"

He doesn't reply, lifting the tray and holding it out to me.

I glare at him. "How do you expect me to hold a tray and eat with one hand?"

He mulls that over for a few seconds before setting the tray down again. "I'm going to unchain you, but don't make me regret it. In case you're thinking of escaping, we are in the middle of a forest in bumfuck Ohio and the nearest property is twenty miles away." He points at the corner of the room, and I hone in on the small camera tucked into the crevice. "We have someone watching you around the clock, so don't try anything."

"What the hell do you think I'm going to try? There are no windows and a steel door. We both know I'm going nowhere unless…you let me go." I press my mouth to his ear. "You know Ben won't stop looking for me. Let me go, and whatever the Russians have promised you, I will get Ben to match," I whisper. "Or, if it's money you're after, I have plenty. Whatever you want, I will give it to you."

"You think I want your *money*?" He spits out the word, and his nostrils flare. I clearly hit a nerve. "This is about respect, and if Ben and Leo had any for me, I would have been treated better."

"They respect you," I protest. "Ben would not have had you guarding Rowan and me otherwise."

"You think that job is a job any soldier wants? I was relegated to the sidelines, like I have been for years. All it would take is Leo or his father speaking up for me, and I would have been promoted. But they made it clear that wasn't going to happen." He scoffs. "My new boss recognized my value immediately. Offered me the promotion I have been hankering after for years." He puffs out his chest. "Now I'm a capo, and the sky is the limit."

I can't even dignify that load of bull with a response. If he's that stupid, let him wallow in it until Ben puts a bullet in his skull. I don't know everything there is to know yet, but Ben has spoken about the importance of loyalty and honor and how *omertá* is their code of silence. I know breaking the oath he swore means he has signed his own death sentence. I wonder if his new boss values him enough to protect him when the weight of the Mazzone *famiglia* comes down on him.

"Here," B says, reentering the room, holding out a blanket.

Ian grabs it off him, dismissing him coldly. "Go watch the camera," he snaps, reaching up to unchain my other wrist.

My arms rejoice as they hang by my sides, still aching but glad to be free of the shackles. With gentle fingers, I probe the torn skin at my wrists.

"Eat, and then I'll bring you something for that," Ian says, kicking the tray across the floor with his foot. Liquid sloshes out of the bowl, onto the tray, and the bottle of water tips onto its side.

I sit down, pulling my knees up to my chest, as I drag the tray over. Ian throws the blanket at me and turns to walk off. He stops at the door, glancing over his shoulder. "You should know I'm not working for the Russians. I work for your father." With that bombshell delivered, he exits the room, slamming the door shut. I stare straight ahead, openmouthed, my eyes wide in shock as he locks it from the outside.

Surely, he's lying, right? My father wouldn't do this. I mean, I know he hates me, but he wouldn't stoop this low. Would he?

TIME LOSES ALL meaning, and I don't know, for sure, how many days have passed since they kidnapped me. With no windows, I can't see the sky to know if it's daytime or nighttime. The only measure I have is my meals, which are delivered like clockwork at regular intervals.

B enters my cell and deposits my dinner tray on the floor beside me before walking off without speaking. This is my third dinner, so I'm working on the probability it's my third day here.

That first day, I deliberated eating for ages, paralyzed in shock and fear. But I realized if they wanted me dead they would have just killed me. The fact I've been kidnapped means someone wants me alive, so I figure the food is probably safe to eat. Briefly, I considered not eating in protest, but I need to keep my strength up if I'm to stand any chance of getting out of here.

I don't know if Ian said what he said about my father to throw me, but I have veered back and forth over his claim, deciding my father is more than capable of it but struggling to understand why. I know he's in bed with the mafia. I know The Outfit was reluctant to join The Commission, and the only conclusion I can draw is that my father is using me to force Ben into doing something. I could be wrong, but that's the best I've come up with.

I pull the blanket up over my shoulders to ward off the perpetual chill, and my fingers brush against my upper arm, feeling the small tracking device under my skin. It's minuscule, and no one would find it unless they knew it was there. I'm hoping Ben can get a signal from the chip and he's on his way for me. I try not to think about the fact it's been three days and I'm still here. In moments when I let my fear loose, I worry The Outfit has done something to Ben and that is why he hasn't come for me yet, but I try to keep those thoughts at bay because they don't help.

I run the tip of my finger over my diamond and emerald ring, and it's the only glimmer of light in my newly dark world. Worry for Rowan is at the forefront of my mind all the time, and I can only imagine how scared he must be. We have only spent one night apart, and I know my absence must be frightening for him. If my father has taken him or done anything to hurt my son, I will hunt him down and murder him myself.

I eat the bland beef stew, stale bread roll, and plain yogurt before washing it all down with warm water. Pushing my tray away, I scrape my ratty hair back off my face, plaiting it with cold shaky fingers. I feel disgusting having not showered, and I'm still wearing the jeans, sweater, and sneakers I was wearing when I was taken.

The sound of muffled voices mixes with approaching footfalls, and I scramble to my feet, crossing my arms and waiting for whichever guards deem to grace me with their presence this time. Besides Ian, B, and Z, five other guards have attended to me. I guess they must be rotating shifts.

The door flies open, and I blink profusely, sure my eyes must be deceiving me, because I must be imagining the familiar woman standing beside Z.

I stare at her pristine pink Chanel skirt suit and high heels. Her blonde hair is styled in sleek waves that tumble over her shoulders, and her makeup is plastered on her tight face. A string of pearls rests on her collarbone, and she holds a small black and pink clutch purse in one hand.

Her nose wrinkles in distaste as her eyes roam the small cell before landing on me. An ugly sneer tilts the corners of her cosmetically enhanced mouth before her lips part and she speaks. "You have no idea how long I have waited to see you languishing in the gutter where you belong, sister."

Her cruel words wash over me, along with all the other mean things Saskia has ever said to me. But it is the acknowledgment that my father *is* behind my kidnapping that threatens to cripple me the most. Saskia would not be here otherwise, and it's clear they are in this together.

She steps right up but keeps her distance, grimacing at the state of my filthy clothes and my stringy hair. "You should have listened to me, and maybe fate would have been kinder to you, but you always think you know best." Her eyes glimmer with pure evil, and I am seeing my sister stripped bare now. There is no more hiding the full extent of the poison that flows through her veins. She revels in it, not wishing to shield anything from me. "I always win, baby sister, but this may be my greatest triumph yet."

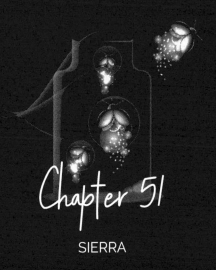

Chapter 51

SIERRA

"YOU WON'T BE needing that anymore," Saskia says, grabbing my hand and wrenching my engagement ring off my finger before I can stop her. Throwing it to the ground, she stands on it, using her stiletto heel to attack the diamond. Frustrated when it only inflicts minimal damage, she spins around, pointing at Z. "You! Get me a hammer."

Curling my damaged ring in her clenched fist, she rakes her derisory gaze over me again. "You look like shit, but it suits you. You have finally found your true place in this world," she taunts, as Z reappears in the doorway, panting.

Did the asshole actually run up and down the stairs to do her bidding?

What an idiot.

With cold calculation, Saskia snatches the hammer from his hand and stalks to the chair, placing the ring down on top of it. Her eyes glisten with devilish delight as she looks at me before lifting the hammer and bringing it down on my ring. She gleefully attacks it, smashing the pretty diamond, breaking the tiny emeralds surrounding it, and battering the platinum band until the ring is nothing but splintered shards on the floor. The seat of the chair is cracked, the legs barely able to hold it upright.

My eyes dance over the broken remnants of my ring, and it feels like my heart is rupturing behind my rib cage. Intense pain settles on my chest, making breathing difficult, but I work hard to hide it. I won't give that bitch any satisfaction. She doesn't know that ring bolstered my courage and fueled my hope every time I looked at it. She doesn't know how precious it is because Ben designed it with me in mind. She won't know I still harbored hope Ben would rescue me in time to make our wedding day.

She will never know because I won't give her any more ammunition to hurt me.

"You were always a petty, spiteful bitch, but that's low even for you," I say, feigning nonchalance.

"Do you want to talk about spiteful?" she hisses. "Let's talk about how you have made it your life's mission to steal everything that should rightfully belong to me!"

I know Saskia is prone to bouts of extreme drama and delusion, but this takes the cake.

She clicks her fingers at Z. "Get me another chair," she snaps, "and make it quick."

Like a dutiful lap dog, he races out of the room, into the next cell, emerging with an unbroken chair. He unashamedly ogles her as he sets it down in front of her.

Ignoring him, she perches her bony ass on the hard wooden chair, pointing at me. "Sit!" she demands.

"I'd rather stand." I flatten my back to the wall and glare at her.

"I said sit, so you will sit," she retorts.

"Make me."

She looks at Z, and he storms toward me, shoving me roughly to the floor. I scream in pain when he stomps his booted foot on my hand. Bones crack, shooting excruciating pain up my arm.

"That's enough," Saskia says, grinning like all her Sundays have come at once. "Stand outside. I'll call you if I need you." He looks like he wants to protest, but one cutting look from my bitch of a sister, and he leaves us alone, closing the door but not shutting it fully.

"We're going to have story time, Sierra. I know how much you love making up fantasies for Rowan."

My claws come out, and I snarl at her as I cradle my injured hand to my chest. "Don't you dare talk about my son. If you even mention his name, I will gouge your eyes from your sockets before your lackey has time to save you," I growl.

She flashes me an amused smile before continuing as if I haven't spoken at all. "You know part of this story. The part where I met a boy from the wrong side of the tracks and fell head over heels in love with him. But you don't know the background. Daddy promised me to Felix when I was thirteen, and the marriage arrangement stated we would wed after I came of age, sometime before I turned nineteen. Felix was handsome, and I knew I would have a good life with him, but I wanted to experience what it would be like to date other boys before I committed myself to one man, so I sweet-talked Daddy into agreeing I could date for eighteen months, provided I remained a virgin."

She shivers in the cold room, rubbing one hand up and down her arm. "The irony is, I only flirted with Ben and agreed to a date as a bet." She giggles. "We met at a club in the city, and I could tell he was dirt-poor. Chastity and Verona said I wouldn't last a week with a man who didn't have the resources or the wherewithal to treat me how I deserved to be treated, and, well, you know how much I love a challenge."

I always wondered how they met and how they ended up dating. Ben is gorgeous, and I've no doubt she had the hots for him, but he had nothing, and ordinarily, Saskia would not have looked twice at him. It's making more sense now.

"He captivated me almost immediately, and while winning the bet indulged my competitive streak, keeping the man thrilled me more. Daddy wasn't pleased at first when he saw how attached I had grown. That's when he started digging into Ben's background. After a few months, he discovered he was the illegitimate son of Angelo Mazzone, and that changed everything. Daddy came to me with a new proposal. I was to get Ben to propose and let him take me to bed. Giving my virginity to another man would render the contract with Barretta null and void, leaving me free to marry the Mazzone heir!"

Her eyes sparkle, and she bristles with self-importance. "Felix was only the consigliere heir. This was a huge step up, and Daddy knew with me on his arm that Ben and I would rule all of New York one day. We had it all worked out. Ben would concede to Daddy as the overall don of La Cosa Nostra, and he would serve as his underboss.

We would have more power and wealth than I ever dreamed of!"

Her eyes glaze over, and I wonder if she is even present. I can picture her daily, sitting in front of her mirror, spewing this imaginary crap, visualizing herself as the new mafia queen.

"And then it all fell apart, and I was enraged." The dreamy expression on her face evaporates, replaced with a scary mask of anger that sends chills up my spine. "Angelo's heir was murdered, and he yanked Ben to New York just as we were making our move."

"You seem to have conveniently forgotten the part where Ben broke up with you."

She darts forward, slapping me across the face. "Don't fucking interrupt me when I'm speaking."

You know, I do believe my sister is insane. I have always known she is cruel and mean and jealous and vindictive, but she is so much more than that. She is a complete whack job.

"We only found out recently that one of Daddy's soldiers killed Ben's half-brother to halt our plans." She cackles, and the sound raises goose bumps on my arms. "Daddy repaid him for that, and I burned his house to the ground," she gleefully admits.

She can only be talking about Terry Scott. This is why he was living in fear. God, Ben will be so shocked when he discovers this truth. But why is she referring to him as one of Daddy's soldiers? And why would Ben ever concede to my father as the main boss? I thought my father washed cash for The Outfit, but it's clear now he is so much more than that.

All the tiny hairs lift on my neck as I try to slot the last puzzle pieces into place.

"Of course, we timed it to perfection." She prattles on. "Knowing it would bring Ben back to Chicago. Bumping into him on the street with Rowan was unplanned, but I thought it would work to my advantage until you had to go and ruin everything!" she screeches, digging her nails into her thighs.

My blood boils, like it does anytime Saskia mentions my son. She has never shown him the slightest interest.

"Not that it's darling Rowan's fault, of course," she adds, wearing a fake adoring smile that snaps the tenuous control on my emotions.

I lunge at her, shoving her off the chair. "I told you not to mention his name!" I yell, crouching down to punch her in the face with my uninjured hand. My fist slams into her cheekbone, and she screams bloody murder just as Z bursts into the room.

He grabs me off my sister, shoving me forcefully against the wall, and I scream in pain as he yanks my hands up over my head, forcing them into the manacles. My injured hand throbs, and the torn flesh on my wrists, barely healed, rips open again. Tears leak from my eyes of their own volition as pain ricochets up and down my arm.

"Are you okay?" Z asks, hovering over Saskia and extending his arm to help her up. His eyes fly to her thighs, bare underneath her skirt that has ridden up her legs.

"Don't look at me like that, you pervert," she snaps, grabbing his arm and pulling herself upright. Once she is standing, she pushes him away. "Leave. And next time, wait to be called. I had it handled, idiot."

A muscle ticks in Z's jaw, and he looks like he could hit her. Silently, I egg him on, but he's got no balls, and he won't follow through. He storms out of the room, muttering under his breath, and I think his rose-tinted glasses have dropped off.

Saskia prods at her cheek, wincing, and I hope I left a nice big bruise. Her eyes narrow with pure hatred as she strides toward me, punching me repeatedly in the gut. "You fucking bitch! How dare you hit me!" She lands another punch to my stomach, and it's starting to hurt. What she lacks in brute strength she makes up for in enthusiasm. "You better pray this doesn't bruise, baby sister. Daddy may have promised Ben he'd keep you alive, but I have no qualms about killing you."

She realizes she's given me vital intel a second too late.

I can't contain my grin, knowing Ben *is* working to save me.

Emitting a frustrated scream, she hits my solar plexus again, with more force this time, and I bite back a whimper as stabbing pain spreads across my stomach.

"I don't know why you look so smug. You're the one chained to a wall like a filthy dog while I'm the one wearing Ben's ring." She thrusts out her hand, waving a monstrous diamond ring in my face.

"Ben would never pick such a hideous ring," I say, risking another punch. "And he would never agree to marry you."

Grabbing her purse, she removes a folded-up piece of paper, thrusting it in front of my face. It's a cutout from *The New York Times*, announcing her engagement to Ben.

What the actual fuck is going on?

All the blood drains from my face, and she laughs. "I told you, you would never marry him," she gloats. "Ben has always been mine. We were always fated to be. He loves me, and he was only with you out of obligation to Rowan." She tucks the newspaper clipping back in her purse. "The whole of New York society will be out in force for our engagement party this weekend and then our wedding two weeks later. But don't worry, I will take really good care of him. Rowan too."

I thrash about in the manacles, barely feeling any pain as I scream and shout at her. "You leave my son alone! He's my baby. Mine!" I don't know what the hell is going on, but I know Ben wouldn't marry her freely, and there is no way he would want her anywhere near our son, so I can only guess this is all part of some plan.

"Not anymore." She smiles. "Daddy is already drawing up the adoption paperwork. They will both forget all about you, as if you never even existed."

"Neither of them will ever be yours," I roar. "Tell yourself whatever bullshit you want, but they are mine!" I thrash about as angry tears prick my eyes. She is lucky Z chained me to this wall because in this moment I want to kill her. I want to grab her surgically altered face and slam it into the wall until she's a bloody pulp with no pulse.

Her entire body shakes with rage as she screams in my face. "Do you know how long I have been trying to have a child!? I had seven miscarriages! Seven. Do you know what that does to a woman?" She paces the cell, running her hands through her hair repeatedly, messing up the careful styling. "I was heartbroken every month when I failed to conceive. Every time when I lost my baby, another part of me died, and then you, *you slut*, you get pregnant without even trying." She slaps me again, much harder this time, and stars swim behind my vision. "I hate you! You tried to steal my life, but I stole it back because you are too stupid to play the game." She taps her temple, reining in her anger. "I haven't always just been more beautiful than you. I'm smarter too."

Add delusional and insane, I snipe in my head. Though I don't articulate it because my sister is unhinged and it's not smart to antagonize her anymore. I don't trust she wouldn't kill me and say I provoked her into doing it.

"How does it feel to know no one trusts you enough to tell you the truth? That you are so insignificant you don't matter to anyone. Even Mom and Serena kept the truth from you when you called them."

I frown before I can stop myself. How does she even know about that?

"They are still lying to you," she sneers. "They chose protecting Daddy's big secret over you."

"I know he's involved in the mafia. Mom and Serena confirmed it." Although they didn't explain *how* involved he is, and I'm newly mad at them all over again.

She laughs. "That's not the secret. Maybe I shouldn't say it, but who cares? You will be out of the country in a few weeks." Her hands ball into fists at her sides as she realizes she just revealed another part of the puzzle.

For someone supposedly smart, she sure fucks up a lot.

"Daddy is Giuseppe DeLuca. Don of The Outfit."

I can only stare at her. This has got to be another one of her delusions. Or is it? I remember everything Ben told me about the mysterious Sicilian boss. The pieces start slotting into place in my head, and it all makes sense. Holy shit. My father isn't just connected to the mafia—he *is* the mafia.

"Didn't you ever wonder why he hates you so much?" She continues goading me.

I brace myself because I know she's preparing to sucker punch me before she leaves.

"You're not his flesh and blood! You're not the only slut in the family. Mom had an affair and she got pregnant with you."

"You're lying," I spit, through gritted teeth. "If that was the truth, Father would have killed Mom when she was pregnant."

"That's what he should've done, but he didn't because the sap loves her for reasons I have never quite understood. She has paid for it though, in other ways. He covered it up and took responsibility for you, but he loathes you with the intensity of a thousand suns."

My heart pounds in my chest, and I'm not sure I can take any more. The weight of everything she has said presses down on me like a ton of bricks, and I slump against the wall, unable to disguise the effect of her revelations.

She gloats, practically purring like a cat. "Don't take it too personally. You're the daughter of a lowly soldier after all. You are just the sum of your DNA, and you were never going to amount to anything." She grabs her purse, palming a hand over her hair to fix it back into place. "Consider yourself lucky you are allowed to live out the rest of your pitiful existence." She straightens her skirt, smoothing out a few wrinkles. "And count your blessings that I'm not in charge, because if it were up to me, I'd riddle you with bullets."

She stalks toward the door, spinning on her heel one final time to leave a parting shot. "Aren't you going to wish me congratulations for my pending nuptials?"

"The next time I see you, you are going to die," I promise. "Even if I have to sacrifice myself to do it."

"I'll tell Ben you wished us well," she says. "Try not to think of him sliding that big cock of his inside me every night. Bennett Mazzone definitely knows how to please a woman. I'm sure it won't be long before I'm pregnant with his baby, and this time, I know fate will ensure I carry full-term."

My heart cracks and splinters down the middle at the thought of Ben fucking Saskia, and I have nothing left to retaliate with. She exits the room, laughing hysterically, and her wicked cackles penetrate my eardrums long after she is gone.

I cry silent tears as I lean against the wall, my arms aching, and my hand throbbing. Saskia is a crazy bitch, and I can't let her get to me. I don't know what, if anything, is fact and what is a lie.

There is one truth I know, and I cling to it like a life jacket—Ben loves me, and he is going to come for me. Whatever he is being forced to do, he is doing to save me, and I won't hold it against him.

I refuse to give up hope.

Not while there is still air in my lungs and blood flowing through my veins.

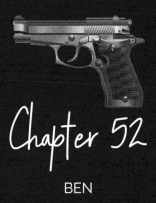

Chapter 52

BEN

STANDING IN THE shadows of the library, I watch Mr. Spielberg explain a math problem to Rowan. His little dark head is bent over the desk, his brow furrowed in concentration, as he listens. Purple shadows linger in the curves under his eyes, highlighting his trouble sleeping.

It's been four days since Sierra was taken, and he's not the only one finding it difficult to sleep or the only one missing her. I have been working from my home office since Sierra was kidnapped because I need to stay close to my son and it gives me an excuse to avoid physical contact with that bitch Saskia.

I don't trust DeLuca to keep his word, and I refuse to let Rowan out of my sight. I replaced all the men at the house because I can't be sure Ian didn't have a partner or partners. Leo has taken them to the city to interrogate them while Alessandro and Frank are guarding my son around the clock. They even take shifts in my bedroom at night. Not that it's necessary. I barely grab more than a couple of hours sleep. Sierra's delicate floral scent still clings to the sheets, and I crawl into bed with a constant tight pain in my chest. Rowan sleeps curled up beside me in our bed, and I need his little body comforting me as much as he needs my comfort.

He misses his mommy, and he cries every night for her. Every anguished sob tears a new strip off my heart, and I want to murder DeLuca and Saskia in cold blood for inflicting this torture on my son. I hate lying to Rowan, but I can't tell him the truth. He thinks Sierra is on vacation with Pen and Esme, but he struggles to understand why she doesn't even call him. I said there was no cell service at the spa, but I'm not convinced he bought that lie. For five years old, he's sharp as a tack.

Natalia is here, playing with him after his daily lessons have ended, because I have work to do. If I'm to rescue Sierra, to bring her home safely, as soon as possible, I need to work every angle, and that takes time. Natalia also wants to be close to Angelo because his days on this Earth are drawing to a close.

He's been in a coma since the kidnapping, and a machine is breathing for him now. His lungs gave up when the sleeping gas infiltrated his system. It's a miracle his heart didn't give out, but he's a stubborn fucker, and he'll fight to the bitter end. I don't even have time to think about the fact he's on his death bed or how I feel about it because I'm too worried about Firefly.

"Boss." Ciro approaches from behind, making an effort to lower his tone. I'm glad he wasn't seriously injured and he's back on the job because I need every man available for duty. "Call for you in your office."

Nodding at Alessandro, I slip out of the library. My dress shoes tap against the hardwood floor as I stride to my office with Ciro on my tail.

"Mazzone," I say, when I pick up my burner cell.

"Everything is in motion," he replies.

"What percentage are loyal to you?" I inquire because we need the numbers.

"Approximately thirty percent."

We can make that work. "Good. I'll be in touch before Saturday."

The line goes dead as he hangs up.

"Knock, knock," Leo says, poking his head through the door.

"Come in." I wasn't expecting to see him until tomorrow, at the earliest, even if I know him to be a fast worker. "What's the verdict?" I ask, pouring a scotch for him and a bourbon for me.

"They're all clean. Ian was working alone. He lured everyone but the guards at the gate to the house with a fake report of men at the rear of the property. Once they were inside, he conveniently disappeared just as the gas was leaked into the system. He gave DeLuca's men the access code to the gate, and they dispensed with the guards on duty before taking Ian and Sierra with them."

We have already replaced the entire security system, changed all the codes, doubled the guards, and the new men protecting my property were all inserted with tracking devices. From now on, I'm making that a requirement for all my soldiers. If they don't like it, they can get the fuck out of my organization.

The one thing I hate is knowing DeLuca is aware of my house now. I have gone to huge extremes over the years to keep the location a secret, and I want to throttle Ian for compromising my safe haven. There is nothing I can do about it now though, and come Saturday night, the secret should be protected again.

"You look like shit," Leo says as I hand him his scotch.

"Saskia paid Sierra a visit," I explain. "She thrust the engagement in her face and destroyed Sierra's ring." I lost my shit when I got that intel and trashed my office, before I composed myself and called the jeweler to design another ring.

"Sierra is shrewd. She will know you are planning something. She will trust you to come for her," Leo reassures me.

I slump in my chair, swirling the bourbon in my glass before lifting it to my lips. "I hate imagining Sierra chained up in some disgusting dungeon thinking I've fucked her sister."

Sympathy splashes over his face. "You haven't touched the bitch. That's what is most important, and you will get a chance to explain it to Sierra when we get her out."

"Am I wrong to do this? We know where she is. I could storm in there and rescue her right now." I lean forward, resting my head in my hands. "I *want* to storm in there and take her to safety. I don't know if I can last another two days." I want to bundle her into my arms and hold her close forever so no one can harm her again.

"I can't begin to imagine what you are going through," he says. "But you *are* doing the right thing. This way we are eliminating the threat permanently. If you ride to the rescue now, you will have shown our hand, and it will mean bloody war. A war where Sierra and Rowan will be the prime targets. You know DeLuca would not let this rest. If you double-cross him, he *will* go for Sierra first."

I lift my head, staring at my friend through tired bloodshot eyes. "I know, but it doesn't make this any easier to bear."

I had tried reasoning with DeLuca, proposing I marry Sierra as planned and I would do his bidding. That way, he would still get what he wants—a DeLuca-Mazzone alliance. At that point, he told me Sierra is not his flesh and blood. If there was time, I'd look into that claim, as I don't trust he's telling me the truth. But it's minor in the grand scheme of things, and I have got to remain focused.

It seems neither Georgia or Serena are aware of Sierra's kidnapping, and I've been told to keep it that way. Right now, I need to look like I'm playing the game so he doesn't guess what I'm up to behind the scenes.

I've had to take extra precautions this week, to ensure our plotting remains hidden.

Now it's set in motion, I'm itching to get it over and done with.

My normal cell vibrates with an incoming call, and I growl as I see Saskia's name flashing on the screen. "She is driving me insane," I mutter, rubbing a tense spot between my brows. She calls multiple times a day, spouting shit I have zero interest in. Her whiny voice grates on my nerves, and my jaw aches from holding back the things I want to say. Faking it is exhausting, but the end is in sight.

Leo doesn't need me to elaborate to know who I'm talking about. "I can't wait to see the look on her face when she finds out you've been acting the devoted fiancé and you really hate her guts."

"Thank fuck, I got DeLuca to agree to no sex before marriage." He didn't want to agree, for a variety of reasons, but I told him that comforting Rowan and preparing him for his new reality was my priority, and he bought it. The truth is, DeLuca needs me, and we both know it. He might be holding Sierra over me, but if he pushes me too far, he could lose my allegiance and his big plan goes up in flames. I'm sure Saskia blew a gasket when he told her it was hands off before the wedding, but I couldn't give a flying fuck what that conniving cunt thinks. She is going to get what is coming to her—they both are—and it can't come soon enough.

Plucking my cell up, I slip my mask on as I press the accept button before I miss her call. Reminding myself of the end game, I use my usual seductive tone when speaking to my despicable fiancée. "Darling. How are the plans coming along for our engagement party?"

"THE OFFICIAL PHOTOGRAPHER has been unavoidably delayed," Alessandro whispers in my ear as I prepare to get into the limo on Saturday night. He smirks, and I can tell he enjoyed that little task.

"And the press photographers?" I inquire, buttoning the center button on my designer tux.

"Will be pulled to the scene of a bank heist before you get there," he explains in hushed tones. "One or two might linger, but if they do, we'll get their cameras after you head into the hotel and destroy them. Phillip and his team are on standby, and they'll remove anything that might pop up online."

The last thing I want is this farce of an engagement party being reported or any photos of Saskia on my arm in existence anywhere. I also don't want press attention when things kick off because I'd like to survive this night without ending up in police custody. The police commissioner—a VIP member of several of my clubs and a close acquaintance—has assured me he will have his men diverted to the bank robbery, but I can't rule out some do-gooder cop with his eye on a promotion stumbling onto events and trying to do the right thing.

"And Brando?" I ask, glancing surreptitiously at the driver. We vet all staff, but I'm extra vigilant at the moment, and I don't want to say anything obvious.

"Has the diamond."

Closing my eyes, I sigh in relief, offering up thanks to a God I long stopped believing in. All week, I have prayed and prayed, offered everything under the sun if this goes off as planned. "Good."

"Benny!" Natalia rushes out of the house, racing down the steps, and flings herself into my arms. "Be careful."

She isn't privy to the facts, but she knows it's going down now. Technically, she should be at my engagement party with her husband. The rest of the New York dons will be there with their wives, but I need her to stay with Rowan, and I want my sister out of the line of fire.

They are barricading themselves in my safe room, along with Frank, and they know not to open the door to anyone. It's an enclosed, secure, impenetrable, fire-retardant space, the size of a luxury suite, with all the amenities they could need. No one can reach them in there, which is why I've had Angelo and Ruthie rehoused for the night too. I won't take any risks. Although I've been super careful to hide my tracks and I've played my part with Giuseppe and Saskia, I wouldn't put it past DeLuca to have a backup plan should I attempt anything tonight.

Natalia has lined up a movie, and she has popcorn and candy. Rowan is excited, and I love seeing a smile on his face again. They have been lacking these past six days. He dragged me into the room before I left to show me the tent with sleeping bags.

"Don't worry. I'll be fine," I assure her. "Thank you for taking care of Rowan."

"Bring her home safely, Benny," she says with tears in her eyes.

"I promise I will."

Even if I have to die tonight, I will ensure Sierra gets out of this alive.

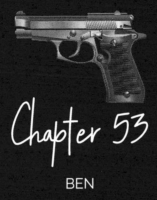

Chapter 53

BEN

"WHERE ARE THE rest of the reporters?" Saskia huffs, pressing her haughty nose to the window of the limo as we pull up in front of the hotel. Three men with cameras linger on the red-carpeted steps, straightening up as the driver kills the engine at the curb.

"Maybe this isn't as newsworthy as you imagined it would be," I say, running low on patience reserves.

She's been pawing at me from the second I picked her up at her hotel, and I'm glad I had the foresight to book a hotel room only five blocks from here so I didn't have to endure her insufferable presence for longer than necessary. All I can visualize when I look at her plastic face and her plastic body, poured into a hideous sickly sweet pink gown, is how she hurt my Firefly, and I want to strangle her with my bare hands after slicing strips from her overstretched skin.

"Don't be ridiculous," she snaps, adding more gloss to her enlarged lips. "This is the announcement of the century."

She truly believes that. She is batshit crazy, I have come to realize. I used to think she was just bitter and jealous, but whatever insanity gene runs in the DeLuca blood has clearly infected her too. If what Giuseppe said is true, at least Sierra has dodged that bullet.

"How do I look?" she asks, thrusting her fake chest in my face. If the dress was any lower at the front, her nipples would be on display.

Saskia used to dress elegantly, back when we were dating, but there is nothing elegant or classy about her now. She is as fake and tacky as they come.

"Like one of those Kardashians." I plaster a faux smile on my face while she tries to work out if my statement is a compliment or an insult. The driver opens my door, and I get out, leaning down to offer her my arm even though my skin crawls every time she touches me.

I only have another couple of hours of faking, so I can stomach the charade for a little longer.

She clutches my arm, preening and pouting for the waiting cameramen as we walk into the hotel.

It takes enormous effort to act lovingly toward my supposed fiancée and to laugh and joke with her father as we enjoy a sumptuous meal in the ballroom of one of the finest hotels in New York, but I do it because I can't tip him off. He's watching me like a hawk, and an offhand look or glint of anger would give the game away.

Around me are two hundred guests I hope won't get caught in the crosshairs. A few of my men have been tasked with discreetly ushering guests outside, in small groups, just before this kicks off, but we can't evacuate the entire room without sounding alarm bells.

I have chosen my guests carefully and vetted all of them on DeLuca's side. Everyone here either has ties to The Outfit, is loyal to the New York dons, or they are clients of my establishments. The hotel owner is one of my best clients, and I send a ton of business his way. He will be compensated for any and all damage, and I'll ensure no adverse press appears in the media about the hotel. That should be enough to assuage him and keep his silence.

No one will speak out about the events here today.

Unless they don't value breathing.

Armed soldiers and bodyguards from The Outfit and the New York *famiglias* surround the room and mingle with the guests. Invisible tension ripples through the air, and the room silently groans in anticipation.

DeLuca stands as the hotel manager materializes, handing him a microphone. I keep my fake smile smeared across my mouth as I listen to him drone on about how proud he is of Saskia.

Serena sits glumly beside Gifoli, at our table, glaring at me any chance she gets. I don't know what DeLuca has told her and Georgia, but they aren't buying it anymore. She's been blowing up my phone all week, but I have avoided talking to her because I couldn't risk incurring DeLuca's wrath. Georgia is putting on a good front, but there was no masking her fear when the dinner started without her youngest daughter. If Serena and Georgia didn't know what was going on before, I think it's blatantly obvious now.

"I'd like you all to stand and raise a toast," DeLuca concludes as Saskia snuggles into my side, tilting her face up expectantly. "To the happy couple."

"To the happy couple" is chorused around the room as champagne glasses are raised.

I pry Saskia off me and stand, reaching for the mic. "I would like to say a few words."

DeLuca sends me a warning look. This wasn't part of the plans for the evening, and he doesn't like that I'm going off course. "Relax," I tell him, snatching the mic from his hands. "I just want to tell our assembled guests how deeply I'm in love with your daughter." I flash him a dark look, pushing him roughly into his seat. "Have a drink. You look like you need it."

Saskia frowns while Gifoli straightens in his seat, glancing around. My eyes briefly meet Barretta's across the table, and shared understanding flows between us.

"Thank you all for coming." My voice projects confidently and loudly around the room. "My fiancée and I are grateful to know so many wonderful people who are willing to share in our joy. You see, I have known my beloved since she was young, and she has always been the love of my life. She is the only one who has ever captured my heart, and it has always belonged to her."

Oohs and aahs ring out around the room as I notice my men sneaking guests out a side door. Briefly, my eyes land on Chantel LaCroix. I suspected she might come with her politician daddy. Her scowl is large enough to cast a dark shadow over proceedings if I gave a shit about her, which I don't.

I continue. "Recently, I discovered she gave me the greatest gift of all—my son."

DeLuca grins, the stress easing from his face. He still thinks I'm talking about Saskia. After all, he wants me to pretend she is Rowan's mother—as if I would ever agree to that.

The main entrance doors to the room open, and my heart thumps wildly behind my chest as Brando's broad shoulders sweep Sierra into the room. I didn't realize how tightly I was wearing my fear—how stressed my muscles were, or how heavy my thoughts were—until this very moment when I lay eyes on the love of my life, and my knees almost buckle with sheer relief.

My jaw slackens as my gaze rakes over her for the first time in six days. She is a vision in an exquisite layered red silk dress that clings to her gorgeous curves. Since her birthday, I have loved seeing her in red. The color compliments her skin tone and her golden blonde hair perfectly. Unlike Saskia's low neckline and gaping cleavage—leaving nothing to the imagination—Sierra's dress only offers a glimpse of creamy skin, hinting at the beautiful breasts underneath. Her hair is newly washed and styled, perfectly glossy and shiny, falling in soft sensual waves down her back. As usual, she isn't wearing much makeup, but she never needs it because she steals my breath every time I look at her.

"Mazzone," DeLuca hisses under his breath, pinning me with a stern look, urging me to continue my speech or end it. He hasn't noticed who my gaze has strayed to, but Saskia has. She swivels on her chair, and it almost happens in slow motion. Alessandro and Ciro emerge to flank Sierra on both sides as Brando protects her from the rear. Sierra holds her head up high as she walks with poise toward me, looking far more beautiful than any other woman in the room.

Saskia almost falls off her chair, and her eyes widen in shock when she sees her younger sister striding toward us. "What the fuck is going on?" she barks, turning around and piercing me with venomous eyes. "Daddy. He can't do this to me!" she wails, standing as I move toward Sierra.

"Ah, there she is. My real fiancée. The only woman I have ever loved and will ever love," I say into the mic, pushing past Saskia and stretching my arm out for Sierra.

She runs the last few feet, and though I want to run to her, I won't leave her exposed. I need to keep DeLuca, Gifoli, and Saskia in my line of vision because I don't trust any of them not to start shooting.

Hushed murmurs and shocked glances float around the room as Sierra throws herself at me. My arm bands around her slender frame, holding her close, and every muscle in my body relaxes temporarily at the feel of her delicate curves flush against me.

"Ben." She places one hand on my hip, cradling her other hand against her chest. It's wrapped in a bandage and clearly hurting her.

I glare at Brando because he never told me she was injured. He has the decency to look sheepish, and I rein in my anger because without him Sierra wouldn't be standing here.

I'm glad I chose to plant a man in the rank and file, just after I found Rowan and reconnected with Sierra. I wanted to have someone on the inside of The Outfit while my family was in Chicago. It's a pity Brando wasn't aware of Ian's betrayal in time to stop the kidnapping, but that was a closely guarded secret for a reason. He only realized what had happened when Ian threw Sierra into the van that day, and by then, it was too late.

At least he has wiped that scourge from the Earth, along with the rest of the assholes who were involved in my fiancée's kidnapping. I know Leo and Frank wanted to be the ones to deal with their cousin, but this could only happen today, a few hours before the ceremony, and I couldn't spare either of them at the last minute.

In a nice touch of irony, I had Brando poison their coffees, before putting a bullet in each of their skulls, ensuring the message was driven home.

There was a slight chance DeLuca might call Ian and become suspicious when he didn't answer, so I had Phillip mess with the satellite signal to cover our tracks. He ensured all telecommunications were down in the area for a few hours.

"Rowan?" Sierra whispers, looking up at me with fear coating her green eyes.

"He's safe," I assure her, pressing a fierce kiss to her head. I want to tell her I love her. That I'm sorry she had to endure what she's endured. How I hate that it took me this long to rescue her, but that will have to wait until after this is done.

"You said no one would touch her," I snap, keeping Sierra against me as I turn us to face DeLuca. Alessandro, Ciro, and Brando crowd around us. Out of the corner of my eye, I spy the other bosses walking this way having escorted their wives to safety.

The moment of reckoning is here.

"And you agreed to marry Saskia. It seems we've both broken part of our arrangement." DeLuca stands, and around me, men reach for their guns as guests start running from the room, sensing the impending battle.

"That isn't all you have broken," I say. "You have crossed one of our most sacred rules," I add as the recording breaks out over the sound system. Phillip has eyes on this room, and that was his cue to play the small segment from that day in DeLuca's car.

"We got rid of Felix to pave the way for this to happen." DeLuca's distinctive voice booms through the speakers around the room.

SIOBHAN DAVIS

The confirmation that he killed a made man, without justification, causes The Outfit's capos and *soldati* to trade angry looks and wary expressions.

Thomas Barretta showed equal anger but less confusion when I played it for him, hours after I left DeLuca at Lawson Pharma that day. Thomas was already suspicious—Saskia's behavior at the church and graveyard had tipped him off—and now he had the proof to confirm it. Taking a risk, I told him everything DeLuca had planned, and he readily agreed to help in exchange for him taking temporary control of The Outfit after we deal with DeLuca and Gifoli. I took it to The Commission who immediately agreed, and a plan was formed.

Gifoli thought he was clever taking my cell from me in the car, but he didn't realize my tie pin had a recording device inside. It's only one of a handful of technical devices my internal team has created for our soldiers' use in the field, and I'm grateful it came in handy.

"Did you really think you could murder my son and get away with it?" Barretta says, pressing the muzzle of his gun to the back of DeLuca's head. No one, except Gifoli, had suspected anything when the consigliere started slowly moving toward him. DeLuca's bodyguards know him as a friend, family, and to most of The Outfit's *soldati*, Joseph Lawson is only the man who washes the money. I'm sure some of them must have wondered about it from time to time, but I doubt anyone guessed his true identity. Why would they? To them, the big boss resides in Sicily. Gifoli is the one they respect. The one they report to. Which is why this needs to happen fast— before the truth is revealed and before Gifoli makes a preemptive strike.

I nod at Barretta as I push Sierra into Alessandro's arms. "Keep her safe."

Sensing the very real threat, DeLuca opens his mouth, shouting so his words carry across the room. "I am—"

"This is for Felix," Barretta says, pulling the trigger.

Saskia screams as DeLuca falls face-first onto the table, the back of his head blown wide, brain matter and blood seeping from his open skull onto the pristine white linen.

Gifoli immediately gives the call, rousing his *soldati*, as our men pull out their weapons and open fire.

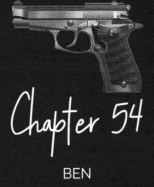

Chapter 54

CHAOS DESCENDS AS shots are traded across the room. While The Outfit's soldiers may be confused as to why Gifoli gave the order and why some of their crew is siding with New York, they obey.

Out of the corner of my eye, I spot Alessandro shielding Sierra behind him as he fights his way to the exit. Leo upends the nearest empty table, hauling it over to the side as I aim and fire, hitting The Outfit men who aren't wearing the small red pin on their jacket pockets. It was a risky move asking them to wear them. If DeLuca had noticed, it might have given the game away, but I guess it shows how little regard he held for his men. Barretta will make a much better boss. He cared enough to protect those loyal to him. To ensure they wouldn't get hit in the confusion.

Several of The Outfit's men are taken down by soldiers who fought beside them at one time, and I know this won't last long. Not once news filters down that Gifoli conspired with Lawson to murder Felix Barretta.

Gifoli must know his days are numbered as I watch him making a beeline for the exit on the opposite side of the room. He is holding a terrified Serena in front of his body, using her as a shield as he attempts to flee.

That fucking coward.

"Cover me," I shout at Leo, moving to go after them as my eyes scan the room for Saskia. Fear prickles my skin when I don't see her.

We can't let her escape.

I find Georgia hiding under the table, her dead husband's blood staining the white linen tablecloth crimson red, but she's alone. "Where is Saskia?" I shout.

"I don't know. She ran off as soon as the shooting started." She stares at me with a dazed expression, clearly shocked.

"Stay there and don't move. I'll come back for you."

I straighten up, and a shot whizzes over my head, narrowly missing me. Leo takes out the shooter as I spin around, shooting the guy creeping up on me from behind straight through the eyes.

A scream rips through the air, and I race around the overturned tables, ducking to avoid more shots as I head toward Serena and her husband. Gifoli is literally using his wife to deflect blows, and Serena is cradling her wounded arm, blood seeping through her fingers, as she screams in agony, wriggling in an attempt to get out of his hold.

What a pathetic piece of shit he is. An embarrassment to The Outfit and made men everywhere. He has no honor, and he deserves to die.

Gifoli shoots at a couple of my men as they aim toward him, and they dive behind tables in the nick of time.

"Sierra. No!"

My head whips around, halting my forward trajectory, when I hear Alessandro call out. They are almost to the side exit, but I wasn't the only one who heard Serena's screams. It's so typical of Sierra to ignore her own safety to come to her sister's aid. Running in her bare feet, she sprints across the room, firing the small handgun curled in her hand at anyone who dares cross her.

"Get down," I scream, spotting the nightmare in pink who rises from the shadows, just behind Sierra. I leap over tables, shoving people and chairs out of my way as I race toward my fiancée. Sierra hasn't seen Saskia. She's too occupied watching her injured sister, and now it's too late. My heart is in my mouth as I watch Saskia grab Sierra from the side, yanking her roughly against her body, pointing a gun at her temple.

I can't take aim at Saskia, not from this angle, without risking Sierra.

"Stay back," Saskia snaps, as I reach them. "Do it, Ben, or I'll kill her."

"Saskia. You don't need to do this," Sierra says in a voice that's unbelievably calm. "I know this isn't you. You need help, and we will get it for you."

"Shut the fuck up, you slut!" Saskia roars, moving back toward the rear side door.

Behind us, the battle rages on, and I trust my guys to cover us. That doesn't mean a stray shot can't take one of us down, so I need to put an end to this now. "Saskia, just let Sierra go, and I'll leave with you." I force a smile on my face and soften my voice, talking as if I was talking to a child. "I have a plane at the airport. We'll go anywhere you want to go. Just the two of us."

"You're a liar," she says, digging her hand into Sierra's arm while dragging her back. "As long as the slut is alive, she'll keep getting between us." She curls her finger around the trigger, and my heart leaps into my throat. I can't shoot her without risking her shooting Sierra first, and panic races through my veins because I don't know what to do. "I love you, Ben. You're mine. You've always been mine."

"Saskia, I—"

"Shut the fuck up, bitch," Saskia roars, digging the muzzle into Sierra's temple. "I am sick to death of your voice. I fucking hate you! You ruin everything!"

Her finger presses harder on the trigger and I raise my gun, aiming it at Saskia's head, but I'm too late.

A shot rings out, and I bellow out a roar, racing toward Sierra. "No! No, no, no." Pain spears me through the chest as I catch Sierra in my arms when she falls forward. She clutches my arms, and my panic turns to relief as Saskia raises a shaky hand to her chest, trying to stem the blood pouring from her body.

"Are you okay? Are you hurt?" I ask Sierra, holding her at arm's length to examine her.

"I'm not hurt." She's trembling, and I wrap my arms around her, holding her tight.

Around us, the fighting has eased to a few final gunshots as things wind down.

"Drop the gun, Saskia," Leo says, appearing alongside us the same time Alessandro does. "Or I will shoot to kill this time."

"Fuck you, Leo." Saskia lifts the gun, aiming it at me this time. "And fuck you, Ben."

I don't hesitate. Pointing my weapon, I fire the same time Leo does. He hits her in the chest, right in the heart, while my shot slings dead center through her skull. The light extinguishes from her eyes, and she's dead before she hits the ground.

Sierra wriggles out of my embrace. "Do something," she pleads, and I reach for her as Alessandro sprints toward the doors where a pale and pleading Serena is trying to keep Gifoli from escaping.

"Let him handle it," I say, reeling her back into the safety of my arms.

At the sound of approaching footfalls, Serena looks around, and some silent communication passes between her and Alessandro. As if it was coordinated, she bites down hard on Gifoli's hand, causing him to drop his gun, before she elbows him in the gut with her good arm and drops to the floor like a pro. Alessandro doesn't flinch or hesitate. He riddles his body with bullets, emptying the chamber in his gun, and the room is eerily silent as The Outfit's disgraced underboss slumps to the carpeted floor.

Gifoli's wide vacant eyes stare at the ceiling as blood seeps from multiple gunshot wounds to his head and upper torso, pooling around him. Alessandro rushes to Serena's aid, gently taking her into his arms. Barretta appears at my side, alongside three of the New York dons. "It's done," he says.

I keep a tight hold of Sierra, careful not to hurt her injured hand. "Where are the cleanup crews?" I ask.

"En route," Leo says, wiping his brow, leaving a streak of someone else's blood across his skin.

"You need to get out of here," Accardi says, approaching with Georgia tucked under his arm.

"Mom," Sierra cries, shucking out of my hold and hugging her mother.

"We all do." I spot the hotel manager cowering in the doorway, and I need to talk with him before we leave. "Take Sierra and Georgia to the car," I tell Leo. "Get Alessandro and Serena to go with you. And call the doc. Sierra and Serena need medical attention. Tell him to bring his portable X-ray unit, and we'll meet him at the usual place."

"Ben?" Sierra turns to me.

"It's okay," I assure her, pressing a soft kiss to her lips. "I'll be right there."

I spend five minutes on the phone with the hotel owner and another five minutes calming the hotel manager down. I check in with the police commissioner as I'm on my way to the parking lot with Ciro at my side, and he assures me that he has it contained. Nothing has gone out on the police scanner or on the web. Phillip has hacked into the hotel camera systems and he's wiping all evidence of tonight from existence. Leo will oversee the cleanup here, and the hotel owner is sending a team of trusted men to hastily redecorate the room, wiping all traces of bullets and blood from the ballroom.

"Let's go," I say when I slide into the back of the limo beside Sierra.

She wraps her good arm around me and tilts her face up, smashing her lips against mine, as the car glides out of the parking lot.

Her lips are soft and warm and familiar, and I haul her into my lap, uncaring we have an audience. I keep my arms around her as I explore her mouth, tangling my tongue with hers while I angle her head so I can kiss her more deeply. Every sweep of her lips unravels the tense knots in my stomach, and I hold her tight, never wanting to let her go again.

I came so close to losing her, and I don't want to experience that again.

A ripping sound, followed by a whimper of pain, finally breaks us apart. We whip our heads around in unison, watching Alessandro tie a torn piece of his shirt around the bullet wound in Serena's arm. "How bad is it?" I ask, sensing Sierra stiffen in my arms.

"I don't think it's life threatening, but I can't see the bullet," he says. "It's deep enough not to be a graze though." Which means the bullet is embedded in her arm and needs to be removed.

"We'll be picking the doc up in twenty minutes," I explain. "He'll fix you up."

"I'm worried about my kids," Serena says. "They are back at the house with some of *his* men. What if they hurt them?" Her voice elevates a few notches.

"I'll get Barretta to call them immediately. Don't worry, they won't touch them."

I hope.

We have a rule about not hurting women and children, but DeLuca broke that when he threw out the rulebook, so I can't reassure her with complete confidence.

I message Natalia to discover Leo has already called her with an update.

When we arrive at the house, a sleepy but eager Rowan is in my sister's arms, waiting for us.

"Rowan!" Sierra screams, racing out of the car and climbing the steps that lead to the front door.

"Mommy!" Rowan runs in his oversized Batman slippers toward a barefoot Sierra, and I battle a wave of emotion as they embrace.

"I can't believe what that monster tried to do," Georgia says, creeping up alongside me.

Ciro comes with us while Alessandro, Serena, and the doc stay in the car. The driver will take them to the back entrance so they can slip into the house undetected. I don't want Rowan to be frightened by all the blood on their clothes or the gaping hole in his aunt's arm.

"You didn't know?" I arch a brow in disbelief as we walk up the steps. Sierra has Rowan in her arms and joyful tears are streaming down her face.

"Not until the engagement announcement was made in the paper." Georgia folds her arms around her body. "I knew he was lying to me, and I wanted to call you, but he forbade it. I've been sick with worry all week. Serena was too. I was so scared he had killed Sierra," she cries, sniffling and swiping at tears as they form in her eyes. "We knew we'd see you tonight, and we planned to corner you and demand answers."

"Daddy! Look, Mommy is home from vacation!" Rowan yells as I approach.

Leaving Georgia, I jog forward, closing the distance with a few long strides. "I told you she'd be home soon, buddy." I ruffle his hair as my arms encircle my family.

"I missed you, Mommy." Rowan rests his sleepy head on her shoulder.

"I missed you too, Firecracker." Sierra peppers kisses into his hair as she smiles at me with glassy eyes.

"Did you miss me too?" I murmur against her ear.

"So damn much." Holding Rowan on her hip, she stretches up, whispering in my ear. "I'll show you just how much later."

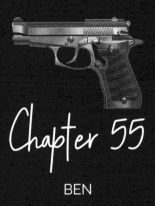

Chapter 55

BEN

"Is HE OKAY?" I ask when Sierra materializes in the main living room a short while later. After the doc set Sierra's hand and wrist in a cast, we took quick showers and changed while Rowan told his grandma all about his new house and his new tutor. Sliding my hands over Sierra's naked body as I washed her in the shower had me longing to bury myself deep inside her, but with a full household and a sleepy child waiting for his mommy to put him to bed, there was no time.

"He's fast asleep though he fought it," she says. Her bright smile reassures me she will be okay, and I'm grateful she is so strong. She has endured a lot tonight and this past week. That she is still standing, let alone smiling, is a testament to her resilience. To think there was a time I doubted she could exist in my world. She belongs in it with me, and I know, no matter what the future brings, we will face it head-on together.

Rowan insisted on sleeping in our bed, and neither of us could refuse him. I guess our proper reunion will have to wait a little longer. But I don't mind. I'm just glad to be going to sleep with my fiancée and son safely tucked into bed alongside me.

"Come here," I demand, pulling her into my arms, because I can't seem to stop touching her.

"You two are so sweet together," Georgia says from her chair in front of the roaring fire.

I snort out a laugh. "I think that's the first time in my life where anyone has referred to me as sweet."

"Own it, my love," Sierra says, swaying in my arms. "Because Mom is right. You *are* sweet." She stretches up, pecking my lips. "I love you. Thank you for rescuing me."

I brush her nose with mine. "I love you more, and I will always rescue you, Sierra, though I hope you will never need saving again." It's on the tip of my tongue to apologize for getting her into this mess, but I hold back because I didn't do this.

This was all on her father and Saskia, which brings us back to why I've insisted on this little heart to heart.

"Amen to that," she says, taking my hand and dragging me toward the couch across from her mother. "How is Serena?"

"Sleeping," Georgia says. "And that nice man Alessandro is watching over her."

Sierra lifts a brow, posing a silent question. I shrug because I've no idea where Alessandro's sudden interest has come from. He held Serena in his arms the entire journey from the city, gently tending to her wound and helping the doc once he got in the car. Now he seems reluctant to leave her side. Not that I'm complaining. I know Sierra will worry about her sister, and she trusts Alessandro, so she'll be happy he's guarding her.

"Doc removed the bullet, and he said she'll be fine," I explain. "Romeo and Elisa are under Barretta's protection, and he's going to personally travel with them to New York tomorrow. I will have Leo pick them up from the airport. We can go too, and bring Rowan, if you want."

She nods. "I'd like that. They are probably scared, and familiar faces will help. Rowan is going to be so happy to see his cousins."

I top off Georgia's glass with red wine before pouring a glass for myself and Sierra. I don't usually drink wine, except at dinner, but I'm afraid if I hit the bourbon tonight I won't stop. I'd like to have this conversation and take my woman to bed. It's been a long day, and we're all shattered. Sierra especially because she's been sleeping on a cold, hard floor for almost a week.

A pang of guilt slaps me in the face, and I make a silent vow to do everything in my power to make up for the six days of hell she's been through.

A contented sigh slips from my lips when I sit down on the couch and Sierra snuggles into my side. I press a kiss to her temple, closing my eyes and relishing the feel of having her pressed up against me. We sip our wine, and I can literally feel a layer of stress rising from my knotted shoulders.

"I'm so happy you found love," Georgia says, her eyes glistening with fresh unshed tears. "I still remember how amazing it felt though it's been a long time for me."

"Is it true, Mom? That he wasn't really my father?" Sierra asks, beating me to the punchline.

Shock splays across her face. "He told you that?"

Sierra shakes her head. "Saskia did."

Sadness creeps over Georgia's face at the mention of her daughter's name. I don't know if she knows I'm the one who inflicted the fatal blow, but I won't apologize. Saskia would have killed Sierra if I hadn't pulled the trigger.

Going into tonight, I had planned to keep her alive. No matter how she treated Sierra, I know Firefly did not want her sister to die. Barretta was always going to kill Giuseppe, and that had to happen. Part of me considered handing Saskia to the cops, to let her take the fall for Felix's death, but giving her to the authorities would have been too risky. She was cunning enough to try to make a deal, and she knew too much. Pity, because the thought of her rotting in a jail cell for the rest of her life held a certain appeal. No, my plan had been to incarcerate her in my dungeon until Sierra decided what she wanted to do with her.

Can't say I'm unhappy with how it turned out.

I'm glad she's dead. She was a crazy bitch, and the world is a safer place without her in it.

Still, it must be hard for Georgia. She *was* her mother. Georgia has lost her daughter and her husband tonight, and I'm not unsympathetic even if I believe she's better off without them in her life. I always remember Saskia didn't have much time for her mother—she was a Daddy's girl, through and through.

"I'm not sorry he's dead," Georgia says as if she's read my mind.

SIOBHAN DAVIS

"But I hate that Saskia died." Tears spill down her cheeks. "I know she was cruel and vindictive and selfish. She had too much of Giuseppe in her, but she was still my daughter."

"She tried to kill me, Mom," Sierra softly says.

"I know, and I'm shocked she did. I'm glad she didn't succeed because I would lose my mind without you." Her tears dry up, and she smiles at her youngest daughter. "I failed her as a mother, and it's one of my biggest regrets. Maybe in the next life, she will finally be at peace."

I hope she's rotting in the fiery pits of hell, but I keep those thoughts to myself.

"How many people know who Giuseppe was?" I ask, needing to understand if there is further risk. Barretta and I already discussed this, but I want to hear it from DeLuca's wife.

"Our personal bodyguards, you two, Serena, and Barretta. Those are the only people who know."

"Are you very sure? Please think carefully. It's important."

Sierra pins me with a perplexed look. "I'll explain later," I whisper, feathering kisses across her cheek.

"There is no one else. At least no one I'm aware of," Georgia confirms after further contemplation.

"Okay. Good." The coils in my stomach loosen a little.

Georgia takes a sip of her wine, staring into space. "We were very much in love when we first met, you know. It was a whirlwind romance, and we were married within six months of meeting. I only found out he was mafia after we were wed. He told me he was the heir to The Outfit, but I didn't really comprehend what it meant." She shakes her head. "I was so damn naïve."

The lovesick look disappears off her face as she eyeballs us. "He started with the whores after Serena was born, and he made no apology for it. He was CEO of Lawson Pharma by then, and he had just taken over as don. The power went to his head, and soon there were very few people he listened to. I hated how he took my family legacy and made a mockery of it by laundering money for the mob."

She gulps back her wine, and her chest heaves. "His attentions

404

blew hot and cold. Sometimes, he treated me so well it was like we were at the start of our courtship, but other times, he was cruel and dismissive, flaunting his sluts in my face. I had an affair because I was desperate for someone to love me and I wanted to give him a taste of his own medicine, but it backfired in a major way."

Pain is etched across Georgia's face, and I hold Sierra close, knowing this is hurting her, rubbing my hand up and down her arm in what I hope is a soothing gesture.

"When he discovered I was seeing Mario, he killed him in front of me. I thought he would kill me next, especially when I told him I was pregnant and he refused to believe the baby was his."

My eyes dart to Georgia's, wondering where this is leading to.

"To this day, I don't know why he didn't kill me. Unless he didn't want the hassle of finding another wife to take care of his kids, or maybe he wasn't entirely unfeeling and he couldn't bring himself to kill a pregnant woman."

I highly doubt it. The man was a psychopath. I doubt he considered that.

"Saskia said he punished you for it," Sierra says. "What did he do?"

"You don't want to know."

"I do. I wouldn't have asked otherwise. I think he kept you alive so he could make you suffer for your sins, over and over again. That's the kind of man he was, Mom. There was no mercy in him saving you and me that day."

Georgia wipes more tears away. "Perhaps you are right," she whispers. "He kept me on a seesaw for years, and it's been exhausting. In public, I had to act the dutiful loving wife. Even in front of you kids. Yet in private, he tortured me mentally and physically. He beat me, only in places you wouldn't see. Forced me to watch as he fucked his whores, and he regularly let his friends rape me."

"Oh, Mom." Sierra slides out of my embrace, rushing to hug her mother. "Why did you put up with it?"

"I had no choice, sweetheart," she says, tucking Sierra's hair behind her ears. "You can't run from this life, and I wouldn't leave any of you with him. Especially not you. He threatened you all the time if I didn't cooperate."

"I'm sorry." Sierra holds her mother tight, tears swimming in her eyes, and I want to resurrect that bastard and kill him myself.

"I know you were hurt that I hadn't told you the truth," Georgia says. "But I never wanted you to know any of this. I was comforted with the fact you were kept protected from it, but there is no point concealing anything now."

"What was my father's surname?" Sierra asks. "Does he have any other family?"

"Sweetheart." Georgia cups her face. "I wish Mario had been your father. He was a good man. He loved me, and I repaid him by getting him killed. The guilt and the pain will never go away, but he didn't impregnate me. Giuseppe DeLuca *was* your father."

"I don't understand." Sierra frowns.

"That makes two of us," I say, leaning forward. "He told me Sierra wasn't his flesh and blood."

"I knew when I was pregnant that the baby was my husband's. Mario and I were always careful in that regard. Giuseppe refused to believe it, so after you were born, I had DNA tests done. They confirmed it conclusively, but still he refused to believe it."

"Oh my God." Sierra sighs, shaking her head. "He really and truly was crazy, wasn't he?"

"I believe so. Or maybe it was a conscious decision. Another way to permanently punish me for my affair. Every time he refused to acknowledge you or he was hurtful and cruel, it destroyed me. I think he continued doing it for that reason." Georgia shrugs. "Maybe, in the end, he said it so much it became his gospel and the only truth in his head."

The conversation pretty much ends after that depressing news, and Sierra shows her Mom to one of the guest rooms while I slip into bed beside my son. His small hand is tucked under his cute face. For the first time in a week, his face shows no sign of unhappiness and he looks settled and at peace.

Sierra pads into the room, and I watch her undress with hungry eyes.

"Stop that," she whispers, stifling a yawn as she pulls a silk nightie on over her gorgeous body. "I'm already horny without your heated stare undressing me."

"We could go to one of the spare bedrooms, and I can take care of you," I murmur, getting out of the bed to retrieve the box from my pants.

"As tempting as that is, Mr. Mazzone," she says, resting her head on my chest. "I'm absolutely exhausted. I just want to sleep with my two favorite people close to my side."

"We'll take a rain check," I say, removing the ring and sliding it on her finger.

"Oh my God," she whispers, looking at the glistening diamond and emerald ring. "Where did you get this?"

"When Brando told me how she destroyed your ring, I was enraged. I called the jeweler and had him make you another one."

"It's different," she says, "but I love it as much as I loved the other one."

"I didn't know if you'd want a permanent reminder of what she did, so I asked him to alter the design a little." The emerald shaping is different, and he placed a fine row of tiny diamonds on the platinum band.

"It's perfect." She stretches up on tiptoe and kisses me.

"You're perfect." I dot kisses all over her face before gently cupping her cheek. "Do you still want to go ahead with the wedding next week or—"

She cuts me off with a kiss. "Yes. I don't care if everything isn't arranged. I just want to marry you, Ben. I don't care about anything else."

Warmth spreads across my chest as I hold her against me. "I can't wait to call you my wife. Nothing else matters to me either." She yawns, and I reluctantly let her go. She's exhausted, and I need to let her sleep.

Sierra gets in beside Rowan, and I crawl in behind her, tucking the covers up over all of us. I know she positioned Rowan on the left side of the bed so she could be close to him and me at the same time. Snuggling against me, she takes my arm, draping it over her waist, before she places a soft hand on Rowan's chest. As if sensing her touch, he moves in closer, pressing up against her, and I feel her melt into the pillows.

"Ben," she whispers, arching her neck so she's looking back at me. "Is it over now?"

"It's over, Firefly." I press my lips to hers as my palm flattens on her silky stomach. "No one will ever hurt you again."

Epilogue

SIERRA

Six months later

"**Y**OU ARE GOING to a lot of trouble tonight, little sis. Anything you want to tell me?" Serena teases, opening the refrigerator and extracting a chilled bottle of wine.

"Can't a wife cook a romantic dinner for her husband without getting the third degree?" I raise her teasing with sass.

"Well, something smells delicious."

"It's meatballs and spaghetti. Ben's favorite. Natalia gave me the recipe. Apparently, it's been in the Mazzone family for generations."

Serena helps herself to a spoonful of the tomato sauce, moaning appreciatively as the flavor explodes on her tongue. "Damn, girl. You should've opened a restaurant not a holistic center."

"That sounds too much like hard work," I joke as I walk around the island unit to the table.

Ben bought a small building in downtown Greenwich for me as a wedding present, and let me tell you, he got laid *a lot* on our honeymoon in Fiji for that amazing gift.

We took Rowan with us on our honeymoon because neither of us could bear to leave him at home. When we returned, we settled into family life with practiced ease. Serena asked if she and her kids could stay a little longer, having no desire to return to Chicago, and Ben willingly handed her the keys to the west wing, telling her to stay as long as she wanted.

Rowan, Romeo, and Elisa all started at a local private school after Christmas, and they are settling in well. I spent a few months setting up my new center and recruiting a small team to work with me, providing a host of different treatments and therapies to local clients. We only opened for business two weeks ago, and it's already booming.

I'm only working part-time because I want to pick up Rowan from school every day and be here with him and my sister in the afternoons.

"Are you eating in here or the dining room?" Serena asks, pulling out silverware.

We have a gorgeous, elegant dining room, but most nights, we prefer eating in the kitchen. It's warmer and more homey. Even though Ben has a helicopter now—which means he comes home from the city every night—it's usually too late to join us for family dinner. Normally, it's just Serena and me and the kids. Plus our bodyguards, of course.

"We'll eat here," I say, accepting the silverware and setting it on the table.

"Is Natalia coming this weekend?" she asks, opening a cupboard and removing two wineglasses. Natalia and Serena hit it off from the instant they met, and we have good fun hanging out together when she's here.

"I'm not sure. She hasn't messaged me yet."

On weekends when she's not visiting her husband, Gino, in Chicago, Natalia comes here with her twin stepsons. I think she needs to remain close to Ben now that their father is gone.

Angelo passed the day after the shootout in the hotel, and Natalia is still grieving.

We had considered postponing our wedding, out of respect, but Natalia insisted we go ahead with it, saying it's what her father would have wanted. She told us how he thought Ben would be the eternal bachelor and how delighted he was when we got engaged even if I wasn't Italian.

Or so we all thought at the time.

Isn't it ironic that I ended up being the traditional Italian wife after all?

It's as if destiny was at work this entire time, and none of us knew.

"I thought Gino was only supposed to be in Chicago for six months," Serena says, pouring white wine into two glasses.

"That was the initial plan, but things are taking longer than expected, and it looks like he will have to stay there for at least another six."

Ben has stayed true to his word, updating me on the details of what goes on in his world. Thankfully, things have settled down in recent months. The Commission is now a united organization comprising all the US *famiglias*. They are still working through the details, but having ultimate cooperation between all Italian American made men, for the first time in years, is a big deal.

A lot of that is thanks to Ben's tireless efforts, and he seamlessly took over as official Mazzone don with no issue. His reputation spoke for itself, and the men already knew they were in good hands. He worked hard to earn their trust and respect, and now he has their unflinching loyalty.

After The Commission orchestrated a successful reclamation of Vegas, Salerno and his scheming daughter returned to Nevada, and the Russians slunk away to lick their wounds and mourn the loss of their ally. We know they will regroup and retaliate at some point, but for now, we have peace and prosperity.

Things aren't fully settled in Chicago, but The Outfit is rebuilding under the expert stewardship of acting underboss Thomas Barretta. Ben explained how Thomas believes he is too old to lead their men and that fresh young blood is needed. So, The Commission appointed Gino Accardi, Natalia's husband, as acting consigliere to work with Barretta in identifying suitable men to take up the vacant key positions.

No one knows DeLuca is dead. (I refuse to refer to him as Father anymore. He lost that right when he kidnapped me and tried to steal my future.) As far as anyone is concerned, he is still calling the shots from Sicily, having thrown his full support behind The Commission and Barretta. The Commission agreed with Ben when he suggested that announcing his death at this time would be too coincidental and might raise suspicion. It would also disrupt The Outfit at a time when things are in flux. So, DeLuca lives on in ghostly form, for now. In

SIOBHAN DAVIS

a few years, when they have a successor chosen and trained and the timing is right, they will hold a funeral for DeLuca and draw a line under his nefarious reign.

"Here." She hands me a glass of wine, and I take it without argument.

I finish setting the table and pull myself up onto one of the stools at the island unit. "Sit down." I pat the space beside me. "Ben won't be home for a while yet, and I take it Alesso is watching the kids?" I asked Serena if she would take Rowan tonight because I want a night alone with my husband. I love having my sister here, for so many reasons, but babysitting on tap is an added bonus.

"The kids are asleep, and Alesso and Frank are playing *COD* on the Xbox in my living room." She rolls her eyes, but I spot the faint blush on her cheeks. Although Alesso is still my bodyguard, when we are at the house, I have noticed his predilection for spending time with my sister when he's not needed. She has denied there is anything going on, stating they are only friends, but I think she doth protest too much! Still, I don't pry. She knows I am here when she needs to talk, and she has been through sheer hell over the past ten years.

I'm so glad that bastard Gifoli is dead. Gradually, Serena has been revealing the truth behind her marriage, and I'm sick at the things she was forced to endure.

Leo tends to stay over on the weekend, and I'm never happier than when all the family is here together and the house is filled with love and laughter. Pen and Esme visit when they can, but with Pen's growing family and Esme's burgeoning legal career, I don't see enough of them.

Mom flies in once a month, but she's crazy busy now she has taken over as CEO of Lawson Pharma. She has thrown herself into reclaiming her birthright, and I can't recall ever seeing her this invigorated. She told Barretta, in no uncertain terms, that Lawson Pharma was done pandering to The Outfit and to go find themselves some other sucker to launder their money. Ben smoothed the transition, and Mom is restoring Lawson Pharma to a fully legitimate organization. Which means she is working nonstop and she doesn't have much downtime.

Serena sips her wine while I pretend to sip mine, dumping some of it in the vase of flowers on the island unit when she's not looking.

"Have you given any more thought to NYU?" I ask.

"I emailed the administration, and they sent me a bunch of forms and information," she admits.

Serena is considering a return to college. To do something she likes, this time, and I want this for her, so bad. "It's your call, sis, but I think you should do it. You deserve to do something for yourself."

"I don't want to be a burden," she says. "And I don't want to neglect the kids."

"You're not, and you never could. You know you can stay here as long as you like. We love having you here." I squeeze her hand. "You can hire a nanny, like we discussed, and you can drive in and out to the city on days when Ben's schedule doesn't suit yours." I lean in closer, smiling. "Do it. Grab something for yourself."

Her eyes sparkle with simmering hope and more than a tinge of excitement. "You're a bad influence," she jokes, sliding off the stool as she finishes her wine.

"I'm a good influence, and you know it."

"Love you," she says, leaning in to give me a kiss. "I'll leave you to get ready for your man. Have fun."

"Love you too, and I intend to."

Twenty minutes later, I'm perched by the front door, waiting for Ben to appear. I heard the chopper land a couple of minutes ago, and I rushed out to welcome him at the door.

A low whistle rings out, and I spin around, grinning as Ben strides quickly toward me, with one hand behind his back. Ciro is snapping at his heels, wearing a familiar frown. There was a time Ben considered reassigning Ciro, but he has proven to be versatile and a good bodyguard. He has grown on me slowly, but he's still a grumpy bastard at the best of times.

"Well, aren't you a sight for sore eyes, Mrs. Mazzone?" my husband says, raking hungry eyes over my body-hugging little black number. He tugs on the gold-trimmed black bra strap peeking out from under the top of my dress. "Is this what I think it is?" he purrs in my ear, grazing my earlobe with his teeth.

"It is, husband dearest. I know how much you love me in skimpy black lace lingerie, and I aim to please."

"Is it my birthday?" he teases, trailing his hot mouth along my neck as Ciro hangs back, giving us privacy. "Or Christmas?" Straightening up, he whips out a giant bouquet of roses, fixing me with one of his signature smirks as he hands them to me. "Or maybe it's yours?"

He never stops spoiling me. The house is always full of flowers, and weekly cupcake deliveries are the norm. I bury my nose in the gorgeous blooms, and my heart feels like it's going to burst I'm just *that* happy. "Every day with you is Christmas," I say, circling my arms around his neck. "I love you so much, Ben. I hope you know that."

"You show me in so many ways, every day. I never doubt your love, and I don't ever take it or you for granted." He takes my hand, pulling me into the house. "And I love you too. I don't think you have any idea how happy you make me."

"I'm about to make you happier," I promise, dragging him into the kitchen.

"Wow." He pulls me into his arms, sniffing the garlic and tomato scents wafting around the kitchen. "You cooked Mazzone meatballs, didn't you? Damn, Firefly. Can I marry you again?"

I place my hands on his chest, gazing up at him in wonder. He is so fucking gorgeous. So sexy and protective.

And all mine.

I have to pinch myself somedays to remind myself he is mine forever and ever. That this glorious life we lead is *mine*. Rowan is the happiest he has ever been, and he worships the ground his daddy walks on, as do I. "I would marry you a million times, Ben, and it would still never be enough." Emotion clogs the back of my throat as he stares at me with so much love and adoration it is almost too much.

"Hey." His brow furrows as he swipes at the tear that has snuck from my eye. "What's wrong?"

"Nothing." I smile as I brush more tears. "These are happy tears."

"Are you sure? If something is wrong, I—"

"I'm pregnant," I blurt, worrying my lower lip between my teeth. I don't understand why I have a sudden bout of nerves when I already know Ben will be thrilled.

Shock splays across his face. "Seriously?"

"Yes." I nod. "I took a bunch of tests, and then Doc confirmed it." I had to enlist Leo's help, and from the shocked expression on Ben's face, I know he kept his word and kept it a secret. I wanted this to be a surprise.

"Oh my God." He lifts me up and gently swings me around. "I'm going to be a daddy again. This is the best news ever, Firefly." Planting my feet on the ground, he wraps his arms around me as his lips descend in a searing-hot kiss I feel all the way to the tips of my toes. He makes love to my mouth, setting every nerve ending in my body on fire, in the way only he can. "I'm hungry, babe," he says when he eventually rips his lips from mine. "And not for meatballs."

I laugh, palming his toned ass as he cups one of my breasts through my dress. "These feel bigger. Are they bigger already?"

I roll my eyes, grinning. "You are obsessed with my breasts."

"Fuck yeah," he says, gently squeezing. "Have you seen yourself? You're sex on legs, Firefly, and if I don't bury my cock inside you within the next two minutes, I'm liable to explode."

His words have the power to render me into a puddle of goo on the floor, and I'm already panting for him. Rushing to the stove, I turn off the heat and put a lid on the bubbling pot.

Dinner can wait.

I spin around, sauntering toward him with slow, deliberate, sensual moves and a tempting grin on my face. Grabbing his tie, I yank him toward me. "What are you waiting for, sexy? An invitation?"

I shriek as he lifts me over his shoulder, much more carefully than usual. He swats my ass. "Now you've done it, Firefly. Fuck dinner. You're my appetizer, entrée, and dessert, and I'm going to devour every morsel of what's available."

"So, get to it. Ravish me, baby," I coax as my panties flood with liquid lust.

He swats my ass again, racing out of the room toward our bedroom. "Your wish is my command."

Stay tuned for more stand-alone romances in this world, coming later in 2021. *STL* is Serena & Alessandro's romance and *FTL* is Natalia & Leo's romance.

ABOUT THE AUTHOR

USA Today bestselling author **Siobhan Davis** writes emotionally intense young adult and new adult fiction with swoon-worthy romance, complex characters, and tons of unexpected plot twists and turns that will have you flipping the pages beyond bedtime!

Siobhan's family will tell you she's a little bit obsessive when it comes to reading and writing, and they aren't wrong. She can rarely be found without her trusty Kindle, a paperback book, or her laptop somewhere close at hand.

Prior to becoming a full-time writer, Siobhan forged a successful corporate career in human resource management.

She resides in the Garden County of Ireland with her husband and two sons.

You can connect with Siobhan in the following ways:
Author Website: www.siobhandavis.com
Facebook: AuthorSiobhanDavis
Twitter: @siobhandavis
Instagram: @siobhandavisauthor
Email: siobhan@siobhandavis.com

BOOKS BY SIOBHAN DAVIS

KENNEDY BOYS SERIES
Upper Young Adult/New Adult Contemporary Romance

Finding Kyler
Losing Kyler
Keeping Kyler
The Irish Getaway
Loving Kalvin
Saving Brad
Seducing Kaden
Forgiving Keven
Summer in Nantucket
Releasing Keanu
Adoring Keaton
Reforming Kent

STANDALONES
New Adult Contemporary Romance

Inseparable
Incognito
When Forever Changes
Only Ever You
No Feelings Involved
Second Chances Box Set
Condemned to Love
Reverse Harem Contemporary Romance
Surviving Amber Springs

RYDEVILLE ELITE SERIES
Dark High School Romance

Cruel Intentions
Twisted Betrayal
Sweet Retribution
Charlie
Jackson
Sawyer*
*Drew^*

THE SAINTHOOD (BOYS OF LOWELL HIGH)
Dark HS Reverse Harem Romance

Resurrection
Rebellion
Reign
The Sainthood: The Complete Series

ALL OF ME DUET
Angsty New Adult Romance
Say I'm The One *
Let Me Love You*

ALINTHIA SERIES
Upper YA/NA Paranormal Romance/Reverse Harem
The Lost Savior
The Secret Heir
The Warrior Princess
The Chosen One
The Rightful Queen*

TRUE CALLING SERIES
Young Adult Science Fiction/Dystopian Romance

True Calling
Lovestruck
Beyond Reach

Light of a Thousand Stars
Destiny Rising
Short Story Collection
True Calling Series Collection

SAVEN SERIES
Young Adult Science Fiction/Paranormal Romance

Saven Deception
Logan
Saven Disclosure
Saven Denial
Saven Defiance
Axton
Saven Deliverance
Saven: The Complete Series

*Coming 2021
^Release date to be confirmed
Visit www.siobhandavis.com for all future release dates. Please note release dates are subject to change based on reader demand and the author's schedule. Subscribing to the author's newsletter or following her on Facebook is the best way to stay updated with planned new releases.

Printed in Great Britain
by Amazon